Eye of the Raven

ALSO BY ELIOT PATTISON

The Lord of Death

Bone Rattler

Prayer of the Dragon

Beautiful Ghosts

Bone Mountain

Water Touching Stone

The Skull Mantra

Eye of the Raven

ELIOT PATTISON

COUNTERPOINT

BERKELEY

Library of Congress Cataloging-in-Publication Data

Pattison, Eliot.
Eye of the raven : a mystery of colonial America / by Eliot Pattison.
p. cm.
ISBN-13: 978-1-58243-566-4
ISBN-10: 1-58243-566-9
1. United States--History--French and Indian War, 1755-1763--Fiction.
2. Scots--United States--Fiction. 3. Indians of North America--Fiction.
4. United States--Colonization--Fiction. I. Title.

PS3566.A82497E94 2009
813'.54--dc22

2009038079

Cover design by Domini Dragoone
Interior design by Megan Jones Design
Printed in the United States of America

COUNTERPOINT
2117 Fourth Street
Suite D
Berkeley, CA 94710

www.counterpointpress.com

Distributed by Publishers Group West

10 9 8 7 6 5 4 3 2 1

For Connor, who nourishes my muse.

Chapter One

April 1760
The Pennsylvania Wilderness

THEY WERE ON the bloodiest ground of a bloody war, and neither side in the great global conflict was inclined to show mercy. With every step the old Indian took through the sleeping enemy camp, Duncan McCallum's heart rose higher in his throat. He had begged Conawago to stay away from the enemy bivouac, had promised he would come back with him on the next full moon, but his companion would not wait. It mattered little to him that the Hurons camped with the French below would roast him alive if they found him stalking through their camp. The spirits had placed their enemy there to test his resolve, Conawago had insisted, and he had begged the young Scot not to accompany him. He had not a moment to spare in his quest to save the tribes, and his mother had taught him that the sacred ochre he needed from the ledge by the camp was at its most powerful when harvested under the full moon.

Duncan watched in abject fear as Conawago slipped between the French officers' tents, then stepped past one sleeping form after another, his linen shirt lit like a beacon in the moonlight. As he leaned forward from the shadows Duncan saw that his friend's hand gripped not the war ax at his belt but the amulet that hung from his neck. A man with blond locks stirred near the smoldering fire as Conawago passed by. The long rifle in Duncan's hand flew to his shoulder, and he kept the figure in its sights until the French soldier settled back into his blanket.

The haunting call of a whippoorwill rose from the opposite side of the camp, where Duncan had last seen the Huron sentry. Suddenly a second bird answered, much nearer, sending Duncan back against a tree, every muscle tensed, every nerve on fire. He had not expected a second sentry, but now knew there was one, near the rock face that was Conawago's destination. Duncan bent low and with slow, stealthy strides eased through the mountain laurel. Not many months earlier he would have thrashed about like a lost cow in the undergrowth, would have been dead after his first few steps so close to the enemy. But after so many months with him in the wilderness Conawago had proclaimed he was no longer a Highland Scot, but a woodland Scot.

The tall, muscular Huron stood in the brush, watching not the camp but the forest, his back to Duncan, his head cocked as if he had sensed something in the deep shadows of the woods. Duncan's heart hammered in his chest as he silently lifted his tomahawk. If he did not disable the guard in one blow the alarm would be spread. But as Duncan raised his arm the sentry suddenly gasped in pain, clutching at his head, then was jerked violently downward, disappearing into the brush. Duncan heard a low moan then a faint rustling of leaves that could have been the sound of something scurrying away.

The sentry was unconscious when Duncan reached him. A dozen frantic thoughts raced through his mind, that one of the nocturnal predators of the forest was stalking them, that they had stumbled into a nest of poison vipers, that he and Conawago were about to be trapped in a battle between the Hurons and their blood foes the Iroquois. Then he saw his friend had reached the exposed ledge that held the ochre. He choked down his fears and rushed to help Conawago extract the sacred yellow powder.

But though he had reached the rock face, his companion was not digging the ochre. With two dozen bloodthirsty enemies before him he was on his knees, arms outstretched at his waist, palms upward, speaking softly to the moon.

"By all that's holy, dig it out!" Duncan whispered, watching the sleeping camp, desperately trying to calculate where the remaining sentry would be.

"All that's holy will tell me if I am worthy," Conawago replied slowly. His months-long quest to reconnect the tribes to their gods, who had so clearly abandoned them, might be the most urgent task of his life, but he would not rush the spirits.

He was waiting for a sign.

Duncan surveyed the camp in grim anticipation. Surely there was no chance now of escaping undetected. But he would not interfere with this courageous elder, who so uncannily reminded him of his beloved grandfather, who had indeed become like a grandfather, and more, to him. Duncan's tribe too had been abandoned by its gods, years earlier in the Highlands of Scotland, his tribe too was nearly extinct due to the greed of the European kings. He had been denied a chance to give his life for his clan in Scotland, but he would not hesitate to offer it up to protect the gentle old Nipmuc.

He freed his knife of the leather strap that kept it tight to his belt then knelt and rested his rifle barrel on a boulder facing the camp. The Huron raiders, always painted with blood, would come first, screaming like banshees, eager for the demons carved on their ax heads to chew enemy flesh.

He heard a whispered syllable of gratitude and looked up to see a solitary goose fly across the face of the moon. Conawago arranged a square of leather below the seam of ochre and began gouging it out with his knife.

They were trotting westward, along the ancient trail that connected the homelands of the Iroquois in the north to the western Ohio country, the first gray light of day filtering through the oaks and hemlocks, when Conawago abruptly slowed. Suddenly his long battle ax was in his hand, its end circling in the air as if about to be launched. Duncan raised his rifle, instinctively cocking the hammer. Conawago pushed the pouch that contained the hard-won ochre to his back to protect it, and he seemed about to charge forward when he spotted a pale oval object on the path in front of him.

Duncan had never known him to show defeat, but now as the old Indian gazed at the turtle shell painted with red symbols an anguished groan escaped his lips. He took a step backward and seemed to sag as a tall warrior stepped out of the shadows. The stranger was unarmed except for a hunting knife hanging from a strap across his bare chest, though the fire in his eyes said he was about to wreak havoc. Conawago dropped his ax to the ground and motioned Duncan to lower his gun, muttering one word, "Onondaga," the name of one of the friendly Six Nations, the Iroquois.

But the man gave no indication of being an ally. He tensed, his fists clenched, as if about to spring on the old man.

Duncan stepped to the side, ready to react when the stranger attacked. He saw now the turtle tattoo that covered half his face, the elaborate painted designs on his arms and chest, exposed under the sleeveless waistcoat he wore open over his buckskin leggings and loincloth. The stranger was no ordinary warrior but a leader of one of the tribes' powerful secret societies. Duncan searched his memory for what he had learned of the Onondaga in his months with Conawago. They were the keepers of the Iroquois Confederation's central hearth, arbiters of disputes, guardians of the ancient secrets that kept the tribes anchored to their past.

"Chief of the Turtle Clan," Conawago added, as if the announcement should quiet Duncan.

"You are outcast!" the intruder hissed. "Since the birth of our people our totems have been safe, honored by our prayers and protected by our gods. Then you steal them like a common thief! You spit on our gods! You are no longer protected by the Haudenosaunee!"

Duncan saw the grief that rose on his friend's face, like a physical pain contracting his features. His mind raced back a month earlier to a small cave above one of the long lakes west of the New York colony, its entrance surrounded by skulls and feathers. Over the opening had been a large turtle shell painted with symbols identical to those on the shell before them. Conawago had insisted Duncan wait outside while he entered the cave. The old Indian had spent the day before in purification rites at a mountain spring and most of the following night reciting prayers in the tongue of his fathers. But Duncan had seen the mote of doubt that had lingered in his eyes for days afterward, and the appearance of the clan chief now seemed to trigger the same emotion.

"The relic I borrowed was left there by my mother in the last century, when I was a boy," Conawago explained in a level voice, pulling from inside his shirt a little ceramic figure of a man that hung from a strap around his neck, "a figure made by the first mother of my Nipmuc tribe, at the beginning of our days."

Duncan inched forward, struggling to keep up with the Iroquois words. He glanced toward the shadows as he did so, sensing that they were being watched.

"It was entrusted to my clan, for all the Haudenosaunee," the man said, using his people's term for the tribes called Iroquois by the Europeans. "I gave a blood oath to protect it."

"It belongs to no one," Conawago shot back. "When my father died my mother took it to the shrine cave to honor his Mohawk people. But it is for all the tribes of the woodlands, all the tribes whose gods are leaving them."

"Our gods stand with us! They flee from no one!"

"Open your eyes! While we fight the Europeans' war for them," Conawago countered, "our women and children die of European diseases. The tales of our peoples have been passed on for generations, but now British rum deafens our young to their elders. Our peoples become dependent on goods they know not how to make. The Europeans sweep up our land as if we don't exist. My Nipmuc people are nothing but last year's leaves blown from a tree. The gods are drifting away, forgetting us because we have forgotten them."

The stranger's face clouded a moment, then his gaze returned to the little clay deity. "I saw you leave the cave that day, but I was unable to follow. I think," he added in a threatening voice, switching to English for the moment as if he wanted Duncan to hear, "you stole a sacred amulet just to sell to some Englishman. Skanawati will not permit it."

"He did but remove a family totem!" The protest escaped Duncan's lips unbidden. He would not let the stranger abuse Conawago.

The stranger's hand went to his knife. Conawago stepped closer to Duncan, a new uncertainty on his face. The announcement of the warrior's name seemed to have shaken him. His hand rose and gestured Duncan away.

"The figure belongs to no one," Conawago repeated, extending it on the strap. "But returning him to his mate gives him new strength." As he spoke his hand slipped inside a pouch on his belt, and he produced a second figure nearly identical to the first, though clearly female.

The sight of the second relic silenced the Onondaga. He stared at it intensely then sighed and lowered himself onto a nearby log. "What is it you seek, old man?" Duncan did not miss the small flicker of his hand, a signal to someone in the shadows.

"I am speaking with the ancient spirits every day and night, reminding them of rites I knew as a child. I am cleaning the dust from their ears, the thorns from their eyes. I am speaking names not heard for years."

"That is the duty of the Onondaga." There was no more anger in his adversary's voice, but rather a rising pain. "You are not even of the Haudenosaunee."

Conawago's eyes flared. He jerked his shirt open to reveal the tattoo of a wolf on his left breast. "I was born of the Mohawk and Nipmuc tribes," he declared in a proud voice, for all the forest to hear, "blood kin to King Hendrick," he said, speaking of the beloved old chief who had died earlier in the war, leading Iroquois braves against the French at an age of over eighty years. "I have been in the court of the French king, given medals by the English king. I have hunted buffalo when they still ran on the banks of the Hudson, spoken with men who knew the great Champlain. And," he said with a simmering voice, tapping the tattoo, "I was made a member of the wolf clan of the Mohawk before you even knew your mother's milk." Duncan had seldom seen his friend so passionate. The two Indians seemed to be drawing each other out, tapping emotions usually buried deep inside.

But it was not the fierce words that choked off Skanawati's protest. His eyes grew round with wonder as he pushed Conawago's shirt to the side, revealing another tattoo on his left shoulder, of a sun with long rays extending down his arm and onto his chest. He ran his fingers over it, the fingertips hovering just above the lines, as if sensing some power emanating from it, then looked up and down, from Conawago's stern expression to the tattoo, before he could find words again. "I thought no man alive still bore the mark of the dawnchasers," he declared with awe in his voice. As Duncan had learned months earlier when he had seen the tattoo on a dead friend of Conawago's, the mark was bestowed only on the elite few who completed an ancient rite, a treacherous, sometimes fatal, twenty-four-hour race across mountain, swamp, and forest to connect and empower shrines of the forest gods.

"I was the last to receive it," Conawago said. "The gods know we have forgotten them," he repeated.

"I thought it one of the lost things. You know the places of the chase, the words that must be spoken?" Skanawati asked with sudden urgency.

Conawago slowly nodded his head.

"Why have you not shared this with our people?"

"It is not worn for pride, or glory."

"We need holy men."

"I have done too many unholy things in my life to become one."

Skanawati looked with melancholy at the little god on the leather strap and slowly nodded, as if he understood the explanation all too well.

Duncan studied the chief anew. There was an air of great power about him, even in his stillness. He was a warrior in his prime, though his eyes spoke of something deeper.

"Come back with me, and we can join the two gods in the cave. Teach me." When Conawago did not reply Skanawati looked strangely shamed. For a moment, in the long shadows of dawn, the Iroquois chief seemed old beyond his years. "Then let me help you." He gestured at Duncan. "I could take this white slave of yours and get many pelts for him in the Ohio country."

Duncan gave no sign he had understood the words, just returned Conawago's sober gaze as his friend seemed to consider the offer.

At last the old Indian shrugged. "I will keep him for now. He is clumsy, but he collects my firewood and cooks my rabbits."

The Iroquois studied Duncan with disdain, then offered a shrug of his own as if to say Conawago would come to regret his decision. He took a step backward, paused, then pulled a little fur-wrapped bundle from his belt and handed it to Conawago. It was what the tribes called a medicine bundle, containing sacred items collected from the forest.

Conawago solemnly accepted the gift, cupping both hands around it then pressing it to his heart. "You have not said what brings you so far from your longhouse."

Skanawati stared silently into the forest, considering whether to reply. "The Warriors Path changes," he said at last, using the Iroquois name for the trail they stood on. "We have been losing warriors along the trail," the chieftain explained, an unsettling darkness entering his voice. "We find their bodies by old shrine trees, mutilated as if by a predator. Sometimes," he said hesitantly, "it is Europeans who are dead." He looked from Conawago to

Duncan, considering them carefully before speaking again. "My mother had a dream," he finally added.

Duncan looked up at the Iroquois. It was a startling revelation. Dreams were intensely private to the Indians. The spirits spoke to them through dreams, linked them to the world on the other side of death. Dreams were fate, dreams had to be obeyed.

Skanawati looked at the dawnchaser tattoo as he spoke. If an Iroquois held a strand of wampum beads in his hand he had to tell the truth. For Skanawati it seemed gazing on the tattoo required him to share deep, urgent secrets. "In her dream she was taken along this trail by an old bear spirit. The bear told her the trail is becoming a crack in the world, that the lives of many men are being stolen on it, that their ghosts form a line pointing to the Ohio country. Then not long after, my mother saw for herself the beginning of that crack and sent me onto the trail. She said when I find the ghosts they will tell me how we leave the servitude of the English king."

They were bold words, terrifying words, for they portended not only much death but a rift between the English and the tribes. If the Iroquois left their traditional alliance the British army would likely seek their destruction, for fear they would aid the French.

"And are the ghosts speaking with you?" Conawago asked.

A chill ran down Duncan's back as Skanawati nodded. "I have looked into the crack in the world," he declared. "There are terrible things to behold. Death walks this trail. Man becomes tree. Man becomes machine. The ghosts call out challenges to me in the night."

Conawago and Duncan exchanged an uneasy glance.

"We are not ghosts," Conawago observed.

Skanawati seemed to consider the point, then solemnly nodded, glancing again at Duncan. "I have heard tales of a crazy old Nipmuc wandering in the mountains with a yellow hair." The Iroquois' gaze drifted back toward Conawago's tattoo. "You must leave this trail. Go deeper into the mountains, stay away from the forts, stay away from the bloody water, or you may fall into the crack in the world. Hide. Not even the children will be safe when the covenant chain breaks," he said, referring to the century-old metaphor for the bond between the British and Iroquois. "More ghosts are coming." He scooped up the painted turtle shell as he spoke.

"Yet you roam the forest without fear," Conawago pointed out.

"I am the answer to the ghosts," the Iroquois replied.

Then without another word he slipped into the shadows.

I have looked into the crack in the world. The lives of men are being stolen. More ghosts are coming. The Onondaga's words preyed on Duncan as he and Conawago journeyed on at the slow, steady trot used by the tribes in the wilderness. Stolen lives meant lives taken without honor. Skanawati had been speaking of murders that threatened the covenant chain. If that chain were broken, the Pennsylvania and New York colonies would become bloody abattoirs. With new foreboding Duncan recalled the sentry in the enemy camp, felled by what had seemed like a ghost.

He was so distracted by the haunting words of the Iroquois chief he nearly collided with Conawago when his friend abruptly stopped. They were almost at a junction with the east-west Forbes Road, the flat bed of which could be seen through the trees. A desperate moaning sound, that of a small mammal in its death throes, rose from the forest near the trail. Conawago surveyed the heavily wooded slope for a moment then sprinted toward a large beech near the trail, Duncan at his heels.

A brown-haired man, a European of perhaps thirty years, sat against the tree, the crimson on his chest glowing in the early morning light. The fresh blood was spreading across the front of his shirt and britches, his left arm was strangely raised along the tree trunk. His eyes were wild and pleading, his breathing labored, and though he kept opening his mouth as if to speak, only moans came out.

"Save your strength," Duncan instructed as he knelt beside him, his medical training in Scotland quickly taking over as he surveyed the wounds. An abrasion to the right temple where the blood was dried and clotted. A deep gash in the thigh, from which blood was pooling on the ground. A wound in his chest, from which blood oozed through his shirt. Duncan raised his canteen to the man's chin, letting the water trickle over his lips. The man coughed, then seemed to quiet as he recognized that help had arrived. Conawago cut a vine and began tying it around the man's thigh. If they did not act quickly the man would bleed to death. More ghosts were coming, Skanawati had warned.

"We must lower him," he told Conawago. But as he gently pulled on the stranger's shoulder the left arm, resting up on the trunk, resisted. He pulled the arm to no avail, pulled so hard it uncurled the fingers that had covered the palm. "God's breath!" he exclaimed. The man's hand was nailed to the tree.

Duncan shut his eyes, collecting himself, then quickly probed the shirt, looking for the entry wound. He found a long tear in the fabric over the center of the bloodstain, then lunged back as he opened the shirt.

"His heart!" he gasped and stared in disbelief. He had heard of men having their hearts cut out by the savage Hurons. But somehow what Duncan saw seemed even more hideous. Pressed into the man's breastbone, pounded into the flesh so that its teeth were embedded in the tissue, was a large clockwork gear. Blood oozed from between the teeth of the gear. *Man becomes tree*, Skanawati had said. *Man becomes machine.*

"There was moss on the bank by the road," Conawago told him, "and spiderwebs on the alder bushes," referring to the tribes' most common treatments for staunching wounds. He opened one of the pouches he kept on his belt, pulling out a bundle of herbs.

Duncan set his rifle and pack on a rock and darted back up the trail.

He was on his knees, pulling moss from the spongy bank, when he suddenly froze. Men were moving along the road nearby. Cursing himself for leaving his rifle with Conawago, he lowered himself into the bracken then watched as two men appeared, not on the road but its northern flank, approaching the old Indian trail. Moments later two more appeared on the south side. They were too stiff, too clean, too uncertain to be rangers, but they had been trained by rangers, who always deployed scouts to parallel the path of their parties. He sensed through the earth, as Conawago had taught him, the drumming of many feet on the forest floor a moment before he actually saw the marching soldiers. More than two dozen men came into view, marching single file, most with short military muskets slung on their shoulders, several carrying the long rifles the French feared so much. There were no regular army uniforms among them, though half a dozen wore identical blue and buff coats and all wore a patch of red cloth pinned to their tricorned hats or the collars of their heavy waistcoats. Militia. Duncan let them pass then slowly rose, and he was about to call out in greeting when an anguished cry split the still air.

"Murder!" shrieked a young, terrified voice. "God protect us! It's the captain! The savages!"

Duncan threw down the moss and ran. He had passed half the men in the column before they could react with more than surprised cries, but several of those who were already running toward the bloody tree spun about, lowering their weapons at Duncan as he sprinted toward them. He wove in and out of the column, ducking a gunstock swung at his head, rising up to drive his shoulder into another as the soldier lifted a tomahawk from his belt. Two muskets discharged, the balls slashing the air near his ear, and someone cursed at the fools who fired so close to the column. He could see Conawago now, saw the confused look on the old Indian's face as the first of the strangers reached him, landing a glancing blow with a gunstock on his shoulder.

The next man charged with a tomahawk aimed for Conawago's skull. Duncan roared with anger and launched himself through the air, grabbing the upraised arm at the height of its deadly arc, his momentum pulling the soldier down. Duncan rolled as he hit the ground, rose, and sprang into the knot of men who hovered over Conawago.

"You mistake us! We are no enemies!" he shouted as he threw one, then another of the men to the ground. Then suddenly a cold blade materialized at his throat. He felt a handful of his long blond hair seized and his head jerked backward.

"If ye be part of this vile work we'll have y'er scalp too," his assailant snarled. Duncan twisted, threw a hand over his shoulder, and grabbed a handful of beard. Then the blade pressed tightly against Duncan's jugular, forcing him to drop his hand.

"We scout for Woolford's rangers!" Duncan gasped, watching in horror as more men joined in the beating of Conawago, kicking him, pounding him with gun butts. "You must stop!" he pleaded. "We are no enemy, I tell you!"

The beating eased as the men looked up, not at Duncan but at the man holding the blade behind him. One of the soldiers put a finger to the neck of the bloody man at the tree. "He's gone, sergeant."

"Y'er friend has killed our captain!" hissed the voice at his ear.

Duncan gazed at the dead officer. His eyes were already glazing, his skin growing waxy and pale. "We found him like this. We were trying to help."

"To hell you say! This savage was leaning over him with a bloody knife! Fixing to lift his hair."

"We are scouts for the rangers!" Duncan repeated, his own anger rising now.

"In that case we won't kill him here," the sergeant shot back. "We'll take him to the fort and have a proper trial before we kill him."

As the pressure of the blade on his throat relaxed two men roughly seized Duncan's arms, holding him tightly as the militia men went back to work on Conawago, with boots and heavy sticks. As the old Indian collapsed to the ground Duncan begged them to stop, cursed them in English then Gaelic, shouted at them, twisted violently to shake his captors off. Then one of the clubs slammed against his own skull. He fell to his knees, his arms still pinioned, unable to cover his head against the second blow. The last thing he saw was Conawago's precious little ceramic god, as old as time itself, being shattered against his breastbone.

Chapter Two

*D*UNCAN BECAME AWARE of the pinpricks of pain on
his forehead first, then on his shoulder, and in his
confusion thought he was back on his prison ship
from Glasgow, where the rats had worked on his flesh while he slept.
He smelled the filth and decay of the ship, sensed the slime of the
moldy walls. A loud screech stirred him, a second caused his head to
roll over, then new spikes of pain pushed open his groggy eyes.

A dead hand, gray with decay, was on his chest, being fought
over by several blackbirds as others pecked at his own flesh.

Duncan's cry of horror came out as a dry, rasping croak. He
pulled himself up, grabbing a club to pummel the scavengers, then
cried out again as he saw the thing in his hand was no log but the
lower half of a decaying human leg. He scrambled out of the shallow pit he had been thrown in, scattering the birds with a handful
of dirt, not stopping until, his chest heaving, he pressed his back
against a heavy palisade wall.

Quickly, still gasping, he took stock of his surroundings. He
was at a large fortress built on a hill above earthworks, where blue-
uniformed artillery officers drilled their men around field guns.

The garbage and days-old detritus of a surgeon's table had been thrown into the pit through a narrow opening in the wall near his head. As he fought a wave of nausea he realized his captors had sought out the pit, had planted the rotting hand on his chest, had, he saw now, knocked down a makeshift scarecrow that had kept the birds away. He closed his eyes, fighting another tremor of nausea, then stepped along the wall until he came to a gate, searching his memory of the military landscape of the western forest. He and Conawago had been less than a day's march from Fort Ligonier, the second biggest of the western fortifications after Fort Pitt.

The scarlet-coated sentry, a British regular, gave him a chilly nod as he slipped through the western gate. Spotting a well a hundred feet away, he waited until an Indian woman in a calico dress finished filling her gourd container then lowered the bucket and drank deeply, rinsed his hands in the remaining water, and emptied it over his head. Beginning to feel alive again, he found a perch in the shadows, leaning against a post of the porch that ran along the front of a long one-story building from which he could survey the grounds.

Small artillery pieces were mounted on swivels along the walls, sentries stationed at each corner. Opposite him men in artillery blue and infantry red wandered in and out of a second long building with several doors, all of the men wearing the small brass gorgets over their breasts that were the sign of rank in the British army. A handful of Indians, the Stockbridge scouts often used by the army, squatted beside a painted animal skin, tossing the white pebbles used in their games of chance. A solitary brave, wearing his hair in the narrow scalplock favored by the Iroquois, sat under a chestnut, slotting small iron arrowheads onto newly fletched shafts. Squads of infantry drilled to the sharp, impatient commands of their sergeants. All around him was an atmosphere of order, discipline, and fear. Although with the fall of Quebec the tide in the bloody war had turned at last in the favor of the British, the fighting was far from over in the wilderness.

"It isn't their knowledge of the spheres as such that impresses me most," came a refined voice from beside him, "it's that they possess it so intuitively."

Duncan turned to see a well-dressed man sitting on a keg by the wall of the building, gazing at the solitary Iroquois. "I'm sorry?"

"The aborigines. All the secrets of the natural world reside within them, yet they express their wisdom not through their words but through their actions. Their knowledge of natural philosophy is instinctive. We barbarians have to have it pounded into our skulls."

The extraordinary words came from an extraordinary-looking man. The stranger was in his midthirties, perhaps ten years older than Duncan. Over a fine linen shirt he wore a waistcoat in whose pockets hung the fobs of not one but two pocket watches. His long brown hair was tied at the back Indian fashion, with a strip of the dyed eelskin used by the river tribes for decoration. Around his neck hung both a small brass snuff box and an amulet wrapped in what looked like mink fur. His hands were unadorned but for a ring of oak leaves tattooed around one wrist like a bracelet. Over his woolen britches was a pair of leggings like those worn by rangers, though his were of doeskin decorated at the top with beadwork. On his feet were the heavy leather shoes worn by soldiers.

"I expressed my admiration for the archery skills of that bronzed Shawnee gladiator this morning as he was casually shooting squirrels out of a high oak. He explained that the force was in the wood of his bow and the accuracy in the lines of the shaft, that all he does is say a prayer to the spirits that loaned him the power of the wood, then point. A more perfect scientific explanation I could not expect from any number of learned professors." He looked up with a bright, curious expression at Duncan. "I am composing algebraic equations that explain the force of the arrow," he declared, tapping a linen bag that hung over his shoulder. "I could show you if—"

He was interrupted by a stocky man in an apron who briefly appeared in the doorway behind them to toss him a plug of tobacco with a quick utterance of thanks.

The stranger glanced at Duncan self-consciously. "Everyone's a friend when you pay off your debts."

"Haudenosaunee," Duncan said.

"Sir?"

"Not Shawnee. He is of the Haudenosaunee. It means people of the longhouse."

The man's eyes went round with excitement. "The Iroquois! The noble empire of the north! I have journals from my dialogues with the Lenni-Lenape, the Susquehannocks, the Shawnee, the Stockbridge, all but a prelude for studying the Iroquois. My studies inexorably lead me toward the heart of their inner kingdom. Might you be an emissary of sorts? Is it true they have ten words for bear, depending on the age?"

Duncan might have found himself grinning at the stranger's odd combination of zeal, intellect, and naïveté were it not for his worry for Conawago. "I seek an old Indian brought in today, under arrest." He paused as he saw a new uneasiness on the man's face, and he extended his hand. "Duncan McCallum," he ventured, "formerly of the Medical College of Edinburgh."

The man's countenance instantly lit, and he pumped Duncan's hand vigorously. "Johan Van Grut of the Hague. Formerly of the university at Louvain and Yale College in the Connecticut colony."

"My friend carries himself like an old monk, wears his hair in long braids in the traditional style, though he was long educated by Europeans."

Van Grut frowned. "New militia from Virginia did arrive with two long bundles like bodies. I only saw from afar as I was sketching a partridge. One was taken into the infirmary, the other dumped by the guardhouse." He pointed to an earthwork ramp that led to a buried structure.

Duncan straightened as he saw that the sentinels at the ramp included not only two infantry regulars with Brown Bess muskets but also a man in the clothes of a frontiersman, a red patch of cloth on his tricorn hat. He spun about, spotting for the first time half a dozen tents pitched in the shade of the oaks at the northeast corner of the fort. He offered the Dutchman a quick salute and strode away.

Moments later he was behind a tree near the northern palisade, studying the little camp, watching the company for signs of leaders, settling on a square-shouldered bearded man addressed by the others as sergeant whose raspy voice and heavy knife confirmed him as Duncan's assailant of that morning. He crept closer, surveying a line of weapons leaning against a rail lashed between two trees. An instant after he spied his own long rifle, he strode out of his cover, casually lifting his weapon and filling its firing pan from the small horn of priming powder he kept in his pocket. He kept his head down as he approached the sergeant, tapping him on the shoulder with the end of his rifle barrel. As the man turned toward him he slammed the side of his gunstock into his belly, dropping him to his knees, knocking the knife from his hand as he reached for it.

The fury in the sergeant's eyes slackened as he recognized Duncan, and he waved away the men who were circling him.

"It's a miracle, boys," the sergeant sneered. "The garbage has been resurrected from the midden."

"So it was your idea to bury me in the infirmary's waste," Duncan growled.

The sergeant made a chagrined gesture toward his men. "That be northern gratitude for ye, boys. We gave him a free hand and here's how he repays us." Guffaws rose from the militiamen. "If they had a doctor or a butcher here we would have poured some fresh blood on ye," he added in a more treacherous voice.

"I'll have my kit."

The Virginian spat toward Duncan's feet, leaving a dark stain of tobacco on the ground. "Gonna to be auctioned off, with that of the savage, to pay for the coffin of our brave captain."

Duncan pulled the hammer of his gun to the half-cock position and aimed it at the sergeant. "I'll have the kit you stole from me, and that of my friend." He ignored the soldiers who began to close around him, keeping his gaze leveled at the bearded man.

"Your red friend is promised a neck-stretching party. All the same to us if you wish to join him in hell. A man who shares his mess with such filth ain't much better himself."

"Son of a *caoineag*!" Duncan spat. The Highland curses shot from Duncan's lips unbidden as he heard himself invoke not just the spawn of a banshee, but the *uruisg*, the *glaistig*, and the one-eyed *direach*, monsters who avenged the innocent. He was barely able to control his fury.

"We be keeping close watch of your heathen's health," the sergeant chided. "If he looks to be dying we'll string him up without the major's verdict. We'll not be cheated of our justice."

Duncan pulled the hammer of his gun all the way back.

"Ye ain't gonna shoot me."

"No," Duncan agreed, and he swung his rifle toward a keg beside a mound of small bundles. "I'm going to blow your powder and supplies. Of course the splinters from the explosion may take a few of you. Ever see a man with three inches of oak in his eye?"

The sergeant cursed. Half a dozen men with clubs began to surround Duncan. The sergeant was beginning to lift his knife from the ground when he froze. Two shadows appeared at Duncan's side.

"'Tis a bonny thing to be practicing maneuvers, to be sure," came a voice thick with a Highland burr. "But we cannot let ye have all the enjoyment."

The men who stepped to either side of Duncan were huge, the spiked halberds in their hands long and lethal. Each wore a scarlet waistcoat over the plaid kilt of a Highland regiment.

The militia sergeant spat a curse. He slowly rose, calling off his men with a flick of his hand.

"Our friend asked for the return of his property," boomed the soldier to Duncan's left, a big ox of a man with curly red hair overflowing from his Highland bonnet.

On a quick, muttered command one of the militiamen slipped inside a tent then reappeared carrying a familiar powder horn, two packs, and nearly all the other equipment Duncan and Conawago had been traveling with.

"An Iroquois battle ax. A red battle ax," Duncan said. It was, he knew, a favorite souvenir for soldiers. The sergeant cursed again and retrieved it himself from a bedroll.

They stepped quickly away from the militia camp. "Sergeant Colin McGregor at y'er service," declared the red-haired man as he thumped his chest. "Such a fine string of Highland invocations be like a salve to me homesick heart. Did I detect the lilt of the western coast?"

"For as far back as memory," Duncan replied, a small grin tugging at his mouth, "the McCallum clan dwelled nigh Lochlash and in the lesser islands to the west. Now my clan is but me and my brother and an old man in the New York colony."

"Y'er brother?" McGregor asked. "Surely not our own beloved Captain Jamie McCallum?"

Duncan paused to study the garb of the men and recognized the dark tartan of the famed Black Watch, the 42nd Regiment of Foot. "Captain of the 42nd no longer." His brother had been branded a deserter after leaving the battleground of Ticonderoga to save a band of Iroquois holy men from ambush and had been declared an outlaw with a sizable bounty on his head.

McGregor fixed Duncan with an inquisitive gaze. "He was reported dead in a skirmish with French Indians last autumn."

"He was reported dead," Duncan agreed, leaving the words hanging.

"Sometimes," McGregor suggested, "it can be difficult to identify bodies when the heathens have finished with them."

"It can be difficult," Duncan agreed.

The big Scot offered a conspiratorial smile, then McGregor gestured Duncan forward. A moment later Duncan halted as he saw he was being led into the headquarters building.

"I need to see the man they brought into the guardhouse today."

"The old Indian? Dead, more than like," warned McGregor.

Duncan clamped his jaw against a tide of emotion. "I need to know."

"Even if he's not ye'll not get near the cell without the blessing of Major Latchford," added the Scottish sergeant. "You can perform your supplication during your interview."

"Interview?"

"Lad, as happy as I be to rescue ye from those damned south-ern planters, truth is we were sent to find ye." McGregor abruptly stiffened as an oily-looking junior officer appeared at the door in front of them.

"They will polish their boots until I say they are done," the officer snapped in a shrill voice to someone over his shoulder, then paused to study Duncan with a disdainful gaze. He dismissed Duncan's escorts with a cool nod then muttered a syllable to some-one in the shadows. A bent, gray-haired soldier appeared with a heavy brush.

Duncan awkwardly let the officer's valet brush the back of his waistcoat, then gently but firmly took the brush from the man's hand and finished the job himself. The officer frowned, stepped aside, and gestured him through the door. Past two tables stacked with maps was an inner office at which a starched and powdered officer sat, sipping from a china cup as he perused an open journal book.

"Your mongrel, Major," the young officer announced in the tone of one expecting a grand entertainment.

The officer frowned, first at Duncan then at his escort. "Fodder, Lieutenant. How much fodder is needed to overnight another fifty animals?"

"I will look into it at once, sir," the lieutenant replied.

"And the junior officers must be moved into tents by tomorrow."

"Of course, sir." The lieutenant offered not a salute but a servile bow of his powdered head then slipped away.

Latchford fixed Duncan with an icy stare. "You think you can wander into my garrison without a by your leave?" he asked in a cool, well-educated voice. "Use our water, watch my troops like some spy, provoke our bereaved comrades in arms?" Latchford,

Duncan realized, had had him under observation from the moment he had passed under the gate.

"If I am not mistaken, Major, I was brought into your establishment by soldiers under your command." He saw the gleam in Latchford's eyes and instantly regretted the words. A man like Latchford delighted in impudence, for all punishments were at his beck and call.

The officer lifted a quill and made a note in the journal. "You have not honored us with your name."

"McCallum. Duncan McCallum."

"I'll know, McCallum, why your friend killed this particular Virginian on this particular day."

Duncan weighed Latchford's words carefully. There was something more to the murder in the forest than he had understood. "My friend killed no one. You should look to the enemy. Last night we observed a Huron raiding party not twenty miles from here."

Latchford lifted a small bronze medallion etched with a tree on one side, a crude W on the other. The strap that until that morning had fastened it to Duncan's neck had been snapped apart. "Observed?" He dangled the disc toward Duncan. "For Woolford's rangers?"

"Nearly twenty men, including two or three French."

"I have had no reports of hostiles."

"The entire point of secret raiding parties, Major, is to operate secretly." Duncan clenched his jaw, chiding himself. Sometimes it seemed impossible not to lash out at such officers. It was privileged and powdered men like Latchford who had hanged his father for a rebel, skewered his younger brother with a saber, and raped his mother and sisters before bayoneting them.

The major's face flashed with anger. He slammed the medallion onto his desk and leapt up. Duncan braced himself, certain the officer meant to strike him, but Latchford moved to a side door, stepped halfway into the hall to bark out orders for a reconnaissance patrol. Through the rear window Duncan could see parties setting up a large campaign tent. The fortress was expecting visitors, ones important enough to worry the commanding officer. Duncan could not afford to linger if senior officers were coming, officers who might have experience in the New York theater.

When he looked back Latchford was at his desk again, lifting an elegant pistol with a metal butt from the desktop. He toyed with it a moment, sighting along the barrel. "Woolford's men are operating along the Saint Lawrence, the last I heard. And you do not have the look of a ranger, McCallum. We have reports of a solitary warrior and a European woodsman making mischief, always evading our patrols."

Duncan shrugged. "I am no woodsman. And Conawago is no warrior, just an old man looking for traces of his family."

The major extended the pistol, raising and lowering it as if practicing for a duel. "It is easy for a man to pretend a new identity so far from civilization. I have orders to deal harshly with deserters and spies."

"Wounds need to be cleansed every day to keep the filth from entering the blood," Duncan said abruptly.

Latchford's brow knitted. "I'm sorry?"

It was a desperate wager Duncan was making, based on the passing remark of the militia sergeant. "Your infirmary is without a doctor. But you have wounded. I attended medical college in Edinburgh."

"You are a wonder, sir," Latchford sneered. "Ranger. Woodsman. Doctor. Murderer perhaps."

Duncan would not let himself be badgered. "Men with wounds can die without daily care. You have amputees. A man who has given a limb for his king does not deserve to die from neglect."

Latchford put the gun on the desk and leaned toward Duncan with a new, intense scrutiny. "If you lie to me," he hissed, "I shall use you for practice with my new pistol." Duncan silently returned his stare for a moment, then the major looked down. "We have half a dozen wounded from skirmishes, another five or six laid up with pox. Our surgeon was summoned to help with an outbreak at Fort Pitt. Our senior orderly is too fond of his rum."

Duncan resisted the urge to press for an explanation. "I can attend your patients in the infirmary."

"What proof do you offer of your competence?"

"Your arm," Duncan said. "Extend your arm."

Latchford smirked but humored his request, resting his free hand on the pistol.

Duncan began by pointing to a fingertip then worked his way up the arm. "Distal phalanx, phalange, metacarpal, carpal, radius, ulna, humerus." When he passed the elbow Latchford held up his hand to concede the point.

"The man with the freshest wounds lies in your brig," Duncan observed.

"You, McCallum, are a hair's breadth from being thrown in with him!" Latchford snapped. "If he dies it shall save us the nuisance of a trial."

"I need to see him."

"You are hardly in a position to make demands."

"Surely you understand, Major, that the entire balance of power in the war depends on maintaining relations with the tribes."

Latchford leaned back in his chair. His hand curled around the butt of the pistol again, as if he were reconsidering whether to shoot Duncan. "His majesty's troops have won the war in North America," he rejoined.

"His majesty's troops won the last season of battles," Duncan countered, "after losing so many before. They are now spread thin over a thousand miles of frontier, mostly along the border of French Canada. Any fool who can read a map knows the real prize of this struggle is the western lands. All the army has done so far is win the right for the king to compete for them. Lose the Iroquois and you'll spend the next five years fighting in the New York and Pennsylvania colonies with no chance of winning the Ohio territory."

"You speak of matters far removed from our little outpost."

"When Lord Amherst hears the news," Duncan said, referring to Britain's military commander on the continent, "your little outpost will be the center of his attention."

"News?"

"Trying a prominent leader of the allied tribes for murder could destroy the alliance. Instead of a buffer of Iroquois warriors protecting the settlements we would have an army of the best fighters in America turned against us. You won't be able to march a hundred paces past your gate without fear of a tomahawk in your skull."

"This man in the brig is an Iroquois chieftain?"

"Conawago has visited Europe, has medals from the king, is a valued intermediary among all the tribes of the eastern forest. He is the most highly educated Indian you will ever meet. Trained by Jesuits. At home in European courts."

"But he is no chieftain." The major sipped his tea, studying Duncan with new resentment. "Is he even an Iroquois?"

Duncan glanced out the window again, trying to control his emotions.

"I am ordered to have that militia in the field," Latchford declared, casually swinging the pistol about, pausing for a moment as the barrel faced Duncan. "And I always obey orders. You and your friend have strained relations between Pennsylvania and Virginia to the breaking point. Someone is going to hang. Someone is going to hang in the next twenty-four hours."

"And what will your commanding officer think when the truth comes out later?"

Latchford pursed his mouth in annoyance. "The truth?"

"I was at the dead man's side minutes after he was attacked. He was not shot. He was nailed to a tree, his heart was mutilated. This was no random killing. This was a ritual performed for a broader audience."

Worry flickered on Latchford's face. "Ridiculous."

"Conawago is innocent."

"A small army of witnesses will say otherwise."

"All they saw was Conawago leaning over a dying man. He was trying to help him."

The major offered another icy grin. "Witnesses will say otherwise," he repeated.

Duncan put a hand on the back of the chair in front of him. "Who was he? The dead man?"

"The captain? Winston Burke? Commander of the militia? Second son of the greatest landowner in the valley of the Shenandoah. His father is a member of the House of Burgesses. We will have a hanging and get on with the work of war," Latchford declared in a matter-of-fact tone. He aimed the pistol at Duncan and pulled the trigger, sneering as Duncan flinched at the spark of the empty weapon.

Duncan worked at a quick, efficient pace among the sick and wounded. Van Grut followed him to assist the orderlies as he progressed along the cots and pallets, changing bandages on wounds and amputations, inquiring when sulfur had last been burned to fumigate the wards, chastising men over the need to keep their wounds clean, even sending an orderly out to gather moss and pine sap when he was told poultices were in short supply. He knew from experience that the fates of such patients were mostly sealed by the time they arrived. Those with flesh wounds would live, those with wounds in the abdomen would almost always die.

He watched as Van Grut became engrossed explaining how to lance a boil, then quickly slipped through a door in a shadowy corner that seemed shunned by the others.

On a table in the center of the narrow, windowless chamber Captain Winston Burke lay now in peaceful repose. By the light of a single candle at the head of the table, Duncan could see that the commander of the Virginia militia had been cleaned of the blood that had stained him, a small ornate dagger placed in the hands crossed over his belly. His long brown hair had been gathered at the back with a fresh blue ribbon. His light blue waistcoat, fastened over his chest, was faced with buff, the makeshift uniform he had seen on the other officers in the Virginians' camp. His brown woolen britches showed little wear, except for the long jagged tear along the right thigh, mottled with the darker brown of dried blood.

He glanced around the chamber, which was used as a storeroom for the infirmary, the shelves on two walls bearing a few large jars of spirits and vinegar, smaller jars of dried rhubarb, powders of Algaroth and Peruvian bark, small crocks of ointments, and a few linens. He slipped a roll of linen bandages into his belt. Far outnumbering the stocks of medical supplies were rolls of canvas, beside spools of heavy naval thread. Duncan closed his eyes a moment, fighting dreadful memories of his voyage across the Atlantic, of the Scots he had sewn inside such shrouds, once joyful men who had slowly rotted away after being condemned to the king's prison ship, their primary offense being the Highland blood in their veins.

His head jerked up as the sound of a deep, shuddering sigh raised gooseflesh along his spine. He turned with a wrench of his gut to the dead man, as if Burke were about to rise from his repose, then realized the sound came from the darkened rear of the chamber. Lifting the candle, he stepped toward the shadows. A middle-aged man in a threadbare uniform of an infantryman was sprawled in a rocking chair, a bottle of rum in one hand, dead drunk.

Duncan turned back to the corpse and paced around the table, touching an elbow, a knee, a wrist. Rigor mortis had begun. He worked quickly, stretching the torn cloth over the thigh wound to study the long ugly gash. The blade had been heavy and sharp, from a hand ax or tomahawk. Despite the Virginian's other wounds, this had been the one that killed him, this was where his lifeblood had drained away. Pressing the flesh back further, he noted the dark central flow in the pattern of its dried blood and the way the wound narrowed where it had cut the artery, then he straightened and pushed up the sleeves to examine Burke's arms. There was none of the bruising that would indicate a struggle, only a raised, jagged scar nearly three inches long, just below the left elbow, still pink from having been recently formed.

Glancing up with increasing discomfort at the man in the chair, he quickly searched the single pocket sewn into the right side of the waistcoat, finding a flint striker but none of the coins that would have been carried there. He studied the waistcoat itself. It had been expertly tailored, of fine wool, using elegant silver buttons with crossed swords embossed on them. But the upper four buttons had been cut away. Only the top four. The killer had been stealing the valuable buttons and been interrupted. Had Duncan and Conawago been so close that they had frightened him from his gruesome work? He glanced back at the figure in the rocking chair, extracted his own knife, and quickly cut away the button that had been covered under the folded hands, stuffing it into his belt pouch.

He studied the silver dagger, which the dead man held like a trophy. The silver wire of its handle said it had been more an object of adornment than of utility. Wealthy fathers often bought second sons commissions, and sometimes commemorated the event with such a token.

Twisting the dagger free from the stiffening hands, he tugged at the handle. It would not come free of its sheath. He set it down to study the hands themselves. A man's hands could tell as much about him as his face. Every trade had its distinctive pattern of calluses and wear, sometimes its own coloration. A professor in his medical college had once traced an unidentified corpse back to a cobbler's shop from the calluses at the tips of his fingers and heels of his hands, as well as the stains along the outside edge of each hand, marks made by the shoemaker's tacks and the dyes of the leathers the man had held steady at his workbench.

He had almost forgotten the terrible wound on the left hand until he pulled the right one away from it, exposing the mangled flesh. The handsome Burke, a man in his prime, with the soft hands of a man of stature and wealth, had been nailed to a tree. The jagged, ugly hole in the palm gave a glimpse of bone and muscle, the back of the hand still showed a smudge of color from the bark of the tree. He paced around the corpse once more as the burly drunk in the corner began to snore, now examining the discoloration at the man's temple. The skin was slightly abraded, the tissue underneath showing the shading of a contusion that had not bloomed to full color because death came so soon after the blow. Duncan lifted the lantern, holding it over each wound in sequence, the head, the thigh, the hand.

"All the doctors I know tend to the living," came a low, whimsical voice from behind him.

Duncan sprang about to see Johan Van Grut pushing the door shut behind him.

"I did what I could for those in the wards."

"And now you minister to the dead?"

Duncan paused. There was no alarm in the Dutchman's eyes, only intense curiosity. "I do not wish to mislead you, Johan. I was arrested and deported before finishing the final phase of my training. I was still learning how to minister to the living, but my professor said I was perfect with those who had already passed over."

"Meaning," the Dutchman asked in a slow, uncertain voice, "you are a reader of the dead?"

"A corpse can be like an open book." He quickly demonstrated what he had learned thus far, pointing to the deep wound on the thigh and the punctured hand.

"Mother of God!" Van Grut exclaimed as Duncan laid open the mutilated palm. "He was crucified!"

"I have seen many violent attacks," Duncan continued as he unfastened the buttons over Burke's chest, "but never have I seen such a piercing, nor the likes of this," he declared as he pulled open the shirt.

The color drained from Van Grut's face as he saw the gear wheel in the dead man's chest. The fear on his face, however, quickly migrated to confusion. "It was not the cause of his death," he observed. "Then why mark the body so?"

"It was done while he yet lived. See how the blood has flowed into the adjoining skin."

"Are there more?" the Dutchman asked with a grisly fascination.

"More?"

"Gears. In Germany once I saw a mechanical woman in a glass box who lifted her hand and waved. Clockmakers in Zurich had constructed her for a prince. People often ran in fear when they saw her. Others dropped to their knees and prayed for her."

The words strangely disturbed Duncan. "Burke was flesh and blood."

"But if he died this way, was he not becoming a machine in the end?"

Duncan stared at Van Grut, not entirely comprehending, then lifted the dagger and with effort jerked the blade free of its scabbard. He twisted the blade in the light, showing a dark red line that ran along its edge, more red that covered its tip. It had been blood that had glued the blade into its case. With the tip of the blade he began to pry up the gear.

"McCallum!" the Dutchman protested. "You know not what you meddle with! We must study the gear's function. In Germany I was told the clockmakers started with a living woman. What if you find another gear connected underneath?"

Gooseflesh rose along Duncan's spine. For a moment he froze, caught up in his companion's irrational fear, then with a wet sucking sound he pried the gear out of the breastbone.

"May the hand of God smite you demons!"

The hoarse disembodied voice sent both Duncan and Van Grut leaping back, gazing in horror at Burke's bloodless face. The Dutchman seemed about to seize the gear to place it back in the chest when a specter emerged from the darkness.

"Unhand the dead, you thief!" the shadow boomed, and one massive hand seized Duncan's wrist as a second rose toward his throat.

A sign of relief escaped Van Grut as he raised the candle. "Corporal, you're drunk!"

The burly man from the rocking chair hesitated, then dropped his hands and stiffened as if an officer had addressed him. "No drop will e'er prevent me from protecting them what gave their lives for blessed King George."

Duncan recognized the thick northern accent and saw now that a Bible was tucked in the waist of the man's britches.

"Mr. McCallum's a medical man," Van Grut explained.

The soldier, tottering slightly now, eyed Duncan suspiciously. "Beg pardon, sir, but this one's beyond servicing."

"In Yorkshire," Duncan ventured, "There are those who sit with the dead and absorb their sins so they can pass on to heaven. It is an honored profession."

The corporal paused as if he had to consider his answer. "It was how my mother, poor widow as she was, kept bread in our mouths. She died all twisted and gnarled for it." He shrugged. "I know most of the dead I sit with. Ye catch the flavor of a man's sins, well enough, when ye sit with his body through the night. Not for me to play a hand in the fate of their soul, just want them to know they ain't alone. As to why I do it, back home a man with but one root lives on alms until the winter, then dies frozen in the gutter." He tapped his right leg and for the first time Duncan saw the worn oaken stump that extended from his britches. "Lost it to a French cannonball two years ago. They keep me on the roster because I do that which no one else will do."

"Like getting drunk with the dead?"

"The dead be perfect company with a bottle. N'er disagree, n'er take a drop, always listen and—" the corporal added with a perverse gleam, "after the first hour or two they sing right along with ye." He punctuated his explanation with a belch, then reached down and carefully straightened Burke's shirt. "A soldier's got to be strong all the way to the end, especially if there be enemy in earshot. I remind them they still be in battle until their final breath. Chin up and mind the colors. N'er let the French frogs see ye weak."

"Mr. McCallum helps the dead, same as you," Van Grut explained. "He reads their body, like an aborigine reads a trail."

The corporal wiped at a spot on the body's brass gorget. "Didn't know this one, hard to read."

"The killer struck him in the head first," Duncan explained, pointing to the bruise at the temple. "Burke was dazed, or unconscious, long enough for his hand to be nailed to the tree, probably with the same ax that laid open his thigh a moment later—" Duncan paused as he looked at the dagger again. He gestured for Van Grut to hold the lantern close to the exposed thigh wound as he pressed back the flesh. "His own dagger was used to finish him. An ax leaves an ugly wound, a crippling wound even, but not always a fatal one. The killer was not satisfied with the flow of blood, so he jammed the dagger into the artery. My friend and I found him minutes later."

"Did he not speak of his killer as he lay dying?" Van Grut asked.

"He seemed unable . . . " Duncan replied, realizing he had no ready explanation for Burke's inability to speak. The jaw did not readily yield when he pushed it, the rigor beginning to hold it tight. The crunching noise when he pushed harder caused Van Grut to visibly shudder, but he held the candle close as Duncan bent to look in the mouth. Pausing in confusion at what he saw, he reached in deep with a finger and scooped out a lump of metal. He extended it on his open palm to his companions as if for explanation. It was a lump of copper, melted and hardened, as if dropped from a forge.

"Jesu' protect us sinners," the corporal muttered fearfully.

Duncan and Van Grut exchanged a confused glance. The metal made no sense, except for that which had occurred to the worn-out soldier. In the old ways that lingered in Scotland and the north country of England metal was used to fend off the devil.

"The major is in a great rush to resolve this killing," Duncan said to the soldier after a moment. "Who is he expecting?"

"They be passing through Ligonier on the way to Lancaster."

"Who exactly?"

"The dignitaries," the corporal replied. "The treaty conference between Virginia, Pennsylvania, and the Indians."

Duncan studied him, confused. "But surely any peace treaty will be made in Europe. And surely there would be no participants from the wilderness."

The corporal shook his head at Duncan's obvious ignorance. "Affairs of the wilderness don't get settled over lace cuffs and tea. I speak of an Indian treaty. Chiefs from the Iroquois towns and western lands be attending, the black-and-white prigs from Fort Pitt along with them."

"Black-and-white?"

"Goddamned Quakers," the corporal spat, then looked down. "Beg pardon, sir. The gentlemen representing the provincial government in Philadelphia. A magistrate and his kin what they sent to run the new provincial trading post at Pitt."

Latchford, Duncan suddenly realized, was trying to hang Conawago before the treaty delegation arrived. "Was it you who cleaned the body, corporal?" he asked.

"I assisted. 'Twas a frightened lad with red hair. A cousin, he said. Weeping so hard he had to stop several times to collect himself. 'Who will tell his mother?' he kept muttering, and 'oh this cursed struggle.' I told him what I tell all the forlorn creatures, that where the good Lord directs the metal is for no mortal to question."

"Metal?" Van Grut asked.

"'Tis always metal, ain't it? Be it blade or ball, 'tis metal that takes the soldier."

Van Grut cast an uneasy glance at Duncan, as if to suggest it had not been a blade or ball but a malfunctioning gear in the man's chest that had killed him.

Twenty minutes later Duncan leaned against a tree in the shadows by the Virginians' camp as they finished their evening meal and began to make ready for the night. Burke's cousin had not been difficult to identify, a young man with russet hair tied at the back who uneasily sat on a log apart from the others, a quill in his hand, gazing forlornly at a half-written letter.

"So what is the tally of heathen bodies heaped about your captain?" Duncan asked, coming near.

The confusion on the Virginian's countenance quickly changed to rancor as he recognized Duncan.

"I once saw an officer tear up a letter being sent by a subordinate treating the loss of a recruit who drank himself to death," Duncan explained. "He explained that those back home must always believe the dead died as heroes, for king and country. He wrote a new letter reporting that the soldier died protecting a family of Episcopal missionaries, with six dead Indians piled at his feet."

The Virginian, barely out of his teens, gestured to the sheet of paper in his lap. "He died at the hand of a savage while scouting safe passage for his troops. That will make him hero enough."

Duncan studied the dead man's cousin. Was there a note of bitterness mixed with his remorse? "What senior officer leaves his troops behind to make a solitary scout?"

"Do you not know who we are?"

"Militia from Virginia."

"We are, sir, Burke's Shenandoah Company. The senior Burke makes the rules."

"And are you now the senior Burke?" Duncan watched the knot of men around the cook fire as he spoke, well aware that the brawny sergeant there had unfinished business with him.

"Far from it, thank God. I do not even bear the name. My mother is a Burke. I am Hadley, Thomas Hadley. There're two other cousins here, both older than me."

"But you are the one who cleaned the body, the one who is writing the difficult letter."

"I had the misfortune of being home from my studies at the College of William and Mary when the company was being raised. My uncle offered a few extra shillings if I would be company clerk. In the past all the militia did was hold parades and ox roasts."

"But here you are."

"I protested when my uncle suddenly ordered us north. I resigned. I packed my books and was on my mule headed back toward Williamsburg when they rode to fetch me," Hadley explained in a hollow voice.

"My uncle reminded me that we keep Virginia safe by fighting Indians in Pennsylvania and the Ohio country. He said my sacred duty was to chronicle the glory of the Burke expeditionary force. That's the way he speaks of us, like we are builders of empire instead of farmers and students. Following in the footsteps of Colonel Washington and General Braddock, who both led scores of Virginians to the glory of early graves in Penn's woods." Hadley's resentment was undisguised as he spoke of the first skirmish of the war, led by Washington, and the first battle, the bloody massacre on the Monongahela that had become the shame of the British army. "Making history on the military and political fields, my uncle reminded me as we left."

"Political?"

Hadley cast a confused glance at Duncan. "My cousin. Surely you knew. He was also to be senior treaty negotiator from the Virginia province."

The words caused Duncan to pause and sit on the log beside Hadley. *This particular Virginian on this particular day*, Latchford had stated. "Tell me, Hadley, where did your cousin keep that little silver dagger?"

"He had a loop sewn into the inside of his waistcoat, whereby to hang the sheath. Why?"

"Because I think whoever killed him knew where to find it. It was that little dagger that killed him, by slicing deeper into the artery, through the wound made by the tomahawk. Did your captain not have any weapons?" Duncan kept the surly sergeant in sight.

"A pistol, and an elegant rifle, a gift from his father, with his initials carved into the stock."

"Where are they?"

"The pistol was found in the bushes nearby. The rifle was gone."

"We arrived minutes after the attack. We would have heard any shots. Captain Burke let his killer get close, without challenge."

Hadley bit his lip.

"I told you my friend didn't kill him. We were trying to help him."

"It means nothing. The killer could have found the dagger by chance."

"How will you feel, having reported to your family that Conawago was hanged for the murder of your cousin, when we later find that the real murderer was someone who knew him?"

Hadley gazed up in confusion. His jaw opened and shut, but no words came out.

The bearded sergeant was looking directly at Duncan now, his eyes flaring. Duncan bent to the young Virginian's shoulder. "Go to the guardhouse at midnight," he hurriedly instructed. "Tell your man there you are relieving him."

The sergeant shoved his way through the throng of men, grabbed a piece of firewood for a club, and was halfway to Hadley's log by the time Duncan disappeared into the shadows.

The sentry argued with Hadley only a few moments before shouldering his musket and marching off into the moonlight. The company clerk was probably the youngest of the Virginian troop, and his every movement betrayed his lack of seasoning. But he was of the Burke clan, and the guard was of the Burke company. Duncan watched from the shadows for five minutes before approaching the earthen ramp, his eyes not on Hadley but on the sleeping provost guard slumped on a stool against the wall at the jail entrance. Duncan put his fingers to his lips as he reached the Virginian, who grimaced but lifted the solitary lantern from a peg on the wall and followed. They paused when they reached another peg near the strap iron door that held a single large key.

"Tell me why I am doing this?" Hadley asked in an anxious whisper.

"Because, like me, you seek the truth."

"All I seek," came Hadley's sullen reply as he lifted the key and opened the door, "is a quick return to Virginia."

Inside there were no more doors, only several low vaulted chambers carved out of rock and earth. The first two held empty gunpowder kegs. Duncan almost passed over the pile of rags at the rear of the third chamber but then glimpsed the familiar pattern of red beads along the edge of a piece of soiled linen.

A despairing cry escaped his lips as he turned his friend over.
Conawago's right eye was nearly swollen shut, the whole right side
of his face an ugly mass of bruises and cuts. Duncan unbuttoned
Conawago's shirt to reveal more contusions and a swollen, oozing
lump over the left side of his rib cage. Duncan's probing brought
a gasp of agony from Conawago. His good eye fluttered open. It
seemed to take great effort for him to focus on Duncan. "That
Onondaga was right," he said in a hoarse whisper. "The gods are
not happy with me."

Duncan fought against a surge of emotion. The ribs under the
swollen lump were badly bruised, if not cracked. Conawago's leggings were torn, the gaps revealing more bloody abrasions. His right
hand was clenched. Conawago groaned as Duncan raised it. The
little finger hung at an unnatural angle.

"They tried to take the other one after they destroyed the first,"
the Indian said, wincing with each exhalation. "But I was disin-
clined to release her. She's old and worn like me, but one day she
may speak to the other gods for me." He had let his assailants break
his finger, Duncan realized, rather than release the little clay deity.

But now his friend opened his hand and extended the figure to
Duncan. "She needs to go outside. Do you have my things? The
pouch of ochre?"

Duncan nodded, then lifted a ladle of water left on a stool
beside Conawago and pressed it to his lips.

The old Nipmuc sipped, then coughed, gritting his teeth
against the pain. "Good," he said after a moment. "Take her now
and put her in a little circle of that ochre in a pool of moonlight.
Someone should sit with her to say words of comfort. If I were able
I would sit with her all night."

"We will do it together soon."

Conawago somehow managed a smile. "Sit with her, tell her the last of the Nipmucs lived with honor." His good hand reached onto the straw to grip something else, the little fur amulet given him by Skanawati.

"No. We will do it together," Duncan repeated.

Conawago coughed again, closing his eyes as if to gather his strength. "Might I ask one more favor?"

Duncan, finding his tongue would not work, nodded.

"Stay near the tree they pick," Conawago said, his breathing labored now. "I would like to gaze on the face of a friend. Then return the little god to her cave. It was a fool's errand." He smiled weakly then slipped into unconsciousness.

Duncan pointed Hadley to a bucket with a rag hanging on its side and began cleaning the old man's wounds.

"He . . . he speaks well," Hadley ventured over Duncan's shoulder.

"I daresay he is the best-educated man in the fort. Conawago was brought up in Jesuit schools. He speaks English, French, and half a dozen native tongues. He knows more about healing than most doctors in Europe." Punctuating his words was a rustling sound from one of the darkened chambers further down the corridor. No doubt there were rats in the shadows. He pulled the linen bandage roll from his belt and began wrapping the broken finger against the adjacent one.

"He had his knife out, McCallum. Why did he have his knife out if he was trying to tend my cousin's wounds?"

Duncan did not reply at first, only searched the tail of Conawago's shirt. After a moment he showed Hadley where a small strip had been sliced away. "To cut a bandage. He is innocent."

"That is for the court to decide."

"Court? You mean Major Latchford, the Indian hater, and a mob of Virginians in the payroll of the Burke family?" When Hadley did not reply Duncan gestured to Conawago's shoulder. "Help me lean him against the wall, so he can drink more."

When they lifted the ladle to Conawago's lips, his eyes fluttered open again. "Not me. You can do more for her," he said weakly, extending a trembling hand toward the shadow.

Duncan hesitated, glancing at Hadley, who shrugged. A muffled cry rose from the darkness.

The two figures were in the deepest and darkest of the chambers, and they reacted to the light of the lantern by burying their faces in the tattered sacks left them as blankets.

"We mean you no harm," Duncan declared. Two wide, shining white eyes emerged from a blanket. The girl, in late adolescence, leaned over as if to protect the second figure, who lay under sackcloth, writhing. Duncan advanced slowly, his hands open before him, and knelt beside them. The figure in agony was a woman of perhaps thirty, her dark, handsome face contorted with as much fear as pain.

Hadley groaned. The lantern fell from his fingers.

"You know her?" Duncan asked as he grabbed the lantern.

Now he saw that Hadley's face too was gripped in fear. "She . . . they belong to Colonel Burke, back in Virginia." He said nothing more.

Duncan lifted the lantern closer to the two prisoners. Their skin was a light cocoa color, African hints in their features.

"Damn the French for toying with lives the way they do," Hadley murmured.

"The French?" Duncan asked.

"Rumors have spread like wildfire back home, from the Piedmont to the ports. Any slave who can make it to the French-controlled

Ohio country will be granted their freedom and given land to work. A cheap way of blocking British plans."

The girl had clearly recognized the Virginian. Tears were streaming down her face. "Mama needs help, Mr. Hadley."

Duncan's companion seemed about to bolt.

"Please, Mr. Hadley," the girl pleaded. "It's the only reason the soldiers found us. Mama cried out from all the pain."

"Mokie . . . no," Hadley answered, retreating a step.

Duncan put a restraining hand on his arm. "I can't do this alone."

"What do you mean?"

"Fetch me clean blankets, even if you have to steal them from the major himself. The officers' quarters may have their stove banked for the night. Boil some water."

"I don't understand."

Duncan threw back the sacks covering the woman. "Your uncle's slave is about to have a baby."

By the time Duncan emerged from the guardhouse the eastern trees were mottled with gray light. His heart sank as he saw men running to the officers' quarters, and he dropped onto a split log bench, too exhausted to worry about the verbal and probably physical flagellation he was about to receive for breaking into the jail and interfering with the prisoners. Yet he was not merely overcome with fatigue. For the moment he was seized also by an odd flush of satisfaction. He had delivered a healthy infant boy. The woman herself, Becca by name, had been more experienced than either Duncan or Hadley, but Duncan had played the role of the midwife.

He had an unexpected longing to write a letter to Sarah Ramsey in the New York colony, who had claimed his heart the year before, to tell of delivering his first baby. Then an officer appeared at a fast, hopping pace, buttoning his gaiters as he moved out of the officer's quarters, spitting invective at the soldier who trotted in front of him. Duncan looked into his hands, stained from the night's work, collecting himself, bracing himself. But suddenly more invective rose from the outer gate, still lit by lanterns. A chorus of new angry voices erupted from outside the walls.

"My God, McCallum," came a weary voice behind him. "I never . . . " Hadley failed to complete the sentence as he dropped onto the bench beside him. "Becca said her son is named Penn. When I was leaving the old Indian called out."

Duncan, only half listening, was watching the officer at the gate. Then the words registered. "Conawago is awake?"

"He asked to see the little boy, to hold him. Mokie brought him, and he whispered in the boy's ear, an Indian prayer, I think, and told her he would have a long and rewarding life."

Duncan kept watching the gate, slowly realizing that the sudden activity marked the unexpected, early arrival of the treaty delegation. "A prayer?" he asked, turning to Hadley.

"Thanking the gods. He said it was a very good omen, that a young one arrives when the old depart, that the spirits were saying they are ready to welcome him today."

"Tell me, McCallum," Latchford demanded, "who is the commanding officer responsible for the rangers in this theater of war?"

Duncan fought to steady himself. He had been at the well, washing his hands, when Latchford's men had dragged him into the major's office. "Captain Woolford is the only name I need to know."

An icy grin grew on Latchford's face. "What is the monthly pay for one of the king's rangers?"

Duncan stared silently at the officer.

The amusement in the major's eyes fanned into a smoldering anger. "What is the official kit issued to a ranger?"

"The rangers, sir, are irregulars. Some serve as the need arises."

"You have the stench of a fugitive. I should clamp you in irons right now, McCallum," the officer snapped, then gestured to a piece of folded foolscap on his desk beside one of the brown envelopes used for army business. "I have already drafted a letter to Philadelphia seeking the truth about you. If I decide you have stolen that badge I will hang you forthwith. I could write the order this morning. A double hanging would be excellent for discipline. We have enough damned Scots in the infantry. We don't need more skulking about the wilderness."

Duncan lifted his gaze from the letter. He could ill afford to have inquiries about him raised with senior officers. He returned the major's stare, the fog in his head beginning to lift as he recognized the note of invitation in Latchford's voice. "What is it you want, Major?"

"This matter must be settled today, immediately."

"The treaty convoy has been arriving since dawn," Duncan noted. "It's a day early."

"It is but the vanguard. The delegates are hours behind. The Virginians have declared that if justice is not served out today they will take the prisoner back to Virginia for punishment. I will not tell my general I lost thirty good wilderness fighters over some aged savage who should have been in his grave years ago."

More importantly, Duncan decided, Latchford could not jeopardize the treaty by conducting a murder trial in front of the treaty dignitaries. "He is innocent."

"There is not a damned Indian on this continent who is innocent. He will hang. Your work in the infirmary was . . . acceptable. You have proven yourself an educated man. What I need from you now is the evidence collected, in a neat package I can send to Philadelphia to explain our actions. I have no time to both attend to the delegation and write the report that is required. I need a summary of the evidence that will be read and filed away without raising further questions. If you need to visit the murder scene I will provide an escort. We can afford no distractions in the work of the king."

"You mean you can't afford to have a killing disrupt the treaty negotiations."

Latchford's eyes flared. "With the right report we can avoid a lengthy trial. And I will refrain from pressing those uncomfortable questions about you." He lifted the envelope and pointedly tapped its corner on his desk.

"The evidence does not say Conawago is the killer."

"You misunderstand. I require the medical expertise you demonstrated to me. I know you secretly examined the body. A vivid description of the wounds. A seasoning of Latin. Wounds made by a tomahawk, a knife, a club. I will officially connect them to the prisoner in my judicial findings. You say the condemned was trained by Jesuits. Obviously a French sympathizer. No one will begrudge us for dispatching another enemy of the king. You were an eyewitness. Perhaps you are ready to reconsider what you saw. Give me the report I need and you will be back in your forsaken wilderness by nightfall."

"I will not help to hang him."

Latchford made a gesture at the sentry. "Then I will place you in a cell where you can watch the old fool twist on his rope. After which you can rot for a few weeks until I write the report describing how you impersonated a ranger. It will give me time to build you a proper gibbet. Help me hang your Indian," the major spat, "or I will hang you."

Chapter Three

UNCAN HAD NEVER truly walked in a forest before until he had walked with Conawago. The old Nipmuc had first taught him how to listen and smell, how to see things he had never seen before, how to move without disturbing the forest floor, but only after subjecting him to long hours of cleansing rituals. The grime of the European world had to be scoured from his skin, washed from his ears and nose, Conawago had insisted. The winter before, they had spent days on a remote mountain building an elaborate sweat lodge, then alternated between the lodge and a pool of icy water as the old Indian murmured to the spirits, staying up for hours each night to watch stars and meteors. Finally Conawago had stood at the edge of a high cliff and shouted up to the sky that this Scot from across the sea was ready for the gods to take notice of him.

The magic of those hours would dwell in Duncan's heart forever, and he embraced it again as he approached the murder scene, trying to clear his mind of the fear he felt for the old Nipmuc who lay, bleeding and broken, in Latchford's jail.

The earth around the scene of the murder had been pressed down with the shoes and moccasins of so many men it was impossible to make sense of the tracks. Duncan paused repeatedly, raising his hand for Van Grut and McGregor to halt as he studied the forest before them, straining to re-create in his mind's eye the scene as he and Conawago had found it. As McGregor took up a position as sentinel, Duncan showed Van Grut where the body had leaned against the big beech tree and pointed out the patch of darkened soil where Winston Burke's lifeblood had drained. The large nail that had pinned his hand was still in the tree, stained with blood its entire length.

"Suppose you are the murderer," Duncan said to Van Grut after pacing along the front of the tree, reconstructing the crime. He paused, considering the intense worry in the Dutchman's face. He had not hesitated when Van Grut had volunteered to join him, welcoming the pair of scientifically trained eyes, but now the Dutchman seemed to be having second thoughts. "You stupefy Burke with a blow of your hand ax to the head then drive the nail through his left hand to pin him to the tree before slashing the leg."

The Dutchman knelt and studied the spike. "Why a nail?"

It was a question Duncan had asked himself during the ride from the fort. Nails were precious commodities on the frontier, where structures were typically joined with wooden pegs, not iron. "I don't know," he admitted. "A sharpened peg would have worked, even a heavy locust thorn. Indians don't use nails."

"They steal from our forge all the time," McGregor corrected him, "use 'em to tip their battle axes, or for trade. Good as money back in their towns, I hear."

Duncan acknowledged the truth of the words with a grimace, then eased the nail out with the edge of his tomahawk, reminding himself that there were many across the sea who would use the metal as a talisman to ward off evil. But here the nail had done the work of the devil. Or had Burke been the devil to be fended off?

The head had an unusual crosshatch design. "Does your forge make this design on its nails?"

McGregor studied it and shook his head.

Other pieces of metal had figured in the death, Duncan reminded himself as he dropped the nail into his belt pouch beside the lump of copper from Burke's mouth. The nail. The gear. The copper. None had been required for the killing. The murderer had been acting on some broader stage. But to what purpose? he asked himself. The objects would have had meaning for someone. Which meant they were intended to convey a message from the killer.

Burke had been scouting, his cousin had insisted. Duncan found the explanation hard to believe, but certainly Burke had been alone and had left his camp before dawn. He reconstructed the scene in his mind's eye once more. Burke's britches and stockings had not shown the heavy dew damp of hard travel through the undergrowth, meaning he had arrived from the Forbes Road, no more than thirty minutes ahead of his men. There had been no fresh tracks on the trail or Conawago and Duncan would have noticed them. Burke had turned off the road up the Warriors Path and gone to the massive beech tree that marked the trail, as if seeking it out.

He looked back at the Dutchman. Van Grut's face was clouding with worry.

Duncan had not forgotten the words first spoken by Latchford. *Why this particular Virginian, why this particular day?* The major had left out another important question. "Why this particular tree?" Duncan asked.

"It is a grand specimen, huge." The Dutchman eyed the road as if suddenly thinking of bolting. McGregor stepped closer to him.

"I've seen larger," Duncan replied as he studied the forest, slowly stepping around the tree, examining now the worn earth and the long shadow that snaked off into the forest. The Warriors Path had been used for centuries by tribesmen traveling to the south and west. He recalled how in their own journey Conawago had led Duncan off it to follow the Forbes Road, which ran near at several points. But none of those other intersections had such a tree. He looked up at the back of it, the north side, and froze.

Over Duncan's head were rows of carved symbols, starting with a line of stick figures and shapes such as Duncan had seen on message belts used by the Iroquois. But here the figures had been carved into the silver bark instead of woven with purple and white beads. The figures of Indians carrying tomahawks were a warning sign. The trail wasn't called the Warriors Path for nothing. Below the signs was another sign, carved not so long before, and not by Indian hands. It was an I and a V, a Roman numeral four. Around the side, to the east, were more signs, five recently carved geometric shapes, squares and right angles, some with small pieces of bark taken out of their centers like dots, not always in the same location on the shape. The first seemed to be a U, squared at the bottom, the next a right angle, tilted so it aimed at the center of the U, the third a right angle with its corner at the left top, a dot tucked into the corner.

He spied curled pieces of bark beneath the signs and knelt, lifting one, bending it, smelling it. The pieces were fresh, not yet dried out, excised no more than a day before. Someone had carved the signs after Burke had been killed, perhaps as it happened. The valuable buttons had not all been cut from Burke's shirt, but the symbols had been carefully carved, as if they were more important than the silver.

He turned to see Van Grut on a log, pulling a journal from the linen bag that never seemed to leave his shoulder, then extracting a writing lead from inside his waistcoat.

"You knew about this tree," Duncan said to the Dutchman.

It was not a question.

Van Grut seemed strangely shamed. "I suspected. I was not certain," he said, his tone one of apology.

Duncan approached the Dutchman. "You were paying off debts at the fort," he said in an accusing tone. "Burke's purse was empty."

The color drained from Van Grut's face. "Surely you don't—"

"In all this broad wilderness, you knew something about one particular tree."

Van Grut once more looked longingly toward the road.

Duncan demanded, "Why this tree? Why these marks?"

"It's not just one tree," Van Grut said. "There are others."

"Others?"

The Dutchman turned with a stubborn gaze then sighed, opened his journal, and began leafing through it. As Duncan watched he paged through detailed drawings of Indians, birds, and mammals, stopping at a sketch of a large tree. It seemed to be the one in front of them, until Van Grut pointed to the legend he had recorded underneath. *Boundary Marker No. III.* Duncan read on. *1 mile SE Forbes Road, 4 miles W. Ligonier. Monongahela Land Co.*

Duncan looked up, suspicion in his eyes. "You didn't come to help me." He shook his head angrily. "You are using me."

Van Grut looked away, at the tree. "My travels, my equipment, are costly. My family lost every guilder in the collapse of the markets in Antwerp years ago. There are three ways one can earn an income while living on the frontier. Trapper, soldier—"

"Or surveyor," Duncan finished.

"It is an honorable pursuit," the Dutchman protested, but the hint of remorse in his voice was unmistakable.

"Yet you didn't tell me."

Van Grut twisted his fingers around the drawing lead in his hands. "I do two or three days of survey work, then two or three collecting specimens." He regarded Duncan apologetically. "They said he was nailed to a tree. How was I to know it was this tree?"

"You suspected it. Why?" Duncan grabbed the journal and pushed it toward Van Grut's face. "Why?" he demanded again.

"Burke," Van Grut whispered. "He was one of the owners of the land company I work for."

Duncan sighed heavily. "All the time in the infirmary, you never said a word."

"Surely it would not have changed anything you did. And he was here in his role for the militia."

Duncan did not argue. He looked back at the tree, seeing again the dying man in his mind's eye. Burke clearly stood at the confluence of many events. Of many mysteries. "Tell me about the land company."

"It is owned by Virginians. A vast tract was ceded to them by some Iroquois chiefs, but the government will not accept the deed without a more definite description. More land claims will come, everyone knows, and they mean to use this tract as the anchor for fixing the location of future deeds."

"It was Burke who paid you?"

Van Grut nodded. "A month's wages."

"When?"

"The day before yesterday."

"Where?"

"By another marker tree, the one with the roman three cut in it. A few miles east of here."

Duncan paged through the book and found the corresponding drawing, complete with the roman numeral and Indian carvings, but none of the geometric symbols found on the tree before them. He pointed to the strangely haunting shapes. "What do they mean?"

"I have no idea."

"You were not curious?"

"I am always curious. They seem to mark out the boundary in some other way. I do not know why, or for whom."

Duncan walked along the wide trunk. "There is a sequence, based on the weathering of the wood. The Indian signs from long ago. The Roman numerals from months ago. These peculiar runes made a day ago. How many of your other trees had Roman numerals?"

Van Grut did not need to consult his book. "Only the ones with Indian signs."

Duncan handed the journal back to Van Grut, who opened it to a blank page and quickly began drawing.

"What else did he say that day?"

"We made conversation. Spoke of the task at hand. He struck me as being in a hurry."

"What exactly about the task?"

"I showed him my drawings. He was most pleased with them, said he would choose ones to buy for his parlor wall when all was finished. Then he changed my assignment."

"How so?"

"There had been another surveyor named Putnam assigned to this region. He disappeared months ago. I assumed it had something to do with him, that they had found him or his records."

"But what was your original assignment?"

"I was to originally record a detailed description of the last fifty miles of the trail, the final western segment of the boundary line.

Two days ago Burke declared that the last tree, by the Monongahela, no longer needed to be visited. In fact he said plainly do not visit it. I took it as an order."

"Burke had the whole wide forest," Duncan said as the Dutchman recorded the marks on the tree, "yet he left his men and came here. As his destination. It must have been to meet someone. He met his killer at a boundary marker just as he had met you the day before at one. Why?"

"A convenient place to meet," interjected McGregor, who had been watching the forest uneasily. "No other tree like it, because of the marks. You can't just say meet ye at yon beechy tree," he added, gesturing to the landscape around them. There were hundreds, thousands of beeches all around them, interspersed with groves of hemlock.

It was, Duncan had to admit, a likely answer. "Who else was in the region two days ago?"

"The Highlanders," McGregor quickly recited. "Three hundred regular infantry. A handful of scouts. Teamsters on the Forbes Road with their wagons."

"Teamsters going where?"

"The western forts have to be regularly replenished. Ligonier, Bedford, Pitt. As many as fifty wagons a week this time of year."

"Coming from where?"

"The Forbes Road goes from Philadelphia to Lancaster, Conestoga, Carlisle, Bedford."

"Who else?"

"That pack of French Indians you reported, looking for fresh stew meat," the sergeant added, referring to the enemy tribes' notorious, though much exaggerated, reputation for cannibalism.

"The tribal politicians," Van Grut added.

"Politicians?"

"The treaty delegations. Representatives of the tribes subordinate to the Iroquois are coming from many directions, with a rendezvous at Ligonier before traveling east. Half chiefs, the Iroquois call them."

"People are looking for peace with these treaties, not murder," Duncan countered.

Van Grut winced at Duncan's seeming naïveté. "Do you understand nothing? The dispute over the Virginians' claim to this tract of land is the primary reason for the treaty meeting."

Anger simmered in Major Latchford's eyes as he watched the arrival of still more treaty participants. The flood of civilians clearly rankled him. The teamsters and their mules brought disarray to his orderly bastion, the merchants who traveled with the convoy defied his orders not to engage in trading out of their wagons, the Indian chiefs ornamented with tattoo, fur, and paint ignored his command to remain in the tribal campsite he had designated in the outer grounds, wandering around the fort like curious spectators. But as Duncan watched the officer from the stable, where he and McGregor unsaddled their garrison horses, it was the half-dozen men dressed in simple black that were the real target of the major's smoldering expression. It wasn't merely that the Quakers were obviously men of affluence or that they gave but cool welcome to the king's troops in their province, McGregor reported, it was that their leader announced that he was commissioned as a magistrate.

Latchford had known the Pennsylvania official was coming, Duncan realized, but had assumed he was not arriving until the next day. The major had lost his race to deal with the murder before the arrival of the Quakers, before the arrival of a civilian with judicial authority.

Duncan watched from the shadows of the stable as a tall, poised Quaker, flanked by a lean blond man of Duncan's own age and a square-shouldered figure of perhaps forty, spoke to the provost sentries at the guardhouse. Duncan, fighting a near-paralyzing fear over the fate of Conawago, watched from the shadows as the tall Quaker pointed toward the barred door, shook a finger at a sentry who seemed to argue with him, then dispatched his companions toward the Virginians' camp before disappearing into the head-quarters building.

Sitting with his back against the stable wall, Duncan had succumbed to his fatigue when he was suddenly seized by the shoulder and pulled to his feet.

"The major commands your presence," barked one of the soldiers Duncan had seen on duty at the headquarters. He proceeded to shove Duncan, groggy from sleep, across the yard.

Inside, the smoke had barely cleared from what had obviously been an explosive argument. The Quaker leader sat ramrod straight in the chair opposite Latchford's desk, fixing the major with a sober stare. Latchford was eyeing his dueling pistol again.

"I was explaining to Magistrate Brindle that all is in hand," he declared to Duncan with a meaningful stare. His hand rested on the brown envelope, now closed with a seal. The letter to Philadelphia that would condemn Duncan. "Your report must be nearly complete."

Duncan gazed from one man to the other. The Quaker looked straight ahead, regarding the major with an expression of sober piety on his narrow face. His hand was on a small black book perched on his knee. In the shadows past Brindle was the tall blond man Duncan had seen outside, watching Latchford warily.

"Captain Burke was killed with forethought," Duncan ventured. "As a result of blows with an ax or heavy tomahawk, then his own dagger, which caused fatal hemorrhaging within minutes of the attack."

Latchford offered a short, uncertain nod.

"There seemed to be a ritual involved with the killings," Duncan added.

"A ritual?" Brindle asked.

"There was a clockwork gear driven into his heart."

The color drained from the magistrate's face.

"It's what the savages do, uncle," put in the blond man in the shadows. "A dead man can be used to send a message."

"A message, Samuel?" In afterthought, Brindle gestured to the tall man. "My nephew Samuel Felton."

Felton stepped closer to the magistrate. "To the other side," he continued.

"A gear in the heart seems more a message for this world," the magistrate observed in a haunted tone.

"A savage who would do such a thing has such hatred for Europeans he wanted to express it for this world and the next," suggested Felton.

Latchford frowned. "What the old Indian intended is of no concern. He will hang all the same."

As Brindle turned toward him, Duncan had the sense of being under the eye of one of the stern priests of his childhood. "Did this Virginian succumb in the territory of Pennsylvania?"

"He died along the Forbes Road, sir. I am given to believe that the Pennsylvania province has agreed to take it over from the army." Duncan glanced at the book again. It was not a Bible. It was a book of laws.

Brindle's smile was thin and lightless. "And did this Indian in the guardhouse kill Captain Burke, Mr.—?"

Duncan looked at the floor. "McCallum. If I am to be a witness, I should not be answering to the judges prior to their proceeding."

"Judges?" Latchford's eyes flared.

Brindle spoke politely but firmly. "As Mr. McCallum reminds us, Pennsylvania has equal jurisdiction in this matter."

The major seemed about to launch himself at Duncan when suddenly the lieutenant appeared, rushing to hand Latchford a note. Duncan inched around the corner of the table, straining to see the paper. It seemed to be a list of names. Latchford settled back with a victorious grin and nodded toward the sentry at his door. "Then by all means let us not delay our justice. Your services, McCallum," he added, "shall not be required."

Moments after Duncan was roughly escorted outside, officers began streaming out of the building, barking orders for soldiers to gather benches from the barracks, which were arranged in two rows before a large table under one of the largest oaks. The trial was to take place outside, with not one but two chairs at the presiding table.

Duncan found himself moving toward the guardhouse, his heart in his throat, his gut churning with fear and anger. For a desperate moment as he watched the heavy door open he found himself studying the horse pistol in the belt of the provost officer, envisioning in his mind how he might rush the man, seize the pistol, and free his friend.

Then suddenly a hand was on his arm, squeezing so tightly it hurt. Sergeant McGregor pulled him away, back into the shadows, as the procession emerged. Conawago paused, blinking, in the sunlight, then stumbled in his chains, falling to the ground but shrugging off the help of the soldiers as he struggled to his feet.

In a daze, Duncan allowed himself to be led to a bench at the rear of the makeshift courtroom. His friend was pushed into a chair flanked by two provost guards with bayonets fixed to their muskets. For the first time Duncan spotted the noose strung from a heavy limb of the big oak.

"He's innocent!" Duncan exclaimed. A sob escaped him.

"It's the wilderness, lad," McGregor said, as if it explained much. He tightened his grip on his charge's arm.

But Duncan no longer was in the wilderness. He was back in Scotland, and English brutes were killing his brother and sisters in the name of the king. He would stop it! He had to stop it! He wrenched his arm free and leapt up, but the burly Scottish sergeant grabbed him again, more forcefully, and pinned him against a tree with an arm across his chest. At that moment Latchford pounded the table with the butt of his pistol, commencing the proceedings.

The two judges moved with sober efficiency, quickly working through the first bench, packed with witnesses from the Virginia militia company. Latchford led the questioning.

"'Twas as cruel a heartbreak as a man could bear," declared Duncan's enemy, the bearded sergeant, the first to sit on the witness stool, "our poor captain's lifeblood spilling out as the damned heathen waited with his knife over him, ready for one more cut at his tormented body."

"A lie!" Duncan shouted out as McGregor tried to clamp a hand over his mouth. "What kind of justice is this, that—" but his words were lost as the shaft of a halberd slammed into his gut. He doubled over in pain, gasping for air.

When he recovered, he was propped against the tree, McGregor squatting at his side. "That was a foul blow," Duncan groused, rubbing his belly.

"'Tweren't me, 'twas the provost who came up behind. That Philadelphia man chided him for striking you, declaring you too would be given your fair time in the witness chair."

Duncan leaned forward and saw another witness now on the stool. Half the witness bench had been cleared. Brindle was taking notes, sometimes pausing to confer with his nephew Felton and his shorter, stockier companion.

"Five witnesses so far," McGregor explained as he recognized the query in Duncan's eyes, "All with the same tale, though some vow that they saw your friend fixing to scalp their officer." Latchford's resistance to Brindle had faded when he saw the list of names ready to condemn his prisoner.

Conawago himself appeared not to be listening to the proceedings. He was studying a red and black bird perched on a limb above him, a tanager, which seemed to be intently watching the men below. McGregor reached into his belt and extracted a scrap of paper. "Passed to the guard for you," he whispered as Duncan recognized the elegant handwriting of his friend.

I can see a hint of dawn between the bars, Conawago's note began. *It will be a fine day to begin a journey. There is a formation of rocks like a chimney on the ridge south of the river. If you happen to be nearby in a year's time I will meet you there. I am Conawago, son of the Nipmuc. Listen to the wind and you shall hear my name.*

Duncan's eyes welled with tears. The old Indian referred to his journey to the spirit world. Despite his training by the Jesuits, despite living in the European world for many years, he was steadfast in the beliefs of the woodland tribes. The journey to the other side took twelve full months to achieve, which is why rituals were held on the one-year anniversary close to the place of death.

Suddenly young Hadley was on the witness stool. Duncan stood up and leaned forward, as the young officer described how he had been at the front of the column and noticed the movement at the big beech tree. He described his horror at discovering the Indian bent over his captain.

"Is it possible," Brindle asked, "that this Indian was ministering to the unfortunate Captain Burke?"

"He had his knife out."

"To cut a bandage perhaps?"

Duncan's heart flushed with hope. The magistrate would not be led by Latchford.

"I saw no bandage."

"It was a bandage!" Duncan shouted as he shot up again. "Conawago was tending the wounds!" Protests rose up from those around him.

Latchford pounded the table. A provost started toward Duncan, then McGregor pulled Duncan down.

Hadley hesitated, looking at Duncan.

"There was no bandage!" The low, insistent words came from the bearded sergeant at the front.

Hadley looked at the sergeant, then at the simmering men of his company, neighbors and comrades all from home, before looking down into his hands. "There was no bandage."

"Why would he nail Burke to the tree?" Duncan shouted. "He had no nails! He had no nails!"

Felton leaned over his uncle a moment, his whispered words bringing a shadow to Brindle's face.

"In the valley where you live," the magistrate asked Hadley, "was there not an incident involving the nailing of hands?"

Hadley's own face darkened. He looked to the bench of militia before speaking. "There was an incident, not many years ago. Some Iroquois were caught taking food. They were punished."

"Punished?" Latchford pressed.

Hadley choked for an instant. The bearded sergeant stood up. "We hanged 'em proper!" he barked. "Then nailed them to a barn by their war path. Now this old fool heathen thinks he takes his vengeance on us."

Duncan stared in disbelief, pushing down his roiling emotions so he could reason with himself. There had to be something he was missing, had to be a piece of evidence that would save the man who, more than any other, was like family to him. The boundary tree, the clock gear, the copper all meant something, but through his miasma of fear and fatigue he could not find the pattern uniting them.

Suddenly McGregor was pulling him up, steering him toward the judges' table. The Quaker magistrate stated Duncan's name in a loud, steady voice.

"Are you landed, Mr. McCallum?" Brindle asked as Duncan took the witness stool.

"Sir?"

"Are you a landholder in Pennsylvania province?"

"I am not." Duncan's mind raced. He could ill afford to have the judge probe his background. If they knew the truth, that he was technically indentured to the family of Lord Ramsey in New York, they would never let him testify, and they would probably order him put in irons. "I am but recently arrived from Scotland," he ventured.

McGregor, standing at the side of the makeshift courtroom, loudly cleared his throat. "Men who volunteer to scout against the enemy heathen, your lordship, be of great service to the province." He was looking not at his major but at the magistrate. Latchford's eyes blazed at the insubordination. The Quaker's brows rose in surprise. But the nod he cast at Duncan was approving. "You were at the scene of violence as well, I take it?" he asked.

Movement at the rear of the assembly caught Duncan's eye for a moment. The young Iroquois he had seen making arrows in the yard was now there, in front of nearly a score of other Indians, watching intently.

"Conawago and I found Captain Burke together. He had already been set upon, only minutes before. We tried to help him."

"But you were not at Burke's side when he died?"

"I ran to retrieve a dressing for his wound, to staunch the flow of blood. The militia arrived as I was gathering it."

Latchford leaned forward, clearly resenting the Quaker's domination of the questioning. "Was Captain Burke dead when you left his side, McCallum?"

"He was not."

"Then how, McCallum, can you testify it was not your friend who delivered the death blow?"

"I examined Burke. The fatal wounds were already inflicted when we arrived. Conawago is no murderer. Someone with a tomahawk inflicted them. He carries no tomahawk."

"Do not practice your sophistry on us, sir!" Latchford lashed out. "In fact you are no witness at all. You did not see the murder. We have had a dozen good men say without hesitation they saw it, and your friend committed it."

"They served the dead man. They hate Indians."

Latchford ignored his protest. "Were you able to see your friend at all times or not?" he demanded. "As he was alone with Captain Burke?"

Duncan's despair was a black, living thing inside him, rising up, gripping his heart, choking him. He turned toward Conawago. His friend's face was open and serene. He offered Duncan the gentle smile that had touched his heart so many times. Duncan looked to the ground. "I did not," he murmured.

Magistrate Brindle gave a chagrined shrug. Latchford leaned back and offered a smug nod to the officer of his provosts.

Duncan did not realize he had been dismissed at first. He stumbled away as if in some terrible dream, barely hearing the pistol butt that hammered the table to close the testimony. He only vaguely noticed that the Indians gathered at the rear were moving about now, whispering, distracted by something behind them.

It was Van Grut who intercepted him and guided him back toward the tree where Sergeant McGregor waited. Brindle and Latchford conferred in whispers for less than a minute. Duncan had already resented Latchford, now he knew he would forever despise the major for directing a provost to make ready the noose before the verdict was spoken.

Brindle asked for Conawago to stand.

"Having dispatched its solemn duty," Brindle began, "this court has no choice but to—" his words died away, replaced by an eerie, high-pitched sound, like the drawn-out attack screech of a hawk. All eyes shot upward in confusion, some men ducking for cover as the sound grew louder. Then abruptly the source of the screech landed in the grass, not three feet from the judge's table. It was a projectile tipped with bone carved into a whistle, an Iroquois signal arrow.

The Indians ran forward, then stopped as abruptly as the arrow when they reached the open space between the judges and the benches. A figure had materialized in the space, a bronze statue of a man wearing leggings, breechcloth, and a sleeveless waistcoat. His skin glistened with oil and fresh paint in the pattern often worn by Iroquois war parties. The young warrior who had been in the fort the day before stood at his side, a bow in his hand, his countenance filled with pain. Duncan saw the way the Indians revered the painted man, then as he stepped closer recognized the tattoo of the turtle on his cheek.

"I am called Skanawati of the Onondaga," the man declared in a voice that would carry miles, his English words slow and carefully pronounced. "I am a member of the Grand Council, keeper of the hearthfire of the Iroquois nations, chief of the turtle clan." Duncan saw that a smear of red paint had been added to the tip of the blade that hung over his chest, and to the blade of a tomahawk in his belt.

Latchford's face twisted into a snarl. His provosts hovered beside him, waiting for an order to clear the disturbance. "What is the meaning of this interruption?" he demanded.

The Iroquois chief waited until the Indians with him had surrounded Conawago, as if to protect him. "I have come to tell you it was I, Skanawati, who killed the Virginian captain."

Chapter Four

A T FIRST DUNCAN did not understand Latchford's furious response to the confession by the Iroquois chieftain, did not entirely grasp the change in the atmosphere. Brindle closed his Bible and clasped his hands as if praying. Then Duncan saw the reluctant nod by Latchford that sent the provosts to remove the manacles from Conawago and place them on Skanawati.

"Blood of Christ!" McGregor muttered. "There's a foot in the kettle."

"I'm sorry?"

"Thank God y'er friend is safe. But the major knows that without the treaty the army will never get Iroquois help in subduing the western tribes. The Six Nations won't even get to the negotiating table if the army hangs their lead negotiator at Ligonier."

"But he confessed," Duncan said uncertainly, looking at Skanawati and the Indians, still not entirely grasping what was unfolding.

"Lose the Iroquois or lose the Virginians. Not even the esteemed and sanctified magistrate will take that decision. 'Twill be for the governor and general to decide how to get the noose on him. Unless the Burke company charges forward," the sergeant added.

Duncan followed McGregor's gaze toward the knot of Virginian soldiers who now surrounded Latchford, their lieutenant haranguing him, angrily pointing at the stone-faced Skanawati, who stood between his new guards.

"Now!" the Virginian officer barked. "While the rope is fresh!" His men would not be denied their justice, or at least their vengeance. The magistrate and governor might be slow in meting out punishment, but Latchford was clearly considering a swifter resolution. Duncan could see the cool calculation in the major's eyes. He was desperate to keep the Virginians in his garrison.

Duncan's mind raced as Latchford announced to the Quaker that the army would have to take custody of the confessed murderer, then Duncan found himself pushing through the crowd toward the judges' table. His words were drowned out by the loud protests of the Virginians, some of whom were now pointing to the noose, eyeing the provosts as if about to rush them. He spoke only to Brindle, his eyes only on the powerful Quaker, then when he realized he was not penetrating the din around him, he placed his palm over the dog-eared Bible in front of the magistrate.

Brindle saw the hand first and followed his arm upward to meet Duncan's gaze, then raised his own hand for silence.

"Mr. McCallum, you were saying?"

"I was saying, sir, that with so many hostiles in the region the garrison has no time to deal with such difficult legal matters. Matters that are, after all, the business of the province."

"I was aware of only one matter," Brindle observed in his level, refined voice.

"Far be it for me to tell your honor his business," Duncan replied. "I was thinking of the crime against the Virginian, of course. Then there is the matter of respecting Iroquois justice if an Iroquois is to be charged while the province negotiates a treaty with them. I suppose it is possible that Pennsylvania may decide the army is responsible for relations with the tribes," he observed, well aware of the constant tension between the Quakers and the military. "But there are still the interesting issues around the new citizen of the province."

The din began to fade as the major, then more and more of the company stopped to listen to Duncan's words. "New citizen?" Brindle asked.

As if on cue the small party transporting Burke's body back to Virginia could be seen by the guardhouse, shoving the escaped slaves toward the gate. As Hadley had warned, the returning soldiers could not resist the reward they knew awaited those who returned Colonel Burke's property.

"Born last night, on these very grounds."

Latchford, who finally seemed to grasp Duncan's direction, lifted his pistol and hammered its butt on the table. "Did you not hear me, McCallum? This court is adjourned!"

Duncan, ignoring the major, leaned toward Brindle. "Born in provincial territory."

The bearded Virginian sergeant, who had been arguing with Latchford, looked at Duncan as if he had spoken sacrilege. "Property of the company proprietor!" he roared. "The law clearly states that the child of a slave belongs to the mother's master! Lieutenant Burke will tell you!" he urged, pushing the new commander of the militia forward.

"So says the law of Virginia," Duncan said, looking only at Brindle. "But Pennsylvania law would say someone born in the province is a citizen of the province."

Brindle followed Duncan's gaze back to where Becca was bravely shielding her infant as one of the Virginians herded her along with a switch. For the first time Duncan saw emotion flare on the magistrate's face. The Quakers were particularly fervent in their views on slavery. Brindle turned and spoke to the Pennsylvania sergeant who had escorted him, who then turned and disappeared into the crowd.

Duncan shrugged. "An interesting philosophical question for the leading province of America. Even if Pennsylvania were to determine this infant is free, his mother is a slave. Yet the boy cannot survive without his mother."

Lieutenant Burke, a pampered-looking man who seemed a reluctant participant, found his voice again. "You go too far, sir!" he shouted as he pushed through the throng. "Do not presume to interfere with Virginia chattels!"

"Pennsylvania has no say over the affairs of our soldiers!" Latchford barked. He seemed to be coiling for a lunge at Duncan.

Brindle stared for a moment at Latchford, without expression, then looked up as the Pennsylvania soldier reappeared, herding Mokie, Becca, and the newborn toward him. For a long moment the Quaker looked at the baby boy, who seemed to return his gaze with a question in his small black eyes, then he asked Duncan, "Does this infant have a name?"

Duncan struggled not to grin as he recognized the shrewdness of the mulatto woman. "His mother has called him Penn."

The announcement seemed to seal Brindle's decision. He stood and turned to the remainder of the squad of militia who escorted him, all of them Pennsylvania men. "After you escort the Iroquois prisoner to my tent," the magistrate said in a loud voice, "you will secure the infant in question, along with his mother. They will all be traveling with us to Lancaster."

His sergeant grinned, summoning his soldiers to his side, square-built men who looked as if they were made of oak.

Latchford glared angrily at the brawny, determined Pennsylvania men, then muttered a command. His own soldiers retreated. But the major lingered, glaring not at Brindle but at Duncan. "You did this, McCallum!" From his pocket he produced a brown envelope. With a chill Duncan recognized it, the letter to army headquarters that would turn him into a fugitive again. The Quakers who ran Pennsylvania might have no appetite to prosecute runaway slaves, but they would zealously enforce Lord Ramsey's property rights in Duncan.

Conawago winced every time his horse's hooves hit the earth. His friend's ribs were badly bruised, his wounds not yet healed, and Duncan had begged him to make camp and wait for them near the fort. The old Indian had readily accompanied him to a bed of moss under a hemlock to rest, but when Duncan had gone back with food an hour later he had found him packing his meager belongings.

"You are in no condition to travel," Duncan protested.

"I do not dare to tarry," his friend said stubbornly.

Nowithstanding that Conawago had been freed, Duncan was still filled with foreboding. "And where, my uncle, will you be bound?"

"Skanawati told us where the troubles start. At the bloody water."

"Surely it is just some kind of symbol, an Iroquois allegory."

"Not at all," Conawago said as he began stripping to the waist. "The creeks at the end of the Warriors Path are full of iron. The rocks rust, tinting the water. It is a name sometimes used for that section of the Monongahela, which can run reddish there after a storm." He pulled the roll of linen bandages from his belt and unbuttoned his shirt. "Now tie me again around the ribs." Duncan watched his friend's face as he pulled the linen tight over his bruised and tattooed chest. Inevitably there was pain on his countenance but also melancholy, and a strange, urgent determination.

"My God," Duncan said as the realization hit him. "You think Skanawati is innocent."

"Look to your heart, Duncan," Conawago said as he began dressing, "and you will find you do as well."

"He confessed. We saw him that very morning, not far from the murder. He has little warmth for Europeans, probably hates us."

"If not to your heart," Conawago said, "then look to the facts. That Virginian came here to fight Indian raiders. He would never have let a strange warrior get so close without firing a pistol, without struggling somehow."

"Burke changed Van Grut's orders before he died," Duncan suddenly recalled. "He abruptly told him to stay away from the last marker tree even though it is vital for the survey. It surely signals the end of the Warriors Path."

"Survey?" Conawago asked. "Orders?"

As Duncan explained what he had learned from the Dutchman, Conawago offered a small nod of acknowledgement, then he turned and began walking westbound on the road. The bloody water and the last marker tree. The dead captain and Skanawati had both been warning them away from the same place, the terminus of the Warriors Path.

The treaty convoy, bound for Lancaster, had left before dawn on the eastward road, with Skanawati, now in chains, joining the slave woman Becca and her infant in the magistrate's huge Conestoga wagon. Brindle had watched with a tormented expression as Mokie and Becca had to be pried apart by the militia. The magistrate had no grounds for keeping the girl away from the family that owned

her. The new commander of the company, the oldest of the Burke
nephews, meanwhile had declared that he and Hadley with four of
the soldiers would travel with the convoy as treaty representatives,
and to assure that Pennsylvania did not slacken in carrying out the
justice due the killer. Hadley himself would be expected to provide
a vivid chronicle of the murderer's hanging.

It was a drunken teamster, passed out in front of the stable, who
had given Duncan hope of a quick journey westward that would
still allow them to catch up with the slow-moving eastbound convoy. He had discovered the man's wagon in the back of the building, its rear axle jacked up, a broken wheel waiting to be repaired
by the smith. If one of the wagons would lag a day or two behind
the convoy, its horses would be idle.

"And why would I part with my brass snuff box?" Van Grut
demanded when Duncan proposed he give it to the smith.

"Because these horses are available today. It shall be the fee for
borrowing them. With good mounts we can reach your western
terminus. With them we can reach the final marker, return them,
and still catch up with the convoy."

"Why the convoy?"

"Because we are obligated to Skanawati. Because his confession
raises more questions than answers. Because," Duncan added, "the
fate of your employment rides with it."

Van Grut frowned. "I still have my orders," he began, then
considered Duncan's words. "What do you mean my terminus?"

"The end of your survey line. The place that Burke suddenly
warned you away from."

"I tend to respect the words of dead men."

"There is a reason men are dying on the trail. I would have
thought you would want to know what it is before you set out
alone again." Duncan needed the answers that were still hidden

in the information Van Grut had gathered for the land company, but even more, he needed the surveyor's resources to obtain the mounts. "No doubt," Duncan said when Van Grut did not reply, "you wish to investigate alone. With the killer in the magistrate's custody you must have nothing to fear."

Van Grut stared unhappily at Duncan, then muttered a Dutch curse, extracted his snuff box, and called out to the smith.

A quarter hour later they had cleared the gates and turned their horses westward at a steady canter, soon overtaking Conawago, who gratefully climbed onto the spare mount led by Duncan. Now they rode in silence, each looking ahead with grim determination. They had gone less than a mile when Conawago shouted in warning, sending them quickly into a thicket to hide as a rider galloped by. With a sinking feeling Duncan urged his horse out of cover and called the man's name.

Hadley wheeled his horse around and halted, saying nothing as Duncan rode in a tight circle around him.

"Desertion is a hanging offense, Mr. Hadley."

The young Virginian hung his head, not looking at Duncan as he spoke. "I said I remembered the murderer spoke with your friend in an Indian tongue, that the Colonel would expect the details of that conversation."

"That is a lie. You never witnessed such a conversation."

Hadley stared at his horse's head. "I am the one who must record what transpired at the boundary tree. It will be published in Virginia with my name on it."

"You mean your words will become the truth."

Hadley looked up uncertainly.

"I have read many words in my time," Duncan declared. "I have read that Scottish Highlanders are the mongrels of God, descended from sinners cast out of heaven, that all Indians are the offspring of wolves and apes."

Defiance flared in Hadley's eyes. "I will write the complete truth, the wholeness of what happened, or I will not write at all. I desire to accompany you, to learn what you learn."

Duncan stared at the young clerk without reply.

"Conawago was freed," Hadley pointed out.

"Did you or did you not see the vine he had tied on Burke's leg? The bandage he cut from his shirt?"

"I don't know." Duncan said nothing. Then Hadley, biting his lip, spoke again. "Yes. But what was the point of my saying so when ten of my comrades sat ready to testify otherwise?" In that moment Hadley seemed but a young boy who wanted nothing more than to run and hide under his bedclothes. "What you did for Becca and her boy," the young Virginian ventured after a long moment, looking uneasily into the forest, "it was an honorable thing." He sighed deeply.

"Surely, Mr. Hadley, an heir to Virginian plantations is not opposed to slavery?"

Hadley's face flushed. "I would like to ride with you, sir," was all he said.

"We ride to find the truth. You seem interested only in truths that are comfortable to you. Which is no truth at all. You still try to obscure your particular connection to Becca and her children."

"They are my uncle's property."

Duncan wheeled his horse around, his back now to the Virginian.

"My father!" Hadley called out in an anguished tone as Duncan rode away.

Duncan turned in his saddle. "Your father?"

"He is permitted to seek distraction with his brother's slaves when it pleases him. Becca is reserved for him."

Duncan brought his mount so close to Hadley's they touched. "Are you saying that Mokie and Penn are your half sister and brother?"

Hadley, again looking at the ground, nodded. "Weeks ago I discovered my cousin Winston secreting packs in the woods near our fields."

Hadley's announcement was so unlikely Duncan was not certain he had heard correctly. "The late Captain Burke, your cousin, was helping slaves escape to Pennsylvania?"

When Hadley nodded again Duncan whistled his companions from the shadows, then prodded his horse into a westward canter.

It was late afternoon when they reached the Monongahela, leading their nearly spent horses, following Conawago, who studied not the ground but the trees for signs. Finally he tethered his mount to a laurel bush near a beech over five feet in diameter, bearing the now-familiar marks of the boundary trees, including a prominent numeral I.

"If this is coincidence, then the gods are surely laughing," the old Nipmuc said as he surveyed the leaf-strewn landscape. Duncan, confused, followed his troubled gaze. A small creek tumbled over round white rocks worn smooth as cobblestones. The spring foliage cast mottled shadows over a field of lichened logs and sun-bleached sticks, several of which Hadley broke as he stepped around the tree. Fifty feet away a wood thrush frolicked amid a patch of red blooms.

"Oh, dear Christ! It's Turtle Creek!" Hadley moaned as he stared at the stream, and he stumbled back to his horse as if to flee.

Van Grut muttered an exclamation of alarm in his native Dutch then stepped to the edge of the creek, bending to lift one of the white cobbles and extend it to Duncan. It was no stone. It was a human skull.

Hadley buried his head in his horse's neck as if he could bear to look no further.

Duncan stepped to the shallow creek and lifted another skull from the water. He counted a dozen within ten feet of where he stood before lowering the one he held to the ground and pacing around the clearing. The bleached sticks were arm and leg bones scattered across the forest floor. What he had mistaken for red flowers was in fact a remnant of scarlet cloth with gold braiding, a rotting uniform.

"They say nearly five hundred men died here that day," Conawago explained over Duncan's shoulder. "The British had never faced the French Indians before, knew nothing of forest warfare. They kept forming up in lines of bright red while their enemy just stayed on the hills—" he gestured to the two small ridges on either side, "—and shot them from hiding."

"You speak of Braddock's infantry," Duncan said as he slowly recalled the published accounts. The elderly British general, commander of all troops in North America, had paid with his life for his gross misjudgment of the enemy irregulars.

"They say King George wept when he heard the news," Van Grut remembered. The Dutchman was holding a crushed and moldy grenadier's cap, bearing the number 48 in tarnished brass.

Hadley appeared behind him, his eyes moist. "One of the only officers not wounded was Colonel Washington. He rallied his

Virginians to hold off the enemy while the regular army retreated. Scores of Virginia children were left without a father that day." Hadley gazed forlornly at the bones. "I knew more than a few of them. This could be them, could be their bones I crushed," he added in a horrified tone.

Duncan surveyed the scene, trying to shake off the darkness that seemed to be paralyzing his companions. He shuddered as he imagined the bloody July day five years before. He knew only too well the chaos, the terror, the bloody axes of an Indian attack. He searched his memory of the accounts he had read. It had been the first battle of the long war for the French Indians. They had been thirsty for blood, rushing in impatiently to take the scalps of the wounded as they lay bleeding on the ground.

He looked back at Hadley, who had collapsed with a haunted expression onto a rock, seeming to have lost all sense of why they were there. Duncan felt himself also succumbing to despair. There was a Highland field near the village of Culloden littered with the bones of those he had known, and loved. He bent and picked up a skull, placed it in a pool of sunlight, then began gathering large flat rocks. Soon Conawago started helping him, joined a minute later by Van Grut. They had built the large hollow cairn nearly two feet high before Hadley stirred from his paralysis. He rose, staggering, as he approached Duncan with a confused expression.

"They *were* your friends, Hadley," Duncan said of the bones they were gathering, "or close enough." He pointed to the skull lying in the center of the hollow structure, then placed a femur beside it.

Hadley nodded his comprehension then winced as Conawago deposited another bone. "I can't touch the . . . "

"You don't need to collect bones, just rocks," Duncan suggested.

Half an hour later, when they had nearly filled the cairn, Conawago paused to light a small fire at the base of it, planting several small dried leaves on it.

"Tobacco," Duncan explained to Hadley. "It attracts the spirits."

Van Grut inserted the last of the remains, another skull, as Hadley began covering the top with a flat stone.

Suddenly Duncan put a restraining hand on the Virginian's arm, then reached in and pulled out the top skull. It was brighter than the others, and it had the jawbone attached. "Where did you find this?" he asked the Dutchman.

Van Grut pointed to a fallen log on the far side of the boundary tree.

"Show me exactly."

The bare patch of earth, still showing the indentation of the skull, was clearly visible. Duncan carefully probed the dead leaves around it with his fingers, quickly finding more bones. Vertebrae, broken ribs, a small, nearly intact skeletal hand.

Van Grut leaned over his shoulder. "What do you find?"

"A female."

"Surely you can't know that," protested Hadley, now at his side. "There's only bones."

"The posterior ramus of the mandible makes it certain," Duncan said, pointing at the skull. He looked up apologetically as he realized he had spoken as if in his old classroom, and he was about to explain when Van Grut excitedly grabbed the skull.

"Here," the Dutchman explained as he pointed to the rear edge of the jawbone that hooked up into the cranium. "McCallum is right! See how it is straight! Look at all the others. The male's jawbone always curves inward there." As if to confirm he lifted another skull from the stream and pointed to the arc in the jawbone.

"But there were no women at the battleline," Hadley said. "These troops had pushed on in a forced march, leaving the supply train with the women behind."

"She wasn't in the battle." Conawago's announcement came from the shadows of the big beech. "Look how fresh the bone is." The worry in his voice told Duncan he too had begun to grasp the implications. "This woman died less than a year ago." Conawago began brushing away the fallen leaves among the tangled roots and produced another skull, as fresh as the first. Duncan caught his eye, then pointed to the vine that twisted in and out of the sockets in the skull.

"You're making no sense," Hadley complained.

"This man and woman died here at the boundary tree," Duncan said, "but in the past few months." He examined the female's skull again, pointing to a narrow crack at the rear. "She was struck from behind and died soon thereafter."

Hadley stared at Duncan as if he were some kind of sorcerer.

"Mr. McCallum," Van Grut explained in a sober voice, "is a reader of dead."

Duncan ran his finger along the crack in the bone. "This is a fracture line. The blow might not have killed her, but it certainly rendered her unconscious." He slid a fingernail inside the tiny crack. It was a clear, crisp fissure. "If she had lived long after, this gap would have started to heal closed."

"You can't know she died less than a year ago," Hadley argued. "It is nothing but bone."

"When you enter the forest you must learn to look as if you never had eyes before, learn afresh how to experience things." Duncan exchanged a glance with Conawago as he spoke. The old Indian had used the very words when beginning to teach Duncan

how to interpret the landscape around him. "Everything is connected, and it is how they are connected that tells their story."
Before lifting the second skull he extended the vine trailing from it
toward Conawago.

"The last two feet of the vine, the part through the skull, is
green," Conawago explained. "That is one season's growth. Last
summer's growth. They died no earlier than July, though I'm
inclined to say August or September."

Hadley looked in wonder again at Duncan, then his gaze drifted
over Duncan's shoulder. Duncan turned to see Van Grut collapsed
on a log, his face in his hands. Something about their explanation
had deeply shaken him. Duncan took a step toward the Dutchman,
only to have a low warbling whistle draw him away. Conawago had
returned to the tree and was now pointing to a nail driven into the
trunk three feet above the ground. Duncan reached into his pouch
for the one he had taken from the tree where Burke had died. He
held the two nail heads together. Each had the same checkerboard
pattern on its head.

Duncan dropped to his knees, joining Conawago's search of the
loose forest debris beneath the nail. They quickly uncovered another
skeletal hand. Though it was incomplete, the bones remaining at
the center of the palm were crushed. Conawago gave a low whistle,
then blew debris away from more bones. Another hand, clutching a
large, tarnished compass. And several small brass buttons.

Suddenly Hadley was beside Duncan, staring at the compass,
then extending his hand to touch the nail, halting, the fingers
trembling before hastily withdrawing as he saw the dark stain on
the wood below the nail.

Duncan extracted the nail with his tomahawk and studied the
buttons, worked with a pattern of leaping fish, before dropping

them into his pouch and turning to face Hadley. "If you came for the truth," he said to the Virginian, pointing to the collapsed Dutchman, "you'll have to start with him."

Van Grut did not look at them, just clutched his arms together and huddled over the little fire. He was visibly shivering.

Duncan, feeling an unexpected anger, leapt forward, yanking the Dutchman up by his shoulder. Dragging him to the far side of the tree, he pulled away tendrils that had partially obscured another set of carvings, six geometric shapes. Van Grut did not react when Duncan reached into his linen bag to extract his journal. He quickly turned to a sketch of still another boundary tree. Previously he had looked for the signs on the sketched trees, now he read the detailed description. It had had a nail driven into the trunk, approximately three feet from the ground.

"Why is someone killing the surveyors?" he demanded.

Van Grut stared at the shapes with wild, frightened eyes. He began to tremble again.

Conawago rested a hand on Duncan's arm. "I will make tea," he suggested.

Taking an ember from the small fire by the cairn, Conawago quickly lit a cooking fire beyond the log. As he set his little copper pot to boil, Duncan, joined by the old Indian, probed the forest floor near where they had found the fresh skulls. Ten minutes later Van Grut let himself be led to the fire, where he silently accepted a tin mug of tea.

"You said there were other surveyors," Duncan prodded. "You never said what happened to them." He dropped a new discovery in front of the Dutchman, a small moccasin of fine doeskin, once exquisitely decorated with dyed quillwork, now stained and mildewed.

Van Grut took a deep sip of the tea before answering. "My employers did not provide many details. It was the sutler in Carlisle where I bought supplies on the company account who spoke of the others, said surveyors must be cheaper by the half dozen. He shared some rum when I sketched his wife and gave him the rendering." He stared into his mug.

"There were three others he knew of in the past few months," he continued. "One named Townsend, the first, a friend of the Iroquois, who was reported dead by misadventure in the wilderness. Another called Cooper, from Connecticut, who traveled with his wife, who was half-Iroquois, half-French, from the Iroquois towns. Very young, very pretty, he said. The only other I know of was the former infantry officer named Putnam, from Philadelphia." Duncan closed his eyes a moment. Townsend and Putnam. Skanawati had mentioned finding dead Europeans on the trail.

"They were to be given tracts of land in payment for their efforts," Van Grut continued. "I asked for cash money, to pay for my travels. It was a big tract, and the Virginians were in a great hurry to get their claims registered. Using only one surveyor could easily have taken over a year."

"Why the hurry?"

"I didn't ask. The job they were offering fit my plans perfectly." Van Grut thought for a moment. "Because of the constant disputes between Pennsylvania and Virginia over land claims. Because no one gets any more big tracts until the Virginia tract is settled. Because the victories over the French have whetted voracious appetites for western lands. Because of the treaty," he added after a moment.

"Did you ask what happened to the others?"

"Like I said, it is a huge tract. I assumed they were working elsewhere."

"Did they assign you only one section then?"

"I was to describe the last fifty miles of the trail, then write my report. I was not inclined to ask questions. It was a great boon, to have my expenses paid for my explorations of the west."

Duncan stared at the Dutchman, certain he knew more than he was letting on. "Were you attacked?"

The Dutchman's face darkened. He didn't reply.

"This pour soul was nailed to the tree like Burke, probably practiced on with a knife like Burke. The woman was no doubt bending over to help him when she was struck from behind. It appears she was then dragged to that log and killed, probably had her veins severed while she was unconscious."

"You don't know with certainty that they were murdered," Van Grut argued.

Duncan went back on his knees beside Conawago, searching the ground again. It was the old Indian who found the final evidence, pointing at it with a grim expression. Duncan stared at it for a long, despairing moment before stepping toward the Dutchman.

"No I don't know," Duncan admitted, his voice tight. "Perhaps his mainspring just wound down with no one to wind him up." He dropped the object at Van Grut's feet. A human breastbone into which was embedded a bloodstained clockwork gear. "This is how you will die, Van Grut, unless you tell us all you know."

The color drained from the Dutchman's face.

"They sent you to replace this one who was killed, to work the section of trail north of here. It's only a matter of time before you become another clockwork man. Shall we place you in a box, then wind you up and charge a shilling for a glimpse?"

Van Grut pressed his hand against his chest, as if to protect his heart. He looked as if he would weep.

"Why are surveyors being killed at boundary trees?" Duncan demanded again.

"Burke told me to go to tree four, the next morning after we met. But I had just been paid, hadn't played a game of whist or touched a drop of rum in weeks."

Duncan stepped closer. Finally he understood Van Grut's fear when he had visited the fourth marker tree. "You were sent by Burke to the tree where he died, the same morning he died? Except you got drunk instead?"

Van Grut nodded, closing his eyes.

"We could sit until nightfall," came Conawago's quiet voice, "and not list all those with complaints against boundary markers and surveyors. Elsewhere the British and French may fight each other because their kings hate each other. But here they fight over the rights to land. When the French leave, the war over land will continue, just fought in different ways. Half a dozen companies already compete for these territories, subject to few laws and fewer lawmen. The Virginians compete with the Pennsylvanians, and both oppose the Connecticut and New York companies. The Pennsylvania Susquehanna Company despises the Philadelphia Land Company. The smaller tribes subjugated by the Iroquois resent them for selling their lands, where they traditionally lived. The Susquehannocks, the Conoy, the Shawnee, the Nanticokes, the Delawares consider the transfer of these lands to be invalid. More than a few Iroquois resent the handful of chiefs who sign away possession."

Conawago shrugged. "There are many possible killers, but surely only one effect. Killing the surveyors defeats the Virginia land claims."

As he spoke Conawago had been studying the tree. Now he dropped to his knees and pulled away the vines that covered part of the lower trunk. The markings near the base were nearly obscured by many years' growth of roots and vines. As he began pulling it away from the base of the tree Duncan joined him. Soon they had cleared a radius of several feet around it.

The symbols at the bottom of the trunk were old, blurred by the growth of the bark, but the representations of the forest animals crudely carved on the ledge stone underfoot were still clearly visible. Duncan stepped back, looking at the stone, then the tree. There were layers of messages, seeming to span centuries. Spirit messages of the Indians. Educated messages of Europeans. Diabolic messages of killers.

Van Grut, his anxiety quickly giving way to his scientific curiosity, dropped to his hands and knees on the stone. Duncan pulled him away. The Dutchman's protest faded as he saw the intense melancholy with which Conawago stared at the symbols.

"Do you have more tobacco?" Duncan asked Hadley.

"Of course," the Virginian answered, then frowned as he grasped Duncan's meaning and reluctantly reached into the bag at his belt.

Van Grut and Hadley followed Duncan's example as he arranged embers from their cooking fire in a semicircle around the old carved rocks, then crumbled leaves of tobacco over each. As they stepped back Conawago began murmuring a prayer in one of the old tongues, with open hands gracefully sweeping the fragrant smoke over the ancient, sacred stones.

"I don't understand anything," Hadley finally said with a sigh.

"It has been Conawago's quest these past months, seeking out these old sacred places. Those who ceded the land used the old Warriors Path as a boundary. Certainly they didn't know that

under their feet was something else, a pilgrim's way as it were, span-
ning untold generations."

"Surely it is too much coincidence."

"Not at all. The geography funnels humans here. The trail
mostly follows the bottomlands, between the high ridges. Anyone
traveling from the north to the rich Ohio country or to the
Virginian settlements would follow this course. And where it
crosses the most important river of the region would be a natural
place for a marker, for a shrine even."

"Before this," Conawago joined in, "before Europeans, the
Iroquois fought terrible wars with the Catawbas and others in the
south, in what you call Virginia and the Carolinas. This is the trail
they would take. Since time out of mind war parties would pass
here, stop for blessings, for purification before crossing over into
the lands where the enemy dwelled, or to give thanks for safe passage on their return."

Duncan remembered Skanawati's warning and looked about
the landscape. The Monongahela was visible through the trees to
the south. *Stay away from the bloody water*, he had said, *or you may
fall into the crack in the world.* As he looked out at the bones still
scattered over the forest floor and the sacred tree scarred by two
murders, he was not inclined to argue the point. The butcher's
ground was not simply a perfect place to commit murder—who
would notice two more sets of bones?—but also its dark air seemed
to speak of more death to come.

"But why, McCallum," Hadley asked as he watched Conawago,
kneeling among the stone carvings, whispering to them now,
"would the Monongahela Company want to interfere with a
sacred—"

"They didn't need to know anything about its history. All
the old trails followed prominent contours in the land, a natural

boundary. Ask an Indian to draw a map, or a land grant, and he would use the trails as a base line as surely as roads would be used in the settled lands. No one knew about the sacred history of the trail, nor needed to know."

"I still don't understand," Hadley repeated.

"Such a place is not for understanding," Duncan said, and he gestured the Virginian to the cairn. "It is for reverence." They silently stacked several more large flat rocks on top. Van Grut watched Conawago at first with fear, then tried futilely to ask the old Indian about the symbols carved in the ledge stone. But Duncan knew Conawago was no longer there, no longer seeing or hearing his companions. He had gone away with the ancestors and spirits of the forest. At last the Dutchman gave up his questioning, took out his journal, and began to sketch the marks on the tree.

"There must be something more we should do for them," Hadley said, staring forlornly at the cairn.

"Give them a Psalm," Duncan offered.

Hadley nodded slowly and thought a moment.

Duncan was so certain of what the young colonial would speak, he almost commenced the comforting Twenty-third's words of shepherds and flocks himself.

"Lord," Hadley began instead, "thou has been our dwelling place, in all generations. Thou turnest man to destruction and sayest, 'Return ye children of men.' For a thousand years in thy sight are but as yesterday when it is past and as a watch in the night."

Duncan's grandfather also had preferred the Ninetieth. To hear the words now gave him unexpected comfort. He mouthed the final words as Hadley spoke them. *We spend our years as a tale that is told.*

After they finished they silently stacked several small colorful rocks on the top of the cairn.

Van Grut was sitting on a log, still sketching, when they returned to the far side of the tree.

"You still have not answered me, Van Grut," Duncan said.

"I don't know, I tell you. I don't know why surveyors are being killed."

"You met Burke only once?"

"By Ligonier, yes."

"Did you show him your journal?"

"I was working on it when he met me. He asked to see it."

Duncan extended his hand, and Van Grut handed him the sketchbook. Each time Duncan held it he saw something new. This time, leafing through, he discovered many portraits of Indians, several with inset sketches of moccasins, pipes, baskets, and other accoutrements of tribal life. "He saw you were beginning to understand Indian life, perhaps read Indian messages."

"Surely that means nothing."

"Who were the first to be killed?"

"Townsend, if you credit the rumors. Then these two we have now found."

"Townsend knew the Indians and their ways. Then this surveyor Cooper and his Indian wife, his Iroquois wife. In Philadelphia there are many surveyors available."

"What are you saying?"

"All the early victims knew something about Indian signs."

"Not the man Cooper who died here."

"Maybe at first they hired an Indian who had a surveyor with her. The most urgent task was to find trees with the Indian markings."

Van Grut's brow wrinkled in confusion.

"Last autumn, after the two died here, several Iroquois died on the northern end of this same trail, by similar markers."

"What are you saying?" the Dutchman asked.

"It wasn't exactly surveyors who died at first." Duncan cast a worried glance at Conawago. "The murderer started with those who can read the trees."

Duncan found all of his companions staring at him. The old Indian seemed about to speak, then suddenly cocked his head to the north. The screams they heard a moment later seemed distant at first, but the war whoops and gunshots that followed were just over the next ridge.

UNCAN AND CONAWAGO darted into the forest shadows, the young Scot sweeping up his rifle, his comrade extending his war club as they ran, not directly at the sounds of battle but in an arc that would put them in the shelter of the rocks above it.

His fear of the forest had never fully retreated despite his months with Conawago, and suddenly Duncan was reliving the terrible moments when he had first ventured alone into the deep forest, convinced that death lurked in every shadow. He struggled to push down his fear, keeping his eyes on his friend. As always, as danger threatened, the presence of the old Indian steadied him. Duncan echoed his movements, listening, instinctively marking the dangers ahead. The deep, throaty roar of rifles being fired close together, the bark of shorter muskets scattered among the trees, the hiss of arrows, the whoop of attacking warriors. They were half a mile from the boundary tree when Duncan glimpsed the small band besieged at the base of a low ridge.

"My God!" came a terrified voice behind him, "this place is cursed for Virginians!" Hadley was gasping, shaking with fear.

Duncan studied the figures ahead and saw that it was, indeed, the small party of returning militia who were under attack. "Do you know how to shoot that thing?" Hadley had at least had the presence of mind to bring his musket.

"It isn't loaded," the Virginian confessed in a voice cracking with fear. He pulled out the ramrod and reached for a ball and cartridge, but his hand shook so much half the powder spilled out of the barrel. Duncan took the ammunition and finished the job as Van Grut arrived, clutching his fowling piece.

"What else do you have in your kit?" Duncan demanded as he noticed the pack on Hadley's back. As the Virginian dumped it onto the ground Duncan probed the contents with his foot, keeping one eye on Conawago, who was creeping closer to the skirmish. He bent and lifted a small piece of carved bone. Hadley had kept the end of the Iroquois signal arrow shot at the trial. Duncan studied the whistle for only a moment before speaking in a low, urgent voice, then made Hadley and Van Grut repeat his instructions before sprinting forward.

Seconds later he was beside the old Nipmuc. Duncan quickly explained his plan, bringing a cool grin to Conawago's face, then stole away to another rock formation a hundred feet away. A moment later an odd raspy sound, the call of a shrike, rose from Conawago's hiding place. Duncan repeated the call and saw one of the raiders pause and look fearfully toward them just as Hadley sounded the Iroquois whistle, followed an instant later by the flat crack of Van Grut's gun. Hadley blew again, then fired his own gun.

Duncan had no faith in the marksmanship of his companions, had told them to simply aim in the general direction of the raiders, but he took a moment to sight his own rifle, selecting a tall Huron who bent over an unseen body with his knife. He hit where he aimed, in the shoulder of the knife arm, knocking the man onto his back. A moment later, as the Iroquois whistle sounded again, the man struggled to his feet, clutching his shoulder, then he shouted several syllables, and the raiders faded into the shadows.

The joy with which the two Virginians still on their feet greeted Hadley disappeared as Duncan explained the ruse, mimicking the signals favored by Mohawk warriors, the fiercest of the Iroquois nations.

"There's no one else?" the younger of the two moaned. "We're all dead! Attacked by a hundred at least!"

"No more than fifteen," Conawago said, then joined Duncan in examining the four men on the ground. Two were dead, two had flesh wounds. "And these Hurons will flee for miles before wondering why they are not pursued. Get across the river with your wounded, find a cave for the night. No fire until you reach Fort Cumberland."

"Can't just leave them," the older soldier said, with a gesture to his dead friends.

Duncan nodded back toward Braddock's battlefield as he began ripping the shirts of the dead for bandages. "They are in good company. No time for graves, just cover your comrades with rocks. Once back at your fort you can have a larger party sent back."

The older soldier grimaced and glanced at his terrified companion. "I reckon we just be making direct for our farms as quick as our feet will carry us. We've had a bellyful of Pennsylvania."

"But they took him," protested the younger soldier. "We can't just—"

"They took a prisoner?" Duncan asked in alarm, looking out in the direction of the fleeing raiders.

"The captain," the soldier said, his voice haunted.

A chill ran down Duncan's spine. "You're saying they took the body of Captain Burke?"

"Aye. The first thing they did, cut out the mule carrying the body."

"Surely they didn't understand," Hadley countered. "A mistake. They saw a mule and thought it was loaded with supplies."

"Witchcraft!" Van Grut muttered in a fearful tone. Duncan and Conawago exchanged a worried glance. The raiders would not have mistakenly taken a dead man. The tribes were usually as wary of the dead as Europeans, but they did indeed have their own witches who sometimes broke taboos in their dark pursuits.

Conawago examined the dead men, leaning over one who held a knife. In his other hand was a chest plate of hollow bones and shells, ripped off the man's attacker. Conawago studied it with worry, then stuffed it inside his own shirt.

The men from Virginia quickly covered their dead companions, departing hastily the moment Conawago finished fashioning a crutch for one of the wounded. "The young one," the old Indian said. "Wasn't she with—" His words were cut off by a sob from Hadley, who knelt behind a low boulder forty feet away. As they rushed forward he lifted Mokie's limp body.

Duncan quickly realized that the raider he had shot had been hovering over the girl. Not merely hovering, he saw as he reached her. The Indian's knife could have killed her in an instant. But instead he had used the blade to cut the rope that had hobbled the girl's legs. The mysterious raiders had come to take not only Burke's body but also the young slave.

The treaty convoy had become a traveling village, its ranks more than doubled since leaving Ligonier. More Indians of the lesser tribes had joined, as had settlers and trappers with business on the Forbes Road who had heard of the raiders and flocked to the long line of wagons for protection.

Duncan and his companions had reached Ligonier in the pre-dawn light, taking Mokie to the infirmary. She had not regained consciousness, though her pulse was strong. "I want her watched over," he had instructed the one-legged corporal. "Clear broth when she awakens."

The orderly had shaken his head. "Soon as the major hears of her she'll be back in the guardhouse. Or, worse, he'll turn her over to the militia."

Van Grut, who had bartered for four scrawny horses, did not argue when Duncan arrived at the stable with the still-unconscious girl, wrapped in a blanket for travel. "My second watch," was his only comment when he saw Duncan examining the mounts. "It took an entire night at the table to win it two months ago."

Now, as Duncan, bone weary from the day's ride, dismounted in the camp and sought out the wagon with the girl's mother, he realized that he might be putting Mokie in still greater danger. There were more Virginians with the convoy, including the arrogant lieutenant now deputized as a treaty negotiator, as well as traders who would be well aware of the rewards paid in Virginia for the return of escaped slaves. As Duncan pulled a blanket flap over the girl's head, Hadley seemed to feel the same anxiety, stepping out in front as if to guard her.

It was past the time for the evening meal, and the fires beside many of the wagons were being banked for the night. Hobbled mares nickered in the twilight as they grazed on the new spring grass. From the high meadow Brindle had chosen for his camp Duncan could see miles of long ridges, like massive waves on a moonlit sea. A ribbon of silver snaked toward the east, the river the settlers called the Juniata. From a teamster camp came the low tones of a fiddle. Somewhere someone read a newspaper out loud, in the tone of a village crier, so that all within earshot knew that in Philadelphia the first lightning arresters, invented by the estimable Dr. Franklin, had recently been installed, and that Mr. Hoyle had published new rules for the playing of whist.

A hulking figure with a musket stood by a tall stump choked with vines near the campsite. "*An tusa a tha ann,*" the sentry murmured.

Duncan had taken two more steps toward the magistrate's wagon before realizing the greeting was in the Highland tongue. "McGregor? What brings you so far from the fort?"

"The Ligonier garrison be responsible for the safety of the convoy," replied the big Scot, looking at the limp girl as Duncan handed her to Hadley. "And the major was right put out by my speaking up at the trial. He said walking to Lancaster and back would suit me and my squad just fine. He sent a company to patrol north of the road, to clear out the raiders from the path of the delegations."

Duncan considered McGregor's position, and his words. If he were worried about Huron raiders, he would be patrolling the edge of the forest. "Surely the camp of the magistrate is not in jeopardy."

"There was a wee fracas yesterday. The prisoner was walking behind his honor's wagon when he was set upon by the Virginians with clubs."

Duncan's jaw tightened and he found himself staring at Hadley, who looked with shame at the ground. "How does he fare?"

"The savages in the convoy came to the chief's assistance. 'Twas not a moment for treaty negotiation, ye might say."

"Is he injured?"

When McGregor offered no reply, Duncan took a step toward the wagon.

"She won't let anyone near," the sergeant said to his back.

Not understanding, Duncan approached the rear gate of the huge wagon, one of the heavy ones made along the Conestoga River near Lancaster. Something flew past his head. Something else struck him in the cheek. The third projectile he caught. A stale biscuit, hard as rock.

"You be getting the pitchfork next if you come near the chief!" came a furious, high-pitched challenge. "The Philadelphia Quakers be here!" the voice added, as if it were the ultimate threat.

Hadley hurried to Duncan's side, holding the unconscious girl. "Becca, we have your Mokie," the Virginian said into the shadows. "The raiders attacked."

The wagon creaked, then Becca materialized out of its deep shadows. She moaned as she saw her daughter, then lifted the girl inside. Duncan and Hadley followed her into the wagon, down an aisle between sacks of flour and other supplies as she laid Mokie down beside Skanawati, asleep next to a large basket that held the infant boy. The baby named Penn was wide awake, gazing at the flame of a candle lantern.

Duncan lifted the lantern and studied the Indian's injuries as best he could without disturbing him. Cuts and bruises on his shoulders, scrapes from the manacles that cut into his ankles, nothing more. "The other Indians," he whispered to Becca, "why aren't they helping to guard him?"

"They did, all day. But when they came to camp tonight they stayed but a few minutes and left, looking like they had seen a ghost. A chief in a fox cap kept muttering something like a prayer, another aimed loud, angry words at the magistrate in the tribal tongue." Duncan saw now that Skanawati's hand was closed around the amulet that hung from his neck. He turned to leave and was restrained by a hand on his arm. "You're a medical man," the woman said beseechingly.

"She has a concussion," Duncan told her. "A bruising of the brain. Some say it means the flux between the inner and outer lobes has been blocked." He saw the pain in Becca's eyes. "Could be hours, Becca, could be days. Even if she were with the best doctors in Philadelphia there would be nothing more a medical man could do. The best thing for her is what only her mother can give her."

Becca choked back tears, then returned to her daughter, lifted her head on her lap, and began stroking her hair, a moment later beginning a soft, whispered song. As he turned to leave he saw that Skanawati was watching through half-opened eyes. The Iroquois prisoner, he suspected, had been awake the entire time.

Outside, Conawago stood near McGregor, surveying the campsite, slowly walking around the six-foot stump that was serving as his sentry post. Confused as to why his friend would not want to see Skanawati, Duncan approached and had opened his mouth with the question when three dark figures appeared by the campfire. Magistrate Brindle consulted briefly with McGregor, who pointed at Duncan, then the Quaker leader called for Duncan to join him at his campfire, which the two other men were feeding with fresh wood.

The magistrate, clearly distracted, quickly introduced his two companions, whom Duncan had seen at Ligonier. Felton, the lanky man who had hovered by Brindle in the major's office, guided the supply wagons that served the provincial sutler's post at Fort Pitt. He had the air of a Philadelphia gentleman, yet moved like a woodsman. Felton nodded at Duncan, then tossed him a piece of the jerked beef he pulled from his belt pouch. The stocky man was Brindle's brother-in-law Henry Bythe, the representative of the province at Pitt. At Brindle's request Duncan explained what he had found at the marker trees, then Hadley described the skirmish on the Monongahela. He was nearly done when Brindle looked up, as if just registering the Virginian's words.

"You say the savages stole Captain Burke's body?" he asked, visibly shaken.

"Taken by the Indians," Hadley confirmed. "I shudder to think to what end."

Brindle shook his head. "'Tis an ill wind that blows in these mountains," he said. "The Indians have all shifted their campfires tonight, as if our presence offended them."

"The raiders would never attack us with so many in our party, uncle," Felton observed. "Their way is to strike where they have the advantage in numbers then disappear into the forest."

Brindle fell silent, his face grave. It wasn't their safety that so worried him. He had one overriding concern on this journey, Duncan knew, and his mood meant he suspected that the treaty was already in jeopardy.

As Conawago sat beside them at the fire Brindle lifted a lantern and stepped to the wagon to investigate his charges. "The wolf shall dwell with the lamb," he observed as he returned, "the leopard shall lie down with the kid, and a little child shall lead them."

Duncan's gaze moved back to Conawago. His friend was upset about something, even deeply disturbed. It was not simply that he was convinced that Skanawati was innocent. Something else, unseen by Duncan, was out of balance. The men around the fire fell into a long silence, broken finally by Brindle's invocation of another Psalm. "Why do the heathen rage," he recited toward the flames, "and the people imagine a vain thing?"

"Now ask the beasts, and they shall teach thee, and the fowls of the air, and they shall tell thee," came a deep solemn voice in response.

The Quaker looked up with a sad smile. "You surprise me, McCallum."

"'Twas not I, sir," Duncan replied.

Brindle lifted his lantern, taking notice of Conawago for the first time. The shocked expression on his face was unmistakable. He looked back and forth from Duncan to the old Nipmuc as if they were working some trickery on him. "Sir?" he ventured.

Duncan recalled that Conawago had not spoken at his trial. He remembered his own first conversation with the Jesuit-trained Indian, when he had awakened after being snatched from certain death, his eyes covered by the bandage that wrapped a slash in his scalp. He had assumed from his voice that his rescuer had been a well-educated English gentleman.

"I too enjoy the Old Testament," Conawago said thoughtfully. "Perhaps you know the remainder of the verse?"

"It is Job, is it not?" Brindle tossed more wood on the fire, as if he needed to see better.

The Indian nodded. "Speak to the earth, and it shall teach thee . . . "

Brindle, although clearly accustomed to teaching by means of the scriptures, seemed confused. "What is your meaning, sir?"

"He discovereth deep things out of darkness," Conawago continued, "and bringeth out to light the shadow of death."

It wasn't the attention Brindle was paying to Conawago that caused Duncan to consider the Quaker with new respect, but rather the sincerity with which he sought to understand the old Indian. "What is the particular light you offer, sir?"

"You must move this camp."

Brindle turned for a moment to Duncan, then to his nephew Felton as if for help. "We will break camp at dawn, of course."

"No. Tonight, if you value the hearts of your allies."

Conawago, looking grim, stood and extended his hand for the lantern. Brindle hesitated only a moment before complying. Following him toward the tall stump, he watched in confusion as Conawago pulled away the vines that remained on it. McGregor brought another lantern. Scores of marks revealed themselves on the high stump, some symbols of animals, others just notches and lines, many Xs with smaller circles or triangles over their tops.

Felton offered an exclamation of wonder. "I must have driven past this post thirty times," he muttered, then ran his fingers over the carvings.

"*Gaondote*, it is called in Iroquois," Conawago explained, then fell silent as he moved the lantern along the rows of markings. His expression grew heavy, and for a moment Duncan saw the patient torment of the sin eaters he had known as a boy. At last the old Nipmuc looked up, as if shaking off his visions. "A war post. Used by raiding parties to tether prisoners. This one was used for many years, over generations. The Xs indicate prisoners, the marks above them signifying if they were male or female. Many were fated to be finished at the stake. They would know early in their captivity, for their faces would be blackened with soot. Throughout their entire journey the marked ones understood it would end with their being burned alive."

Conawago looked up at Brindle. "Though you may not sense the pain and darkness in this place, I assure you those of the tribes do. The fear, the hate, it all still lives here. The tribes assume you chose this place to torment Skanawati. You have an Iroquois prisoner proceeding to his death on a British rope."

"Burn it," suggested McGregor.

"There is something else the magistrate needs to fully understand," Duncan interjected, turning to his Nipmuc friend. "The significance of the nails was mentioned in passing at the trial. What exactly do the Iroquois remember about men being tortured with nails?"

"Surely it has nothing to do with—" Brindle's objection was cut off by Duncan's upraised palm.

"The English and the Iroquois have not been antagonists for a long time," Duncan said. "But the nations begin to sense what the English truly think of them, at the worst possible time. Tormenting Skanawati by placing him beside the captive post. Flaunting the nailing of men to barns and trees. Why do the heathen rage," he said, repeating the Psalm.

Conawago gazed at the post as he spoke. "Since before memory Iroquois raiding parties have gone up and down the Warriors Path, through the Virginia country to reach their traditional enemies. But then one year an Iroquois raiding party found a farm across its ancient path. They halted, debating whether to turn around. But the militia had already been alerted and confronted them. The Iroquois said they simply wanted passage down the trail, as was their custom, promised not to harm any settler. The militia refused. The Indians had little food, expecting to live off the land. When they took some corn from a farmer's field, the Virginians called it war. The Indians were outnumbered. Some fled north, a dozen were captured, beaten, tortured, some hanged. Those who did not die right away were nailed to the side of a barn facing the Indian trail as a warning. Some took a week to die."

Brindle studied Conawago in silence, then gazed at the wagon, under which several of his party were already bedding down. "We will move camp," he said with a sigh. "Call out the militia and teamsters to assist us. And I will ask Brother Conawago to extend our apologies to the chiefs. We are but strangers in a strange land."

The moon was high by the time they finished moving the Quakers' camp to the flat below the crest of the ridge, where half the other travelers had already bedded down.

Magistrate Brindle was disquieted, and despite the late hour he had his nephew hang two lanterns beside him so he could read his Bible. His thin face had the expression of one staring into the murk of the wilderness for the first time, a strong man facing evils he never knew existed. The first time Duncan had entered the wilderness he had crawled under a rock and hidden.

"Have you been to treaty meetings before?" Duncan asked McGregor, keeping an eye on the shadows along the treeline. Conawago had disappeared during the shifting of the wagon.

"Aye. In Albany. Grand affairs."

"With as many Indians as here?"

"Here? This is a mere three dozen or so. When the trunks are finally opened expect a hundred or more."

"Trunks?"

"A few chiefs may come to make their marks on the king's paper. But the rest come for the gifts. Blankets will be distributed, and muskets and knives and bolts of cloth. If the gifts aren't there, the Indians won't talk." The big Scot gazed at the row of fires along the edge of the woods, where the Indians had camped. "Except the savages with us keep sharpening their knives and tomahawks. As if they expect an outbreak of hostilities instead of a treaty."

With deep foreboding Duncan ventured toward the Indian camp, desperately hoping for a glimpse of Conawago, nagged again by fear for his friend. It was as if death, having been cheated of him

at Ligonier, still hovered near. A dog barked from a lean-to of
pine boughs built against a wall of ledge rock. The soft voice of
a woman comforted a child, the sound of rushes scouring a pot
came from near a dying fire. The quiet domestic sounds reassured
him. He quickened his step and ventured closer to the lines of fires
along the edge of the woods, pausing at each in turn to look for
his friend.

At first he thought he had tripped on a root, not realizing
until too late that it was a pole deftly levered between his legs.
As he stumbled, the Indian wielding it slammed the pole against
Duncan's knee while pushing with a twisting motion at his shoulder. Suddenly Duncan was on the ground, with four warriors
atop him, pinning each of his limbs. The one kneeling on his left
shoulder held the edge of a tomahawk to his throat. The words that
rushed out in the Iroquois tongue were whispered, and too fast for
Duncan to understand. But the tone was unmistakable.

They hit him, striking repeatedly with small clubs on his
legs, on his arms, not enough to break bones but enough to hurt,
enough to bring bruises that would last days. The two men holding
his legs uttered sounds of amusement. The one with the tomahawk
leaned closer, hissing at Duncan, the hairs of his amulet brushing
Duncan's neck, the turtle tattoo on his cheek visible in the moonlight. It was the young warrior from the fort, who had stood at
Skanawati's side when he had made his confession. His eyes shone
fiercely as he slammed the blade of the tomahawk into the earth
inches from Duncan's ear.

Suddenly one of the Indians at Duncan's feet gasped as he was
lifted bodily away. As a second assailant mysteriously rose Duncan
could see Henry Bythe calmly standing with a lantern while Sergeant
McGregor and two more kilted soldiers methodically removed the
attackers, lifting them and tossing them away like sheaves. Duncan

did not understand why the warriors did not resist, why they did not even rise up from the ground where they landed, then saw that they were looking not at Bythe or the Scots but at a figure in the shadows, an older Iroquois wearing a headdress made of a fox skin, the head of the animal perched over his forehead.

"This is what happens when we journey with such devils," the Quaker said as the Scots faded back into the darkness. Bythe seemed entirely unafraid of the warriors around him.

Duncan struggled to his feet, rubbing the pain out of his limbs as he tried to grasp which devils the Quaker spoke of.

"They have no place in a treaty. The war does not affect them like it does Pennsylvania and New York." Bythe began brushing off the dirt on Duncan's back as he spoke. "They should go home to their easy southern life."

"The devils you refer to are the Virginians?" Duncan asked, about to point out it had not been colonists who had attacked him.

"Of course. What happened here was naught but revenge for the Virginians' attack on our prisoner. The southerners cannot be trusted. If it were up to them we would be driven to abandon this very road."

"The road?" Duncan asked, confused again.

"The Forbes Road. They were furious when General Forbes decided on the Pennsylvania route two years ago. The general even intercepted secret correspondence from their Colonel Washington seeking to reverse the decision. They insisted the western lands were already theirs, that the road to Fort Pitt should run from Fort Cumberland, to ease the travel of Virginians."

Duncan had not appreciated the political significance of the road. It did indeed open the western lands to Pennsylvania settlers.

"'Twas but a game. Those bucks meant to frighten, not seriously injure you," Bythe declared.

Duncan rubbed his shoulder, realizing that indeed the aches from the blows were already receding. "How could you know what they—" Duncan's question died away as the Indian wearing the fox headdress stepped to Bythe's side with a casual nod at the Quaker.

Bythe lifted a hemp bag from where it lay by his feet and extracted a slab of bacon and sack of flour, dropped them back into the bag, and handed it to the Indian. "Johantty is Skanawati's nephew," Bythe explained with a gesture toward the youth who had led the attack, "the others also from the chief's village." As Bythe explained to Duncan, Johantty rose, glowering at Duncan, then motioned his comrades back into the shadows.

"The future of the western lands, Mr. McCallum," Bythe declared in a genteel voice, "is properly a matter between the Iroquois and the Penn province."

Duncan considered the words for a long moment, uncertain whether he was meant to take warning or invitation from them. "Would you consider it possible, sir," he ventured, "that Skanawati is innocent?"

Bythe did not hesitate. "We would consider it certain, sir," he countered, "that even if Skanawati killed a solitary Virginian that act would not explain all the other deaths along the Warriors Path this year."

Duncan stared at him in astonishment, then reminded himself that Bythe was the provincial emissary at Fort Pitt, which meant the nations he dealt with were not European.

"The surveyors Townsend, Putnam, young Cooper, and his bride," Bythe recited. "Brother Brindle and I sent out secret inquiries about them months ago."

"Skanawati himself was seeking to understand the deaths," Duncan observed.

"So my friend Long Wolf has led me to understand," Bythe said, with a gesture to the Indian in the fox headdress, still at his side. "Perhaps you have not met the chief of the Mingoes, the western Iroquois?" The chieftain nodded silently at Duncan. "He is one of those who understand our true enemy is the French. Just days before Burke's death Skanawati warned him of Hurons in the area of Ligonier."

"Yet you let your brother-in-law hold Skanawati as a prisoner."

Bythe raised a hand to cut off Duncan's protest. "Simply because he warns friends about raiders does not mean he is not secretly allied with them. That is a question we are still seeking to settle."

The two men looked at Duncan expectantly. "Does Long Wolf perhaps know of the signs on the trees?" Duncan asked Bythe awkwardly. "Conawago suggests that—"

Bythe interrupted by holding a finger to his lips, then pointed to the chieftain, who gestured for Duncan to follow toward a lodge at the rear of the camp.

Duncan hesitated as Long Wolf disappeared into the entrance of a structure made of skins draped over a framework of bent saplings.

"The fire is made and the smoke rising," Bythe said, motioning Duncan inside.

"I'm sorry?"

"It means a council has been called."

Duncan eyed the Quaker uneasily, then saw that Johantty and his companions were standing nearby, watching him, and stepped inside.

Conawago sat on the earthen floor of the makeshift shelter with Long Wolf and three other Indian elders, sharing a long stone pipe of tobacco. Knowing better than to interrupt the intense, fevered conversation that was underway, Duncan found a space and sat cross-legged on the floor, wondering for a moment why the five Indians sat in a lopsided circle, with an empty place at the far side.

The others took no notice of him and continued speaking in low, fast voices that allowed Duncan to catch only a few words, though not the sense of the overall discussion. *Wolf,* he heard, then *tree, turtle, Onondaga,* and *Skanawati.* The solitary life he led with Conawago gave him few opportunities to listen to conversations between Iroquois, and now as he gave up trying to make specific sense of their words, he opened himself in the way he'd been taught to listen in the forest. There was eloquence in the voices, but also something else. Conawago had told Duncan if he listened carefully he could tell the difference between the call of a young owl and an old one, for the older bird spoke with wisdom and melancholy over all the death it had witnessed. The voices he heard now were those of old owls.

He lost all sense of time and became lost in the spell of the rapid dialogue and the random images it summoned. The haunting piles of bones at Braddock's battlefield, Captain Burke nailed alive to a survey tree. The bizarre symbols, unknown to Indian or European, on the boundary trees. Mokie about to be carried away with Burke's dead body.

A touch at his knee brought him back. "Will you speak to us of what the dead man teaches?" Conawago asked.

"I'm sorry?"

"These chiefs from the Grand Council of the Iroquois have spoken about Skanawati, and his actions these past weeks. I have spoken of the events since the first day near Ligonier, of Skanawati's confession, and of the trees. They are disturbed that raiders took

Burke's body. I have told them you come from a lost land, where you were taught how to make the dead speak. I told them you, too, sought out his body, touched it."

Duncan looked from one man to the next, each face as inscrutable as the one before. Even if one of their own had confessed to murder, what concerned them most was the theft of a dead body. The oldest of the Indians, whose wrinkled, leathery face spoke of great age, nodded to Duncan.

"Old Belt of the Mohawks desires you to share your knowledge," Conawago said.

The old chief extended the long pipe toward Duncan, gesturing, moving over to make room for Duncan at his side.

Only after Duncan had settled by Old Belt and inhaled deeply of the fragrant tobacco offered him did the chief speak, this time in English with a heavy French accent. "My people, guardians of the eastern door," he said, using the traditional Iroquois description of the Mohawk tribe, "are accustomed to returning from a victory with a prisoner. But never have we heard of a dead man being captured as if he were alive. Did you perhaps see that one come back to life and fight those raiders?"

The way Winston Burke, days dead now, still preyed on him, Duncan was tempted to agree. The Virginian's ghost cast a long shadow over the treaty convoy. "No. He was bound and tied inside a blanket."

"Perhaps the blanket was writhing the way a cocoon writhes just before the butterfly emerges?"

Duncan shuddered, then studied the chiefs. He was looking at the heads of the tribal treaty delegation, he realized, and now knew why there was an empty place in their circle. They still considered Skanawati an active member of their delegation. "No," Duncan said quietly. "He did not come back to life to fight the Hurons."

The chief in the fox headdress spoke at last. "Not Hurons,"
Long Wolf said, pronouncing his English words very slowly.
"Renegades. Outlaws. What is the word when your king hires those
German soldiers?"

"Mercenaries."

The Mingo chief nodded. "Mercenaries." He pointed to an
object by the little fire, the bone-and-bead breastplate Conawago
had found at the ambush. "This is Nanticoke, or maybe Conoy,"
he said, referring to two of the smaller tribes that traditionally lived
along the Chesapeake and its tributaries. "Most of them have lost
their ways. Some would kill for the leg of a chicken."

"But we saw them," Duncan said. "Conawago and I were at
their camp. They were French Indians."

"Some were," Conawago agreed. "But not all, I think. If such
men were paid to kill English, might they not be friendly with the
French?"

"But who would use such killers?" As the question left his
lips Duncan realized it was what the men around him had been
asking themselves. By the worried glances they exchanged he realized they thought it possible it was someone within their own
confederation.

They sat in silence.

"The great chiefs of the Iroquois League," Conawago finally
said to Duncan, "will never sign a treaty without understanding
what the dead man was trying to say to you. Those on the other
side are watching what is done here."

Duncan reminded himself that these chiefs too would have
heard that there was a crack in the world that seemed to be spewing out ghosts. The English members of the treaty party desperately
wanted to forget the killing at the tree, dismiss it as something

unrelated to their mission. But the Iroquois knew all things were related, and ghosts from the Warriors Path had joined their negotiations.

With an outstretched hand Old Belt cupped smoke and directed it to Duncan, letting it wash over him before offering the pipe again. He meant to bring the spirits into Duncan's heart before he spoke. But Duncan could find no words.

"If it is as you say," said the Mohawk, doubt lingering in his tone, "then they took him so he would stop sharing his secrets with you."

Duncan realized the Indian had grasped the truth that had been eluding him. "They are taking him to another who understands the language of the dead," he agreed. *But why?* he desperately asked himself. What on the body had he missed?

"Captain Burke was a man not used to physical labor," he began, at least offering what he knew, "a man not at ease in the forest." The Indians were much more interested in the details of the murder than the English had ever been.

"What did his tattoos speak of?" Old Belt asked.

"He had none, only a little scar like a bolt of lightning."

The announcement triggered a worried exchange among the Iroquois.

"His hand was nailed to the tree," Duncan continued. "He could not stop his killer from cutting away his silver buttons. And this—" He lifted his pouch, pulling out the lump of copper and dropping it onto the ground in front of him. "This was in his throat."

The announcement was punctuated by a gasp. Long Wolf seemed to have stopped breathing. Old Belt sagged. "That explains it. Why he does not speak with you."

"You mean it blocked his tongue?" Duncan ventured.

"No." Long Wolf lifted a kindling stick and pushed the lump back toward Duncan, gesturing for him to put it away. The copper scared him. "It is his soul," he declared matter-of-factly, "shriveled and melted. Without a soul the dead will never speak, never see, never find the other side."

An unnatural chill gripped Duncan's spine. He too was now strangely scared to touch the metal. He pushed it back into his pouch with a fingertip.

Old Belt produced a little bag of deerskin and upended it by the fire. Three more molten lumps dropped out. "The killer did the same to the warriors Skanawati sent," he said in a mournful tone. "We cannot let this happen to Skanawati." He stared pointedly at Duncan. "He is the best of us. We will need him on the other side."

Duncan looked to Conawago for help. But the expression on his friend's face said he too was frightened, more than Duncan could have imagined.

"Tell us what the words of the dead say on the trees. Perhaps it is how they speak when they have no tongue." Long Wolf tossed wood on the fire, making it flare up for more light. He then carefully extracted and unfolded a square of finely tanned doeskin, laying it beside the fire. The skin showed signs of wear, of being folded and unfolded and handled often. A shiver ran down Duncan's spine as he saw the geometric shapes painted on the skin. The treaty chiefs had recorded eight groupings of the shapes from the trees. He returned the somber gaze of each man in turn. The chiefs were trying to reconcile the deaths in their own way.

"I have not unlocked the magic of these shapes," Duncan replied, "but I can tell you each set marks a death along the Warriors Path. I think it is the killers, not the dead, who make them. And," he added, "I am aware of only four, maybe five." He reminded himself that the surveyor Putnam had never been accounted for.

"The three members of the turtle clan Skanawati sent down the trail late this winter," the old Mohawk chief said in a heavy voice. "They were killed at such trees as they tried to clean the old shrines."

"Why?" Duncan asked. "Why would he have sent them?" He stared at the molten lumps. They would be a perfect shield for a murderer among the Indians. Any body discovered with such a lump would be taboo. No one would have touched it, no one would ever have tried to learn more about it.

"Skanawati told them the old trees, the marker shrines, needed to be cleansed, needed to have the dust removed from their eyes and ears."

Duncan looked at Conawago. The chief was referring to a greeting ceremony, like that performed at the edge of the woods between travelers. It was what Conawago had performed at the western tree. Skanawati had guessed the other trees were also ancient shrines.

"None of this explains why they wanted the dead Virginian," Conawago pointed out.

Long Wolf frowned. "There is a French shaman who could put more of those wheels in his chest and make him live again," he said. "Neither warrior nor soldier could stop such a creature."

The words hung in the air. Duncan wanted to dismiss them as absurd. But then he saw the frightened way the other chiefs reacted to them.

"Before he left for the western lands," offered Old Belt, "Skanawati argued to the Grand Council that the world was coming to an end, that the Iroquois had brought it upon themselves by ignoring the ancient, honored ways. There is an old tale told at our campfires of how our world will end with a great monster of rock eating everything." The chief paused, drawing deeply on the pipe, letting the smoke slowly waft out of his mouth as he seemed to consider his own words. "After Skanawati left, an old woman of our tribe had a dream that a monster came to her village, some sort of European man machine with a chest of metal, and he began eating the village, starting with the children."

Duncan wanted to shake the chiefs, to reason with them, to tell them it was impossible. But he dared not break through the solemn, anxious atmosphere. Dreams could never be ignored or denied, for they were considered messages from the other side. And the moment a man had been found with a gear in his chest, the terrible vision had become possible.

"You are the one who possesses the power to reach across the edge of the worlds, to the spirits of your tribe," Old Belt declared to Duncan. "You must ask them to speak with the Iroquois spirits on that side. Ask what we must do so our children will not die."

It was Duncan's turn to despair. He did not know how to say yes, was not certain what was being asked of him, yet could not bear to refuse the wise old man, who reminded him of so many Highland chieftains he had known, vital, courageous men, now in the ground, whose children, whose world, *had* been destroyed. He found himself struggling against one of his recurring visions of his dead family, reaching out for him.

"We will need more tobacco," Duncan said at last.

The despair that seized him every few weeks was like a living thing, a beast that burrowed into him, devouring his vital organs so that Duncan could not see, could not feel, was sometimes not even conscious of his whereabouts. It was a cold winter dusk when he had found himself sitting on the lip of a hundred-foot cliff with Conawago an arm's length away, ready to grab him.

"You need to let them go, Duncan," the old Indian had said. "You need to let your dead family go."

Duncan flinched. As ever, Conawago's arrow had hit the mark. "It's a dark, cold spot in my heart that seems to ebb and flow like the tides. I don't think it will ever go away."

"How old were you? Eleven? Twelve?"

"Ten," Duncan replied. "I was ten when the English killed them."

"And hundreds of miles away at school. Do you possibly think you could have stopped it?"

"I would have died with them. I should have died with them."

"I was the same age when the Jesuits took me away," Conawago said after a long silence, "promising I would return with knowledge to help my people. When I finally came back I had all the knowledge but my people had vanished. I spent most of my life looking for them. You must not spend the next fifty years looking for ghosts." The old Nipmuc extended his hand to guide Duncan back from the edge.

An hour after leaving the council fire Duncan sat on a solitary ledge, the moon high overhead, scanning the low starlit horizon of the lands below. He gazed down at the Indian camp three hundred feet beneath him, where he had sat in silence after the haunting words of the chief, letting the tobacco smoke waft around them, until finally Conawago had turned to explain.

"I spoke about you," he had said in a near whisper, "and of our time in the great woods. Old Belt believes there is a reason men like you and me survive the loss of our tribes, believes that we have special voices that reach the spirits. He says the Iroquois must learn all the ways to connect to those spirits. Word has come to him of a plaid man who can make the voice of the old ones."

When Duncan had raised his brows in confusion Conawago motioned toward the shadows. There he saw his friend had brought his tattered haversack into the lodge.

Understanding at last, Duncan had taken the bag and disappeared into the darkness, alone. Conawago knew well the solitary communion Duncan now needed as he unpacked the bundle wrapped in tattered muslin. With slow, reverent motions he laid the intricately crafted pieces in a pool of moonlight before assembling them. The first test of a reed brought a reply from a whippoorwill.

"You are clan chief," a familiar voice called from inside him, in the tongue of the Highlands, "which means you must show the others the right thing to do." Though he had first heard them spoken at his father's investiture many years before, his father often repeated them to him in his dreams. "Never mind that we will never see the Highlands again," an exiled countryman had declared to him the year before. "Your clan is all those under the boot of the world."

At last the bladder bulged with air, the reeds were wetted and set, the drones tuned. He clamped the blowstick in his teeth and began fingering the chanter. He could not have foreseen how every fear, every resentment, every longing for the justice that always seemed to elude him would crest in that moment when the first notes sounded, sweeping over him in a heart-thumping crescendo. By the end of his first tune he thought he would weep. By the end of the second he was no longer mournful, he was fighting, he was standing against the world, he was the last pipe speaking for the lost clans and dying tribes, and in that moment he would have charged a line of infantry alone, sword in one hand and pipes in the other.

He did not know when Conawago arrived to sit on a moonlit rock nearby, did not see the painted Iroquois bucks who had earlier assaulted him arrive to sit facing outward as if to protect him. He played the rally songs of long-ago battles, the airs from Highland romps, the ballads of women sending their men to do battle against impossible odds. As the moon crested he discovered the great brute McGregor sitting beside him, sobbing like a bairn.

Chapter Six

MAGISTRATE BRINDLE WAS ill-pleased with Duncan's musical performance, his nephew Felton reported as Duncan rose up from under the wagon after a few hours' sleep. Horses had been spooked. Several of the Welsh teamsters had insisted a banshee was descending on the convoy. As more grievances were recited, McGregor appeared at Duncan's side. Something like rancor flashed across the gangly young Quaker's face, then he shrugged, offered an exaggerated bow of his head, and retreated.

As Duncan made ready for travel he glanced up at the high ledge where he had played the pipes. Conawago was there, stretching in the dawn light, waking with the Iroquois chiefs. They had arrived the night before with wondering eyes to listen as he had played, had nodded solemn approval when he had finished. When Duncan had left them they were settling down on a bed of moss as Conawago pointed to the sky. "*Ootkwatah*," he had heard his friend say as he stepped away. "Pleiades." He was explaining to the chiefs the European names for the constellations.

Van Grut now approached, extending a tin mug of tea, which Duncan ravenously swallowed. He uneasily eyed the four young red-painted warriors who had followed him back to the magistrate's camp. They had been highly animated since hearing his pipes, pointing at Duncan and making low exclamations to each other, words that might have been praise or might have been the opposite. He no longer knew whether they plotted to protect him or harm him, though he had no doubt about their intentions for the breakfast the Quakers had been cooking.

"Yo ha!" one of them suddenly moaned and held his cheek, dropping a piece of bacon he had furtively lifted from the breakfast pan. When a companion bent to retrieve the meat a pebble flew from under the wagon and hit him in the temple. He cursed, but the other bucks laughed and pointed to a diminutive shape hiding behind a wagon wheel.

"Mokie!" Duncan called out and scooped up the girl as she darted toward him. He found himself embracing the girl with more emotion than he would have expected. He released her, turning her around to examine the wound on her head. "I proclaim you healed," he offered good-naturedly.

"They say it was you making that music last night," the girl said. "I heard it like in a dream, far away but asking me to come to it. Something kept pulling me back, but I went toward the music. Then suddenly I opened my eyes, and I was in Mama's arms."

"Bagpipes, lass. I breathe into a little pipe, and the voices of all my grandfathers come trilling out the other end."

She embraced him again, then insisted he sit while she brought him a meal of bacon and bread, the best breakfast he'd had in weeks. She disappeared inside the wagon with more food, but was chased out by her mother, who declared they would eat in the fresh air. Becca climbed down from the high gate then reached up. To his surprise it was Skanawati who handed down the infant, Penn, then with a rattling of chains the Onondaga chief climbed down. He smiled not with his mouth but his eyes as he recognized Duncan, then cupped his hand over his heart and swept it toward the sky. "I too heard your grandfathers," he said. "My heart was soaring."

Duncan grinned for a moment at the man then, without thinking, reached out to examine the cuts and bruises on the chief's arm where the Virginians had beaten him. Skanawati pulled away, sitting down on a log to gulp down a tankard of water brought by Mokie. With intense curiosity Duncan watched a small group gathered near the front of the wagon. Magistrate Brindle was leading his Quakers in morning devotions, his nephew Felton now reciting from the Bible.

"In the village of my family," Skanawati suddenly declared, looking north, "this is the moon of the singing—" he paused and made a hopping motion with his hand.

"Frogs," Duncan offered.

"Singing frogs. The children catch them on the leaves where they dwell. They bring them into the longhouse to hear them sing at night and laugh when they see their throats swell up with air. Frogs and children share great joy in the spring."

They watched the teamsters hitching the mules and oxen to the wagons. Some began moving down the road.

"A young woman was killed at that last boundary tree," Duncan announced. "An Iroquois woman, we think. And her husband, a man named Cooper."

The news brought pain to Skanawati's eyes.

"You knew them?"

"She was adopted into our village when her family was killed. My mother took her in like another daughter."

"Did she understand the old things? The signs made by the ancients?"

"She would speak with me, yes, even come with me to the cave where the old gods live."

"Help me understand why she died."

Skanawati shrugged. "She was called away. It is not for us to say why."

Duncan extended one of the clock gears from his pouch. "Where do these come from?"

"It is a European thing."

"What does it mean, having one of these in the breastbone?"

"Asking so many questions is a European thing as well." Skanawati turned and studied Duncan. "Do not trouble about me, McCallum," he said, pronouncing Duncan's name slowly. "I am my own man."

"Others have died. Others may die. I must find the truth."

Skanawati ate a bite of the bread Mokie brought him before answering. "You mean you must find *your* truth."

The words strangely stung Duncan. The people of the woods may have sprung from the same stock as Europeans, but with a few words such as these it seemed they were from different planets. Despite his months with Conawago he still struggled to understand the many dimensions of truth in the Indian world. They were the most straightforward, honest people he had ever known, but truth for them was not simply a matter of never lying. With a sacred wampum belt in his hand an Iroquois was as likely to lie as to sprout wings and fly, but one still had to be careful with the words that came out, could not truly understand them without understanding the spirit of the man who spoke them. Among the tribes, truth was something between a man and the spirit god that was always with him. Each man had his own truth, for most vital of all was that each, in the Indian way of speaking, maintained his own true skin.

Duncan realized that he was staring at the small bundle of mink fur with tiny red and yellow feathers sewn around its top that hung from Skanawati's neck. Inside would be a token of the spirit animal that guided the chief. He flushed as the Iroquois noticed his gaze, then looked away as Skanawati pushed the amulet inside his shirt.

At that moment a running figure caught his eye. Hadley, eating with Van Grut, had tossed aside his mug and was darting toward a copse of bushes. "Unhand her!" Hadley shouted. Duncan leapt up and ran.

He arrived at the thicket in time to see Hadley launch himself at one of two large men wearing the colors of the Virginia militia. The second was carrying Mokie over his shoulder, a gag in her mouth, her legs bound with rope.

The man Hadley knocked to the ground rolled over and deftly unsheathed his knife as he sprang into a crouch. He paused, confused, when he recognized his assailant.

"She be Virginia property, sir!" the soldier declared in a plaintive voice. "Y'er uncle's property."

"Put her down," Hadley growled. Mokie began pounding her assailant's back with her fists.

The soldier with the knife crouched as if to attack. But suddenly there was a sound of rattling chains and a blur of movement at his side. The knife flew from his hands, his legs flew out from under him, and he was on his back with Skanawati's foot pressed so tightly against his windpipe he began to choke.

Duncan put a restraining hand on the Iroquois. "The girl is under the protection of Pennsylvania province," he declared to the militiaman with Mokie.

"That be only her mother and the infant," the soldier protested.

"Not since the attack at Braddock's field. She was there when your captain's body was taken. They sought to take her as well. She knows matters important to the investigation. She has become a witness required by the magistrate."

It was only partly a lie, yet enough to make the man hesitate. Mokie squirmed, bit her captor through her gag, and rolled off his shoulder. In the next instant she lifted a rock and smashed it down on his foot. The soldier hopped backward, clutching his boot.

"Ye little black bitch!" he howled. He seemed to consider whether to charge at the Iroquois who had pinned his companion when a hulking presence loomed at Duncan's side. With one look at McGregor the man limped away, his companion frantically following the instant Skanawati lifted his foot from his throat.

Mokie was at first so relieved, then so preoccupied with untying her feet that she did not notice that the pouch she had tied around her neck had slipped out of her shirt, or that the paper inside it had nearly fallen out. But Duncan saw and grabbed the pouch before the girl could react.

"No! You mustn't!" The mulatto girl was fast, and surprisingly strong, but Duncan was prepared for the tug of war. He held on with one hand, the other on Mokie's shoulder, until the leather strap broke in her hand. She erupted into tears. Duncan released her and stepped back to the wagon, knowing she would follow.

The markings on the paper were crudely made, but they were unmistakable. The geometric symbols from the marker trees he had visited had been transcribed. There was writing on both sides of the paper. Behind the rows of symbols duplicated from the trees was a crude map of the trail showing its starting point and the places where it crossed the Forbes Road.

"Where did you get this?" Duncan demanded as Mokie ran into her mother's arms.

Becca's eyes flared when she saw what Duncan held, and she seemed about to snatch the papers away. "You think we just wander into the wilderness and expect to be free?" she asked with fire in her eyes. "Freedom is hundreds of miles away. We need supplies to travel so far."

"You go north because the French offer freedom and land. Are you saying they actively assisted in your escape?" Duncan asked.

"What duty do we owe to *your* king?" Becca demanded.

The words stung, in more ways than one.

"People have been killed because of the boundary trees, and these markings seem to lie at the heart of the evil being done. More may die yet."

"I pray, Mr. McCallum." Brindle appeared from behind the wagon. He had been listening. "Do not foment more fear among our party. We have but one crime, and one who has already answered for it."

Duncan turned to face the magistrate. "I beg you not to be deceived by appearances, sir. So far I have seen these runes on two trees, and at both, men were nailed to the trunk and then slain. There is reason to believe others have died in the same fashion these past few months."

Duncan marked that there was no surprise in Brindle's reaction. "There are no other bodies. There are no other complaints to the authorities. We have but one crime," he repeated. "Surely that is more than enough."

"How many more boundary trees are there?" Duncan asked. "Fifteen? Twenty? The Pennsylvania colony will run out of surveyors before this is over. You might view it as one crime, but it has meant multiple killings." He faced Becca again. "Winston Burke helped you escape, did he not?"

Brindle stiffened.

"He helped you and perhaps died for it," Duncan pressed.

The Quaker seemed about to protest but instead looked at his brother-in-law Bythe and grimaced.

Defiance still burned on Becca's handsome face. Then the infant, Penn, in a basket inside the wagon, stirred, offering a cooing sound, and her expression softened. Her son's fate, and that of her daughter and herself, were in the hands of the Pennsylvanians. Tears filled her eyes. "Shamokin," she whispered, referring to the large Indian town on the banks of the upper Susquehanna. "A man in Shamokin was to give us supplies if we brought these to him. He would give us directions to the place where slaves are settling in the French country." She put her arms around her daughter, as if the confession placed them in new jeopardy.

"And the trees?"

"The trail was to take us all the way to Shamokin. When we reached the wide Susquehanna we were to tell the Indians at the village there that we sought the great bear and they would ferry us across."

Duncan realized there was something else in Mokie's pouch. A chill went down his spine as he upended it and a clock gear tumbled out.

"That was there when we received it," Becca quickly explained. "We never understood. But it wasn't ours. We didn't dare remove it."

"The gears," came Hadley's frightened whisper as he looked toward Duncan. The Virginian understood the reason. The killers had stopped the Indians from pursuing them with lumps of molten metal. Here was another defense in case the slaves were taken. "Word already spread about the killings, and the gears in the bodies. If they found such a gear with escaped slaves," Hadley said with a shudder, "they will assume it is the slaves doing the killing. None will ever be brought back alive."

By the time Duncan had discussed his discoveries with Conawago, the magistrate's massive wagon was nearly half a mile down the road, the treaty caravan already stretching nearly a mile before and behind it, lines of Indians on either side like an honor guard for the prisoner. Shamokin, Conawago quickly explained, was the population center for both the tribes of the Susquehanna and the southern villages of the Six Nations themselves, the southern capital, as it were, of the Iroquois empire. At least a dozen tribes were represented there, as well as sutlers who sold wares to the Indians, missionaries, fur traders, and Pennsylvania's Fort Augusta, guarding the colony's northern border, sometimes garrisoned with militia.

"This news of Shamokin," Duncan said, studying his friend's face, "brings you new worry. Why?"

Conawago seemed reluctant to reply. "We should go, Duncan. Back into the forest. That is our place, that is where my work lies."

"Why?" Duncan pressed.

"Because Shamokin is full of renegades and outlaws. And there will be many there who oppose a new land treaty, whether or not the Grand Council seeks to sign it."

Duncan began his loping run toward Brindle's wagon with the intention of warning the magistrate, but by the time he reached it he realized there was someone else he must speak with first. Long

Wolf, the chieftain of the Iroquois living in the Ohio lands, was walking beside the team, admiring the heavily muscled mules.

"You spoke last night of a French shaman," Duncan said. "Where will I find this man?"

"He is a man of powerful medicine. He goes where he wishes."

"If you were to seek him where would you start?"

"Do not seek to interfere with the work of nations," came a stern reproach from behind. He turned and looked into the wrinkled face of Old Belt.

"Did you not come here," Duncan asked, "because you think the treaty important?"

"There is a covenant chain that links our peoples since the days of my father's father. We protect their borders. The British provide us with clothing and goods." Old Belt cast a long, worried glance toward the wagon where Skanawati lay in manacles.

"What happens to the chain when the British decide the Iroquois are killing all their surveyors? There will never be another treaty."

"But we are not killing surveyors. We will tell the British so."

"If I place a burning ember in your hand and tell you it is ice, which will you heed, your hand or your ear? Someone is making it appear that the Iroquois are killing the surveyors. If they succeed you will return home with empty hands, Skanawati dead, and the covenant chain shattered."

The two chiefs spoke with each other in low, worried tones. "Shamokin," Old Belt finally announced. "The Frenchman you seek is in Shamokin."

Duncan spent another half hour in search of the magistrate, who had ridden forward to hurry the convoy along. When he finally came upon Brindle's large black mare, his nephew was leading it. Felton explained that his uncle had joined a group of teamsters trying to hoist a heavy wagon to shift a broken wheel.

"Impossible," the magistrate replied when Duncan explained his proposal. "I will not surrender escaped slaves to you. And I will not let you force us into greater difficulties. Already the treaty hangs by a thread, the Virginians ready to steal away Skanawati to hang him, the Iroquois ready to attack them if they try. I will not entertain your fantasy that some broader conspiracy is afoot."

"Only Mokie need go with us. Let Mr. Hadley accompany us so that you can tell the Virginians she is in the custody of a member of the Burke family."

"Us?"

"Van Grut and Conawago will come with me."

"Mr. Hadley is an official record keeper of the treaty proceedings. And of the trial."

"You will take nearly a week to reach Lancaster at the speed of these wagons, more days to organize the proceedings. Give us fast horses to get to the river and we can meet you there with no disturbance to your schedule."

"I will not have you destroy my treaty over a few rumors," Brindle replied in an insistent tone.

"The government of this colony cannot make light of this trial. You know it will need to be precise, correct in every detail, if you are to carry out justice and still maintain relations with the Iroquois. Letting us go shows them that Europeans are trying to get to the bottom of this affair. Do not forget I can offer the precision of science in my report."

Brindle looked at Duncan with new interest but said nothing.

"Of course," Duncan continued, "a scientific expert is duty bound to tell the complete story. I will speak of another murder, at a different boundary tree, exhibiting the same method. Hanging one man for one act in the drama will solve nothing. The Iroquois will be wrathful, as will the Virginians. When the truth reaches Philadelphia you won't find a surveyor ready to set foot in the wilderness for years to come. And when the treaty is ruined the news will be passed on to the king and the Parliament, to the proprietor," he added, referring to the heir of the godlike William Penn. "You will have single-handedly brought to pass the worst interruption in relations with the Iroquois since the covenant chain was formed over a century ago."

For the first time since Duncan had known him he saw heat on the Quaker's face. He had gone too far. "You are insolent, McCallum! A feral Scotsman does not dictate affairs of state!" As Brindle fixed Duncan with an angry gaze his nephew rode up, leading the magistrate's horse.

"The Scottish highlands were scoured clean of resistance in but a few short years," Duncan shot back. "The Pennsylvania wilds and the western forest are vastly bigger. It will take twenty, maybe thirty years to clean them out if the Iroquois fight back. Thousands will die. Expansion of your province will be a distant dream if you alienate the tribes. Fort Pitt will be gone in a day if they choose to attack."

"The biggest threat to our treaty conference is you yourself, Mr. McCallum. I should have heeded Major Latchford's warnings and banned you from our company." Brindle paused. "Before we left Ligonier the major informed me he had sent a dispatch rider to Philadelphia with written inquiries about you."

Brindle mounted, but before riding away he gestured Felton on and turned back to Duncan. "For many weeks Mr. Bythe has been investigating the matters that so upset you. He is fully capable of reconciling the facts to appease the tribes. The tribes will see that we of Philadelphia are their true friends, and the army can stop troubling itself."

"The army?" Duncan asked uneasily.

"You cannot use a smith's hammer against the hornet when it stings."

"Sir?"

"The army is incapable of dealing with stealth, with spies. Bythe knows the tribes, and the nature of the war. It was not by coincidence he was sent to run the provincial outpost at Pitt. He has been collecting evidence of French saboteurs. And if you breathe a word of it I will have you in chains."

"The best chance the French have now is to turn the Iroquois against us," Duncan observed.

"I am painfully aware that if we lose the Iroquois nations the bloodbath will last a decade. There are hundreds of brave young families on the frontier. Many years ago I had the misfortune to arrive at a frontier village just after a raid. There was but one sobbing old woman left, twenty others hacked to pieces, several of them my own relatives. She said there was no warning, not even a barking dog. She said they just rose up out of the ground, sent by the devil himself." Brindle's voice trailed off, as though he was revisiting the horror of that day. After a moment he turned and spoke in a near whisper. "Bythe found a French spy among us."

"Here in the convoy?" Duncan asked in alarm. "How could he know?"

"The man's a n'er do well, a Delaware who sometimes mingles with the army scouts. Bythe saw him carrying the rifle of Captain Burke, his initials carved into the stock. He fled to the north when Bythe tried to press for an explanation."

Duncan glanced about, looking for the sturdy Quaker. "Sir, I pray you. Let me speak to Bythe," he urged. "I will gladly assist him."

"He is gone, since before dawn. He sat with your friend Van Grut and went through his journal last night. Afterward he asked for a small, sharp knife and said he knew what had to be done now."

It was nearly noon, and the two of them were sitting on a ledge rock watching the convoy descend onto a river valley floor when suddenly Conawago pointed out a mounted figure galloping from the east. Even from the distance they could make out the scarlet uniform of a military dispatch rider. The soldier did not gallop past the head of the caravan as expected but reined to a halt, speaking with the lead teamsters.

"Let us go, Duncan," his friend said. "It will not be welcome news for us." There was a boundary tree they meant to investigate, not more than a mile away, at one of the places where the Warriors Path ran close to the road. Conawago had pointed out the likely location, close to the head of the river, where the road made a sharp horseshoe curve beneath a narrow waterfall.

But Duncan kept watching. The messenger was clearly seeking out Brindle. He looked to the big Conestoga wagon with its escort of McGregor's squad and braves. The Virginians, not far ahead of the wagon, were carrying their muskets in front of them, as if ready for action. The night before, mischief had been afoot in their camp, with flour sacks slit open, shoes cut apart, dirt thrown into the frizzen pans of muskets. Their patience with Quaker justice was growing thin. Duncan was gripped with foreboding, and a new helplessness. None of them wanted his help, none seemed to sense the explosion of violence that he was certain approached.

"We have other business in the forest," Conawago reminded him, as if now proposing to abandon the convoy entirely.

Duncan sighed in frustration, then rose and turned toward the north. With a few steps off the road he could be back in the life he had grown to love, roaming the forest with the serene old Indian, who still had so much to teach him.

Suddenly frantic cries rose up from the valley floor. Every wagon stopped. From front and back men were running toward the center of the convoy.

Conawago pulled at Duncan's arm, then saw the determined expression on his companion's face and grimaced. "Ten minutes, no more," he said, and he gestured Duncan down the road.

They found Brindle sitting on a log by the stream that tumbled from the cliff above in a waterfall at least thirty feet high. The army dispatch rider had joined McGregor in pushing back the onlookers that were for some reason gathering.

The magistrate gestured sternly with the envelope he held. "I have orders to arrest you," he declared in a hollow voice as Duncan approached. "One of Philadelphia's leading citizens has sworn out a warrant against you."

"Philadelphia?" Duncan asked in disbelief.

"Do not dishonor me, McCallum, by pleading ignorance of your indenture to Lord Ramsey." Brindle seemed strangely weary, as if he hadn't the strength to rise. "There is a bounty on your head of thirty pounds. What, pray tell, did you do to him?"

Before replying Duncan gauged the distance to the thicket at the base of the cliff, taking a step closer to it as he eyed the soldiers. "I caused the loss of his New York estate. I caused his daughter to sever ties with him."

"The bounty is greater than any I have ever heard, even for a murderer."

"I wounded Ramsey's pride," Duncan said, knowing that had been his greatest crime of all.

Duncan now saw something unexpected in Brindle's eyes as he looked up. It appeared to be despair. He realized the Quaker was struggling to control his emotions. "But divine Providence has other plans," the magistrate slowly said.

Duncan hesitated, not certain he had heard correctly. "I'm sorry?"

Even when Brindle pointed at the center of the waterfall Duncan did not comprehend, did not at first grasp the oddly rhythmic movement of the round rock in the center of the current, not until Van Grut, shielding his eyes from the sun, gave a gasp of alarm.

Duncan stepped out of the sunlight and looked up again at the strange shape in the waterfall. It was Henry Bythe, the magistrate's brother-in-law. His body, thrown into the stream above, had been caught in the rocks in its descent so that the head protruded out of the rushing water. Wedged there, buffeted by the cascade, the dead Quaker was nodding at them.

"Go," the magistrate instructed Duncan in a haunted voice. "Go to Shamokin and bring me back your terrible truth."

Chapter Seven

*T*HE PENNSYLVANIA WILDERNESS unfolded mile after mile,
the steep, repetitive ridges finally yielding to the broad
Susquehanna, the vast river that had served as the region's
north-south thoroughfare for centuries. They paddled relentlessly
now through the shallow waters, past the river's hundreds of tiny
wooded islands, their canoes aimed like arrows at the heart of the
Iroquois nation.

In his infrequent rests from the paddle Duncan found himself
gazing at the silent, determined men in breechcloths who accompanied them. When the others had met Duncan at the boundary
tree above the waterfall, where he studied its freshly cut symbols,
Van Grut had explained that Conawago had adamantly refused
Brindle's offer of Pennsylvania militia as an escort. The old Iroquois
chiefs had a suggestion more to Conawago's liking. Johantty and
the young Onondagas who had assaulted Duncan, only to later be
transfixed by his piping, had intercepted them an hour later, leading
them back onto the Forbes Road ahead of the convoy, where Felton
waited with fresh horses. The bucks seemed to have aged somehow,

grown more solemn, the rough ways displayed earlier replaced by a wary determination. Their elders had spoken with them, and now they were on a path of war against an unseen enemy.

"You run with death," Brindle's nephew had warned Duncan as he handed over the horses. "Sleep with one eye open if you value your hair. Henry Bythe died because he did not understand the depths of the treachery afoot."

Duncan studied the wary way Felton watched their escort. "Surely you do not suspect these Iroquois now. Bythe was convinced it was the French behind the murders."

"And what got him killed was his failure to see that the line between the two has blurred. The Iroquois lie between us and the French. More than a few are married into French families. Skanawati is Iroquois," Felton reminded Duncan. The Quaker paused to watch the cloud of dust as the others trotted away. "Shamokin is a nest of vipers. What do you hope to find there?"

"I don't know. A clock. A rifle."

"Burke's rifle? That is gone, friend. I saw it, in the hands of an Iroquois fur trader headed into the deep Ohio forest."

Duncan looked at the Quaker with new interest. "You did not question the man?"

"I saw him with the gun, a memorable piece, but did not know what I had seen until I heard the Virginians describe the carving on the stock. He was gone by then."

"What did the chiefs say of this man?"

Felton grimaced. "Why would I tell the Iroquois?"

"Because they have suffered murders too. Similar murders, ritual murders."

"Nonsense. If that is what they tell you, they toy with you. Everything those Iroquois chiefs do is about negotiation, another move on some great chess board. Their truths are like quicksilver."

"Was Bythe's murder a move on that board?"

"God rest his soul, yes. Bythe meant to root out the French sympathizers among the tribes, to strengthen the alliance. I have vowed to my uncle that we will even the score before this war is over."

"Bythe's murder was almost identical to Burke's," Duncan observed. "Skanawati was in chains at the time."

"Skanawati has confederates," Felton replied. "And while one murder might mean a personal feud, more than one surely means it is part of the war. The Iroquois begin to glimpse that English expansion will be unfettered if the French lose. Have you not wondered why the army has found no signs of the raiding party you yourself reported?" The Quaker did not wait for Duncan's reply. "Because the army scouts are all Indians allied with the Iroquois. The army has gone blind and doesn't yet realize it."

Duncan considered Felton's words. "Did Bythe understand that?"

"Of course. Which is why I have been his trusted eyes and ears these many months."

Duncan mounted his horse. Felton rode alongside for a moment. "I admire your courage, Scotsman. Murderers in front of you and bounty hunters behind."

"Lord Ramsey is in Philadelphia," Duncan countered.

"His money reaches far beyond the city. News in the wilderness spreads like it has wings," Felton said as he wheeled his horse about. "Every teamster in the convoy will know by tonight. You'll have a few days at most before word of the bounty reaches Shamokin. Thirty pounds is enough to tempt even the most saintly of Christians. Whether they take you for the bounty or kill you to stop you finding their treachery, either way they will be fighting over scraps of your hide by the end of the week." The Quaker pressed his heels to his mount and was gone.

Duncan watched Felton gallop away, puzzling over the threatening tone that had risen in his voice, then turned to catch up with his friends. But suddenly he reined his horse around to watch Felton disappear down the road. Bythe had told the magistrate that Burke's rifle was headed north with a renegade from a smaller tribe. Felton, Bythe's trusted eyes and ears, who seemed to be urging Duncan to flee, insisted it had vanished with an Iroquois into the west. Either the dead provincial official or the zealous Quaker scout had lied.

As they climbed the ridges he pushed down his fear of bounty hunters by revisiting the murders in his mind. It was easy to assume the murders were a consequence of the war, but Duncan's every instinct said otherwise. Bythe had started out thinking he knew those responsible, had assured the Pennsylvania government he would expose the French agents behind the murders. But that had been wishful thinking, since such a solution would have avoided enmity between the tribes and the English. After Burke's murder what Brindle and Bythe had hoped for was a solution that would show that Skanawati had been manipulated by the French, allowing them to declare him their mutual enemy's unknowing victim. But there had been no signs of a French raiding party at the tree where Bythe was attacked, only tracks of two men in moccasins in addition to Bythe, and no one outside the convoy could have known Bythe would be going to the tree. The Quaker emissary had paid for his misjudgment with his life.

Duncan found himself wondering why the dead Quaker had so abruptly decided to go to the boundary tree. He recalled his conversation with Brindle. Bythe had seen Van Grut's journal, after which he told Brindle he understood what had to be done. He had discovered new information in those pages that changed his perspectives on the murders. *The code.* What he had seen on those pages, Duncan now realized, had been the code. Bythe had recognized the code, had known its workings, and had gone to the tree with a borrowed knife to use it.

Above a patch of blood on the tree had been four symbols and an incomplete one, all with slash marks through them, with another, longer set of complete ones carved overhead. Based on Van Grut's sketches the Pennsylvanian had thought he had found a way to leave a message for the killer. But what he found at the tree had been the killer himself, who recognized that Bythe, though no surveyor, had learned enough to be dangerous.

There had been a hole in the bloody tree, three feet from the ground. Bythe had struggled, ripping out the nail that had fastened his hand. Duncan had followed the path of blood to the stream above the waterfall. The Quaker had stumbled to the water, where the killer had finished him, then had returned to carve his death message on the tree.

The four warriors accompanying them set a merciless pace. They insisted on paddling at night under the bright gibbous moon as the others slept in the bottom of the two large canoes. When Duncan tried to join them, he struggled to maintain their rhythm, but finally surrendered and lay back on the packs. It was one of the most beautiful nights he had experienced in years, and it put him in mind of moonlit sails among the Hebrides taken with his grandfather as a boy. The two sturdy canoes, readily offered to them when they had reached an Indian village at the river's western bank, were like creatures of the night, the water singing at their prows, the silver ribbons of their wake pointing ever north.

For long, calming moments, Duncan thought not of the terrible mystery that drove their journey, but only of the deeper mysteries that animated the strong, silent people of the wilderness. He had come to realize that the poetry in the souls of Conawago and Skanawati, even of the four braves in the canoes, was something that would forever elude the logic of Europeans. The most Duncan could hope for was to experience it, the way an artist experienced the impossible crimson and gold of a sunset.

"When he sleeps," an unsteady voice said near his ear, "the chief keeps the skin of a snake pressed close to his heart."

He turned to see Mokie's face in the moonlight. She was frightened. "You mean Skanawati."

The girl nodded. "Near scared mama to death when she first saw it."

Duncan gestured the girl closer. "The tribes consider the birds to carry messages to the gods," he explained. "But snakes are especially sacred. Snakes bring dreams, and in dreams, the tribes say, you visit the spirit world."

"You mean he talks to ghosts?" There was now more curiosity than fear in the girl's voice.

The words gave Duncan pause. He had almost forgotten Skanawati's words from the first day they had met him. He had embarked on the Warriors Path to speak with ghosts, not just to speak with them, but to be told how the Iroquois would leave the servitude of the English king.

"I was talking to ghosts that night with my pipes," Duncan said.

The girl nodded again, yawning. "I think it was them who brought me back from that dark place." She nestled into Duncan's shoulder to sleep. "I hope they take him where he needs to be."

The girl's last words strangely disturbed Duncan. He could not shake the feeling that the truth he so desperately sought was indeed bound up between Skanawati and his ghosts.

When he looked away from the sky again he saw that Conawago was awake, half-turned to look behind the canoes. More than once in their voyage Duncan had seen him looking over his shoulder. "Are we being followed?" Duncan asked.

"I feel it, yes. But it is a busy river. I could be mistaken."

"The killer has only struck on the Warriors Path," Duncan reminded his friend.

"The killer," Conawago countered, "makes ritual murders on the trail. Off the trail he may not need to be so fastidious."

By the time they landed below Shamokin the next morning, Mokie had repeated, without Duncan's bidding, what she and her mother had been instructed to do were they to reach the Indian town alive. Find the trail that rose above the southern edge of the town, they'd been told, and go to the fort that was not a fort, then ask again for the great bear.

"Was it Captain Burke who gave you those instructions?" he asked.

"On a piece of paper from Captain Burke," the girl confirmed. "We had to burn it after, he said. Captain Burke, and Mr. Hadley, they teach mama and me how to read and write. Captain Burke, he would say that he would see we would always have jobs in the house, not out in the weather."

"Why, then," Duncan asked, "did he change his mind? What made him help you flee?"

"Don't know. We couldn't make the sense of it. He just took us into the summer kitchen and said we deserved better, that he had a way to help us, help everyone. Mama made him swear on a Bible he was not tricking us."

"Help everyone? What did he mean by that?"

But the child only shrugged.

As Van Grut and Hadley disembarked, Duncan stood on the bank and stared with foreboding in the direction of the settlement, its existence marked by the many plumes of smoke rising over the low ridge before him. In English he recited Mokie's instructions for all to hear. The declaration brought a stifled laugh from Johantty, who translated it for his companions, raising more laughter.

"Do you know this bear?" Duncan asked.

Johantty raised a hand and pointed further down the ridge. "The bear's den is on the ridge," the young Iroquois declared then, exhausted, curled up for sleep on a bed of moss.

Duncan had been to Iroquois villages with Conawago, and at Shamokin expected something similar, on a larger scale, long bark houses with fields of corn, squash, and pumpkins stretching out from them. But it was no metropolis of longhouses he saw as they crested the ridge. The town seemed to consist of pieces borrowed from several different communities, haphazardly jammed together. Close to the river, on the long, curving flat at the junction of the north and west branches, there were indeed several longhouses, though half appeared abandoned. Here and there were clusters of log cabins, connected by muddy byways and most surrounded by primitive snake-rail fences that kept in milk cows. Scattered about were more prosperous-looking cabins, with even a few substantial

stone houses standing out amid rich fields of bottomland. A small
stone church stood by a graveyard. Beyond everything, just above
the fork, was a log palisade structure, the fort used by the militia.

The hammer of a smithy by the river rang out, near which several men labored over a new bargelike vessel resting in a log trestle.
Kegs were being rolled from one of the heavy cargo canoes that
plied the river. Duncan watched their progress, spying a substantial
cabin against which more kegs were stacked. A tavern. Two familiar
figures emerged from the trees and walked toward the church. Van
Grut and Hadley had agreed to explore the town as Duncan and
Conawago escorted Mokie to her mysterious rendezvous.

When he first looked down on the compound below the laurel
thickets, Duncan thought they had found another military fort,
then saw that the structures were old and in disrepair, placed not
for defense of the river forks but more for a view of the town. As he
approached he saw that not all was tumbledown. The central gate
had been recently rebuilt, and the dominant building appeared to
have been created by constructing a hall against an older structure
with the appearance of a church. Years earlier, he suspected, the
compound had been built as a mission. Now it was alive with
industry, men in buckskins and breechcloths counting and tying
furs in bundles, others operating one of the heavy wood-screw
presses used to compress stacks of hides for shipment. Several
Indian women were hanging fish on long drying racks. On the wall
of the new construction he saw a huge bearskin. Fighting a fresh
foreboding, wishing he had not left his gun at the landing place,
Duncan turned to tell Mokie to remain with Conawago while he
explored further. But she was gone. He looked frantically about and
spied her running through the open gate with Conawago trotting
to catch up with her.

He nearly collided with his friend as he darted through the gate moments later. Conawago was frozen, staring at a huge device made of wood, leather, and bone. It was spinning about, propelling several Indians in a circle as they sat on short planks suspended on ropes. Duncan gazed in disbelief at the machine, which was built around a heavy wagon wheel mounted horizontally atop a thick post functioning as an axle. Extension poles had been strapped with leather to the spokes of the wheel and hung with the rope swings at their ends. Antlers and small skulls adorned the end of the poles. Impossibly, it was a carousel, a particularly Indian carousel. Three small Indian children swung with cries of glee as an older Indian man propelled the machine by pulling on a rope hung from one of the extension poles. Two adolescent girls and a woman sat on the other seats, making no sound, their eyes filled with wonder.

A shriek from inside the large building broke their spell. Duncan and Conawago darted inside, past a sleepy Indian propped on a keg beside the door who sounded a surprised, halfhearted warning at their sudden appearance. Conawago's hand was on his warclub, Duncan's on his tomahawk, as they sprang into a large chamber.

They were met by high-pitched laughter. It took a moment for Duncan to realize that it came from Mokie, pointing at them in amusement, as if they were performing on her behalf. She sat at a long table eating bread and honey off a wooden plate beside a man with a great black beard. With one foot on the bench beside the girl, he was tuning a fiddle.

The stranger began a lively reel, bowing in greeting without stopping his music. He leaned over Mokie, playing with great speed and skill, finishing with a flourish and a hearty laugh that shook his well-fed frame. He nodded his head toward his two new guests.

"The mademoiselle has her first sweet taste of liberty. Surely worthy of a celebration."

"It looks like only bread and honey to me," Duncan observed.

"The plantation masters are far away," the man replied, stiffening. "The mountains are high."

"You are French," Duncan said, at once embarrassed by the unnecessary observation but unable to hide his surprise.

"A label bestowed by birth is impossible to deny." The man pushed the pot of honey closer to Mokie.

Conawago paced about the long table, eyeing the man with the same distrust Duncan felt. He paused at the only refined piece of furniture in the chamber, a little cherry table on which sat a solitary cross and a Bible. In the dust on the table he drew two letters with his fingertip. An S and a J.

The Frenchman's smile dimmed for a moment. He stepped to the table and erased the marks with a sweep of his hand. "That particular label I was able to abandon."

"For the profits of a merchant," Conawago shot back.

Duncan looked from man to man, unable to grasp what was passing between them.

"I came into the wilderness to aid the last uncorrupted people on earth."

"I believe the doctrine says we all are corrupted," said Conawago.

"That doctrine was devised by arthritic old men in Europe who never walked in the bowers of Eden." The man had grown serious, almost somber. "Sault St. Louis?" he asked of Conawago. "Swegatchy?"

Conawago did not respond.

Duncan stepped to the bench to stand behind Mokie. The girl pushed a heel of bread toward him.

"So you left the Society of Jesus in search of Adam and Eve?" his friend asked.

A Jesuit. At last Duncan understood. The Frenchman had been a Jesuit priest and had asked about two of the Jesuit missions that operated in the northern Iroquois lands. Though Conawago had never entirely embraced their faith, he had been in the care of Jesuits in Canada and Europe for much of his youth and had great respect for many of them.

The Frenchman set his fiddle on the table and paced around the old Indian, studying him with a new intensity. "I came not to search for Adam and Eve but to ensure Eden might become the fortress they need to withstand the onslaught from without."

"A mission by another name then," Conawago replied.

"My name is Rideaux, old man. My Jesuit robe was ripped off my back before I had the chance to throw it off. And I tend to take criticism only from my friends, not trespassers."

Conawago gave a small, bitter grin.

"You redeem the Indians by building carousels and fur presses?" Duncan broke in. "Your mission has a decidedly commercial feel." He studied the man's huge beard, which covered most of his face. "You are the great bear?"

Rideaux's eyes flared. "Who are you?" he demanded, his gaze shifting from one man to another. "No one invited you inside my walls."

"Like you," Duncan offered, "seekers of truth. Believers in new beginnings. Escorts for a young slave girl."

"Slave no longer. Virginia property rights do not extend to our country."

"Your country?" Duncan asked.

"Iroquoia."

"I thought we were in the province of Pennsylvania."

"You are misinformed. This land has never been legally surrendered. Technically the colony's boundary ends miles to the south.
We recognize no European sovereignty here."

"We?"

Rideaux did not answer, but looked past Duncan. Duncan
slowly turned to see a dozen Indians, both men and women, watching from the shadows at the back of the chamber. "Your business is
done here," the Frenchman muttered. "We thank you for delivering the girl."

Mokie linked her arm with Duncan's. "We were promised supplies," she said. "In Shamokin there would be supplies."

"Not here, mademoiselle. In town. The log cabin with two
floors. I will take you there."

Mokie shook her head. "I am with them. If they say I must
return to the Virginians I will do so," she said with a conviction
that quite astonished Duncan.

Rideaux's expression darkened. Something seemed to pass
between him and the Indians. Duncan rose and stood beside
Conawago. The questions that had leapt to his tongue suddenly
seemed far less important than finding a safe egress from their
host's strange compound. Several of the men, sturdy warriors all,
began advancing, one with a length of rope, one with an iron bar,
one with an ax.

"Skanawati!" Mokie suddenly blurted out. She darted from
Duncan's side to stand between himself and the Indians. She
pronounced the name again, like a loud command. The company
froze.

Rideaux stared as if dumbstruck. "What did you say, *ma
petite?*"

"We come from the Great Chief of the Iroquois!" She spoke
still loudly but faster, as if rushing to get all her words out before

her nerve broke. "Mr. McCallum and Mr. Conawago are trying to keep him from being hung from a Pennsylvania gallows! Mr. Conawago was going to die when my master was nailed to a tree, and Mr. Skanawati took his place, and the Hurons attacked us in a field of skulls to take an old smelly body, and they tried for my scalp but I fought them off with stones!"

Rideaux's eyes grew round with wonder, then he shot several quick syllables toward the Indians in the shadows. Two of the men darted out the door. A woman came forward with a heavy clay jug and several wooden cups. The Frenchman's dangerous glint softened, and a narrow grin returned as he gestured to the table. "I think we shall have some cider," he announced.

The telling of a story, Indian fashion, was never in the linear style of Europeans, Duncan had learned. Now he saw that their taking of a story was much the same. He began to explain the death of the Virginia officer, then one of the Indians insisted on hearing about the field of skulls. He described Conawago's arrest and the trial at Ligonier only to be interrupted with questions about whether Iroquois were scouts at that garrison. When Mokie mentioned Penn's birth the night before the chief's confession, an Indian woman broke in to inquire about the stars and moon that night, to Conawago's approving nod. At last, after nearly an hour the violent and bizarre events of the past week were out, spread on the table before them as it were, where they continued to be dissected and digested.

"Did Skanawati wear paint when he confessed?" one of the men asked.

Duncan's confirmation brought a flurry of quick, worried whispers among the Indians.

"The trees you speak of," an aged woman asked. "Are they all on the old Warriors Path?"

Conawago slowly nodded.

"They tried once before," she replied.

"Tried what exactly?" Duncan wanted to know.

"The Virginians attempted to take our land. In 1744. They came to a treaty conference and took away a piece of paper from some Oneidas that said they owned all the Ohio country."

"What happened?"

"Everyone lied," the woman replied.

"The Six Nations agreed to sell rights to the valley called Shenandoah," Rideaux explained. "Afterward the Virginians said the wording included all the lands in the west."

Conawago and Duncan exchanged a worried glance. There seemed too many reasons why an Iroquois chief might want to kill a man from the Shenandoah.

"The Six Nations had no right," the woman interjected. "It was always Shawnee country, not that of the Iroquois."

Her words stilled all conversation. One of the men with his hair in the Mohawk fashion snapped an irritated word at her. For the first time Duncan realized the gathering included members of several different tribes.

"Is he safe?" Rideaux asked at last.

"Skanawati? For now he is protected as part of the convoy en route to the Lancaster treaty talks. But then there will be a trial."

"You said he confessed."

"Even if he were the killer there could be circumstances that might avoid a hanging."

"You act as though you don't believe him. He is a chief of the Grand Council."

"The killings continue. At the southern boundary tree we found two who had been murdered last summer. Was Skanawati on the Monongahela last summer?"

Rideaux chewed on Duncan's words. "He stayed close to his family's village," he revealed in a low voice. "There was sickness, much sadness."

"But you misunderstand the Virginians," the Frenchman added after a moment. "To their leaders the world is divided between those who have land and those who are slaves in one fashion or another. They are wise to the ways of the tribes."

"I'm sorry?"

"A powerful chief like Skanawati is the perfect killer as far as they are concerned."

"But hanging him will only excite the tribes against them," Duncan countered. "They could hope for no more land, no more treaties."

"To the contrary, Skanawati will never be permitted to die," Rideaux said. "Have you not heard of condolences? When someone in the tribes is slain the killer's family has the right to offer payment. Blankets. Flints. Baskets of corn. When the victim's family accepts the gifts the murder is resolved, harmony is restored."

"The Virginians have no need for blankets and corn."

The Frenchman rolled his eyes upward as if praying for patience to deal with the thick-skulled Scotsman before him. "For Virginia, this new treaty is all about perfecting its claim to the western lands. The Iroquois have protested that the new contract is not valid, that it was signed by minor chiefs in some tavern. But apart from Old Belt himself, Skanawati is the most revered chief in all the Six Nations. They will do most anything to save his life."

"Land." Duncan whispered. "They would play with his life over land?"

"Based on what you have explained lives have been played with for several months over that land. And now Skanawati has made himself the most important bargaining chip of all in the treaty talks," Rideaux concluded. A strangely sad air seemed to descend over the former priest. "You come on a fool's errand. The murders are unimportant. The land is everything."

"Skanawati would not barter away Indian lands for his freedom."

"He might for his life, and that of his village."

Duncan studied the Frenchman. "You said there has been great sorrow there."

"Thirty miles up the western branch. Their suffering this past year has been of Biblical proportions. Disease. Dissent. Crop failures. A flood. Ten of their people crossing the river ice this winter broke through and were swept away. If the Iroquois open up negotiations for condolences his life will be saved, meaning the treaty will be saved, and he will get the supplies to save his people."

"Except," the Shawnee woman noted. "He was wearing paint."

Duncan turned and looked at her questioningly.

"War paint," was all she said.

Duncan stared into his cup a long time. He had not heard the whole truth, he was certain, but much of what the renegade Jesuit and his flock had told him had the ring of truth. He absently looked toward the hearth. Mokie was petting one of the large black dogs that slept there. Conawago was gone.

He rose from the table, uneasy for his friend, taking a step toward the door. Then Mokie screamed.

In a blur of panicked motion the girl launched herself onto the top of a nearby barrel as one of the dogs began barking and leaping up at her. Rideaux cursed, and two of the Indians ran for the second animal, which ran braying in fright toward the door. It was not a dog, but a young bear.

"He is very troubled since his mother died," the Frenchman offered with a shrug, then he darted outside after the animal.

Mokie's screams quickly subsided as Duncan lifted her from the barrel and took her to a window perch, where she could see the chase for the bear. The beast spun around the piles of fur, tipping several kegs over, knocking down a stack of furs, then a rack of drying fish as its pursuers kept slipping on the soft, wet earth. Low giggles began to replace Mokie's sobs, and soon she wiggled free of Duncan and ran outside to join the pandemonium.

Duncan was about to follow her when he realized he was the only one left in the room. Quickly he explored the doors on the far side, finding first a kitchen, its beams hung with dried apples and quarters of venison, its table bearing baskets filled with wild onions and fern fiddleheads. A dry pantry held baskets of grain on the floor, tobacco on its beams.

The third room was lost in shadow. He took a step inside, pushing the door open to allow enough light for him to discern three benches and a table. Beyond these was deeper shadow that had the feel of a cavernous space. He took another tentative step then pushed back against the wall, his heart suddenly racing. Something alive lurked in the darkness beyond the table. He could not make it out, but sensed its presence, could even, incredibly, hear a low sound like the beating of a heart.

Pressing against the wall, Duncan sidestepped to the door then slipped out and shut it. He closed his eyes for a moment, gripping his fear, then lit a candle and opened the door again.

The flame illuminated a circle of only a few feet. He edged along the benches, studying the careful drawings of animals on the walls before lifting a paper from a bench with words in three columns. Moon, *lune, ehnita*, read the first words in each column. Man, *homme, ronkwe*, and water, *eau, ohneka*, the next two lines. Someone was not only teaching English and French but they were also devising a system for writing down the Iroquois tongue.

The table, he now saw, was more of a workbench, covered with wood shavings, carving knives, files, the small bars of lead used for making bullets, plus a number of oily rags.

He halted, gazing into the darkness. The heartbeat was growing louder. Knowing the crowd outside might return at any moment, he clenched his jaw and stepped forward.

After two steps he gasped in terror, nearly dropped the candle, and would have fled if he had not been paralyzed by the monster before him. His heart was in his throat, his feet were leaden.

It was some primeval beast of the forest, a bear and more than a bear, a black fanged thing of nightmares, its jaw moving up and down as if preparing to consume Duncan, its yellow eyes shifting back and forth as if to see what other fresh meat might be approaching.

Yet curiosity began to overcome his fear. The eyes moved without ceasing, the jaw shut in time with the eyes, and with the heartbeat. He lifted the candle higher, advancing, seeing now how a bearskin had been stretched over a frame that gave exaggerated bulk to the shoulders and kept the forelegs extended like encircling arms. It was a bear and not a bear. Over its shoulder were draped other skins, with heads intact, of a red fox, a mink, and a marten. Here and there feathers from birds of prey had been sewn along the forelegs. He stepped warily around the creature, discovering that the rear was uncovered, exposing the intricately constructed frame of carved wooden struts joined with straps of sinew that gave it its shape. Its heart was a box of clockwork gears, from which a wooden pendulum swung, its shaft extending through the gearbox into the head, so that each swing not only gave motion to the black and yellow discs suspended in the eyeholes but also tripped a lever that opened and shut the jaw. From the rear the rhythmic ticking of the clockworks was unmistakable. The fur had muffled the sound, softening it to the heartbeat he had heard.

He returned to the worktable, setting down the candle as he lifted the rags. Underneath was another gearbox, this one largely disassembled, its gears, pinions, and screws piled beside it. With a thrill of discovery he lifted one of the gears, equal in size and shape to the largest one he had found at the murders. As he spun it between two fingers a floorboard creaked. Too late he sensed the movement at his back, too late he smelled the animal grease with which braves anointed their skin. As he turned, a club slammed into Duncan's skull, and he sank onto the floor.

Chapter Eight

A CONCUSSION COULD BRUISE the brain, a distant voice recited, sometimes destroying all function of the limbs. A crack in the skull plates made vital fluids hemorrhage, causing slow death as the victim descended into lunacy. Duncan hovered in a distant place, where lecturing voices seemed to come down a long pipe. He had the sense of being carried, but he was strangely disinterested in reacting, simply wanted to linger in the warm, welcome lethargy of this lightless place. Duncan wasn't conscious, he was having a strange dream of being conscious. In his dream came the sound of water lapping on rocks, a wetness on his legs. He was dropped onto something hard, with an object protruding so painfully into his belly that it seemed to stir a new voice, one screaming at him to awaken.

"Duncan!" came the frantic, forlorn cry, followed by splashing. "You must come back to us!"

His eyes flickered open. As he floated away Duncan watched dreamily as Conawago frolicked in a pool of water.

A gust threw cold water onto his face. He blinked, becoming aware of the river and the log that was rapidly carrying him out into the treacherous main current. He shook his head and saw Conawago struggling in the water as he tried to save Duncan, then saw his friend disappear under the water. Suddenly he was painfully awake, and he saw death before him. He rolled off his log and dove.

Conawago had never learned to swim. He had told Duncan that his spirit protector was a creature of land, as if it excused him. As Duncan swam he could not see his friend through the clear river water, could only see one of the many deep holes that pockmarked the bottom of the Susquehanna. He surfaced, gulped more air, and dove again. Downward he went, deep, into the hole, flipping his legs like the seals he had swum with as a boy, down until the light began to fade. Then finally Conawago was there, not trying to swim, his arms extended as if to embrace someone, his eyes open and puzzled as he hung suspended in the murk.

Duncan emerged coughing, with barely strength enough to drag his friend's body onto the pebble shore, frantic that he could see no movement in Conawago's chest. He turned him over and pounded his back, wondering at the strange voice beside him until he realized that the desperate prayer in Iroquois was coming from his own mouth.

Then suddenly, miraculously, the old man was coughing, spitting up great quantities of water, and there were feet running on the pebbles, hands reaching down for them as Duncan collapsed onto the beach.

He awoke under a stack of blankets on a cot set next to a blazing fireplace, basking in dull, splendid warmth.

"God's bones, McCallum, you both nearly died." Van Grut handed him a steaming mug.

"Conawago—"

"Is just beyond the door, drying in the sun."

Duncan sat up, sipping the mug. It was not tea but a beefy broth. He drank half then quickly surveyed his surroundings. He was in a spare but comfortable room. The split log that served as fireplace mantel held a small wooden cross, a Bible lay on a plank table surrounded by rough-hewn benches. The needlepoint sampler hung by the door spelled out a blessing in German. From one of the two partially closed doors behind him wafted the smell of baking bread.

"Moravians?" Duncan asked as he drained his mug, referring to the German missionaries who often lived among the Indians of Pennsylvania.

As if in answer a girl with two blond braids stepped into the house, accompanied by two Indian children, a boy and a girl. All three carried small writing slates, covered with chalked words from the Bible in English and German.

The children watched in apparent fascination as Duncan swung his legs onto the floor. The boy wiped his slate clean and began working with a piece of chalk.

"Did you see who did this?" he asked Van Grut, rubbing his throbbing head.

"Greta—" the Dutchman nodded toward the blond girl, "—saw Conawago running into the water, shouting in fear, and ran for us as we sat with her parents. We saw you lying limp, adrift on the log, and realized he had gone to rescue you."

"He can't swim," Duncan said, shuddering at the memory of his friend suspended as if dead in the clear river water.

"But you!" the Dutchman exclaimed. "You were like a beast bred in the water."

"I nearly was," Duncan absently said as he stepped to the doorway, checking his clothes. The small pouch that usually hung from his belt was gone, and with it the evidence taken from the murders. "We were a clan of the islands." He could see Conawago now, sitting cross-legged on a flat ledge stone jutting over the broad river.

"Do you suppose I could get another?" he asked, extending his mug toward Van Grut. He found himself shivering. The cold of the water had seeped into his bones.

"The kitchens of the Dutch and Germans overflow with warm concoctions," Van Grut replied with a smile, and he disappeared behind the door nearest the fireplace.

Duncan turned to Greta. "You brought our rescuers," he offered in a grateful tone.

"We prayed for your deliverance," came the reply, not from Greta but from the native girl beside her.

The boy held up his slate. At the top he had drawn an image of a great fish spewing up two men. Duncan studied the trio. The Indian children were as well-groomed, as well-fed, as the German girl.

"God watched over us as he did Jonah," Duncan agreed, then watched as the boy covered the fish with his hand, showing another image at the bottom, a series of concentric circles.

The boy, apparently lacking the language skills of his sister, pointed meaningfully to the strange circles. "Lenni-Lenape," he said, then repeated the words, the native term for the Delaware Indians. Duncan was about to press the two girls to explain when Van Grut returned with another steaming mug, announcing that a meal would soon be served.

Duncan took the nourishing broth outside and sat beside Conawago. "Thank you," he said.

"I was an old fool," Conawago muttered. "Nearly got us both killed."

The river had harrowed him to the core. Duncan had never seen his companion so pale, never heard before this hollow tone in his voice. He remained silent a long time, watching a flight of geese, staring at the living, rippling water of the mighty river, worrying with all his heart about the old Indian. "The cold of the deep water is like no other," he said. "I've seen it affect people in many strange ways."

Conawago did not reply, nor did he react when Duncan set the hot mug on his leg and wrapped his fingers around it. "Drink. Please."

After a moment the old Nipmuc abruptly looked down at the mug, as if he had not heard the words, only sensed its heat.

"You need to push the chill from your belly," Duncan urged, and finally Conawago complied, sipping at first, then quickly draining the contents down his throat.

Duncan watched with relief as the color slowly returned to Conawago's cheeks. "Did you see who put me on the log?"

"Just their backs. Two bucks, one with an eagle feather dangling in his braid, the other with red leggings with tattoos on his back."

"You saw them carry me from Rideaux's compound?"

"No. I was behind it, circling it, trying to understand it. I have never seen such a place."

"Nor I," Duncan agreed, and he quickly described the clockwork creature he had found.

"It was meant to be a bear?"

"More like an amalgam of many forest creatures, or a symbol of all."

"Or the mother spirit of the forest."

"Yes," Duncan said slowly. There had been benches facing it, as if the thing were an altar. He explained finding gears on the table, in addition to those in the machine. "In all the vast wilderness," he pondered aloud, "where else could a killer find such gears?"

"With all the vast wilderness," Conawago said, as if to correct him, "why would the killer trouble to find such gears?"

The ring of a small bell broke their troubled silence.

The dining table had been carried outside and extended with planks to accommodate not only the four visitors but also six Indian schoolchildren and four of their parents, including a somber middle-aged Onondaga named Moses, who led them in a long prayer before the bread was broken. Duncan suddenly found himself famished, but had difficulty keeping up with Hadley and Van Grut, as the good-natured German matron replenished their plates. The shad were running up the river, and the tasty fish, fried in cornmeal, seemed in limitless supply.

Duncan made polite inquiries of Reverend Macklin, their host, about the history of the mission and the sprawling settlement of Shamokin that was, he learned, the second-biggest community in the region after Philadelphia. The most cosmopolitan of Indian towns, it was home to a dozen different tribes, as well as European settlers, trappers, and merchants. An enterprising Welshman had set up a business employing Indians to make baskets and brooms for shipment to the European settlements, and a German settler had hired several others to harvest and dry the shad, which, split and salted, could be seen drying on long racks along the long curving bank of the river.

"You have the town well organized, it seems," Van Grut observed to the missionary.

"Me?" Macklin laughed. "I am busy tending to our own small flock. The Iroquois Confederation runs this town, runs the region. It is for all intentions their southern capital. The Conoys, Conestogas, Delawares, Shawnee, Nanticokes, and the others all are subject to the Grand Council of the Iroquois, represented by the chiefs who reside in the longhouse villages nearby."

"You make it sound as though the Iroquois have an empire, with subject states," Hadley said between mouthfuls of shad and spring greens.

"But they do, boy. Many an Indian village along the river was bathed in blood in the last century until the tribes pressed for peace with the Iroquois League. The local tribes can run their local affairs, but may not meddle in relations with other nations, European or otherwise. No treaty concerning the realm from the Saint Lawrence to the Ohio country gets signed without the approval of the Grand Council and the marks of its leading chiefs. Several passed through just last week to join the new treaty negotiations."

"Old Belt," Duncan offered. "Long Wolf."

The German slowly nodded, studying his guests with new interest. "You are involved in matters of state?"

"Did the chief named Skanawati ever put his mark on such treaties?" Duncan ventured, with a worried glance at Conawago. His old friend, who had remained taciturn for the entire meal, seemed to be sinking lower and lower. His thoughts were secret, his mood growing morose. Something Duncan did not understand had come between them. It had started with Skanawati's confession but had been strangely magnified by his near drowning in the river.

"I daresay no treaty would ever be signed without his approval," Moses explained. "He may not sit at the first place, whose seat is always left empty in honor of long-dead Dekanawidah, our league's founder, but his position would be no lower than fifth of the fifty great chiefs who sit on the council." Duncan listened carefully.

"The fifth seat, and the most important in this region," Moses continued. "I was born in Onondaga, the capital of the Iroquois League," he added. "And even though he may be fifth, there is no other chief like Skanawati."

Duncan glanced at Conawago, who still appeared lost in other, darker thoughts.

"The chiefs of our council are called peace chiefs," Moses continued in his rich, careful voice. Not for the first time Duncan gave silent thanks to the missionaries who had for decades been teaching the Indians to speak English. "They are the wise ones that guide the tribe, in consultation with the wives and mothers. It is no good for a people to be governed by those who feel the heat of war, so the supreme chiefs like Old Belt never lead war parties, seldom even lift a battle ax. Except for one. For as far as memory serves, only Skanawati has the honor of being both a war chief and a peace chief, for his skills are needed in both realms."

Conawago abruptly rose and left the table.

Hadley restarted the conversation as new planks of shad were passed around the table. "Do you sometimes join with the mission on the hill?" the Virginian asked the Moravians. The words were slow to register in Duncan's consciousness, for he was watching his friend disappear around the corner of the Germans' cowshed.

"Mission?" Reverend Macklin asked.

"I believe there is a Jesuit compound above the town, is there not?" Hadley asked.

It was the Moravians' turn to be struck dumb. The Indians pushed their food about on their plates, glancing uneasily at their spiritual leader.

"There is no mission," Reverend Macklin corrected in a tight voice. "There is no Jesuit. There is a tormented soul whose deliverance we pray for daily." With that the German rose and directed the children to begin clearing the table. The other adults, seeming eager for an excuse to leave now, quickly joined in. Only Moses, sitting across from Duncan, lingered.

"But Rideaux *was* a Jesuit," Duncan said to the Onondaga, "he was a missionary."

The Iroquois nodded his head. "Though the Jesuits were aligned with the French, my people allowed them to have a mission in our country, so long as they did not seek to assist their army or their king. I was there when it happened," he added. The Onondaga's wife, a handsome middle-aged woman in a red dress decorated with quillwork, appeared and settled on the bench beside him.

"When what happened?"

"When the frock was ripped from his back," Moses replied. "They even made him surrender his crucifix. We thought he would kill himself." The Indian's wife nodded sadly.

"Why would they do such a thing to him?"

Moses' face darkened. The question seemed to torment him. His wife spoke a low, quick sentence in their native tongue. Her husband nodded. "Because he loved his flock too much."

Hadley, who had been helping the children, sat down beside Duncan. Van Grut had retreated to a bench by the shed, working with his sketch pad.

"You mean," Duncan ventured after a long moment, "he became closer to the Iroquois than to his church."

"A clock. He lost his black robe over a clock."

Hadley's head shot up. Duncan leaned closer.

"I was in the mission as a boy," Moses explained. "They taught me my first writing, taught us French but also English, so as not to alarm the English who sometimes visited. There was an old church building that was not used by us, a small chapel with an altar and a room at the back where one of the aged Black Robes, who had been in these lands for over fifty years, had taken up residence. He had a clock from France that rang every quarter hour. He put it in that old chapel on the altar with a cross over it. It was a trick the Black Robes used in the last century when they first went among the Hurons and other northern tribes. He still had the old ways in his blood, would sometimes treat the Indians who had not been baptized like dumb animals. Clocks were magic, they were sorcery, they were beyond the comprehension of the tribes. That clock proved the power of the European God. I remember being taken into that chapel by my uncle when I was no higher than his waist. Many of our old people would not go to the rituals of the Black Robes, but they would sit for hours in front of that clock, and whenever it rang they would exclaim in Christian words taught to them by that old priest. It became a god to them. My uncle told me a little sacred man lived in that box, who spoke to the Europeans at night. The Indians would leave him offerings, bits of fur and feathers, little carvings, in front of it. Every time it rang my uncle cried out 'Hallelujah! Hallelujah!'

"Rideaux loved our people like no others among the Jesuits, began learning our language as soon as he arrived, soon was more fluent in it, in all our dialects, than any of the other Black Robes. He would sit up all night with our sick, wouldn't stop our medicine men from doing their work like the other Jesuits did, even tried to learn Indian medicine." Moses' wife spoke again into his ear. She clearly understood the English but was not comfortable speaking it.

"She remembers the others would try to interfere with our burials," Moses related, "try to sprinkle their holy water on them as our dying breathed their last, put rosaries in their hands when they

died. But Rideaux never did. He would come to our death ceremo-
nies but never recite the Christian words unless he was asked."

"The clock?" Duncan pressed.

"Father Rideaux spent much of his time in other camps, traveling with the tribes. He never knew about it, thought it merely a
matter of the older Indians going in to pray with the priest who
lived there. Then one day he tried to find the old priest. He went
inside, found twenty Iroquois worshipping the clock, the priest
drunk on a cot in the back. He was furious, started shouting so
loud the other priests came in. He declared we Iroquois were not
puppets to be played with, that worshipping machines was like
worshipping false idols, that his countrymen were arrogant sinners, pretending that owning better machines made them better
people. He said he would match the soul of an Iroquois to that of a
Frenchman anytime. He destroyed that clock with an ax, scattered
the gears all over the floor.

"He was ruined. Some of the priests wanted him burned for a
heretic. They did not wait for their bishop to act. He was thrown
out of the order that very day."

"But now," Duncan observed, "he works with clocks himself."

"Now," Moses corrected, "he seeks to make the tribes understand that machines are not magic, that we can make them too. He
bought a clock from some settler and took it apart for all to see,
bought tools to work with it. He has Delaware and Iroquois carv-
ers who make wooden gears, then he shows them how to assemble
them. He shows them how such things are but products of their
hands, like a good bow or a canoe."

"You're saying," Hadley suggested, "that he wants the Indians
to understand they can live without the help of Europeans."

"Just as Africans can have lives without Europeans," Moses
added.

Moses' wife finally tried her English. "He . . . stop the rum," she said. "He stop the guns."

"He runs off the gun and rum traders whenever he finds them here," Moses explained.

"Does he know Skanawati?"

Moses hesitated before responding, his expression troubled.

"Last autumn Skanawati called a gathering of chiefs. He arrived with war paint on. He demanded they eject a natural philosopher from Philadelphia who was—" Moses searched for words, "doing experiments with Indians. I think that's when Rideaux met Skanawati, when they realized they both were striving for the same end, trying to wean the Iroquois off the ways of the Europeans."

"It is why I too try to reach out to him," a new voice broke in. Macklin was standing at the end of the table. "I tell the Frenchman what he and I are doing is not so very different. But he scorns me, asks why our converts wear European clothing, live in European houses, are given European tools. I explain that it is only Christian to provide for their comfort. But he laughs, says his Bible provides for the comfort of souls but says nothing of German forges and British tea. He says all I am doing is forcing them to bite at the forbidden fruit. He said we fail to grasp the miracles of the wilderness. He ejected me the last time I tried to speak with his Indians, months ago. I have seen him do great kindnesses. He has the touch of Saint Francis in communing with animals. But he also can have the touch of the rabid dog. He has perverted our technology to create an abomination in his house, a monster of gears and fur."

"People are being killed along the boundary line," Duncan announced, "with clock gears pounded into their hearts."

Moses went very still. He translated in a hoarse voice for his wife. "They will look to Shamokin," he said. Fear was heavy in his words.

His companions had grasped what was at stake faster than
Duncan. There seemed little doubt now. If the European settlers
knew about the gears in the hearts—word would soon come out—
and the strange role of gears in Shamokin, they would not wait for
soldiers or a magistrate, they would march on Shamokin in their
own frantic fear, with guns and torches. Settlements of Indians had
been burned for less.

"The first place they will go to is Rideaux's compound,"
observed Van Grut, who had joined the table. "Word was already
spreading through the convoy when we left. Bythe's murder may
be the spark that ignites the powder keg."

"Mokie!" Hadley cried out. "Do you have your gun, McCallum?"
the Virginian asked.

Duncan looked up. "At the canoes with our gear."

"We must get her out of there."

Duncan had not forgotten Mokie but found himself dreading
the prospect of returning to Rideaux's compound. He lingered only
long enough to make a quick inquiry of Moses, then led Van Grut
and Hadley on a brief detour.

The two-story log cabin that served as a store appeared to be a
prosperous establishment, with barrels and crates of goods stacked
along its porch. Duncan did not hesitate when he spotted a stout
European in an apron sweeping the end of the porch.

"It is a bold thing to be openly supplying runaway slaves," he
declared loudly, standing close as the man turned.

The man grabbed the broom like a staff as if to defend himself.
"Surely I don't know—"

Duncan seized the broom himself and used it to shove the merchant backward, pressing him against the wall. "I do not seek the
slaves, but I will know who is paying for their supplies."

"I am but a clerk, sir. If one of the blacks arrives the proprietor takes them in the back room, gives me a list of supplies to gather." The clerk glanced uneasily at Hadley and Van Grut, who now flanked Duncan.

"Where do we find your proprietor?"

"Mr. Waller's gone, sir. Left for Philadelphia. All of a sudden he said he had to leave, though last night he spoke of how he and I would scrub out the smoke house today."

"Then I'll see his books."

The clerk took a deep breath and glanced in both directions to assure there were no eavesdroppers. "No need, sir. I have taken my own secret looks. There is naught but a credit shown. Runaways, it says, and when the account is low it is replenished from Philadelphia."

"Tell me this," Moses asked. "When exactly did Mr. Waller depart?"

"Not two hours ago."

"Two hours," Van Grut said as they walked away, "was when someone tried to kill you, Duncan."

"Two hours, more precisely," Moses observed, "was when someone failed to kill you."

The faces of their little party were dark as they finally approached the palisade on the ridge, rifles at the ready. Van Grut's eyes were round with wonder as he saw the carousel in the yard. Things were much as Duncan had seen before, with Indians cleaning skins and packing furs, but as the men in the yard saw Duncan they stopped, looking up in surprise, murmuring to each other. Reverend Macklin and Moses appeared out of the brush by the gate to step protectively to Duncan's side. Conawago, though still withdrawn, accompanied them. The Indians, all appearing to be from the minor tribes, seemed to ignore the missionary but nodded uneasily at Moses. The looks the Christian Indian exchanged with them reminded Duncan of the complex relations within the tribes themselves. While the tension between them could simply be that between the baptized and the unconverted, it just as easily could be because Moses was Onondaga and they were of the tribes subjected by the Iroquois.

Rideaux seemed to be expecting them. He led them to his table, where a jug and cups awaited, then held a finger to his lips and pointed to the hearth, where two mounds of black fur again were arrayed in front of the coals. Curled up around them, her head on the back of the young bear, was Mokie, lost in slumber. As Macklin stepped inside the Frenchman hesitated, first fixing the missionary with a cool gaze, then frowning as he turned to Duncan.

"As you can see, there is no need for firearms," Rideaux said in a near whisper.

Van Grut instantly set his fowling piece down, pulled out his sketch pad, and began drawing the sleeping figures.

Duncan did not give up his rifle. "The last time I visited someone tried to kill me."

"The last time you were here I believe you frightened us more than we frightened you."

Duncan returned Rideaux's steady gaze, fighting an impulse to snatch away Mokie and flee from this unpredictable man. But suddenly a gasp of surprise came from Reverend Macklin. He was holding one of the slates Duncan had seen in the larger chamber. "You are devising an Iroquois alphabet?" he asked the Frenchman.

"We use the roman alphabet," he replied with one of his unsettling grins, "just reduce the sounds to letters. So as not to handicap the Europeans."

"We?"

Rideaux opened the door that led to the kitchen, revealing two Indian men busy with quills and paper at a large table, putting Duncan in mind of monks illuminating manuscripts. Moses rushed into the room, greeting the two men as old friends and leaning over the table to examine their work. Conawago looked on.

"When we are done," Rideaux declared, "we will make a great library to memorialize the Iroquois civilization."

"Civilization?" Macklin's expression was skeptical.

The doubt in his tone brought color to Rideaux's face. "You come to make them dream of the savior's blood, but in the end you would put chains on them as real as those this poor girl's family wears. In a hundred hundred ways the Europeans make them feel inferior, when it is we who should feel inferior to them for their uncorrupted souls."

"The lambs of God enter his flock from many paths," Macklin observed.

"I once gave last rites to an old Mohawk woman," Rideaux shot back. "She said she knew she was going to hell. I asked why she would say such a terrible thing, and she said white people always said so, and they were the ones who could read words, the ones who would know such things."

The former priest paused, surveying his uneasy audience, then lifted a small wooden chest, a traditional Bible box, from the mantel over the fireplace. He produced a key from his pocket, opened it, and began to lay tattered papers on the table. "1705," he said. "A letter from the governor of Pennsylvania assuring the Nanticoke tribe perpetual use of the lands along the Susquehanna below here. Today it becomes crowded with settlements. 1720," he continued, lifting another paper. "A Quaker deed purporting to show that the Delawares ceded them a huge tract at the Forks of the Delaware,

though the Delawares insist they never signed such a document."
He lifted one more sheet from the box. "Someone in Lancaster gave
a Conestoga family this in exchange for half their corn crop, saying it would assure them safe passage through all European lands
forever. It is nothing but a receipt for a wagonload of lumber, but
they didn't know. They treasured it, kept it protected, wrapped in a
sacred wampum belt for twenty years. An old Iroquois once told me
all the storms and wars of the past century cause but minor troubles
compared to the devastation done by the pens of the colonists. By
quill and ink we commit the sins that break the souls of these noble
people. We share the same shapes, but the hearts of Europeans and
Indians are as of different creatures."

"These noble people," Hadley asserted in a near whisper, "have
slaughtered thousands of settlers. Witnesses have seen them cut out
the hearts of living men and eat them."

"The ways of the forest are absolute. You may as well condemn
the bear for his claw or the lion for his fang. They may draw the
blood of a few of us, but we draw the words that deny their entire
race their future. Is this what eighteen centuries of Christ has meant?
That the country with more power has the sacred right to destroy
the lesser?" Rideaux leveled his gaze at Duncan. "McCallum is a
Highland name. Where is your clan today?" he asked pointedly.

Duncan shook his head. "There is no man here who is an
enemy of the tribes."

"Then stop interfering."

"With what?" Duncan demanded. "Your secret protection of
runaway slaves? Your efforts to keep Europeans from aiding the
Indians? Murder of innocent men on the Warriors Path? The
unnecessary hanging of a chief desperately needed by his people?
Those behind the murders are seeking to make it appear Shamokin
Indians are behind them. *Your* Indians in fact, for the killers are

using the slaves you give shelter to, leaving clock gears behind. You would have us not interfere with the mob that will surely come looking to spill Indian blood? They will start here, I tell you. They will annihilate this settlement. And your compound will be the spark that ignites the flame."

"You understand nothing."

"I understand your notions of societies and civilization in the great frame of history are more important to you than the deaths of innocents here and now."

Rideaux's eyes flared again. "In that case, Scotsman, you *do* begin to understand me." As he spoke the Frenchman looked toward the window, sudden worry on his face.

The sound outside had been growing steadily louder, nagging at Duncan's subconscious, until suddenly it broke through. Conawago cocked his head then darted outside with Rideaux. Duncan was a step behind. The Frenchman cursed as he saw the yard had been emptied, and he cursed louder as he seemed to recognize the din rising from the other side of the ridge. Reverend Macklin and Moses pushed past, running toward town. The screaming, the musket shots, the frenzied whooping were unmistakable. The battle Duncan had dreaded had already arrived.

Rideaux darted back into the house, fear shining in his eyes now. *"Tewaarathon!"* he shouted at the Indians still inside. "Make ready!"

Chapter Nine

UNCAN RAN BEHIND the men from Rideaux's compound, watching with horror as they stripped off
unnecessary clothing, pulling knives and war axes
from their belts. It had begun. There would be no treaty, no saving Skanawati. The Frenchman sprinted past, carrying bandages,
murmuring what could have been a frantic prayer. The men ahead
of them reached a low rise above one of the wide fields, and with
a collective cry the Indians leapt to the fray. *Tewaarathon!* Rideaux
had shouted. *War!*

Duncan checked the powder in his frizzen pan, saw Hadley
and Van Grut do the same as they arrived panting at his side, then
looked to the field in confusion. The Indians who had been with
him were not charging into the melee below but instead were running toward a group of women and children at one end of the long
rectangular field. Duncan hesitated. *Tewaarathon.* It meant more
than war. Brother and war. Not just brother, but younger brother.

The Indians threw down their weapons onto a blanket already
stacked high with other weapons. In exchange each grabbed a long
crooked stick with netting woven from the tip of the crook to a

point nearly halfway down the shaft. Every man on the field held such a stick, and at the center of the battle, they fought over a small leather ball.

"It is for good reason the Iroquois call it Little Brother of War," Macklin said as he reached Duncan, carrying more bandages. "There are full battles with fewer casualties."

"*Tewaarathon* is a game?" Duncan asked incredulously.

"That is the Mohawk name for it. The Onondaga say *dehuntshigwa'es*, which translates as *man hitting a round thing*. Fortunately this is just an impromptu practice. Later in the year, especially after the crops come in, there will be lacrosse games— that is the French name—played all day, or even over several days." As he spoke a dozen men leapt onto the man with the ball. When the knot cleared two men lay moaning on the ground.

"What are the rules?" Hadley asked, the confusion on his face replaced by a budding excitement.

"Few enough," Macklin said. "The opposing team must get the ball to your goal to score. The goals today are those old stumps—" the Moravian pointed to two large stumps at either end of the field, more than a hundred yards apart. "They may never hold the ball. They scoop it and carry it in the racquet or with their legs and feet, and the other side tries to stop them using only their bodies or their racquets."

"There're Europeans!" Van Grut exclaimed, pointing to a score of pale-skinned men with their shirts off at the far end of the field.

"Nearly every able-bodied man beneath the age of forty plays. Today it looks like the Iroquois against the smaller tribes and the Europeans."

"Those men on the ground," Duncan said, indicating the two victims of the last pile-on. "They need help."

"Not likely. Mostly the only thing that stops a player is a broken bone." Macklin cast a worried eye toward the tavern. "Afterward the ale will flow for hours." As if on cue the two men on the ground, one pale with red hair, staggered up and set off a slow, limping trot toward the mob that surrounded the ball. More men went down, some leveled by vicious blows to the knees or ribs with opposing racquets, others downed by deliberate collisions that would fell a horse. Still, Duncan could see no rancor on the players' faces, only a spirited joy.

The first player with a broken bone was carried off the field, by two Shawnee who spotted Rideaux and left the victim in the Frenchman's care. The man's shaven temples and short braid at the rear combined with his dark skin to assure Duncan he was of the tribes, until he pressed a splint against the man's arm.

"God's wounds, man!" the patient spat in a thick Welsh accent. "Leave the bone, and take my stick! Ye can't let those Mingoes hoard the ball like that!"

Duncan replied with a low laugh, but then saw the anticipation in Hadley's eyes. He picked up the man's racquet and tossed it to the Virginian, who caught it with a wide smile then began stripping off his shirt.

Duncan found himself focusing on the little deerhide ball, marveling at the skill of the Indians who deftly juggled it as they ran, cheering when a colonist wove through a line of Iroquois defenders to score. As a Swede was brought in with broken fingers, Van Grut too pulled off his shirt and launched himself into the melee with an uncertain but joyful cry.

An hour later, battered and smiling, the players staggered off the field as bells starting calling them to chores and supper. The Iroquois had won, though only by one goal. Three men still lay on the field, and he now ran to join Rideaux and Macklin as they examined them. Two had cracked ribs. The third, a Delaware, lay motionless on his side. Duncan heard Macklin's mournful cry before he reached the young warrior and knew there was no hope as soon as he saw the purple color of the man's face.

"His windpipe was crushed," Duncan declared, pointing to the deep, ragged bruise at the front of the throat.

"It's meant to be a game," Macklin sighed, then murmured a quiet prayer.

"Whoever did this played no game," Duncan replied.

Rideaux stared at Duncan. "Surely it was an accident."

"Trust me. I have attended many corpses in medical school. This required a deliberately aimed blow with tremendous force behind it."

"Just bad luck, surely," Rideaux said.

Then a hand reached out to push the dead man over onto his belly, revealing a large tattoo of concentric circles on his shoulder. "I saw this pattern today, at the river bank. He died in the way he meant for you," Conawago declared. "Choking for air."

Duncan looked at the dead man, then remembered how the Indian boy had sketched such circles on his slate, trying to tell Duncan something about his would-be murderer. *Lenni-Lenape*, the boy had said, the tribes' term for the Delawares. The Indian who had attempted to kill Duncan hours earlier had just been murdered on the lacrosse field.

"He failed to kill you," Conawago ventured, "so he had to die." He untied a familiar doeskin pouch from the dead man's belt and handed it to Duncan, who dumped its contents onto the packed earth of the playing field. Out fell the two nails from the boundary trees, the buttons he had collected, his own flint and steel. Nothing seemed to be missing. Rideaux reached with a tentative hand, roll-ing the nails in his fingers so he could see their heads, then picked up one of the buttons with the fish worked in the metal.

Duncan watched as worry mounted on the Frenchman's face. "Do you recognize them?"

"I knew someone . . . " the Frenchman murmured, his words trailing away.

"There was a fine young man from Connecticut, named Cooper." Reverend Macklin picked up the explanation. "Trying to make his way as a surveyor. He lingered a few months here, and in the little English settlement called Penn's Creek across the river. He took up with the daughter of an Onondaga village. They showed great affection for one another . . . " the Moravian said awkwardly.

Rideaux took over the story. "They gave offense to Reverend Macklin's wife. She told the congregation she saw them swimming under the moonlight, bare as fish. Cooper promptly asked the good reverend to marry them so no one would think them sinners. The surveyor had the buttons made as a gift to his bride. Everyone laughed when they saw the fish."

Rideaux stared at the buttons in his hand, watching in silence as Duncan took them and returned them to his pouch.

"She was not from *any* village," Macklin reminded them. "She was from Skanawati's village, from his own hearth."

Rideaux lifted one of the long nails. "And these?"

"Used to nail the hands of the victims to their trees. One went into Cooper's hand. He probably was still alive as they murdered his wife in front of him."

Rideaux's face sagged. He stared at the nail, squeezing it until his knuckles grew white. "What do you want from me?" the Frenchman asked in a hollow voice.

"Did you send this man to kill me?"

"Like lots of the tribesmen, he appears every few weeks to wander about town. They called him Ohio George."

"Did you send him to kill me?" Duncan repeated.

"No. I just want you to leave us alone. There are other ways of getting rid of you without committing such a sin."

"Like hiding your involvement with the escaped slaves. Like warning the merchant Waller to leave town. Like pretending you know nothing of intrigue over land claims."

"I did not warn Waller," Rideaux said in a brittle voice. "As far as I know he is but doing his Christian duty in helping the slaves."

"You can either deal with us or else with two hundred vengeful settlers when they hear of Shamokin Indians brutally slaying surveyors. What do you know about this Ohio George?"

"What I know," came a new voice, "is that we should not speak over his dead body." Moses was kneeling beside the corpse now, removing the lacrosse stick still clenched in his hand.

Duncan conceded the point with a nod. "Does he have family here?"

"Not likely. He's a Delaware, from the Ohio. We will take him to the compound. His body should be cleaned for his journey to the other side."

It was a slow, silent procession up the hill, the body on a blanket carried at each of its corners. They set it on a trestle table in the yard of Rideaux's compound. As an older woman brought water to wash the dead man, Rideaux gestured for Duncan to follow him back outside, leading him down the path to town. They stopped at the lean-to sheltering the smith's forge. The Frenchman lifted a hammer left on the anvil where it lay beside half a dozen newly forged nails and extended it to Duncan. Confused, Duncan turned it over in his hands then understood as Rideaux held up one of the fresh nails. The head held a rough crosshatched pattern, identical to those used in the murders.

"It's just something the smith does, to distinguish his work. He smashes the heads with this hammer. I've never seen it elsewhere."

The striking end of the hammer, Duncan saw, was scored with crossed lines.

"Anyone could have taken these nails from here," Rideaux pointed out. "Settlers buy them. A passerby could lift them from a basket."

"Ohio George wasn't acting alone. Someone here silenced him, not just because he failed in killing me, but because if he were captured he would have had much incriminating knowledge to divulge." Duncan fixed Rideaux with an inquisitive gaze. "Is there anyone here who might have employment for a man like Ohio George, work that would take him west from time to time? Someone, perhaps, who would buy these nails from the smith?"

"Not many can afford to buy nails. Pegs are used for most construction. Mostly the nails go into making heavy doors." The Frenchman took a moment to contemplate the community. "There are merchants using the nails for making stronghouses to store their goods."

"Merchants," Duncan ventured, "who may trade in the west, who would know about Europeans traveling on the frontier. Surveyors who bought supplies."

"Some hire Ohio Indians to help convey their goods to the western forts and trading posts." Rideaux considered the town once more. "There is a shed behind one of Waller's storehouses where some of them sleep when they are here."

Duncan bent with one of the nails and drew shapes in the soil, the five geometric shapes from Burke's killing tree. "Do you recognize these?"

His companion shrugged. "Secret signs. A code."

"Jesuits and spies use codes," Duncan asserted.

"Often," Rideaux agreed. "But Jesuits use alphabet codes, keyed to a Bible passage. This is altogether different."

"It is not an Indian thing."

"Of course not. It is European. Secret societies use them. The Freemasons. The guilds."

"Where in America are Freemasons?"

Rideaux shrugged again. "New York. Philadelphia. Virginia."

The shelter to which Rideaux and Moses led Duncan was a drafty lean-to fastened to the log storehouse behind the store they had visited earlier. They were a stone's throw from the landing dock where boats bound for the settlement upriver at Wyoming boarded, and as Moses explored the shadows inside, Duncan watched a flatboat slowly wind its way upstream. In two days a fast canoe in that direction could reach Edentown, where Sarah Ramsey and her company of Scottish workers were building a new life.

When he emerged a minute later Moses was herding a muscular Indian who was using a lacrosse racquet as a makeshift crutch. The young stranger spat curses at the older Indian, clutching a small clay ale pot tightly to his chest as he staggered toward a bench along the wall. He lowered the crutch and fingered a tattered shoulder pouch decorated with lewd figures, pushing it behind him as he sat. Moses motioned for Rideaux and Duncan to approach.

"This sinner at first claimed he never heard of Ohio George," Moses declared in a disapproving voice as the young Indian slopped more ale down his throat. "I told him he could then have no claim on the possessions of the dead man he had stuffed under his pallet, that we would gladly take them for the use of the church."

"He is an Ohio Indian as well?" Duncan asked.

"Red Hand is Shawnee, from west of the Susquehanna," Moses said. "I have known this one since he was a boy. His parents died of fever, and we brought him to the mission to live with us, but he always fled into the forest. He consorts with a band of renegades, most of them orphans who ran away from missionaries, ready to work for anyone who will buy them rum." He shook the drunken Shawnee. "Did you kill Ohio George?" he demanded.

Red Hand offered a drunken laugh. "He had no family," he said with a sneer. "No one to complain."

The words, as good as a confession, startled Duncan at first. Then he realized that Red Hand was saying that in the tribal world there was no need to account for the killing, for there was no one to be held responsible to.

Moses stared at the Shawnee with a cold fury. The Christian Indians took a very different view of murder.

Duncan stepped into the lean-to, quickly surveying the tattered furs that hung on the walls, the bundles of cedar boughs used as pallets, the stringless bows and battered lacrosse sticks in one corner. Picking up a pack decorated with a faded pattern of concentric circles that was half-covered by a pallet, he took a step toward the door then paused. Kicking aside the boughs, he exposed a much smaller, crudely made case of heavy buckskin bearing a similar pattern of circles.

He carried both outside and dropped them in front of the drunken Shawnee. As he upended the contents of the pack on the ground the Indian began a low, whispered chant. The words, unintelligible to Duncan, lit a fire in Moses' eyes. He snapped a command at Red Hand, who ignored him. Then to Duncan's astonishment, the Christian Indian slapped the man, so hard it cracked open his lip.

"He is without honor, this Shawnee!" Moses spat.

"I don't understand." Duncan scanned the faces of his companions for an explanation.

"He is invoking vengeful gods," Rideaux explained, as Red Hand laughed at Moses, then touched his bleeding lip. His eyes flashed with defiance as he drew lines on his cheek with his own blood.

"It is a sacred thing to invoke those spirits," Moses said in a simmering voice. "Not for one who would kill his own mother for his next jug."

"What will you do, Chris—tian?" the Shawnee taunted Moses, drawing out the last syllables. "Your master forbids you striking another man. Run now, and beg forgiveness. Your white god makes you a woman!" he mocked.

As he spoke Rideaux appeared from inside the lean-to, carrying a rifle. "This is too rich a gun for the likes of these," he said. "It was hidden under the boughs along the wall."

Red Hand's face clouded as Rideaux handed the gun to Duncan. It was a finely worked piece, with an elaborate carving of the owner's initials on the stock. WB. He thrust the stock into Red Hand's face. "Did you kill him? Did you kill Winston Burke?"

Red Hand silently drained his pot of ale. Duncan studied the gun as Moses took it and leaned it against the wall. It meant one or both of the renegades had come from the Forbes Road, had probably been following them, and had no doubt warned Waller. It meant that Samuel Felton had lied to Duncan.

Duncan kept a wary eye on the man on the bench as he sorted the possessions of Ohio George. A pair of tattered moccasins. A lacrosse ball, its hair stuffing hanging out a deep gash in one side. A broken bullet mold. A small oval-shaped piece of wood with several threads attached to it. A glass ball, perhaps an inch in diameter. A bundle of leather straps. Six more of the long nails with the crosshatched heads. A twist of tobacco. He lifted the tobacco and smelled it. It was neither the leaf cultivated by the tribes nor the cheap plug tobacco traded in sutlers' stores, but an expensive leaf, the kind Winston Burke might have brought from his home in Virginia.

As Duncan contemplated the meager possessions of the dead man, Moses probed them, then peered into the empty pouch. He saw the query on Duncan's face. "Our missionaries have never been killed during their service with the tribes. But one has been missing, one of our only female missionaries, a longtime friend of the Macklin family who left Bethlehem two years ago for the Ohio country and was never seen again. We watch for any sign of her. The Reverend is leaving for a meeting with the church elders soon to discuss resuming the search for her." As he spoke he shook the pouch again. A second, very small bag fell out onto the ground.

When Duncan opened it and tilted it over his hand four silver buttons fell onto his palm. Two were worked with the same fish as those he had found at the Monongahela, two were embossed with crossed swords.

"The dead Virginian," he explained to his companions. "Had silver buttons cut off his waistcoat." He reached into his own belt pouch and produced the button he had taken from Burke's corpse. It was identical to the two with swords from Ohio George's pouch.

Duncan then began pulling papers from the separate, smaller case he had found hidden in the lean-to. Tattered letters from a lawyer in Philadelphia to Francis Townsend, hectoring for a debt. A small worn New Testament bearing Townsend's name on the inside plate, which he handed to Moses. A broadside advertising a public display of Dr. Franklin's experiments with natural fire, on the back of which was the beginning of a letter. *Dear Catherine,* it said in a careful hand. *Fair weather makes for a quick journey. I look forward to my return with resources enough to hire carpenters.*

"This man Townsend has been to Shamokin more than once," Moses said. "The last time as a surveyor, heading down the Warriors Path. He went west and never came back. A magistrate sent inquiries, but there was no trace of him."

Red Hand began to laugh.

"Did you kill him too?" Duncan demanded. "Did Ohio George kill him?"

"Not us," the Shawnee crooned. "He said it was his job, to carry out punishment."

"Who? Who killed him?"

Red Hand leaned forward, swaying back and forth as if he were going to be sick. "I was there. I saw him kill Townsend. Saw him stab Townsend." The Shawnee made a screwing motion over his chest. "I put my mark on a paper that says so."

"Who?" Duncan shouted.

"Skanawati."

The name shattered the air like a cannon shot.

"Surely you must be—" Duncan began, but had no time to finish his sentence.

The Indian leapt into action, slamming his makeshift crutch across Moses' knees, kicking Rideaux's thigh as he jumped up, no longer as drunk as he appeared. Both men dropped to the ground in obvious pain. Duncan made a futile leap for the prisoner, landing in the dirt as the Shawnee disappeared around the corner of the storehouse.

The moon was high over the broad river when Duncan ventured out of the Moravians' house, leaving the pallet he had been given

by the hearth after Hadley and Van Grut had offered to stay with
Mokie at Rideaux's. He could not sleep, could not penetrate the
mysteries that gnawed at him, could not even focus on them for
the worry over his friend. Conawago had retreated back inside
himself, leaving the cabin with murmured thanks for the evening meal shared by the Moravians but without another word to
Duncan.

He found the old Indian on the ledge that jutted out over the
moonlit water and sat with him in silence for several minutes.

"You must listen to me carefully, Duncan," Conawago said at
last. "I beg you to heed my words."

"No one's words are more important to me," Duncan replied,
suddenly frightened by the frailness in his friend's voice.

"You must leave. Go back to Edentown. Hide somewhere from
those who would throw you in prison. But leave this place, go
anywhere but Philadelphia, where Ramsey will kill you. Leave the
mysteries of the tribes to the tribes."

Duncan must leave *him*, Conawago was saying. "You know I
am trying to help, to stop the killing, to stop the hanging."

"You only help to increase the pain." It was, from his comrade
and mentor, a stinging rebuke.

Duncan could find no reply.

"What that Frenchman says, about the hearts of the Indian and
the hearts of the Europeans being different, it is right. It is not for
you and me to pretend otherwise." There was a wrenching tone of
surrender in Conawago's voice.

"I have seen European and Indian marry, build families
together," Duncan offered, his voice tight. "The Moravians bring
comfort to the hearts of some in the tribes." Even as he spoke them
Duncan's words felt hollow. For that which Conawago invoked
there were no words.

"You will bring more death, Duncan. The spirits have their own ways of dealing with evil. I worry that you interfere with them."

"There is too much death," Duncan said, a hoarseness rising in his throat. "My people became like the leaves on the autumn tree. I do not want the clans of the woods to die too."

"I think what you and I want matters little to the fate of the tribes."

For a moment, Duncan wanted to weep. He could not bear to think this was the end of the life he had started only months before, the end of his time with the remarkable old man.

They sat for a long time, gazing into the stars reflected on the river.

"Will you tell me one thing, Conawago? What happened in the water today?"

His friend gave a trembling moan. He was silent so long Duncan assumed he would not answer.

"I had never been deep in the water like that," Conawago finally said. "Not like the land world. So cold. Dark and yet not dark. I found a gateway to the other side."

The hairs stood up on Duncan's neck. "Gateway?"

"My mother was there, Duncan. I saw her plain, looking as she had the day I was taken from her as a boy. She was smiling, gesturing for me to come to her. She held a basket, like she was waiting for me to go gather summer berries."

The realization of Conawago's meaning stabbed Duncan like an icy blade. "You are not going to die, my friend. More years lie ahead. The tribes need you more than ever. I need you."

"My mother needs me. I think there is trouble on the other side. Maybe that is where the fate of the tribes is being determined, maybe that is where I can best help." Conawago turned to Duncan. "That day at Ligonier," he added, "it was my fate to die. I was ready to cross over. That baby boy had been born to take my place. Skanawati should not have stepped in. He thought he should help me, protect me because of what you and I were doing. But he is more important to the tribes than some dried-up old Nipmuc. I cheated death, don't you see, and by my doing so bring the death of a chief who is like a saint to these people, the only chieftain with a chance of leading our people back to the old ways. At Ligonier death was cheated by a lie. Today it was cheated by the happenstance that you were near. It is wrong to trick the spirits."

Even had Duncan been able to think of a reply, the words would not have gotten past the great swelling in his throat.

"We will meet again, Duncan. I will visit you from the other side." The Indian rose and descended the rock. Ghosts, Conawago had once told him, revealed themselves only to closest family members.

A tear ran down Duncan's cheek. As if it were dispatched from the spirit world a large canoe appeared and nudged the pebble beach below. He watched as though in a dream as Conawago slipped into the vessel and four shadow warriors paddled him onto the silvery water.

Chapter Ten

I MPOSSIBLE!" RIDEAUX SPAT. "They will roast you alive!"

"Then I will shout out my questions from the stake," Duncan shot back. "One way or the other I will see the family of Skanawati." He had been waiting at the Frenchman's gate at dawn, seeking a guide. "The west branch, thirty miles upriver." A weary Rideaux, looking haggard, had gestured him inside for a cup of birch tea.

"What use could they possibly be to you?"

"I must know what Skanawati has been doing these past weeks. I must know why his adopted sister and her new husband were sent to the western boundary tree. I must know why Skanawati sent men out to investigate old markings on the Warriors Path. I must know what he thought he would learn from the ghosts there."

Duncan dared not reveal the most important reason of all. He had sat for another hour by the river the night before, watching the shadows where Conawago had disappeared, considering how the Indians in the silent canoe had all been from Skanawati's village, then considering again each piece of the puzzle. Finally he had understood that the Iroquois had been thrust into the violence because Skanawati's mother had a dream.

"I will paddle myself," Duncan vowed, "if I cannot find help."

"Not by yourself," came a voice from the shadows. Van Grut sat up from his pallet.

"Fools!" Rideaux snapped. "Any man who consents to guide you will earn the enmity of Skanawati's clan. You understand nothing about them, nothing about the trials they have endured. No one could guarantee your safety."

"Yesterday you asked what you could do to help."

Rideaux buried his head in his hands for a moment. "Word about bounties spreads like wildfire, McCallum," he said when he looked up. "Thirty pounds is a princely sum. The word came in last night with a trader from Lancaster. Stay anywhere near Shamokin and if the killers don't finish you the bounty hunters will take you for certain. Thirty pounds would solve most of the problems of Skanawati's village," he warned.

"You asked what you could do," Duncan repeated.

"Your stubbornness will get you killed," Rideaux sighed. "I will give you supplies, and a canoe. I already have men looking for Red Hand. He went south."

"On the river?"

"On the trail toward the settlements. Tulpehocken. Reading. He stole a horse. He was going fast."

"What is past Reading?"

"The road to Philadelphia," Rideaux said with foreboding.

Van Grut began stuffing his belongings back into his pack.

"It is too dangerous," Duncan said to the Dutchman.

"If you don't tell them I'm a surveyor," Van Grut said with a tentative grin, "I won't tell them there's a bounty on your head."

Duncan offered a grim smile and gestured to the other sleeping forms, flanked by the dog and orphaned bear, which was snuggled against the girl. "Tell Hadley and Mokie to wait for us here," he told the Frenchman.

As they carried their canoe into the water a tall figure emerged from a path through the alders. "If you go," Moses warned, "what you see will visit your nightmares for years."

Van Grut hesitated, growing pale as he gazed at the Moravian Indian. There was something wilder, less civilized about Moses. The day before he had been another mission Indian, but today he seemed more the warrior crusader.

"I will not allow Skanawati to be hanged," Duncan said as he followed the Dutchman into the canoe. "There are secrets only his family knows, secrets that might save him yet."

"That village," Moses sighed as he stepped toward their vessel, "is worn out. Soon it will be no more."

It was, Duncan realized, all the explanation the Indian would give. Without another word Moses shoved the canoe from the bank and climbed in behind them.

As the sun rose toward the zenith they pulled hard against the current of the narrowing river, paddled fiercely, into the rugged lands the tribes called the endless mountains. It was early afternoon when Moses began to turn the canoe toward the north bank. Duncan could see no sign of habitation but with relief spied a cluster of beached vessels that included the large one Conawago had left in the night before.

They had progressed only fifty paces up the worn trail that rose along a shallow creek when Moses halted. He seemed to sense something that his companions could not. His face sagged. "It is what I feared most. This is not the day to be here. We need to leave, make camp until tomorrow."

"Is his family here or not?" Duncan demanded. In the distance he now heard the sound that had stopped the Moravian Indian, the soft, steady throbbing of a drum.

Moses gave a melancholy nod. "There are too many dead here today."

Van Grut's face darkened, and he retreated several feet down the trail before seeing Duncan's determined expression. He grimaced, checked the priming of his gun, and pushed past Moses to follow Duncan up the trail.

They emerged at the edge of a large field that lay below a cluster of five longhouses surrounded by a decrepit stockade fence. The village appeared to be empty except for a ragged dog that barked once and fled. Duncan walked slowly toward the buildings, searching in vain for any other sign of life. Van Grut nervously lifted his gun as they passed through a gate of rotting logs. A smoldering fire sent up a wisp of smoke from the front of one of the longhouses. The only living creature to be seen now was a solitary raven on a log watchtower.

Duncan paused at the entrance to each of the longhouses. Two, with gaping holes in their elm bark roofs, appeared to have been abandoned. The others held the meager belongings of an impoverished people, arranged along the hearths reserved for each family. Tattered clothing hung from pegs on roof posts. Rattles of dried, folded bark lay beside a rotting water drum. Dried apples hung in strings from rafters beside haunches of venison. Birch buckets with bark lids were caked with the drippings of the maple syrup the Iroquois prized. In the dirt lay a tattered doll made of cornhusks that had been cleverly bound and knotted. In the largest structure of the ghost village most of the belongings appeared to have been wrapped in blankets and tied with leather straps as though for travel. In the distance, beyond the second gate, the low drum sounded like a heartbeat.

A shadow on the wall caused Duncan to spin around, his gun raised. Moses lifted a hand as if to restrain him. "The village has had great pain this past year, lost many children and old ones. The fields are no longer fertile. They begin moving soon to a new village, but first they must say their farewells."

Still not comprehending, Duncan stepped slowly to the far gate, pausing to look up at the silent raven, which seemed to be intently studying him. In a flat below the village he at last saw its inhabitants, no more than fifty men, women, and children. They seemed to be engaged in some sort of rhythmic motion, bending, lifting, digging as one of the few young men beat on an immense hollow log.

"It is the ancient way," Moses explained. "Many of the Iroquois have stopped the practice, but Skanawati was adamant that they do it this year. It is easier when platforms are used, but that is not the way of these clans. They have been waiting for his return, but they know they can wait no longer if crops are to be planted at the new site."

Van Grut shaded his eyes with his hand, trying to see the villagers better. "Christ in heaven!" he moaned as he finally understood what they looked at. The Indians were digging up their dead.

"There is a solemn feast," Moses continued. "The names of the dead are revived. The bones will be cleaned and lovingly wrapped for a new group grave. Gifts will be offered to the dead. Final leavetaking must be made, for the dead will no longer be near the calls of the women and the laughter of the children. Skanawati helped dig the new grave before he left, helped trap furs all winter to line it."

"How do you know these things?" Duncan whispered.

"My brother married a woman of this village."

"He is here?"

"He was killed fighting with the British at Fort Niagara."

No words of greeting met Duncan as he advanced, his gun and pack left at the gate. As he approached he realized he knew the drummer. Johantty, covered with soot, frowned as he saw Duncan. The oldest of the women, clearly in charge, shot up from where she sat and began shouting at him, the words unintelligible but her gestures unmistakable. Every villager straightened, eyes on Duncan. One man lifted his iron shovel like a weapon, another raised the sharpened stick he was using to pry at the earth. Then an energetic voice called out, and Duncan's would-be assailants hesitated as Johantty left his drum and ran to the woman's side, pointing at Duncan, speaking in low, hurried tones. The woman scowled then uttered a few low syllables that sent the villagers back to their sober task.

"Stone Blossom," Moses explained at his shoulder. "She has been the undisputed head of this village for decades."

Duncan watched uneasily as Moses stepped forward and spoke in quiet, earnest appeal with the sturdy, aged woman. She frowned again but did not object when the Moravian began to help arrange the old bones in fur bundles. Though somber, the atmosphere was not altogether mournful, more like that of a reunion of friends who had suffered much since last meeting. The only ones looking disturbed at all were the women who worked with knives to clean lingering flesh from bones of the freshest graves. Duncan clenched his jaw and approached them, hand on the hilt of his own knife.

"Tell them, Moses," he said, "tell them that in my country I am considered a friend of the dead."

The women stepped back warily, surrendering their task to Duncan. It was no different than working with the cadavers in his Edinburgh college, he told himself as he put his blade to the first muscle.

He watched as Van Grut inched away, poised to flee at any moment, and saw how the Indians watched the Dutchman with angry suspicion. Van Grut approached with a sideways motion when Duncan gestured for him, clearly repulsed by Duncan's chore. Duncan rose and leaned into his ear.

Van Grut sighed in exasperation as he heard Duncan's suggestion. "Do it," Duncan said, "or return to the canoe. This is no place for an onlooker."

"I haven't enough paper," Van Grut protested.

"Make them small."

The Dutchman sighed, then reached into his pack.

Ten minutes later Duncan lowered his knife and approached Stone Blossom, the matriarch. "Do you have English words?" he asked.

"A little," the woman said stiffly. "My son Skanawati teach me."

Duncan paused, then realized he should not be surprised that the woman who was clearly the matron of the village was also the mother of Skanawati. "The spirits have empowered my friend's hands," he said. "He wishes to help you leave something of yourself with your lost ones."

"We have readied gifts for them," the woman said, confused. "Old prayers have been spoken over their new grave, since before dawn."

As Duncan looked back the Dutchman was approaching, tearing away a quarter of the sheet in his hand. The woman hesitantly accepted the paper, then cried out in fear as she saw her image sketched on it. She threw it down and began chanting words that had the sound of a curse.

Moses was suddenly at Duncan's shoulder, speaking reassuringly to her. Calmed, she bent and tentatively touched the drawing. A younger woman leaned over it, her eyes growing round before she snatched it up with an exclamation of awe.

"There are witches in the tribes," Moses said, "who sometimes are burned just as in old Europe. Stone Blossom said it was witchcraft, but I told her no, it was the spirits speaking through this stranger, who came from across the big water to honor the village of Skanawati. I said he was making a tattoo of her memory, to leave with loved ones."

Duncan offered a grateful nod. He had grown to greatly respect the Christian Indians, not just for their spiritual fortitude, which often exceeded that of Europeans, but for the adept way they navigated the ground between worlds.

The work went speedily now, with more and more spirits lifted as Van Grut offered one and then another sketch of the villagers. Young girls returned to the village and carried down wooden planks laden with cornbread, smoked eels, and crocks of fresh water. As the others ate Duncan slipped up the trail toward the new communal grave, toward the scent of fresh tobacco burning with other herbs.

Conawago sat cross-legged on a blanket, rocking back and forth, chanting prayers to sanctify the new grave. Duncan slipped onto a boulder in the shadows of a sassafras tree and watched, the Nipmuc seemingly oblivious to his presence. The gentle voice worked like a salve to his tired, aching body. He did not know how he would find the strength to continue down his treacherous path without Conawago at his side, but at least for now his friend was where he belonged, standing in for Skanawati, the father the village had lost.

At last he retreated down the path, realizing he was famished. He ate heartily of the eel and cornbread, then helped the villagers finish wrapping the last of the bones in swathes of fur as Van Grut completed the last of his sketches.

He heard a new pitch in the conversations, a new strain in several voices, and looked to see that the Indians were now addressing bundles of bones, saying farewell as the bones were covered for a last time, slipping the sketches done by the Dutchman into the bundles before tying them tight. Tears were flowing freely, and several women clutched small bundles to their breasts, whispering the last words of a mother to her child.

Finally the slow procession began up the path to the grave overlooking the river.

"I am grateful to you, McCallum," came a quiet voice by his shoulder. Moses was solemnly watching the single file of mournful villagers. "Every European I have known who encountered this practice has been revolted by it, condemned it as barbaric. I have always thought it very civilized. I know Christians who bless new homes, but it has always seemed better to me to bless the homes of the old ones. If we do not respect those who have gone before, how can we respect ourselves?"

Duncan, nodding in agreement, recalled another cemetery, that of his clan, which had been dug up and ravaged by English raiders. They had hung the corpse of an uncle branded as a traitor, then destroyed most of the markers. But his parents and grandparents had banished the horror by digging new graves and summoning the clan for a gathering—illegal under English law—to reconsecrate them.

It was not the time to ask the questions he so wanted to ask the villagers. It would not be for hours.

"Where will they go?" he asked Moses. "I mean, where is their new village?"

The Moravian's eyes narrowed in warning. "Do not ask them. There are hidden valleys, in uncharted land. Skanawati wants them far from English rum, far from English traders. He asked me to visit them, with some of Rideaux's Delawares, to teach his people how to write sounds on paper. He wants his village to record all the old stories, the names of all the old spirits."

"Do you believe with Rideaux, that those of the tribes have uncorrupted hearts?"

Moses considered the question a long time. "I believe many Europeans have lost the way of their hearts."

"They have lost their true skins." The words left Duncan's tongue unbidden.

Moses nodded. "You have had a good teacher."

Duncan looked up the trail to the new grave, where Conawago still chanted. In that moment he wanted more than anything to steal away with the old Nipmuc to one of their mountain hideaways and leave the rest of the world behind.

When he finally returned to the new grave, behind the slow, murmuring procession, Stone Blossom was seated beside Conawago. As each bundle was placed in the wide pit, lined with fur and moss, those carrying it spoke, raising the bundle toward the sky and calling out the name of the dead, sometimes twice, even three times before setting it down and arranging the gifts that would be buried with it.

He saw the old woman reach for the bundle of white fur that had been used to wrap the first set of bones he had cleaned, one with heavily tattooed skin. He found a place behind her and sat to listen as she lifted the bundle and spoke. Her words brought the sound of new lamentation among the villagers, many of whom offered their own short prayers. When she finished, ready to place the bones on a bear fur at the center of the mass grave, she raised them one last time and called to the sky.

"Skanawati! Skanawati! Skanawati!"

A chill ran down Duncan's spine. He looked about, trying to understand. Skanawati was in the hands of the magistrates, waiting to be hanged. Skanawati had been in the Shamokin and lands north for the past six months, yet Red Hand had insisted he had been in the western lands, killing a surveyor. And now Skanawati was being buried, having died months earlier.

As the village arranged the pots, blades, and combs that were the final gifts to the dead and began filling the grave with soil, Duncan turned to Moses. "I ask you, my friend. Explain to me how Skanawati can be in so many places."

"There has always been a Skanawati," Moses said enigmatically. Then he saw the tormented way Duncan looked at the bundle of white fur as it disappeared under the soil. "Perhaps there is something you must learn about the high chiefs of the Grand Council. When a man is raised to a seat of the council he takes its ancient name."

Duncan considered the words for a moment. "You are saying the Skanawati held by the magistrate has only had the name for a few months?"

"Less than a year. The old chief died of the pox, and the title was given to his nephew, who had trained to take on that burden for many years."

Duncan's mind raced. The chief awaiting hanging could not have killed the first surveyor, Townsend, but the prior Skanawati could have. "What was he like, the last chief?"

"A great and noble warrior, as was his duty. Stone Blossom says there is an essence that passes from one Skanawati to the next."

Duncan at last understood the most important question. "And who was the foe of this last warrior chief?"

Moses did not reply, but looked to the old woman, who, Duncan now saw, had been following their conversation.

"We met Skanawati on the old trail," a familiar voice interceded. With an uneasy glance at Duncan, Conawago settled on the other side of the woman. "We spoke and we listened."

The woman's eyes lit with something like joyful anticipation. "I only knew you were wise in the ways of the old prayers. Johantty did not tell me you were also the one my son met on the trail!"

Duncan did not at first understand when she gestured to Conawago's shoulder, but his friend did. Loosening his buttons, he slid his shirt off his shoulder. She stared at the sign of the dawn-chasers in silence, wonder rising on her face as it had on Skanawati's when they had first met him on the trail.

"Jiyathondek!" she suddenly cried, loud enough for all to hear. *Hearken!* In moments a dozen villagers had crowded round, looking at the tattoo with the same awed expressions. The woman called out Johantty's name, and the drumming faltered a moment as the drummers changed. "Johantty and his uncle, Johantty and Skanawati, found what they think is the beginning of the dawn-chaser path," she declared, glancing again at Conawago's tattoo with the excitement of a great discovery.

His uncle. In the Iroquois world, a boy's maternal uncle played a much bigger role in his life than his father. Johantty had been at the chief's side at Ligonier and had played a role at every stage of the violent drama since. Skanawati had been preparing him.

"Tell them," the woman said to the youth.

"Rocks like a—" he turned and asked a quick question of Conawago, who offered a whispered reply, "—like a chimney. Signs of animals carved in the rocks, below a sign of the rising sun."

"A giant cottonwood at the opposite side of the clearing," Conawago put in, and Johantty nodded excitedly.

"Skanawati was like a boy when he returned that day," the woman continued. "It was a sign. He went to the Grand Council in Onondaga," she explained, referring to the capital of the confederation. "He said we could say no to the Europeans now."

"No?" Duncan asked.

"No. No to everything."

It was, he realized, the beginning of the chief's efforts to return his people to their own traditions. "What happened?"

The woman shrugged. "He spoke for hours that night, won many chiefs over. But the next day British traders arrived with new guns and rum and bolts of red wool. When he came back he said he had misunderstood, that the sign was meant just for our village. That is where we are moving, to be close to the old shrines."

As Johantty bent with his wooden shovel to toss on a final scoop of loose soil, the objects around his neck swung outward, an amulet pouch, and on a separate strand something else Duncan had not fully seen before. He remembered the feeling of long hairs dangling on his neck the night Johantty had jumped him and had assumed they were bundled with his amulet. Now Duncan plainly saw the separate object, a piece of wood with threads, not hairs, fastened to it. He had seen an identical one the day before, in Ohio George's horde of stolen objects.

When Johantty finished Duncan gestured to the strange necklace. "Did you make that?"

The youth shook his head. "Magic spider. Dances in winter."

Not comprehending, Duncan tentatively reached out. Johantty let him touch it, lift it. It was incredibly light. He saw now that the wood was a small oval cork, the threads silk. "Where did you get this?"

It was Stone Blossom who replied. "His uncle brought it back from the settlements. A friend there gave it to him to be remembered to Johantty, as a gift."

"Settlements? You mean Shamokin?"

She shook her head. "The Quaker city."

"Why?" Duncan asked urgently, knowing he was touching again on the mysteries of the boundary trail. "Why did the chief of the Grand Council go to Philadelphia?"

Stone Blossom looked back over the new grave. "I like the sound of the river from here. It makes a singing over the rocks."

She was as inscrutable as an old monk, Duncan thought to himself. He gazed at the villagers as they retreated toward their houses. He saw sadness but no despair. All about him, in this town that was the most removed from European influence of any he had ever known, was a harmony such as he had not experienced since leaving the Highlands. The matriarch rose and began walking toward the stockaded town, as Johantty joined a half a dozen children sitting on the slope below town and began speaking to them with gestures toward the sky. The sun was fast sinking.

"Skanawati made that young one spend a year at the seat of the Grand Council," Moses said over his shoulder. "Hours every day Johantty sat with the old men and women to learn all their stories, the rituals, the names of chiefs long dead. Skanawati places great hope in him."

The village quieted as the sun disappeared, the inhabitants gathering near their hearths, a small group at the central fire pit continuing the prayers to the spirits, led by Stone Blossom. It was two hours later, the evening meal finished, the other villagers retired to their pallets, when Duncan approached her at the fire, dropping an object from his pack onto the ground in front of her.

The matriarch did not react at first when she saw the soiled, crushed moccasin in front of her. It had the look of a beautiful thing that had died, a dead flower of the forest.

"She was killed with her new husband at the boundary tree by the bloody water," Duncan began. "I think she had started to clear away the debris that would show it to be one of the ancient shrines."

"My grandmother's grandmother," the woman said at last, "and all the grandmothers before, taught that such places were what rooted our people into the earth, like the—" she looked to Moses, sitting nearby, for help, "—the heavy weight that holds boats safe."

"An anchor," Moses offered.

"Like the anchor that keeps us safe in all weathers. For centuries the old shrines were maintained and our people lived as one with the spirits of the land. I am to blame, and my brothers and sisters, for it was in our lifetime that the shrines were forgotten, that the children and grandchildren lost interest and stopped tending them."

"You sent your adopted daughter to clean the shrine," Duncan said.

"She was one of the few who bothered to learn the old ways." The old woman looked down at the moccasin with a desolate expression. "It is time we moved on. Too many of our buds shrivel before they can blossom." She turned to Duncan. "They had a Christian marriage in Shamokin, for her husband's sake, after a bonding ceremony here in the village. There was a great celebration. It was then that Skanawati and I learned she was going with her husband to that far end of the Warriors Path." The woman looked up, first at Moses, then to Conawago, before turning to Duncan with apology on her face. "If we could open the old root shrines, let the Grand Council know they had been discovered again, we thought all the great chiefs would have the strength to stop selling our lands."

Stone Blossom lifted the shoe, futilely rubbing at the stains on the pale doeskin. "I made these for her, in the winter. I would get out of my blankets in the middle of the night and work on them so she would not see. By a fire in the snow I whispered old songs over them to bring her good luck." A tear rolled down her cheek and landed on the moccasin.

Duncan looked into her haggard face. "Grandmother," he asked after a moment, "how many of your village did you send to find the old anchor shrines?"

"Three. The three who had spent the most years learning the old ways. Then my daughter went with her husband. All gone now. When my son told me of the first two dying I said the spirits must have needed them on the other side more than we needed them here. He said that could be true, but it also could mean someone was trying to keep the old shrines from being reopened along the Warriors Path. He and I did not believe what all those fools said about those lumps of metal being the remains of their souls. He said we owed condolences, to reach them on the other side."

But condolences were given by the guilty party. Duncan knew better than to push the old woman to explain. As he struggled to understand her meaning, a familiar voice solved his dilemma.

"Skanawati is both war chief and peace chief," Conawago reminded him. Duncan did not know how long he had been there listening. "Our Skanawati has more of the peace in him. Perhaps his uncle had more of the war." Something about his day with the dead had calmed his friend. He was still distant, but the anxiety, the strange longing, was gone from his eyes.

As Stone Blossom nodded, another tear rolled down her cheek. Duncan's mind raced back to the words of the renegade Red Hand and, as he looked into the old woman's face, he realized they were probably true. The prior Skanawati, who had died of the pox the year before, had killed the first surveyor. The tribes may not have continued the violence on the survey line, but they may well have started it, playing to the hand of a distant conspirator.

"The spirits we need," the matriarch said in a tortured voice, "are not the ones awakened by blood."

They sat in silence. Moses heaped more wood on the fire and joined them as they watched the sparks mingle with the stars. The spring frogs chirped.

"When that first surveyor died," Duncan asked, "was it known in Shamokin?"

"I don't understand," Stone Blossom replied.

"The killers now are trying to make it look like Iroquois from Shamokin are responsible for all the deaths."

It was Moses who answered. "There was some survey equipment. One of the warriors with the last chief sold it in Shamokin for rum. When he got drunk he did not mind speaking about what he and the old chief had done, killing an enemy of all our peoples."

Stone Blossom rose and disappeared into the nearest longhouse, returning a moment later to drop a doeskin packet into Duncan's lap. "I was going to bury it," she said. "It is tainted."

He unwrapped it to discover an elegant little wooden box, of a kind made for jewelry or keepsakes. It was artfully worked, with an inlaid pattern of diamonds across its front. But a crude design had been scratched into the hinged top, in the shape of a turtle. On the bottom was more scratching, though in very careful block letters. *F. Townsend,* it said, *1756.*

As Duncan turned with more questions a low rumble rose from the direction of the new grave. Someone was beating the great log drum.

"Johantty said you must join him after the moon rises, to sing the dead." Stone Blossom gestured toward a dark object at the edge of the ring. Conawago had retrieved his pack, with his pipes.

Duncan solemnly nodded. "Can you first tell me when Skanawati learned he was to be a negotiator for the new treaty?"

"He had already gone down the trail," the chief's mother said. "A messenger was sent to him with the news from Old Belt. Johantty is one of our fastest runners. Even so Skanawati had gone very far west."

"But Skanawati had been here, preparing the rituals, readying for the move." It was the closest Duncan dared approach to the dream that had changed the chief's plans.

Stone Blossom stared into the fire a long time. "I do not know you well enough," she said.

"All the leaders of my clan were killed," Duncan whispered to her. "I will not let it happen to yours."

The old woman studied him with new interest. "A message came from the other side. When I showed him he knew everything had changed."

"Showed him what, Grandmother?"

"I took him to the sacred place that once anchored our village. I showed him the crack in the world."

Although they left just after dawn the next morning, when they pulled their canoes onto the bank two miles upstream, Johantty was there with his three companions, tending a fire by a small sweat lodge. The youth had not slept, Duncan was certain, for the two of them had drummed and piped at the graveyard, looking over the river, long past midnight. Wary of asking more questions, Duncan watched as Conawago began stripping to a loincloth, then Johantty pointed to a small wooded island opposite the lodge. They had to cleanse themselves before venturing to the sacred place. Stone Blossom appeared from behind a shrub, wearing nothing but a woolen breechcloth herself, and entered the lodge, into which the other youths were carrying hot stones cradled with sticks. Johantty tossed Duncan a length of wool. Duncan stripped and arranged it like a kilt before stepping into the purifying steam of the lodge.

An hour later Duncan warily watched the island as Conawago, Stone Blossom, and he approached it. From a distance it had appeared to be just one more wooded hump of rock in the center of the river, an island perhaps two hundred feet long. But in a river filled with little tree-covered islands this one stood out for its dramatic rock formations and clump of misshapen beech trees at the northern end.

Duncan kept as silent as his guide, watching the old woman, then mimicking her action as she plucked a sprig of sweet cedar from a small tree. Yet even when she stopped and placed the sprig on a flat slab at the highest point of the gnarled ledge rocks and looked at him expectantly, he did not understand. But then he heard the gasp of surprise behind him, and he turned to see Conawago staring at the rock at their feet.

What Duncan had taken to be cracks and seams in the rock were carvings, dozens of primitive symbols of animals and men, trees and fish. They were very old, even ancient, and the effort to make them with stone-and-wood tools would have been extraordinary.

The styles and size varied, some of the carved petroglyphs so worn by weather that they were barely visible. And almost none were entirely visible, for they had been attacked.

Hammers or axes had been taken to the signs, cracking and splintering the rock, obliterating the stone so that in some cases there was nothing but a rough, shallow bowl of freshly exposed rock left.

But that was not the worst of the damage. With a long, quivering wail that sent a chill down Duncan's spine, Stone Blossom knelt at the largest of the carvings, a three-foot-long image of a raven. It was the centerpiece, as if the bird were the leading deity. But the raven was dead, split down the center by a narrow crevasse that continued for over ten feet to the end of the ledge. As the old woman laid her arms on either side of the image and bent low, whispering to it, Duncan followed the crack to the side of the exposed ledge and saw the black burn marks there. Knowing it was made by gunpowder did not change the effect of seeing the crack. It was gut-wrenching. The most remarkable Indian shrine he had ever seen had been destroyed, desecrated by European tools. He could not argue with Stone Blossom's perception that it portended something terrible for her world.

"It was here we came to on festival days," Stone Blossom explained when she was done. "When I was a child, when I was a young woman, when I was a wife and mother. Even as a boy Skanawati would come and sit here for hours. It was always a place of great power." Her voice choked with emotion as she gazed over the destruction. When she spoke again it was in her native tongue, answering questions softly asked by Conawago.

Duncan roamed around the wide-open ledge that gave a view of the river in every direction. The symbols were everywhere, and as he found several still intact at the rim of the broad ledge he thrilled at the thought of the ancient hands that had reverently chiseled them into the stone. He touched one of the overhanging beech trees, twisted and stunted by the river winds, and saw how thick its trunk was. It too was ancient. It had witnessed the reverence, heard the chants that would have been used to empower the completed figures.

He paused, studying the way the rock fell away at the north end. Crude steps, long ago overgrown with lichen, had been cut there. He bent and pushed through the laurel along the edge, dropped off the ledge, and followed the barest shadow of a trail that ran from the bottom step. Broken stems hanging over the bushes indicated that others had recently found the shallow cave at the end of the trail.

Ancient hands had also worked the walls of the cave, some with chisels like on the ledge above, some with pigments. Most of the images had been recently scraped away with a blade, some covered with bear grease, but he could see features here and there of hunters with spears, of huge oxlike creatures with short horns, of moose and bears three times the height of the human figures. As he stepped inside, an unmistakable odor rose from the rear of the cave. Someone had defecated against the back wall.

"She weeps," Conawago said behind him. He pulled a heavy branch back to let more light into the cave. "She weeps," he repeated.

The pain on his friend's face was so deep Duncan expected to see tears there too. But Conawago's grief was tempered by an intense fascination, an awe he could not hide. Gazing reverently, his eyes came to rest upon the most intact of the little images. It was a human figure facing one of the ruined bears, holding out not a spear but what looked like the skull of another animal. "This," he said, "is who we were."

He walked slowly along the walls, pausing at each image. "For generations, she says, since long before the formation of the confederation, people of her clan have come here, left offerings, sat under the full moon and performed their chants. Even in the middle of a war the enemies could come here and be as one."

Duncan could hear the excitement in Conawago's tone. Their journeys during the past months had been in search of such places of power. "This is who we were," Conawago repeated as he gazed again at the image of the man reaching out to the bear, then gestured toward the feces on the wall that had ruined another painting. "This is who we become."

"Surely it was Europeans who did this."

"Stone Blossom knows who did it. Shamokin Indians, town Indians. Some Iroquois, some town Delawares out on a trapping expedition. They had little success and were on their way home. An English trader going up the river found them camped here and bartered a keg of rum for the few skins they had taken. They spent the day getting drunk here. One of the Indians had been instructed by missionaries and told the others their bad luck came from these graven images. They spent hours drinking and destroying. At some point one remembered they could sell the old images to collectors in Philadelphia, so they tried to pull some up. There used to be a shrine of old human skulls, holy men of the tribes, some from many generations ago. They threw them all in the river."

"When Skanawati found out he beat several of them within an inch of their lives. He told his mother it was a sign, that the village had to move into the endless mountains, to the other place he had found, to protect it and keep it secret."

"You mean his hidden valley?"

"It has another shrine, she says, below a high ledge with similar carvings, where a raven makes its nest."

"They should have moved then."

"It takes much preparation. They had to wait until warm weather, gather syrup from the spring maples, make the new grave." Conawago rubbed at one of the grease-stained images, saw that the grease was carrying away the pigment, and gave up.

They found Stone Blossom on her knees, gazing again at the shattered images. She stood as they returned, gesturing them closer, then taking a hand from each of them in her own. "You have been purified in the heat of our lodge," she said. "You have each spoken to our dead. You have come to this same place from different paths." The matriarch looked at them expectantly.

"What is it you wish, Grandmother?" Conawago asked.

"You must help us through this. Together," she said pointedly, steadily regarding him. She had seen Conawago's despair. "I dreamt of two outsiders coming to help our village. I could never see their faces, until now."

Conawago went very still, closing his eyes for a moment before glancing at Duncan. "We are here," he whispered.

"Every guide we have sent to find our path has failed," she said. "But the two of you know things together you do not know apart." The old woman nodded at them solemnly, then released their hands and bent to lift bundles of rushes she had gathered from the river's edge. Duncan and Conawago each took one, and they knelt with Stone Blossom to clean away the debris from the little gods.

Only when they had finished did Duncan speak. "Why," he asked Conawago, "during such an important time for the village and his clan would Skanawati go to Philadelphia?" The new chief would have just taken over from his predecessor and had already told his people they had to move their village.

Conawago repeated Duncan's question to the woman in her tongue, triggering a low, hurried conversation. "Last year," his friend finally explained, "she says there was an Englishman who had been trapping, who stopped in Shamokin. He came in from the endless mountains. Skanawati spoke with him, at Rideaux's place. The man had told Rideaux he had seen the old shrine on the ledge. Skanawati's shrine."

Duncan looked up with new despair. "Surely he did not try to destroy that one as well?"

"Not at all. He said merely the mountains had no good fur left."

"But that does not explain . . . " Duncan started, but the woman was done, turning back to the canoe.

"Moses told me the rest last night," Conawago said, pain rising in his voice now. "That Englishman was Francis Townsend, the surveyor killed months later on the Warriors Path. Skanawati learned from Rideaux that he had not just been trapping. Townsend was educated, knew how to look for minerals. He had drawn a detailed map with the plan of selling it in Philadelphia. He had been at the shrine, had drawn it on his map. And he had marked that its valley was rich in minerals and Indian artifacts."

"So Townsend went back to Philadelphia to sell his map?"

"A piece of paper like that could be worth more than a wagon of pelts. Skanawati left for Philadelphia an hour after learning of the map, even though he had never been there, had no idea how to find this man. When his brother learned that Skanawati had gone to Philadelphia he too left, a day behind. Skanawati returned a month later, alone. He said nothing of what happened until just before he left the village three weeks ago. He said then to his mother, pray for the spirit of his brother, her second son, for he had died a warrior's death in the city of the Quakers."

Duncan considered the words. "Why would his brother have followed him to Philadelphia?"

"His brother had been earning money to buy seed corn for the village."

"What are you saying?"

"He did not understand the scratchings Townsend made on his papers. He did not know about Skanawati's plans for the new village until he returned. But he had been the guide for Townsend when he drew the map."

Chapter Eleven

OCRATES MOON WAS the name Conawago assumed in
the European world, the swarthy exotic traveler who had
crossed the Atlantic several times, looking and speaking
the part of the educated gentleman when need be. Duncan watched
with a weary grin as his friend completed the transformation by
donning a crumpled waistcoat he kept rolled in his pack over his
linen shirt, covering the long trail of hair gathered at his back.

"You will put me to shame in the taverns," Duncan chided.

"No. Because you are staying here," the Indian said, with a
gesture toward the little clearing they had found in the forest overlooking the city. It was an argument that had risen with increasing frequency during their days of hurried travel from Shamokin.
"Lord Ramsey is somewhere on those streets," Conawago reminded
him again. "He will have you in chains a moment after he spies you.
And once he has you, Duncan, you will be lost forever." The old
Nipmuc had once told Duncan that Ramsey was a manifestation of
the malevolent spirits that dwelled in certain corners of the wilderness, waiting to commit mayhem.

They eyed the city that stretched below. "It is a big city," Duncan observed. "And he but one man. In all the city he is the only one who knows my face."

"Only London is greater in the English world," Conawago said. "But the places we need to visit are ones likely frequented by Ramsey. He despises you. He considers you a traitor to his house, knows you removed him from the affection of his daughter and caused the loss of his New York estate. His evil cannot be defeated, Duncan, only avoided."

"I will not hide. Every hour the hangman's noose is closer to Skanawati's neck. Every hour the real killer draws closer to another murder."

Conawago frowned. "Are there no words I can say?"

"I seem to recall Stone Blossom saying we were fated to find the path together."

Conawago sighed, then reached into the pack hanging from his horse and unfolded a second waistcoat, lent by Rideaux. It was threadbare in spots but would cover Duncan's own shirt, tattered and soiled from hard travel.

Rideaux had remembered the Englishman whom Skanawati and his brother had followed the year before. "Townsend came back weeks later with a commission as a surveyor," the Frenchman had confirmed. "A quiet, intelligent man. Thin like a rail." Townsend had stayed at Rideaux's compound en route to Philadelphia and had exclaimed over the grandeur of the mountains and shown his map. The Frenchman had been the one to describe the markings on Townsend's map to Skanawati. "It was as if I had kicked him in the belly," Rideaux recalled. "He wanted to know who else had seen it. As far as I knew, no one, and I told him so. He then asked me to tell no one else, never say such a map existed. He asked me to write Townsend's name on a piece of paper. He asked for some food, and a second pair of moccasins."

"Moccasins?" Duncan had asked.

"It meant he was going on a long journey. I put everything in a pack, and off he went, running like a deer. Next day his brother comes in, cheerful and laughing. But the moment he heard that Skanawati had abruptly left for Philadelphia his merriment stopped. Notwithstanding my vow I knew I had to explain to him about the map, and when he learned it showed Skanawati's secret village site, he suddenly turned grave. Minutes later he was gone. I never saw him again. Later I discovered he had asked for some paint, as if going to war."

Rideaux had searched their faces, seeing the worry. "The fastest way to Philadelphia," he offered at last, "is on horse, over the trail to Reading."

"We have no horses," Duncan said. "We have no money."

The Frenchman left them to engage the group of Indians working outside, soon returning to retrieve a heavy wooden box from a cabinet. He counted out a stack of coins and pushed them toward Duncan. "Horses will be in the yard in five minutes. A canoe will take your friends back to the treaty delegation. Go with God."

Now, walking slowly, they led their horses toward the sprawling city. A hundred things could happen when they stepped onto the cobblestone streets, almost none of them good. Duncan's foreboding was so great that only when he heard Conawago negotiating with him did he notice the stout bearded man who offered to stable their mounts.

Minutes later, their packs and weapons entrusted to the stableman for an extra coin, Duncan walked uneasily into America's metropolis. The smoke of hundreds of stoves and fireplaces drifted over the rooftops. Small, well-tended farms stretched from the outskirts, many with children hoeing rows of vegetables. Ox-drawn wagons stacked high with firewood, charcoal, or sacks of grain lumbered toward the city.

Duncan had almost forgotten that a visitor to any city first experienced it through his nostrils. Wafting through the underlying scent of sewage and wood smoke were lighter hints of tallow, freshly tanned leather, and beeswax. Soon came the sounds of hooves on stone, smiths at forges, hammers on the planks of new houses.

The street underfoot felt unnatural, like solid ground after months at sea. The two men exchanged uneasy glances and kept moving. A girl chased hens away from a bed of tulips. A boy loudly hawked a slim broadsheet. A youth in a white apron pushed a hand-wagon stacked with freshly baked loaves.

Conawago approached the boy and proffered a coin, speaking with him as he took a small loaf, half of which he handed to Duncan. "I asked where one goes to find maps of the frontier," his friend reported. "He replied that he surely doesn't know, but if it's men of learning we want, best go closer to the government house and the steeples." Conawago gestured toward the white towers extending above the trees in the distance.

Half an hour later they stood below the glistening spire of Christ Church, splashing their faces with water from a stone trough. Twice Duncan stopped passersby to inquire of Mr. Townsend, receiving only frowns for his trouble. Then he spied a man in a black robe weeding headstones in the small cemetery.

"Excuse me, father," Duncan began, then saw the wince on the man's face and corrected himself. "Reverend. We are travelers seeking a family named Townsend."

"I could think of a dozen who answer to that name," the pastor replied in a tentative voice.

"Our man is a surveyor. In the western country last year."

"Francis Townsend?" The pastor's face darkened. "A tragedy, that." He studied Duncan, as if suddenly suspicious. "See for yourself," he said and pointed up the street. "Three blocks up, one toward the west."

A squad of soldiers marched by as they proceeded up the street. A man in dark clothes carrying a long staff walked past them, a constable on his rounds. Reaching the intersection, they surveyed the buildings. "The Townsend residence?" Conawago inquired of an elderly woman with a cane, who used it to point before hurrying on.

They looked in confusion to where she had indicated. It was the ruins of a house, burned nearly to the ground. The few scorched timbers and mortared stones that remained were weathered, weeds growing among them. The fire had been months ago.

Conawago nodded to a tavern across the way, where they sank gratefully into chairs at a table by the front window.

"That was the Townsend place?" Duncan asked when the proprietor brought them two mugs of strong cider.

"Aye. A damned shame."

"Did the family suffer injuries?"

"Only Townsend and his maiden sister lived there, neither hurt. A sad case, always down on his luck. An educated man, you know, but forever restless. Off in the wilds and such. Trapping, prospecting, trying to get this book on birds or that on animal husbandry commissioned."

When they ordered a second round the proprietor brought them a length of dried sausage on a board with a knife. Seating himself, he cut several slices, taking one before pushing the plank toward his customers. "'Twas a night no one will soon forget. I still have nightmares. The heathen beast hallooing, the new fire brigade scrambling, the neighborhood carrying away their belongings in panic, certain the whole block would perish."

"Heathen?" Duncan asked, dreading the answer.

"Aye. The real thing." The barman twisted his face as he stared at the ruins. "Though something of playacting about it, too, it seems when I think on it. Theatrical if ye understand me."

"I'm not sure we do," Conawago said, slowly chewing on a piece of the tough, spicy meat.

"There were two of them. Indians, I mean. Why the proprietor lets them come and go in the city is beyond me. Because of our brotherly love, is why," he answered himself in a bitter tone.

"The fire?" Duncan prodded.

"The two knocked on his door in the afternoon, wearing blankets over their shoulders as if to conceal their identity. They wanted something of Townsend's, but he wouldn't admit them. He shouted from the door, something about it being locked in his desk and would remain there. Then that evening one returns. He starts stripping down to a loincloth under the corner lantern," he said, indicating the whale oil streetlight, "then daubs on paint. On his face, on his arms, on his chest, all the while chanting some gibberish. Right out of the tales you read about the savage raiders. I sent my boy for the constable. Then I see him coolly light a little torch from the lantern and start igniting little piles of kindling and branches he had stacked against the house. He opens the door and yells out for those inside to leave as if planning to ambush them on their way out, and starts prancing by the fires, making an unholy racket, calling down his war gods, they say."

"Did he? Ambush them?"

"It was damned curious. When they appeared, he quieted and just gestured them along to the street before starting his dance again. By the time the fire company arrived there wasn't much to do but water down the house next door. All the while that heathen stayed, speaking in his devilish tongue."

"They arrested him?"

"Most wanted to lynch him on the spot. But that is not the way of the Quakers who run this town. Words have to be spoken first to make things right. They trussed him up like a wild bull and held a proper trial the next week. He never resisted, never argued."

"And?"

"We hanged him, of course. Most of the town turned out. He was one of those whose neck didn't snap. He just hung there and twisted, slowly strangling."

Conawago buried his head in his hands. Duncan stared into his cup. "Did he speak in the end?"

"Nary a word. Except when he climbed the scaffold he called out, not in protest, just shouted toward the sky. One of the farmers who spoke a little heathen said he was calling his name to the spirits, to let them know he was on his way."

Duncan and Conawago exchanged a tormented glance. They needed no further explanation. It was clear that Skanawati's brother had not understood what Townsend had drawn on his map. That a white man would capture a sacred place on paper would have been unimaginable. Yet it had happened, and to prevent Skanawati from taking suicidal action he had taken his own, donning his war paint and correcting his unforgivable mistake, burning down the house to be sure the map was destroyed.

"What happened to this Townsend afterward?" Conawago ventured.

"Like I said, a restless soul. A week after the fire he came in and declared he had a new commission as a surveyor. There was new coin in his pocket. He said he would be soon gone and wanted to pay advance board for his sister to sup here twice a week, for three months, though that ran out months ago. Never saw him again.

Dead in the wilderness, people say. Without his support, his sister's had to take up household service."

"Surely becoming a surveyor requires an apprenticeship," Duncan observed.

"This colony suffers from land fever. Private companies being formed every day to acquire land, usually in competition with each other. All the trained surveyors have their hands full with the local conveyancing. The companies, what they need is gross work, one might say. More like rough mapmaking, and most of that in secret. The more definite a claim the more likely it is for the courts to uphold it. Hell, at this point I think anyone who can read and write and has the spine to face the Indians can find a commission."

"Where does one go to hire such a surveyor?" Duncan asked. "Do they have a hall?"

"Lord boy, this is America. We have no guild halls." He grinned as he rose from his seat. "But we have taverns. Down near the river, below Walnut Street, that's where they go. The Broken Jug, mostly, after the supper hour."

Duncan pulled out one of the clock gears from his pouch and spun it between his fingers. "Meanwhile we seek a clockmaker."

"Which one? This be Philadelphia. Most American clocks are made here. You could spend a day and not visit all their shops."

"The nearest then," Duncan pressed.

A quarter hour later they stood by the worktable of a middle-aged bespectacled man leaning over a small vise, assisted by a candle mounted with a lens that collected the light onto the gear he worked on. He had assessed them with a quick glance when they stepped into his shop, apparently concluding they were not potential customers, so he kept them waiting as he worked with a tiny file.

Finally he looked up with a barely tolerant expression that softened only when Duncan produced one of the gears and spun it like
a top on his bench.

The man wiped his hand on his leather apron, snatched up the
gear, and studied it a moment before passing it back. "Your complaint is not with me," he declared.

"I beg your pardon?" Conawago asked. His refined tone caused
the clockmaker to hesitate.

The man frowned. "When someone appears with a piece taken
from a gear works, it is to complain. They think because they have
dropped the clock or suffered it to travel over rutted roads that it is
the maker's fault when it fails to respond."

"How can you be so certain it is not your work?" Duncan
wanted to know. He extended one of the other gears, a pinion, and
displayed it on his palm.

"I import most of my gears from England. Yours is meant for a
farmer's clock, a crude but cheap machine. Although that one never
saw the inside of a case."

"How can you know that?"

The craftsman sighed, extended his palm for the gear, then
lifted an instrument like a tiny awl to point to an imperfection in
the gear teeth, a place where whoever filed it had slipped, causing
an irregular spacing. "An incompetent apprentice," the clockmaker
groused.

"And how many incompetent apprentices are there in
Philadelphia?" Duncan asked.

The clockmaker snorted. "In those workrooms making mantel
instruments for the low trade? Probably one in every shop."

"Why mantel clocks?"

"The pendulum meant for this gear is nine inches long." The
man saw the confusion on Duncan's face and gestured for Duncan

to hand over the second gear in his palm. He held up the small one. "The pinion that fits into the wheel has six teeth—" here he set the larger gear against the pinion, meshing the teeth. "The large wheel has seventy-two teeth. That is a combination for the short, fast pendulum of a mantel clock." The man gazed at his candle a moment. "Which gives you perhaps three or four likely candidates, all in the cheaper shops along the waterfront, below Walnut."

"Near the Broken Jug?" Duncan ventured.

"All within a short walk of the old Jug," the clockmaker confirmed, then cocked his head in confusion at Conawago. As they stepped out onto the cobbled street the man was still staring at the miniature cairn of gears Conawago had made on his table, topped with a yellow feather.

They had eliminated one of the likely clock shops and were approaching another when an urchin ran past, calling out details of a new hanging as he hawked a broadside. Shuddering, Duncan saw his friend staring at a large nondescript brick building on the river side of the street. It appeared to have been built as a ship chandler's storehouse, though there were no ships' masters conducting business, no sailors milling about, no heavy wagons, only a single stylish carriage parked near its door.

Without a word Conawago swiftly crossed the street and tried the front door, then began pounding on it when he found it locked. Duncan glanced at the passersby, already casting suspicious glances, then tried to pull his friend away. Instead Conawago set his face against a window and peered inside.

"You forget there are constables!" Duncan warned. They had noted a half dozen of the large men with staffs since leaving the first clockmaker. "If they see you looking into a building they will surely question you!"

Conawago paused, then let Duncan pull him away, across the street in the direction of the next clock shop. But he would not proceed without first stopping to study the two-story building as if interested in its construction. Duncan tried in vain to make sense of his strange actions. Surveying the structure himself, he noticed the strange metal spikes mounted along the roof, the cradles on the sidewalls once used for holding heavy rope, the winch under the eaves for loading cargo through an upper hatch. Conawago touched his arm and pointed to the main entrance of the building.

The frame of the main entrance had been decorated with ornate, abstract patterns of brick after the Dutch fashion, but the pattern on the lintel over the frame suddenly congealed. With purple and white paint someone had carefully depicted figures from a wampum belt, the stick figures of straight Indians and triangular Europeans holding hands in friendship. A peace belt.

As they gazed at the surprising pattern a brilliant flash erupted through the window of the upper floor, as if gunpowder had been ignited. But there was no explosion, only a long moan of pain, loud enough to be heard through the window glass. Duncan grabbed Conawago by the arm and pulled him down the street toward a line of clock shops.

The fifth shop they visited was a rundown establishment nearly in the shadow of the Broken Jug tavern. As they stepped toward the entry Duncan paused to study an establishment across the street. *Coppersmith*, its sign proclaimed, and at the rear was a furnace building for melting the metal, a building where small lumps of molten copper might be found.

Inside the shop, two young men sat at a table indolently work-ing pieces of walnut with small planes, surrounded by chips of wood and several incomplete cabinets for mantel clocks. The older of the pair looked up with a sleepy expression.

"He's out for refreshment," he declared. "Three doors down, at the Jug."

"I have a problem," Duncan said, producing the defective gear.

The apprentice examined the gear only when Duncan pushed it nearly under his nose, then glanced nervously toward the dimly lit room at the rear of the building. "Surely you don't mean to make your own repair," he said with a sneer. "We'll need the entire works."

"The only thing wrong is this gear that was badly cut," Duncan said in a dissatisfied manner. He extended it, pointing to the flaw. All traces of the youth's confident air melted away. He glanced at his companion, who leaned over his work without looking up, and flushed with color. "In the other shops," he complained, "they get special lanterns, even lenses, and fine tools like jewelers use."

Duncan stared at him expectantly.

"He'll have my hide if I take a gear from his good stock."

"Tell me this," Duncan tried. "Do you trade with Shamokin?"

"What, sell clocks to the damned heathens? Not bloody likely." He looked out the window toward the tavern, then watched Conawago for a moment with an uneasy expression. "I can get a new one," he offered. "Just between us, right?"

Duncan's own gaze lingered on the tavern. "How often do you bring your drinking companions back here?"

The silent youth working the wood sprouted a narrow smile.

"It's not allowed."

"But sometimes your master leaves town," Duncan suggested.

"I'll get a new one," the apprentice repeated, and he disappeared into his master's work chamber.

Duncan silently accepted the new gear from the sullen youth and was about to retreat when Conawago stepped to the table.

"That old brick warehouse down the street," he said. "Who occupies it?"

"A lunatic, most say. His calling card says natural philosopher. More like Lucifer, for all his deviling with nature."

A door at the rear of the building suddenly opened and shut. The boy shot up from the table, pushing Duncan and Conawago to the door. "Those who ask too many questions get called to the constable," he warned in parting.

They walked quickly down the street, casting strangely guilty glances back at the shop, drifting with the flow of foot traffic toward a little square where a freestanding plank wall held handbills, newspapers, and notices. Duncan was gazing absently at the bill board, trying to fathom what the Library Company advertised on one sheet might be, when Conawago indicated a recently posted bill at the end of the wall. Thirty pounds sterling, it declared in large type, for the capture of a runaway. Duncan's mouth went bone dry as he read the name. *Duncan McCallum*, it stated, *Scotsman*, followed by an exact description of him and instructions to contact Ramsey House. *Considered violent*, the poster concluded, *Keep under Restraint.*

As the sun was setting they sat in the corner of the Broken Jug picking slowly at miserly portions of cold shepherd's pie, one eye on the stout German proprietor, whose cooperation had been purchased with one of their last coins. He had advised them not to divulge the tract to be surveyed if they were looking to hire someone, only the length of the assignment and the fee to be paid. Retaining a surveyor in Philadelphia had apparently become an affair of intrigue. "If it's too far west," the tavernkeeper added, "they may be asking for guards as well."

The trickle of customers grew into a steady stream as the working day ended. Men with hands stained with ink from printing presses took a corner table with a pitcher of ale. Two customers shook wood shavings out of their hair as they entered, speaking of a shipment of mahogany from the Indies. Duncan found himself filled with a strange longing. It was another world these Philadelphians lived in, a world without murders and bounties and hands nailed to trees.

After an hour, during a lull in the evening's business, the proprietor paused to sit with them.

"What if it *is* Indian country?" Conawago asked abruptly, in his earnest English voice.

The man stared at Conawago intensely, leaning forward as if only now noticing his customer's bronze skin. "Don't advertise it. There's still a war on."

"We heard of a Mr. Townsend."

"Gone these many months. Some say he journeyed to the Carolinas. But he ain't sent for his sister."

"For whom was his last commission?" Duncan inquired.

"Like I said, the land companies are secretive. It's all to do with competition."

"How long after the burning of his house did he go?"

"Stayed around for the hanging of the heathen what done it. Too many drunken savages allowed on the streets, if ye ask me."

"Were you there?" Duncan asked. "At the hanging?"

The proprietor nodded, seeming to take pleasure in the turn of conversation. "A great crowd turned out. They started gathering at dawn for the best seats, even with hours to wait. I sold two barrels' worth and cursed myself for not bringing two more."

Duncan stared at the man, trying to control his emotion. "You sold ale at a hanging?"

Their host stood and wiped the table with a rag. "A city tradition. Hangings be as good as a king's holiday. Stalls with ale and
little cakes. Boys blowing pennywhistles. Eggs by the dozen."

"Eggs?" Duncan asked.

"To throw, ye fool. Funny thing, when it started the only one
to try to stop it was Townsend himself. He got as many yolks on
him as the damned savage. Out of his mind over the loss of his
home, folks said."

Over the next hour the tavern nearly filled. Duncan studied
each newcomer, increasingly certain he had found the place where
the dead surveyors had been hired, though not sure if he was any
closer to knowing who had hired them. Several men came in and
sat alone, nursing tankards of ale, some reading news journals.
One played with a writing lead on his tabletop. Several others
congregated at the opposite side, aiming small throwing knives at
splintered planks painted with bears and wildcats, two men in tri-
corns performed a balancing act with a ball on the side of their feet,
passing it to each other as they hopped around the tables.

Duncan found his gaze drifting toward the half-walled corner
from which the landlord dispensed his drinks. Above his head a
stuffed crow presided over the chamber, sitting on a shelf where
other oddments had been arrayed. A tall angular hat, in the style
of another century, that could have been worn by old Penn himself. A wooden shoe. A portrait painted on a board, of a bewigged
aristocrat whose bulging blue eyes and large nose identified him
as King George the Second. He glanced back at the men amusing
themselves with the ball, taking dares and bets now over their performance. Their antics had the flavor of a lacrosse game.

The solitary man with the writing lead gazed in drunken
puzzlement at the stuffed crow, as if perhaps he had seen it move.

He ran his fingers through his long hair, then looked back uneasily at the bird. With a nudge from Conawago, Duncan regarded him more closely. His ear had been cut off.

"They say," Duncan declared as he slipped into a chair beside the man, "that ours is a new fraternity of mercenaries."

The man turned with a dull, resentful look, then Duncan lifted the hair at his temple to expose the long, ragged scar along his scalp.

"God's breath!" the man gasped, jerking Duncan's hand down. "Have you no sense! The mark of the savage is like the mark of the devil to these city folk."

"Then you are not of the city?"

The man answered cautiously, all signs of drunkenness gone. "Bethlehem, in the north."

Duncan knew it only by reputation. "The Moravian town?"

"*Ja.* But here I take my education," the stranger offered in a hollow voice.

"As a surveyor?"

The man nodded. "I am an excellent surveyor. Though I fear I lost my equipment in the wilds."

"Along with your ear?"

The German winked. "I expect it's now being worn on some savage's necklace. My father declared it was a sign I should return to mission work. Missionaries be protected by God."

"I hear surveyors are needed for the Virginian claim in the west."

"I hear," the man shot back, "they require as many grave diggers as surveyors." He accepted an apple from a servant girl who wandered among the patrons with a basket of the fruit. Duncan sipped from his tankard as the man unfolded a pocketknife and cut the fruit into wedges.

"Suppose a man were desperate enough," Duncan said. "Who would he see?"

The Moravian pushed an apple slice toward Duncan and ate one himself as he studied the crowd. "There is a tobacco merchant who sells Virginia leaf and pipes to smoke it, a Potomac man."

"How many has he hired?"

"Half a dozen perhaps."

Were there men still out there, Duncan wondered, unknowingly proceeding toward their deaths? "How long since—" his words died in his throat. The men playing with the ball had stopped, had taken off their hats, and were standing at the corner counter where drinks were dispensed. A familiar figure stood at the front of the group, staring directly at Duncan now. The notices declaring a bounty on Duncan would be meaningless to the residents of the city since they would not know Duncan's appearance. But Samuel Felton, the magistrate's nephew, knew his face. One word from Felton and every man in the room would turn on Duncan.

The lanky Quaker caught the eye of first one, then another of his group, both broad-shouldered beefy men with the sunburned faces of those who worked the river boats. Conawago was on his feet now, his hand instinctively going to his belt, where his war ax usually hung. But they had left their weapons at the stable. They had no weapons, only the barest acquaintance with the alleys and streets outside the door. Eyes began drifting toward Conawago, who had lifted a heavy stick from the hearth, bracing for a fight.

Suddenly the door of the inn burst open and a dark-hooded figure appeared silhouetted by the light of the street lanterns behind him. A murmur of recognition rippled through several of those present, and they began to back away as the cloaked man, carrying a large wooden box, took several steps inside. The shapeless garment he wore extended nearly to the floor, its hood obscuring his face.

"Ave caesar! Morituri te salutamus!" the mysterious figure called in a ragged voice. Impossibly, he was speaking Latin. *"Ecce ignis! Ecce ignis!"* he repeated. Duncan stood, inching toward the door as he watched not the stranger but the crowd, frantically trying to see where Felton had gone. He looked back at the intruder in confusion. *Hail Caesar,* he had called in Latin, *we who are about to die salute you,* the call of the gladiators, then *behold the fire.* The men who had backed away had stopped as if they sought only a safe distance. The proprietor watched from his corner with an expectant, almost amused expression.

The same Latin words were repeated, rising in volume to a crescendo. A drunk at a table near the front threw a heel of bread. With a quick, deft motion, the stranger opened the hinged lid of his box, produced something like a wand with a metal ball at the end, and aimed it at the drunkard, extending it to within inches of the man's face.

A bolt of lightning leapt out and struck the offender's nose.

The room erupted into chaos. The man who had been struck screamed, tumbled off his chair, and crawled under the table, whining in terror. His companions leapt up and fled to the far side of the room. Except for Conawago and Duncan, the half of the room nearest the door was emptied. The stranger turned his contraption toward Duncan for a moment, muttering, *"Apage!"* with a short, quick gesture toward the street before stepping closer to the crowd. *Begone!* Several onlookers began crossing themselves, one even lifted a cross from his neck and extended it in front of him.

"Tanta stultitia mortalium est!" the cloaked figure cried, making a jerking motion toward another drunkard, who promptly fainted. *What fools these mortals be.* One fearful spectator swung a

poker from the fireplace at the stranger, who aimed another bolt of lightning at him. The lightning hit the iron poker, and the man yelped in pain, dropping it to the floor. From the rear came hoots of amusement, from those closer more fearful prayers.

Duncan turned and darted out the door.

Chapter Twelve

*H*E DID NOT know what direction he took through the darkened streets, did not care, only became aware of Conawago passing him. Minutes later they stopped, gasping, the river wharves with their ranks of ships looming on one side, a hulking building on the other, with a row of low wooden structures like cages along its rear wall.

"Where are you—" Duncan began as Conawago tested the latch on the building's back entry. A snarl erupted from one of the cages.

His friend cut him off with an upraised hand as the door opened under his touch. "Let us not disturb the neighborhood when safety is so near at hand," he warned, and he stepped inside.

Where they were, he now realized, was the warehouse with the Iroquois markings on the front door.

They moved through a large chamber that seemed part kitchen, part workshop, into a hallway that connected the front and rear of the building, then settled onto the floor near a patch of moonlight. His eyes shifting from the rear door to the front entry, just visible beyond the shadows, Duncan relayed his conversation with the

Moravian surveyor in the tavern. As he finished, the latch of the front door rattled. A solitary man entered, laughing to himself, whimsically reciting the Latin words Duncan had heard in the tavern as he set a large box on the table by the entry.

They warily rose, retreating back into the shadows as the stranger lit a candle before stepping into the hallway. Duncan touched the knife he kept at his waist, his only weapon.

The stranger did not seem surprised to see them. "Excellent!" he exclaimed. *"Veni vidi vici!"* he concluded cheerfully. "They know not what a gift it is," he added as he pushed back the hood of his cloak, "to have the channels of their brains reenergized." He handed the candlestick to Conawago, leading them to a door in the middle of the hall before gesturing them to wait as he trotted to lock the rear door. Lighting a second candle from the first, he opened the door and led them up a steep, winding staircase that took them into a spacious chamber, where their host began lighting several oil lamps.

"Dr. Henry Marston," he announced with outstretched hand.

Duncan did not immediately respond. He gazed in confusion at one of the oddest chambers he had ever seen. The long troughs, designed for feeding livestock, that lined the two sidewalls were filled with salt. In the center of the room was a large, bizarre device of wood and glass. Along the front wall, behind a heavy wooden chair whose arms held straps for restraining its occupant, was a long table on which sat several large glass jars pierced through the top by metal rods. What appeared to be a brass ball hovering over their heads proved on closer examination to be connected to a long brass rod extending up through the ceiling. Duncan recalled the metal spears on the roof. On two smaller tables were an array of glass containers, strips of metal, and discs of what appeared to be hardened tree resin.

The worried query on Conawago's lips suddenly transformed into wonder. "Electrical flux!" he exclaimed. Vigorously he shook Marston's hand, then introduced himself and Duncan.

Marston beamed. "All creation can be reduced to the four main elements of earth, fire, water, and air." He finally removed his cloak as he spoke, revealing himself to be a slight, bespectacled man in his forties. "But it is electrical fluid that binds them all, the great common essence. We have wrung it out of the air to create fire, captured it in the water of the Leyden jars," he said, pointing to the glass containers on the table, "and used it to reduce any number of minerals to their base earth. We shall one day change the world with it!"

"We?" Duncan asked in a stunned voice.

"Dr. Franklin and I. Of course there are other practitioners today, but I was there in fifty-two to help launch his kite that first wonderful night when we captured the power of the storm in a jar. Such a spectacle! Newton had his apple, Archimedes his bath, Dr. Franklin his kite! When he returns from England I shall require days just to demonstrate the advances I have made since his departure!"

Conawago stepped to the strange device in the center of the room, nearly six feet long and almost as high. The near end was a tower of two wooden pillars between which a glass globe nearly twelve inches in diameter was suspended on wooden spindles. At the far end was a large ornate wooden wheel mounted between two short posts, with a leather belt wrapped around its rim connected to one of the spindles of the globe. "A variation on Nollet," Marston announced, as though they would surely recognize the name.

Conawago touched the handle extending from the center of the wheel and looked up at their host. It was all the invitation Marston needed. He would not be drawn into answering Duncan's questions until he had shared his thrilling advances with them.

"This afternoon," Duncan said as Marston showed Conawago how to turn the handle to spin the globe, "we saw flashes of light coming from here."

"Which is when I noticed you approach the building and study the lintel. I saw instantly that you recognized my signs. As you left I saw your friend's hidden braid and his bronze skin. I would have come immediately had I not been with a patient."

Duncan was more confused than ever. "You practice medical science as well?"

Marston lowered a finger to within an inch of the glass globe. "Here," he explained proudly as a spark leapt up to his finger, "is the primogenitor of all future science. Dr. Franklin and I began treating paralysis years ago with electrical fluids. Patients come now with toothaches, the cramp, sciatica. We have even seen some success with deafness."

The scientist gestured Duncan toward the table, took his arm, and extended his open hand over one of the glass containers. "A Leyden jar, with only a small charge left," he explained, and as he slowly lowered Duncan's hand toward the brass ball extending from the jar a small sparking arc leapt up and connected with his fingertip. He jerked his hand back in alarm. For an instant he had felt a burning sensation, but quickly confirmed there was no damage to his hand.

"Tonight at the tavern," Duncan said as he rubbed his hand, wondering at the tingling sensation that lingered in it, "you were not coming for a patient." He looked inside an empty jar. It held a small brass chain resting on the bottom, the top end brought up through a large cork stopper, then wrapped around a rod terminating in a ball. "But for us."

"I was walking along the river and saw you enter."

"But you could not have known we were in danger."

"As the night wore on there would be those who would recognize Mr. Conawago's features, trust me." As he spoke Marston
gestured them through a side door, into a pleasant parlor that overlooked the street. "More than a few who frequent the Broken Jug
have been set upon by Indians in the wilds. And red men arrayed in
European clothes have not always been friends of our city."

Duncan studied the eccentric scientist as Marston lit several
lamps. "We have heard of the great festival when the last Indian
was hanged," he declared.

The words seemed to shake Marston. He turned toward the
window to gaze into the night.

"You were the one making spirit fire at Shamokin," Duncan
ventured.

"That was never a term I used."

"Why would you go two hundred miles to conduct your
experiments?"

"My partner believed it would be a valuable way to learn about
the upcountry. Our new upcountry."

"Your country?" Duncan asked.

Marston turned with a troubled expression on his face. "We
had an alliance, the two of us. He would stake out new claims for
our land company, sell half of them in Philadelphia, then use the
proceeds to build there. I would have an edifice dedicated to my
science, a temple of learning in the wilderness."

Duncan stared at the man uneasily, wondering now if they had
been lured into a trap. "Does your partner have a name?"

"Francis Townsend, of course."

Duncan looked at the man in disbelief. Surely the coincidence
was too much. "You and Townsend had a land company?"

Marston shrugged. "Many a new land company gets formed
over cups in Philadelphia taverns. Most don't endure past the

last round of rum punch, the others usually last a few months at most. The Dutch had their tulip craze, London had the South Sea bubble," he added, referring to two well-known financial disasters in Europe, "Philadelphia has its land companies."

Marston's voice grew distant for a moment. "Yet our bubble too was burst." He sighed heavily. "I used what was left of my inheritance to pay our expenses. Francis, ever the adventurer, went on into the mountains, looking for likely tracts, seeking minerals that might have value. I stayed in Shamokin with my projects."

"Projects?"

"There is much important work to be done. I correspond with Dr. Franklin. He and I agreed on a course of research to penetrate the mysteries of negative and positive particles and the role of electrical fluid in the human body. There are reports from France of the dead being revived with doses of flux. But," Marston added, "not all the city fathers share our enthusiasm."

From behind them Duncan heard a sharp intake of breath. "God's teeth!" Conawago exclaimed, "you were using Indians for your medical dogs!"

Marston stepped to a wingback chair and collapsed into it. "We forced no one. They were always compensated."

"What exactly," Duncan asked in a brittle voice, "did you do?"

"Flew some kites with wires into jars of brass dust. Charted individual tolerances to negative and positive flows. Energized open wounds. There were some possums brought back to life, a lot of frogs." The scientist looked up. "Dr. Franklin killed a turkey once with a flux machine," he added earnestly, though Duncan was at a loss as to whether this was an apology or a justification.

"Then why leave a proving ground as fertile as Shamokin?" Conawago wanted to know.

"I was going to stay until Townsend came back from the mountains. There was a man called the French bear. He had a lot of influence with some of the chiefs. I explained the French were in competition with us English for advancement in the sciences, and that it was their duty to help their English allies. But he told them I was experimenting with ways to extract the spirits from Indians."

Duncan lifted a candle in a pewter holder and explored the shadows of the parlor. Scattered about tables and chests were more Leyden jars. On a work table near the window were pieces of cork being carved into oval shapes, beside a spool of silk thread, with four completed spiders identical to the one Johantty treasured. In the winter, the youth had said, he could make the spiders dance.

"Testaments to our science," Marston explained. "Teaching instruments I give to the uninitiated." He saw Duncan's confusion and gestured to the adjoining table. "The largest jar still has a charge."

Still uncertain, Duncan lifted one of the cork spiders by the thread glued to its back and held it over the brass rod extending from the jar. The legs began to move as they approached the jar, jerking up and down when he placed it directly over the rod.

"When it is cold and dry you can rub fur or wool together to much the same effect," Marston said.

Duncan stared at the little spider in fascination, moving it in and out of the invisible flux field. But as he did so a vision of Johantty sprang into his mind, Johantty somberly, desperately, playing his graveside drum, followed by an image of Stone Blossom weeping over her ruined island shrine.

He lowered the spider and took a seat in a chair beside Marston. "Did you first meet Skanawati at his village or at Shamokin?"

Marston's head jerked up, and he stared suspiciously at Duncan. "Who are you?"

"Friends of the Iroquois. They have too few in Philadelphia."

Marston pursed his lips, then slowly nodded. "I met him at Shamokin." His voice trembled as the scientist spoke of the Onondaga chieftain. "He was fascinated by my work, brought several of his clan to watch. He beseeched me to return with my equipment to his village."

"Did you?"

"It was full of smallpox," Marston explained. "He thought if I ran electrical charges through the infected it might help them. I knew there was no hope, but I couldn't say no. He wanted to pay me in furs, but I refused. They all had such desperate hope in their faces when I touched them with my jars. Beautiful children. Old men and women, even some warriors built like bulls who had lost all their strength. Eight out of ten weren't going to survive the week. I didn't argue any more with the French bear. Not long after, I packed up my equipment and came home."

"But Skanawati knew how to find you."

"I gave him a piece of paper with my address on it, then placed the Iroquois signs on my door. His people moved me. I had seen too many Indian drunks and beggars on our streets. The city becomes like a trap to them. The missionaries fill them with grand ideas about the equality of all men, the tavernkeepers fill them with rum. Some are kept at the alehouses to perform tricks like tamed bears, throwing tomahawks, shooting arrows and such. Most die of drink, or of some European disease. I wanted to do what I could. . . . "

Townsend and Marston, in their own peculiar way, had been friends of the Iroquois, Duncan realized. It was perhaps not so great a coincidence that Townsend's partner had appeared at the Broken Jug tavern, for that was where the two had met in the first place, nor too great a coincidence that Marston had recognized Conawago and gone to help him.

As his guests digested his troubling words Marston seemed to reflect on Duncan, his brow knitting. "At the tavern, McCallum, it wasn't Conawago who seemed to be in danger, but you."

"There is a gentleman now residing here who seems to think I am in bond to him. A man who knows my face was unexpectedly in the tavern tonight."

Marston frowned. "The law is not sympathetic to those who flee from indenture."

"The bond was transferred to his daughter. She takes a liberal view of my obligation. But he has sworn otherwise in an affidavit. He is a vindictive man, and I caused him much shame last year."

"Might I know his name?"

"Ramsey."

Marston's jaw dropped. "Bestowed with the title of Lord? Cousin to the king?"

"A distant cousin."

The scientist sagged. "You pick your enemies well. Since he arrived last year Ramsey has bought his way onto the council of the city, has the governor's ear. His house is like a palace, he is one of Philadelphia's self-declared royalty. If he knows you are in the city he will have men on every street."

"We will flee soon," Conawago said. "We only seek a Shawnee named Red Hand here."

Marston shook his head. "As I said, the Indians come and go. And when in the city most stay in the shadows."

"We can linger but a day," Conawago cast an apologetic glance toward Duncan. "Our real business waits in Lancaster."

Marston cocked his head. "Lancaster?"

"The treaty conference. Where Skanawati awaits trial. We mean to keep the rope from his neck."

Marston's face darkened with the news. He opened his mouth several times but seemed unable to find words. Finally he rose, pulled a news journal from a table under the window, and dropped it onto Duncan's lap. It was an edition of the *Pennsylvania Gazette*, dated the day before. The first page was nearly filled with notices of ships arriving and departing, listing their cargos and ports of call. There was only one headline. *Treaty Conference Adjourned to Philadelphia for Hanging of Iroquois Murderer.*

When he spoke, Marston's voice was tight with emotion. "He dies as soon as a Philadelphia judge hears the evidence and confirms the sentence. A formality. He has two, maybe three days."

Duncan stared numbly at the paper and did not see Marston leave, only saw him return, carrying glasses and a bottle, which he wordlessly uncorked. "Let us have full explanations, all around," Marston offered solemnly as he poured out the claret.

Duncan and Conawago told their story first, starting with their discovery of Captain Burke and proceeding through their tour that afternoon of watchmakers, interrupted only by the appearance of a serving woman in a dark blue dress and apron who left a tray of ham and bread. As he listened Marston ate, then cleaned his spectacles on a napkin, looking up with a worried expression as they finished.

"The governor of the province had demanded a treaty," he observed, "and convinced the general that the success of the British military in the north would be meaningless without a settlement of the many issues around the western lands. When Magistrate Brindle reported that the Indian delegations threatened to decamp over the imprisonment of Skanawati, the governor then invited all the delegations to Philadelphia. There he could personally court the Indians, attempting to repair the damage they say Brindle has done. The governor this very night has hosted a dinner for the chiefs in the state house. But the Virginians worry him as much as the tribes. They still thirst for vengeance."

"The governor understands the tribes. Surely he will arrange for appropriate condolences for Skanawati to be freed," Conawago said.

"And break with the Virginians? It will be a hollow accord indeed if that is the price. As bad as that Virginia land company may be, they are private owners. If they do not succeed, the Virginian governor will press official claims, in the name of the crown colony. Do not forget Pennsylvania is but a proprietary colony, while Virginia is held in the name of the king."

Duncan pushed down his bile. He was well-acquainted with the way men's lives could be ruined when those in power invoked distant kings and proprietors. "Magistrate Brindle is a reasonable man," he offered. "If only I could speak with him."

"It is all out of his hands now. And were he to be seen speaking with you, a fugitive from justice, his own office would be jeopardized. He may be an honored judge, but Ramsey is on the council that reigns over Philadelphia and has the governor over to dine frequently."

"Operating in the shadows, you mean, like the Indians," Duncan shot back.

Marston sipped at his claret. "You speak of codes on trees," he said with the scientist's curiosity. "Tell me of them." He listened in rapt attention to Duncan's description, then brightened. "The pigpen code!" he exclaimed. "Boxes and three-sided squares? Open triangles and dots?"

Duncan leaned forward excitedly. "You know it?"

Marston's enthusiasm ebbed. "Know of it. Called the pigpen because it is a matrix onto which the alphabet is overlaid, like a mass of pens, some enclosing empty spaces, some dots. But I don't know the arrangement, nor the details of the code."

Duncan sighed with disappointment. "But in Philadelphia there are people who know such codes, other learned men?"

"Assuredly. But their codes are secret, and a man's use of such codes always so as well."

The pigpen. It aptly described the morass of clues in front of Duncan.

As Duncan now lifted the carving knife and a fork to work on the ham, Marston watched with interest. "You cut with the precision of a surgeon."

"I completed three years of my medical studies at Edinburgh."

"Edinburgh! Why, it is the capital of all medical science! This is destiny!" Marston exclaimed. "You can assist me. I need—"

"The treaty," Duncan reminded him.

"Forgive me," their host apologized. "Where was I? . . . The governor assumes that eventually the Grand Council of the Six Nations will come around to the compromise since they will be shamed if they go home without his bounty."

"Compromise?"

"It has been the talk of my friends' dining tables ever since we heard of the convoy reaching Lancaster. Virginia receives no land but has its revenge by the hanging. The Iroquois avoid having the covenant chain broken by agreeing that the crime was the work of one man, not an act of war. Pennsylvania maintains the peace, getting all to agree the killings were contrived by the French, emphasizing the need for us all to stay together in common cause. And confirming need for troops at Fort Pitt. That," Marston said with a bitter flourish, "is the stuff of statecraft. It is how we deal with friends of the French."

The words brought an unexpected sound from the shadows, a choked-off sob. The maid had lingered in the hallway.

"Catherine!" Marston gasped. "I meant no—" He fumbled with his words, then gestured the woman forward. She was a plain, sturdy woman in her thirties, her careworn face averted as she inched into the room.

"Do you require anything further, sirs?" she asked in a brittle voice. "Some more claret perhaps?"

She was, Duncan realized, trying desperately to control her emotions. He looked in confusion at Marston, understanding neither what had aggrieved the woman nor what caused the scientist's discomfort.

"What I would like most of all," Duncan ventured, "is to ask if you are acquainted with other serving women in the city. I am looking for an unmarried woman, the sister of Mr. Townsend."

Catherine burst into tears. "I believe, Duncan," Conawago said as he guided her to a chair, "that we have found her."

Duncan flushed with embarrassment. He should have known. Marston had taken in his partner's sister when Townsend was lost.

"As Catherine steadfastly reminds me," Marston said, "there is no proof certain that her good brother is dead."

Duncan sighed and looked away for a moment, dreading the pain of the words he had to say. "Your brother had an elegant wooden box, with a clever sliding lid and an inlaid pattern of diamonds on the front."

"I gave it to him when he finished his schooling!" Miss Townsend exclaimed.

"I have that box in my pack. It was returned to me by some Iroquois. With tribal markings scratched on the cover."

The woman quickly turned away. She brought her apron to her face.

"No one has produced his body," Marston asserted.

"I fear the wilderness swallows up bodies," Conawago observed.

The woman, Duncan reminded himself, had first reacted not when Duncan had mentioned her brother but when Marston had mentioned the French. "Many good souls have fallen in the western country these past months," Duncan said. "Captain Burke. A surveyor named Cooper and his Indian wife. Mr. Bythe."

At the mention of the Quaker's name the woman's grief disappeared. "The devil collected that one at last," she spat, and for the first time Duncan heard a hint of Irish in her voice.

"Bythe had been investigating secret French involvement in the killings," Duncan told her.

"A pox on him! My brother was no traitor! He was a leader of men, hired to assure the others it was safe and honest work. He was only being a good Christian when he helped the others get hired."

Marston handed the woman a glass of wine.

Duncan lifted one of the ladder-back chairs and sat close to her. "Mr. Bythe," he explained, "has suffered the same fate as Captain Burke. Those particular bodies I have seen. What exactly was Mr. Bythe suggesting?" Duncan asked.

The reluctant answer came from Marston. "When surveyors began disappearing there was a meeting called by Justice Brindle. It was just the war, he told us, the price we all pay when kings feud. We should just stay away from the frontier until the hostilities end, he warned. But someone asked how Philadelphia surveyors were marked for death by the French, how the French could know them all. It was as if half a dozen particular birds had been scattered across the wide wilderness, someone said, yet each one found and dropped by the French. The meeting grew unruly. Men started shouting that the French were being told, the surveyors were being betrayed.

"Some trader pointed out that the French could slip in and out of Shamokin with impunity. A trapper pointed out that Townsend had been moving in and out of Shamokin, that he was the very one to have arranged for the first surveyors to venture west, the only one to know them all."

"Simpletons!" Miss Townsend cried. "Francis never so much as whispered against the king!"

Marston, in obvious discomfort now, quickly finished his tale. "Bythe's appointment to the trading post at Fort Pitt allowed him to investigate. Some say it was why he was given the appointment in the first place. He held rank as a militia officer, took out militia patrols sometimes hoping to capture the raiders who worked with his suspected spy, make one talk. There were reports, even in the *Gazette*, of runaway slaves carrying messages for the French. A clever ploy, that. A runaway would already have great incentive to avoid notice. Bounty men from Virginia are known to keep watch even in Shamokin sometimes."

"Would your brother have reason to speak with such runaways?" Conawago asked.

The woman shook her head from side to side.

"Then tell me something else," Conawago continued. "Your brother arranged for other surveyors. But who arranged for him?"

"There's a Virginia merchant," Marston said. "He runs tobacco and timber ships up Delaware Bay."

Marston had not answered the question. "Did he hire your brother, Miss Townsend?" Duncan pressed.

"Not that merchant. He but takes messages. All of the surveyors were hired directly by the company, by one of the gentlemen directly," she replied. "He even invited us to dine at his booth in the City Tavern. Francis was the key. He knew the wilderness, had just come back from it, told everyone how safe it was, how the Iroquois had behaved like perfect gentlemen, how our burned house was a different matter altogether. Francis was hesitating at leaving us so soon after his return, but we had lost the house, and the gentleman said he would publish one of his works on American birds after the survey was complete."

"Which gentleman?"

"An owner of the Monongahela Company, the Virginia land venture. Winston Burke. After my brother agreed, they sat together to interview the others. A young man from Connecticut. A Dutchman with two watches. One or two others."

Duncan stared at the woman, then stepped to the tray, poured himself another glass of claret, and drained it. He wasn't fitting pieces of the puzzle together, he was simply finding more impossible pieces.

"There is a small band of tribesmen," Conawago inserted after a heavy silence. "Banded together to no good purpose. Where would such men shelter in the city?"

Marston shrugged. "The ones on respectable business visit me or stay at a government house. The others could be anywhere."

"I have heard of places," Miss Townsend put in. "Especially one. Most unsavory. I heard a gentleman say it was a blight, as bad as an opium den in London, but he was grateful to have a den that drew the drunken savages from our streets."

"You know this place, Catherine?" Marston registered disbelief.

The woman seemed to summon up her dignity. "Acting as a housekeeper puts me in the market with many serving types. Tongues can wag."

"And this is a place where a fugitive might shelter? Do you hear of specific warriors? Red Hand? Ohio George?" Duncan asked.

Her eyes now grew wide. "Ohio George? You seek Ohio George?"

"Surely you did not know the man?"

"There was an entertainment staged months ago. Real warriors demonstrating their savage ways, war whoops, arrow shooting, dancing about a fire in a big iron pot," Miss Townsend blushed. "Some of the ones who spoke English told of attacks on other tribes. This Ohio George told of fighting fifty Hurons, of being captured and taken to a great western ocean where he fought terrible sea monsters. He pranced back and forth in his nakedness, with naught but a cloth over his loins!"

All of which meant that Ohio George had made himself known in Philadelphia as a violent, English-speaking Iroquois, one not above engaging in deception if it put money in his pocket.

"This place," Duncan asked, "the lair of the tribal castaways, can you tell us where it is?"

"A great barn in the fields above the northern docks, used for a dairy herd before they were moved farther from the city."

"You're not going into that nest!" Conawago protested. "If they wanted you dead in Shamokin they have even more reason now."

"Red Hand has all the answers," Duncan shot back. "I will not be a coward with Skanawati about to be hanged. We will return to the stable for our weapons. The night is yet young."

After a moment Conawago spoke in a slower, more contemplative voice. He looked with new query at Marston. "No. We need no weapon if our shield is strong enough."

Chapter Thirteen

THE CONSTABLES WOULD not be looking for a family strolling back from an evening engagement, so Marston and Catherine Townsend had put on more elegant attire to join them as they walked along the Market Street cobblestones. With a tricorn hat and full waistcoat borrowed from Marston, Duncan played his part, even responding to Marston's banter about the celebrated Dr. Franklin as they passed the compact, comfortable-looking house where the great man lived when in Philadelphia. As they approached the brick wall that surrounded the large structure that was their destination, Conawago slipped into the shadows and shed his waistcoat, letting his braids down over his shoulder, affixing a feather to one of them, even lifting his ever-present amulet from underneath his shirt. By the time they reached the squad of militia that sleepily guarded the gate, Marston and Miss Townsend had faded into the shadows and Conawago and Duncan were engaged in a lively, loud discussion in the Iroquois tongue.

"Have we seen you in the treaty delegation?" inquired the soldier who appeared to be in command. He lifted his musket across his chest and blocked the gate.

"God's blood, corporal," another guard guffawed, "they all look the same to me."

Conawago shot back an impatient torrent in Iroquois words, using Brindle's name twice.

"You're no red man, sir," the corporal pressed Duncan.

"The tribal delegation is permitted advisers, corporal," Duncan replied in an impatient tone. "It would be indeed unfortunate if we had to summon Magistrate Brindle."

The soldier hesitated, then stepped aside.

The government house that had been set aside for the tribal delegation was a commodious two-story brick house, sparsely furnished but large enough to accommodate a dozen visitors. Conawago seemed to know his way around the building, leading Duncan straight through a large sitting room, then a dining room, and through a kitchen where four members of the house staff sat playing whist in a candlelit corner. They looked up but said nothing as Conawago led Duncan out the rear door.

As Duncan should have guessed, the Indians had no use for the house. Blanket canopies had been erected against the brick wall of the rear courtyard, under which several mattresses had been dragged from the house, most of them occupied by sleeping members of the delegation. But those they sought were awake and sitting at a fire that had been lit in the center of the kitchen garden.

Duncan waited as Conawago approached the chiefs and spoke in low, respectful tones. After several minutes Old Belt himself turned and gestured Duncan into their circle. He lowered himself onto a fragrant bed of sprouting chamomile and listened as Conawago completed the traditional exchange between travelers meeting after a long journey. Duncan studied the revered tribal leaders, saw that new lines of worry had been etched into their faces. At last Old Belt sighed. He raised an intricately carved red stone pipe, filled it from a pouch, then lifted an ember with two green sticks to light the tobacco. He drew deeply, letting the aromatic smoke waft over the little circle, before extending the pipe to Duncan.

"*Denighroghkwayen*," he offered in solemn invitation. *Let us smoke together.*

"You have made hard travel since last we met," Old Belt said when the pipe had been shared by all in the circle.

"There is a great deal to learn and little time to do it," Duncan replied.

"You worry much about people who have been summoned by the spirits," Long Wolf broke in. It was, Duncan knew, his way of reminding the Scotsman that questioning deaths was little different than questioning the gods.

"In my clan," Duncan said after taking another draught of the pipe, "my sisters, my brother, my mother, in all over fifty children and helpless women, were killed by the bullets and blades of my people's enemy. They were not invited by the spirits to cross over, they were shoved into the next life without preparation, by men with evil in their hearts. Because no one stood up to stop that evil my people were destroyed. Ever since, when evil crosses my path, I resist. The spirits of my people require me to do so."

Long Wolf seemed to consider his words, then offered a slow, approving nod.

"That is a heavy burden," Old Belt observed.

Duncan looked up at the stars before replying. "It is heavier some times than others," was all he could say.

"Is it true," Old Belt asked after a long puff on the pipe, "that Stone Blossom took you to the sacred island?"

"It is true."

Long Wolf reached into a pouch and solemnly laid a short belt of white beads over Duncan's wrist. "We are willing to hear what you would speak about your journey."

Duncan rested his arm on his knee and extended his wrist so that the belt was plainly visible to all. It seemed to glow in the moonlight. With the wampum on his arm he could not tell a lie.

"I have looked into the crack in the world," he began, "and I have followed the trail of blood that flows from it."

More than an hour passed as Duncan and Conawago explained what they had found in the north. They answered the chiefs' many questions, listening as Conawago asked them, too, of their own progress, listening to the account of great disruption as the delegation made camp at the army barracks in Lancaster only to break it a day later when summoned by the governor to Philadelphia. When some of the tribal delegation had complained about Skanawati's imprisonment, the Virginians had appeased them with demijohns of rum. Old Belt had ordered the drunken Indians home.

There was no hesitation when Duncan explained what he needed. They left the compound with Old Belt and four of his Iroquois guards, attired and equipped as if for a predawn raid.

The huge stone-and-timber barn had once been a magnificent structure but was now in disrepair. There were still horses, but the odor from the pile of manure in the corner of the paddock made it clear that most of the barn's occupants were human. Through the open entry way wafted the smoke of cheap tobacco, snippets of bawdy ballads in English, and slurred, drunken shouts in more than one tribal language. In the stall nearest the entry six men, four Indians and two Europeans, sat on bundles of hay covered with flour sacks, playing cards on a plank. One of the Europeans stood up, swaying as he stepped toward them.

"Rum in the next bay, y'er honors," he declared in a Welsh accent. "If ye got the coin, it's by the mug or by the jug," he added with a guffaw at his own wit.

Old Belt whispered to his escort, and two of the men took up station at the entry. The drunken Welshman seemed about to protest but halted as he looked at the axes on the warrior's belts and hastily retreated to his game. One of the two remaining escorts lifted a dim lantern from a peg and led Old Belt, Conawago, and Duncan down the central bay of the barn. The warriors knew Red Hand by sight, Old Belt had explained, so Duncan did not interfere as the two Iroquois led the search of the musty stalls. In the first, half a dozen Indians lay in drunken stupor on piles of straw. The next was much the same, though two Europeans in tattered, soiled clothes were present as well, one of them performing an unsteady drunken jig to earn a swig of an Indian's jug. In the third an angry warning snapped out, and a naked Indian woman threw a man's shoe from her pallet as she covered the head of the European beside her with a blanket, leaving the rest of his chalky nakedness for all to see.

The heads of two horses extended from the half wall of the last stall, and from the low moans arising from the stall before it Duncan expected to see more rum drinkers. But at the sight of the forlorn shapes in the straw he rushed forward. Three Indian women and three children lay in the dim light. One woman propped against the wall was in the discomfort of pregnancy, but she watched them silently, making no complaint. Another was clearly stricken with fever, lying between two children who held her hands, trying to console her. The third cradled a boy of four or five in her arms, rocking him back and forth, trying to make him forget his obvious pain. Duncan knelt first by the fevered woman, gesturing for the lantern to be held closer, taking her pulse, lifting an eyelid, laying a hand on her forehead, then stroking it as her body was wracked with violent shivering.

"Hold there!" boomed an angry voice. "No one be touching the squaws but if I—" The stout, heavily whiskered man who stormed into the stall hesitated as he saw Old Belt. "This be private property," he said more tentatively. "No one—" his protest completely died away as the two braves stepped from the shadows. These were not the city Indians, weakened from drink and sickness, that he was accustomed to, but towering warriors of the wilds, in their prime. One of the Iroquois slipped behind him, blocking the door.

"T'ain't no public thoroughfare is all," the man muttered.

Duncan fought the impulse to strike him. "You will get fresh water for these people, now! Then fresh straw."

"Ye have no right."

"Now!" Duncan repeated. Conawago quickly gave instructions to one of the braves to escort the barn's proprietor, who lost all color when he saw the warrior remove the war ax from his belt. He nodded and backed away.

"She has malaria," Duncan explained. "Shivering fever. With Peruvian bark we can cure the symptoms." He turned to Old Belt. "Magistrate Brindle would no doubt be responsive if you requested a physician to bring some tomorrow." The Iroquois chief nodded his agreement. "Ask him for a large supply. She needs to be out of here, back in the Iroquois towns, where she can be cared for away from the miasmas of the city."

The woman with the boy was reluctant to let Duncan touch her son until Old Belt stepped closer. She uttered an exclamation of awed surprise, obviously recognizing the great chief, then nodded to Duncan. Instantly he saw that the boy had a broken arm, the

skin an ugly mass of green and blue from coagulated blood, one end
of the bone protruding into the muscle.

Conawago spoke with the woman in a comforting voice, then
explained to his companions. "The boy was carrying food up the
ladder when he fell. She fears he will never be whole again. In the
village of her youth a boy who could not shoot a bow was considered worthless, abandoned by his people."

"He will shoot a bow again," Duncan promised, then spoke to
Conawago. "I need some of the broken harness I saw hanging on
the wall, two small planks, and some of the flour sacking from the
first stall."

By the time Conawago returned Duncan had the boy stretched
out on the straw, his mother holding his good hand. He cut a four-
inch piece of the heavy leather and told the boy to bite it whenever
he felt the pain grow sharper, then began shaping the splint as
Conawago ripped apart the sacking. Duncan began singing a low
song, a Scottish sea shanty of his youth, repeating the chorus in a soft
voice. He rubbed his fingers along the broken bone then, nodding
at the boy to bear down, with a single smooth stretching motion
snapped the bone back into place. He wrapped the arm in one layer
of the makeshift bandage, then tightly wrapped the splints with the
remaining sacking, and finally made a sling out of the leather.

"For two moons," he said to Conawago, not trusting his own
translation, "tell her to keep it like this for two moons and the boy
will be whole again."

Duncan smiled as the woman gripped his hand in both of hers
and thanked him, again and again.

"He broke his arm taking food into the loft," Conawago observed.

Old Belt needed no further prompting. An unfamiliar energy
had entered his eyes, the fire of an aging horse remembering tricks
of his youth. He bent over the oldest of the children for a moment,

whispering. "There is a secret room up there," he reported as he straightened. "With chairs and pallets and Europeans belongings. And there is a ladder at the far end that will take us up without being noticed."

Duncan was inclined to ascend the ladder alone but did not object when one of the Iroquois braves shot past him and stealthily disappeared into the darkness above. As they gathered near the top of the ladder moments later, they could plainly see the sentinel at the far end, cocking his head toward them, and just as plainly see the long arm that materialized around his neck, dragging him into the darkness.

The second brave pressed ahead, taking up a station on the other side of the door, as Duncan pushed past to enter the chamber. The room had been cleverly built of rough planks on the exterior but was lined with finished boards on the inside, giving it the character of a comfortable habitation. Sacking had been tacked to the floor for a crude carpet, castaway furniture scattered around the room. One Indian was in repose, his head sagging onto the back of his chair, and another four were sitting at a blanket in the center of the floor, rolling the colored stones that were the Indian equivalent of dice, each with a stack of European coins beside him.

The four men on the floor shot to their feet as Duncan entered, hands to the knives that hung on their chest straps. Duncan watched uneasily as they spread out, their muscles coiling, the blades suddenly out of their sheaths. They did not mean to parlay, did not even mean to challenge their intruders before attacking. The man closest to Duncan lifted a long tapered wooden club, a marlin spike used in ships' rigging. It was lethal looking, and Duncan crouched to defend himself against a certain blow, when suddenly the four men froze. They stared in amazement at Old Belt, who had appeared in the doorway, fixing each in turn with a

stern, disapproving gaze. As recognition sank in they sagged, lowering their weapons, two muttering low, reluctant syllables of respect
for the revered Iroquois leader.

"We will have the Shawnee called Red Hand," Old Belt quietly
declared.

Duncan bent to a pallet by the wall. "Still warm," he reported.

The man in the chair, a Nanticoke, judging by his oyster shell
adornments, awoke and cast a sour look at the intruders. "We know
no one by such a name, old man, just get—" He never finished
his sentence. One of Old Belt's escorts tapped his head with the
ball end of his war ax, and the man collapsed to the floor. No one
reacted.

"We will have the one called Red Hand," Old Belt repeated.

Duncan sprang forward the instant one of the Indians glanced
toward a shadow in the far corner. In two leaping strides he found
himself going down a short, narrow passageway into a storeroom,
then spotted the open hatch used for loading supplies by pulley and
rope. He leapt to the opening, steadying himself by grabbing the
rope that still swung in the darkness.

Red Hand, having made good his escape, stood in a pool of
moonlight fifty paces away, his arms thrust toward the sky as he
taunted Duncan. There was no hope of catching him. By the time
Duncan slid down the rope and reached the pool of light the Indian
would be lost in the labyrinth of the city.

"He comes and goes," Conawago reported as Duncan returned
to his friends. The Nipmuc dropped onto the table a tattered pouch
on which lewd figures had been drawn over old tribal decorations,
the pouch Red Hand had carried at Shamokin. "His kit."

Duncan upended the pouch onto the table. A deck of stained
and dog-eared playing cards. A gold cross on a strand of beads.
The remaining two silver buttons from Winston Burke's uniform.

Three of the crosshatched nails from Shamokin. The chipped head
of a small china doll. Several soiled silk ribbons, two tied around
locks of delicate blond hair. The meager, macabre belongings of
an Indian outlaw. Duncan pushed the ribbons aside and lifted an
object from underneath them. A glass ball, nearly an inch in diameter, larger and more refined than a gaming marble, identical to the
one found with Ohio George.

He pocketed the ball, then turned toward the Indians who had
been in the room, lined up against a wall now. As he did so one of
the Iroquois guards appeared, shoving another Indian in front of
him, speaking quietly to Old Belt.

"This one was in the jakes," the chief explained, "using this."
The guard extended a black book, a prayer book. Nearly half the
pages had been torn out, starting in the rear.

"Some will take such books because they are sacred," Conawago
said with a sigh. "Others take them for pages to wipe themselves
in the jakes."

Duncan lifted the bloodstained book and opened it to the first
page. Inscribed in a refined hand across the top were a date, *1749*,
and a name. *Henry Bythe.*

Conawago paced along the Indians at the wall, who fearfully
watched Old Belt, then spoke in low, terse syllables to each, striking
up a conversation with the last man in line. "Red Hand owes this
one much money," he related after a moment, "and told him he
would soon have it. Red Hand bragged about what fun he would
have earning the money."

"Fun?" Duncan asked.

"Red Hand said to expect the money tomorrow night since
he had to earn it before Skanawati's trial. He said," Conawago
explained ominously, "that he is going to kill a black girl, a runaway
from Virginia."

It was Old Belt himself who insisted they stop at the magistrate's house despite the late hour. Brindle was sheltering Becca, Mokie, and the infant, Penn, in his own household pending the decision of the governor on their fate. What's more, the magistrate had confided to the Iroquois chief that he was keeping hours past midnight every night with his law and philosophy books, seeking an answer to his treaty dilemma.

The door to the large clapboard house was quickly opened by an austere woman wearing a white apron over her black dress. She did not greet them, did not react to the tall warriors who positioned themselves on either side of the door as sentries, simply ushered the visitors into a spacious room lined with bookshelves. Magistrate Brindle sat staring at the embers in his fireplace, the candlelit table by his chair heaped with documents bearing the wax seals of the courts, beside a law book whose pages gently stirred in the breeze coming from the open window beyond the fireplace.

Old Belt, motioning for Conawago and Duncan to wait, stepped forward. The Quaker looked up with a melancholy nod. "My servants say I should be abed. But we workhorses feel the harness every hour of the day."

The chief said nothing, just placed Bythe's prayer book on the table. The magistrate's hand trembled as he lifted the bloodstained volume. He opened it and stared at the inscription for a long moment before looking up.

"Your brother-in-law discovered the killers," Conawago declared as he approached. "But they were not the French, as he sought."

Duncan hung back in the darkness, acutely aware that he was a fugitive in the house of a high-ranking judge. When Brindle spoke it was in a near whisper, directed toward the little Quaker book. "When we took his body down there was a long spindle gear hammered into his eye." His voice cracked. "There were bloodstains around the eye. I think your medical friend would say it means he was still alive when it was done."

"We have seen other such gears," Conawago reminded the judge. "And in Shamokin we have seen the death of one of those responsible. Another walks these very streets. Perhaps in the employ of a merchant named Waller."

Brindle's countenance swirled with dark emotion. "I am no longer responsible for dealing with the deaths. With the murder of a family member I was considered too close to the crimes."

"A great benefit for those behind the killings," Conawago observed.

Brindle looked up. "I do not understand."

"Are you not still responsible for the treaty negotiations?"

"That duty has not yet been removed from me. We speak for hours every day, but little seems to get done," Brindle acknowledged. "We arrange and rearrange chairs at tables, organize meals, listen to speeches about why each of the delegations deserves the greater esteem."

"Not all at the table are telling the truth," Conawago ventured. "What does the Psalmist say? The words of his mouth are smoother than butter, but war was in his heart."

"His words were softer than oil," Brindle continued the verse, "yet were they drawn swords." He leaned forward. The Iroquois had their wampum for assuring a listener's attention. Magistrate Brindle had his Psalms.

"Your removal from the murders keeps you from seeing that they are just one more device being used to manipulate the treaty."

Even from the shadows Duncan could hear the Quaker's sharp intake of breath. After a moment he rose from his chair and laid another log on the fire. "Day unto day uttereth speech," he recited, "and night unto night showeth knowledge." He lifted a quill to continue the notes he had been taking, then nodded to Conawago. "Speak to me, my friend."

As the old Nipmuc began to relay the events of the past ten days, the log flared and Duncan stepped back, deeper into the darkness. His heart shot into his throat as someone touched his elbow. The stern woman who met them at the door had materialized beside him, gesturing him into a spacious kitchen with an immense stone fireplace, then lifted a glass of milk from the counter and handed it to him. Duncan was about to whisper his thanks when he saw a figure huddled on a stool by the remains of a small fire in the huge hearth.

Duncan did not return Van Grut's greeting when he rose from the stool, only grabbed the front of his shirt and pulled him close. "You lied to me!" he growled. "You were with Burke in Philadelphia! He's the one who hired you!"

The Dutchman sagged as Duncan released him. "It didn't seem important. Not a lie exactly. I told you I was hired by the Virginia company. He was part of the company."

"You heard me puzzle over connections to Philadelphia and never said a word about how Burke was here, in Philadelphia. You knew the killers were trying to implicate Indians in Shamokin and never said a word."

Van Grut dropped back onto the stool. "Surely it was only happenstance that he was in Philadelphia. And there *were* Indians in Shamokin doing the killing . . . " The Dutchman paused, as if beginning to recognize there could be several reasons for Burke's presence in Philadelphia, not all innocent.

"Hired by someone else," Duncan snapped. "If I had known of Burke's connection to Philadelphia I would have looked here sooner, before so many bounty hunters were breathing down my spine."

"Surely his presence here had nothing to do with the killings. There *were* Indians," Van Grut repeated.

"Are you certain? You wager your life on that slender belief."

"Duncan, I never..." the Dutchman began, then Duncan's words seemed to register. "My life? But the killers are on the survey line."

"Every instinct tells me otherwise. The treachery on the line is being orchestrated from Philadelphia. If someone in Philadelphia wanted all the Virginian surveyors dead, what do you suppose they will do when they find one walking the streets here?" There was a rustling of linen at the door. The taciturn maid had been listening, but now disappeared.

For a moment, looking at the stricken Dutchman, Duncan almost felt sorry for him. He did not believe Van Grut was one of the plotters, only trying to keep open all his options for a livelihood. The odds that Duncan would ever get to the truth were slim, and Van Grut wanted to be able to take money from whichever land company emerged successful in the treaty negotiations.

"No," the Dutchman said woodenly. "This is Philadelphia," he added, as if trying to convince himself. "The streets are safe. There are constables." He looked up with new energy. "I will help you, Duncan, I swear it. Tell me what I can do."

Duncan frowned. "That merchant from Shamokin. Waller. See if you can locate him." He hesitated, then reached into his pocket and produced the glass ball taken from Red Hand. "Two of the killers had these. Not beads. Not made by Indians. Not common even in towns." He dropped the ball into the Dutchman's hand. "If you want to help, tell me its story."

"Fine work," Van Grut said with an uneasy glance at Duncan, as he rolled the ball between his fingers. "Flint glass, without a flaw. American made, I wager. Instrument makers here will recognize the work, know the fabricator."

Duncan left Van Grut staring at the glass ball and again stole within hearing distance of the three elders who conferred by the library fireplace. He watched as worry grew on Brindle's face, marking how Conawago, and sometimes even Old Belt, cast wondering glances at the scores of books on Brindle's shelves. Inching closer, he strained to catch the low voices.

"Surely you do not suggest the governments of Virginia or Pennsylvania have been corrupted!" Brindle protested.

"It is not the governments that benefit most directly from the land depositions," Conawago pointed out. The words seemed to wound his host. When the magistrate pressed his point no further, Conawago relayed the final chapter of his tale, ending with the events in the barn an hour earlier.

"Philadelphia is the lair for miscreants of all colors," Brindle stated. "It means nothing that this man you seek fled to Philadelphia."

"That can be determined when he is caught. Meanwhile, as I explained, he means to slay the young girl in your custody."

"I shall alert the constables immediately."

"No. He is too clever to be caught by your constables."

"There is nothing more I can do." Brindle studied the two Indians. "Surely you are not suggesting I become a player myself in this drama."

"You already are, as your brother-in-law was."

"Do not presume I will bend the laws of my province!"

Duncan stepped into the light. "Then Skanawati's death will be on you." They were harsh words, brutal words, but they seemed to tear at something in the magistrate as he turned to see who had spoken them.

"You!" Brindle gasped. "How dare you, McCallum! A fugitive of the law in my household! You give me no choice but to send for the constables."

"It is the constables we must speak of."

Brindle's face was a storm of emotion as he rose from his chair. "I am obligated to inform the courts of your appearance, to tell the one who swore out the warrant against you."

Old Belt stepped to Duncan's side. "Answer me this, my friend. Until the treaty is concluded do you not have the Virginian runaways in your—" he turned and leaned toward Conawago with a whispered question.

"—your custody?" Conawago finished the question.

As if on cue the muffled cry of a hungry baby came from somewhere in a room above them. "I do."

"Then I shall keep McCallum in my custody," replied the Mohawk chief.

Brindle winced. "Mr. McCallum is answerable to a much more powerful authority."

"In the end of this affair," came Conawago's quiet voice, "that will be the conundrum, will it not?"

Brindle's brow wrinkled. "Sir?"

"In the end there is an authority supreme even over the great houses of Philadelphia."

The Quaker dropped back into his chair and gazed into the flames of the fireplace.

Duncan stepped close enough to read the documents on Brindle's table. "The documentation for the Susquehanna Company," he observed, studying the magistrate with new interest. Companies were only formed by act of the government. Brindle had removed the documents from the court records. "Why, amidst a crisis in the treaty negotiation, would the lead negotiator be investigating the ownership records of a Philadelphia land company?"

Brindle grimaced. "Do not be fooled by appearances, you told me once."

"Even in the Old Testament there were wolves in sheep's cloth-ing," Conawago observed.

"This company has become the largest, the most active of the land ventures," Brindle said. "If the Virginia land claims are defeated, it will mean Pennsylvania will be in line for those lands."

"And if Skanawati hangs for killing a Virginian, there is no way the Iroquois will ever cede land to the Virginians. Meaning the Susquehanna Company will have the most to gain from the hang-ing of Skanawati," Duncan concluded. As he saw the tormented way Brindle stared at the documents he realized the magistrate had already reached the same conclusion.

Brindle sighed. "Great things doeth he which we cannot comprehend."

"If I am not mistaken," Duncan said, "those words were written about Lord Jehovah, not Lord Ramsey."

Brindle fixed him with a level stare. "Your bitterness over your indenture clouds your vision, sir."

Duncan gestured to the papers. "Who are they?" he asked. "Who are the owners?"

"The records are incomplete. I can find only the initial pro-moters and owners of the company," Brindle explained. "Good solid citizens. Old Philadelphia families. Leading merchants. Christians all."

"Shares get sold," Conawago suggested. "Especially when new wealth arrives."

Brindle glanced at the doorway. "Be careful what you say, sir."

"This is America," Duncan shot back, "not the fiefdom of a few aristocrats."

"I daresay not all aristocrats agree," came Brindle's quick reply. The Quaker grimaced, as though regretting his words. "The company was formed before Lord Ramsey arrived in our city, yes." He gathered up the documents into a pile. "It is beyond my powers to learn more."

"Officially," Duncan said.

Brindle did not reply. "Even if I do not call the constables down on you, Mr. McCallum, I am not sure I do you any favor. There are handbills with your name on them at every corner."

Duncan paused, studying the Quaker a moment. "I encountered your nephew tonight."

"He is idle while the treaty delegation lingers in the city."

"Of all the bounty hunters, he is the only one who knows my face."

Brindle gazed into his folded hands and sighed. "He is a proud lad, trying to make a good start in life. It is no sin to assist the law."

"A good start? Is he not already gainfully employed?"

"He wishes to buy a stake in a commercial enterprise on the frontier."

"He tried to convince me to flee into the wilderness instead of going to Shamokin."

Brindle offered a lightless smile. "He read a romance about a Scottish highwayman. Perhaps it made him sympathetic to your plight. But now he can't be blamed for joining the ranks of those pursuing the bounty."

"What if he were working for Lord Ramsey?" Duncan asked abruptly.

Brindle's eyes went cold. "Impossible. If you are seeking to have me stop him I cannot. And I have not yet decided myself what to do with you."

"Do as you will with me, your honor," Duncan offered. "But after tomorrow. After we catch Red Hand. I am convinced he has the answers to all our questions."

"How do you propose to work that magic after he has eluded so many so long?"

"Call off the constables around the northern docks. Red Hand is, after all, just another mercenary. Tomorrow evening he shall find an irresistible target, an easy bounty for the taking. In the middle of our trap."

"No, Duncan!" Conawago protested. "He is a cold-blooded killer!"

Brindle glanced from Duncan to Conawago, then sighed as he understood. "You are suggesting the bait will be yourself?"

As he spoke Old Belt turned toward the shadows behind an overstuffed chair at the far end of the room.

"We will let word spread in the taverns near the Indian barn that I have been seen by the ships," Duncan explained, "as if I am trying to steal away on the evening tide. Some of the Iroquois guards can hide on the wharf to help me. It's the best we can do," he added in a determined tone.

"Not the best," a young, soft voice broke in. Mokie sprang up from behind the chair, where she had obviously been listening. "We know whom he seeks."

"Never, child!" Brindle gasped.

"Tomorrow at sunset!" Mokie declared defiantly as she inched toward the wall. "The north docks!"

An instant before Old Belt reached her, she leapt through the open window and was gone.

The Philadelphia waterfront was so alive with activity Duncan wore himself out watching it from the high east-facing window of Marston's attic. Ships and boats of all sizes and shapes were astir under a steady spring breeze. Fat shallops heaped with shad and oysters were delivering their loads to the kitchens of Philadelphia. Slow-moving barges stacked with lumber were poled into the city from upcountry. Stevedores swarmed over square-rigged merchantmen bound for Europe or the Indies.

Duncan watched as one of the big ships was towed to the center of the river and slipped away for the broad Atlantic. It would be such a simple thing, to dart out of the house and leap onto the deck of one loosening its moorings. Such far-ranging vessels were always in need of able-bodied sailors and would not press him for his real name. He could leave everything behind, make a new life. As a tutor perhaps. Maybe he could even establish himself as a doctor in a distant port town.

The sound of the thin plank door scraping on the floor broke him from his reverie.

Expecting Conawago with news of Mokie, Duncan did not turn right away, then heard a groan and spun about to see Conawago and Marston carrying Van Grut to the low bed at the wall. The right side of the Dutchman's face was bruised and swollen, his hair matted with blood. Duncan's quick examination showed four broken ribs—not cracks but clean breaks that would greatly pain Van Grut when he regained consciousness, long bruises on his forearms from fending off clubs, several slashing cuts on his scalp, and a stabbing wound in the thigh.

The Dutchman's eyes fluttered open and shut several times before he seemed to recognize Duncan. The guilt in his eyes was obvious even through his pain.

"Perhaps you understand now," Duncan said. "This was not someone trying to send a message. You're lucky to be alive."

Van Grut's words came out garbled, and he paused, confused, rubbing his cheek. Duncan pushed away his hand, studying the bone underneath. "They fractured your jaw as well as your ribs," he explained. "Not broken clean, but it will take some weeks of healing." He showed Van Grut how to press the jawbone in place to speak.

"At the Broken Jug I heard there was a lacrosse game, at a field north of town." The Dutchman's words were twisted and slurred, as if his tongue were swollen. "A dozen Indians, as many townsmen. I think they were after me in the game, trying to kill me like they killed Ohio George. I was tripped several times with the sticks. An Indian jumped on me, but an Englishman fell on top, then scolded the Indian for forgetting to take his knife off before playing."

Van Grut paused as Miss Townsend tipped a glass of water onto his lips. He winced as he swallowed. "I was so tired afterward I wasn't paying attention, just wandered toward town to find some ale. Four of them cornered me by that big barn where the Indians stay. One was that Shawnee who knew Ohio George. Red Hand. He kept shouting encouragement as they used their sticks on me. They were dragging me toward the barn, would have finished me, but some of the European players came by and assisted me, started yelling that the Indians shouldn't be bad sports because they got beaten, that if they wanted a fair match they shouldn't come to the game half-drunk."

Van Grut winced as he pulled on his watch chain, the only adornment left on his body. The device was smashed, its crystal shattered, the face and case dented. He stared at it forlornly. "My father's," was all he said.

"Half an inch to one side and the blade in your thigh would have slashed an artery. Like Burke."

Van Grut's eyes widened. "Red Hand! He stood back from the others, with a hammer and something else in his fingers. Christ in heaven!" he gasped. "They weren't taking me to the barn, just to the wall. He was going to nail me to the wall!"

"What did you expect?" Duncan's voice held little sympathy. If Van Grut had not held the truth back he would be days ahead in his search for answers.

Marston cast uneasy glances at the two men. "I will get more bandages," he said and retreated.

"You were gambling again," Conawago deduced. "You were at the Broken Jug."

It took a moment for Duncan to understand what his friend was saying. "My God, Van Grut, surely you weren't hoping for another offer of work?"

The Dutchman winced and pushed at his jaw again to speak. "I lost everything but my watch in a card game in Lancaster," he confessed with downcast eyes. "Burke had allies here. I thought if they saw I was not intimidated, that I was still willing and able to work in the Indian country, they would hire me. If need be I would step forward and declare myself to the Virginian delegation, saying they must honor the contract made by Captain Burke. Once the land claims are settled by the treaty they will need more surveyors than ever. The right men in the colony could get me a teaching position at the College of William and Mary." Van Grut seemed to see the anger in Duncan's eyes. "I would never do anything to hurt you, I swear it! It's just that . . . I must make my own way in the world, McCallum. What choice do I have?" he asked in a cracking voice.

Duncan looked out the window as he spoke. "You'll need rest, weeks of rest. I will impress upon Marston that you are a man of science. He is seeking a collaborator for writing up his experiments. He may be willing to let you stay here. But your jaw will need to be wrapped in place. It will be egg in milk for you, through a reed."

Van Grut did not try to speak again until Marston reappeared with strips of linen and a basin of steaming water. "I tried to help," he said in a pleading tone. "I discovered there is a glassmaker named Wistar who specializes in fine containers and instruments."

Duncan looked up. He had almost forgotten his request of Van Grut.

"His agent in Philadelphia recognized the little ball when I showed it to him, said it was unmistakably from the Wistar works. But the rest of his explanation made no sense."

Duncan signaled for Marston and Conawago to prop up the Dutchman as he wrapped his ribs. "What explanation?"

"Smaller balls they sell as marbles, for those who can afford something more than clay balls," Van Grut said with a wince of pain. "But he has a special customer for the larger balls. He sold a gross of them last autumn to him, to one of the Philadelphia aristocrats."

Duncan looked at Conawago. His whisper was full of foreboding. "Ramsey."

Van Grut nodded. "He labels them as trade baubles in his invoices."

Conawago sighed, then pointed out the window at one of Old Belt's men, approaching from the docks, and slipped out of the room.

Duncan was showing Miss Townsend how to change Van Grut's jaw bandage when Conawago returned ten minutes later and sat heavily on a dusty stool by the window. "Mokie is moving in and out of the market. She stole an apple at one stall, upset a basket of onions at another. She is," Conawago added pointedly, "better than that."

Duncan instantly grasped his friend's meaning. "She is trying to be seen, letting it be known there is a runaway slave girl working mischief near the docks." Several watchers, including Marston,

Miss Townsend, and some of the Iroquois, had been trying to find the girl since dawn. But Mokie would not be caught unless she wanted to be caught, and she would gladly face Red Hand if it would help her friend Skanawati.

"Will Brindle cooperate?" Duncan asked.

"Call back the constables? Not likely. I don't think he has the power to do so. Not now." Conawago reached into his belt and dropped a copy of the day's *Pennsylvania Gazette* on the table. In the bottom corner of the cover page was a primitive cartoon, with an image of a man with the face of a cat tied at a pole, encircled by Indians with torches. On the man's chest in crude letters was written *Brindle.* Underneath was the uncharitable caption, *The stink begins to rise from the polecat.*

"Then I shall rely on Old Belt and his men."

"The bounty on your head will draw the constables like flies. They will surely take you."

Duncan noticed a short article on the page, above the cartoon. *Iroquois Chief Rots in City Prison*, read the headline. "The girl will be dead a moment after Red Hand sees her. Saving Mokie and capturing him will be worth the price. Easily worth six more years of indenture."

Conawago watched the ships with Duncan in silence. "You know you wouldn't survive another year, Duncan. Once in Ramsey's hands, hidden from public view, he will eventually kill you. Or sell you as a slave to some Jamaican sugar plantation. Either way you die in months."

"Sarah will hear. His daughter can stop him."

"That prospect will serve only to accelerate his plans."

Another ship began pulling away, its deck laden with cut lumber.

"It seems to me," Duncan observed in a distant voice, "we should focus on the certain death on a gallows two days from now, not the merely possible one months from now."

"You're a damned fool, Duncan McCallum. Ask Skanawati and he would tell you to stop interfering, just flee to safety in the wilds while you can."

"Then we all agree. I am a damned fool," Duncan replied, and he began outlining his plan for sunset.

The lamplighters had begun their evening rounds when Duncan and Conawago slipped out of the building, one of the soot-stained men walking in advance with a ladder and keg of whale oil to fill the city lanterns before they were lit. The day sailors and fishermen were moving home, a woman who had been selling fresh oysters lowering her baskets into the river for the night.

Conawago grabbed Duncan's arm as a long droning whistle broke through the background of sounds. Iroquois bowmen with signal arrows had been concealed at the head of every other pier, and the signal they heard came from one of the docks above Market Street. They moved at the fast, stealthy pace used when chasing deer in the forest, in and out of the shadows, slowing when the cover diminished, arriving at the dock five minutes later. An Indian rose up from behind stacks of crates and pointed to a diminutive figure perched on a mound of thick hawser rope.

Where are the constables? Duncan asked himself. Conawago had convinced him that a trap would indeed be set for him, but there was no sign of the city's enforcers. He inched along in the shadow of a row of tall hogshead barrels, then used the cover of a slow-moving freight wagon to reach the foot of the long pier that extended from the wharf that fronted the river. Mokie seemed to sense something behind her, but turned and saw nothing. Duncan, with no cover left, strode purposefully toward the girl. He was perhaps forty paces away when a shape materialized in the gray light behind Mokie. Red Hand had been under the wharf, hidden in the timbers below, and now he climbed out only a few feet from the girl.

"Mokie! Behind you!" Duncan shouted, then sprang forward. Another signal arrow sounded. A shout rose in Iroquois from the shadows of the warehouses. The girl spun about and screamed as Red Hand coolly approached, his long knife glinting in the dusk.

Duncan was in the air, leaping toward the Shawnee as he reached the girl. He hammered the Indian's knife hand down from its killing stroke. Red Hand delivered a savage kick that knocked Mokie to the ground then turned to Duncan with hatred in his eyes.

Waiting with a blade half as long as his assailant's, Duncan feigned a thrust as Red Hand charged him then landed a vicious kick on his enemy's knee. Red Hand rolled onto the planks of the pier, grinning now, and was instantly back on his feet. He fixed Duncan with a treacherous gaze, then paused as he heard the running feet on the wharf. The Indian grimaced, not with fear but with disappointment. "Another time, Scotsman," he spat, then turned and ran.

Duncan turned to quickly scan those approaching. Only his Indian allies, no constables. Had Brindle used his influence after all? He spun about to pursue the Shawnee. The Indian had fled not toward the town but further down the adjoining wharf, where two wide ships were berthed so closely together they could provide a platform to leap across to the adjacent dock, where no pursuers awaited.

Red Hand's outstretched knife warned away the sailor standing sentry at the gangway of the first ship, allowing the Shawnee to vault onto the wide deck, but a group of sailors emerging from a hatchway spotted the intruder, causing him to veer away. Duncan made a frantic leap onto the ship's bow and discovered that the rigging above was in the process of replacement, leaving several lines hanging down from the yards. He grabbed one near the far rail, pulled it back, and with a running leap and a swing across the open water he propelled himself onto the deck of the second ship. By the time Red Hand reached it Duncan was standing before him, a heavy marlin spike in his hand. The Shawnee eyed him for an instant, glanced at the pursuers, then launched himself up the shroud lines of the mainmast. It was a large ship, so large its upper rigging disappeared into the night shadow above. Duncan leapt onto the shroud lines on the opposite side of the mast and scrambled upward.

Red Hand was like a spider on the ropes, scampering over them without hesitation, leaping, twisting in midair, catching a strand as he flew. But Duncan had spent his early boyhood playing in ships' rigging, was as at home among the ropes and spars as any seasoned sailor.

It was a bizarre game of cat and mouse fought in the air. For long, agonizing moments Duncan could not see Red Hand, but each time the Shawnee was betrayed by the moonlight reflecting off his proudly oiled skin. Up the shrouds and ratlines, running out on a yard, leaping onto a stay to propel himself hand over hand from the foremast to mainmast, dropping into the broad platform of the main top, Red Hand moved with amazing stealth and speed. Pausing for a moment to study the pursuers on the wharf searching the stacks of cargo, he glanced at Duncan and disappeared. There was only the mizzenmast then the dark water of the Delaware, where Duncan would surely lose him. Duncan grabbed another stay and half-climbed, half-slid toward the main-top, watching for any sign of the Shawnee in the rigging beyond. Missing his footing as he landed on the platform, he landed with a staggering fall. The stumble saved his life, for Red Hand had concealed himself behind the broad mast and greeted Duncan with a violent lunge that would have gutted him had he not fallen. He flung out with a fist, knocking Red Hand off balance long enough to regain his feet.

The Shawnee mocked him as Duncan lashed out futilely with his own blade. "Your god is waiting for you," Red Hand called out.

"McCallum!" came the gruff tones of Sergeant McGregor from below.

"McGregor!" Duncan called back.

Red Hand, knowing he would be an easy target for the soldiers' guns once he was spotted, cursed, then slashed one of the stays and swung away. The Indian was, Duncan suddenly realized, retracing his path in the rigging, bound not for the river but the city. "McGregor!" Duncan shouted again. "The girl!"

Mokie still stood by the mound of rope, watching the pursuers as if it were a grand entertainment. There was still no sign of constables, but McGregor's entire squad had appeared and was trotting with their long muskets at the ready.

Red Hand descended to the deck as Duncan swung across the gap between ships, then leapt onto the long bowsprit that extended over the wharf near Mokie. Duncan recklessly shoved off with another rope in hand, shouting Mokie's name as he swung. The girl wandered a few steps down the wharf, looking up in confusion as through the shadows a new band of men emerged. Seeking protection, she ran to the side of the lampman who had been filling the lanterns and was still looking down the long pier when Red Hand landed a few feet away. Duncan dropped down a backstay, burning his hands on the rope, landed on the deck, and vaulted over the rail.

As the Indian ran toward the girl the lampman fled, abandoning his keg and ladder. From the opposite direction came a solitary figure, charging at Red Hand. Hadley had no weapon but his fists. Red Hand took a step backward as Hadley reached him, and with a stroke of his tomahawk knocked the Virginian to the ground. The sound caused Mokie to turn. She screamed but was paralyzed with fright.

Duncan was seconds away when he saw one of the men from the street wrestle with a soldier, pulling away his musket. He froze. The soldier was down, being pummeled by three ruffians, and beside them Felton was aiming the gun directly at Duncan as more of his companions fanned out to surround Duncan. The men from the street had come not to help the girl but to help Felton trap Duncan. Red Hand, seeming to understand, grinned, then saw the soldiers approaching from the wharf, McGregor in the lead.

With a lurch of his gut Duncan heard Felton pull the hammer back, saw the fiery discharge. The bullet hit not Duncan, not Red Hand, but the keg of whale oil that Red Hand stood beside. As Mokie darted away the keg exploded into white flame, propelling its contents upward. An instant later, the volatile oil soaking him, Red Hand burst into flame. The tomahawk fell from his hands as the Indian desperately, futilely, tried to rub the flames out. His loincloth and leggings ignited, his lock of hair ignited, his very skin caught fire as with a terrible bloodcurdling groan he staggered toward Duncan, his oil-soaked body now completely in flames.

"Mother of God!" McGregor moaned. The smell of charred flesh bit into their nostrils. The sergeant grabbed a musket from one of his men and fired. Red Hand jerked backward then dropped to his knees, raising his burning arms to the sky as a second soldier fired. He collapsed in a ball of fire to the planks of the pier.

Duncan lingered for a breathless moment then leapt to the wharf's edge and dove into the black waters below.

Chapter Fourteen

D UNCAN SWAM UNDERWATER with the long, sweeping strokes he had learned as a boy, keeping overhead the lighter shadow that marked the gap between the ships, swam until his lungs screamed, then surfaced to gulp fresh air and submerged again. With every stroke he was moving closer to the way of the outlaws, defying the entire city now, with every stroke the prospect of freedom and a new life tugged more strongly at his aching heart. He could climb up onto any of the great ships coursing out into the spring tide and leave his misery behind. Surfacing, he held on to the anchor rope of a dory left beyond the moored ships, watching as more and more torches were lit, as more and more men ran up and down the wharfs. Some searchers were being lowered on ropes to scan for him under the docks. A woman screamed, then another, as a crowd gathered around the charred remains of Red Hand.

Releasing the rope, he let himself be pushed by the current down the broad river, past another wharf, then another, letting several ranks of the big ships pass, until suddenly a large vessel loomed over him. He let the merchantman pass, then without thinking

grabbed a trailing manline. For a moment, as he climbed up the
rope enough to rest against the great black hull, he was free, for a
moment he was on the way to the Indies. With an instant's effort
he could pull himself onto the deck and all would be behind him.
The lights of Philadelphia passed alongside, and as they began to
fade he looked up with longing at the ship's rail and dropped away.
Minutes later he found an algae-covered ladder built into a pier and
climbed back into the world.

The guard had been doubled by the time Duncan arrived at the
tribe's compound a quarter hour later. He watched from behind the
trunk of a great elm, then slipped into the shadows under the high
brick wall, worried now that the militia may have started patrols
around the government house, worried too that the new fortune on
his head might mean bounty hunters seeking him at all hours. He
had no refuge left. His link to Marston was too thinly concealed for
the scientist's house to be safe now. Barns and outbuildings would
be searched. By now, for all he knew, his gun and kit had been
found and confiscated. If by Ramsey's men, the lord would order
his pipes be burned, as he had tried to do the year before. Duncan
braced himself against a tree, fighting what seemed an overpower-
ing weakness. He was cold and wet and bone weary, and hope
seemed forever beyond his reach.

Breathing deeply, refusing to succumb to despair, he suddenly
sniffed the sweet, acrid scent of the tobacco used by the tribes and
was buoyed for a moment by the memory of sitting in a sweat lodge
with Conawago. He edged along the ivy-covered wall, discovering a small door, which he tried and found locked. Then hearing
footsteps coming down the street, he launched himself into an
awkward, desperate ascent, using the thick vines for support. He
reached the top and rolled over, dropping onto the soft, moist earth
of the garden.

The Indian camp was quiet, its occupants all asleep save for the two men who were replenishing the small fire in the herb garden.

Conawago said nothing, just reached out and embraced Duncan when he approached. "Still playing the fish," he observed, his voice cracking with emotion.

Old Belt threw more wood on the fire, then gazed at the lighted window of the kitchen. "I believe," the Iroquois chief declared with whimsy, "we shall ask our servants to make us some English tea."

Mokie had been escorted to Brindle's house by McGregor and his men, the Indians reported, while the charred remains of Red Hand had been wrapped in a sailcloth and taken to the pauper's cemetery.

"Felton will have drinks bought for him for a month," Conawago remarked. "The Quaker hero saves an innocent girl, kills a fugitive murderer."

Duncan leaned over the fire, soaking up its warmth. "When the Shawnee died the truth died with him," he stated.

"With the Shawnee gone," Conawago rejoined, "you can concentrate on making yourself safe."

Duncan did not have the strength to argue. He hovered over the fire in silence, pushing the river chill out of his bones, then watched with amusement as Old Belt led a small parade of the house staff out the kitchen door, the English servants carrying a tray with a teapot and fine china cups, chairs, and a small table. They watched in silence as the table was set for them by the fire and grinned as one of the women delicately poured out the tea and sliced a fresh loaf she had brought with it. Finding himself famished, Duncan quickly covered his bread with butter and chewed as Old Belt described the day's futile treaty deliberations.

Suddenly the chief paused, grabbing his belt ax at the sound of a cry in the shadows. Long Wolf appeared, dragging a man bleeding from several scratches. Hadley grinned sheepishly as he saw Duncan and Conawago, did not resist when Long Wolf shoved him into the firelight.

"This fool," the Mingo chief declared, "climbed over the wall into a bed of thorn roses."

Duncan knelt at the Virginian's side, first inspecting his head to confirm that Red Hand's tomahawk had done no serious damage, then handing him a napkin to wipe away the blood on his arms.

"When I came to, she was gone," the Virginian reported in an anxious voice.

"Mokie is safe for now, back with Brindle," Conawago said.

Hadley gave a sigh of relief then reached inside his shirt and handed Duncan a tattered piece of paper. "You wanted to know about the owners of the Susquehanna Company. Being a Burke has its advantages. I spoke to the man who is the tobacco merchant who acts as agent for the Virginia land company, then the family banker here. They made some inquiries. Before leaving for the pier, I took their reports."

The paper contained a list of eight names, with numbers beside each indicating a number of shares. "Eight of the original owners have sold their shares. Each of them had a tale of reversals. A ship lost at sea. A sugar mill burned in a southern colony. An unexpectedly adverse judgment from a Philadelphia judge. Orders for timber or turpentine cancelled. Contracts with the army suddenly terminated. They all suddenly needed cash."

"And Ramsey bought them out," Duncan suggested.

Hadley nodded. "He promised to do it quietly, so as not to cause public humiliation. It seems he now has a controlling interest in the company opposing Virginia for the western lands." He pushed Duncan's hand back when he tried to return the paper.

"No," Duncan said. "Get this to Brindle. Tell him everything you've just told me. Tell him if he looks he will find Ramsey's hand in at least some of the calamities that forced the sales of shares."

Hadley nodded and secreted the paper back inside his shirt.

"And ask the magistrate's help in finding the merchant Waller. We must know who replenishes his accounts, who instructed him in dealing with the slaves."

The Virginian nodded again. "I will ask if I might stay in his stable, to help watch over Becca and Mokie and the little one." He hesitated, looking up at Duncan. "What did you mean, the girl's safe for now?"

"In the race to protect Mokie," Duncan replied, "has no one asked why they want her dead? She is still somehow a threat to the killers."

"But she is only—" Hadley began, then paused.

Voices were being raised in the house. In the light cast through the open window Duncan saw something fly across the kitchen, heard the shattering of china dishes and the frightened cry of a woman.

"What kind of bull have they released in there?" Conawago wondered out loud as a pot flew out the window.

It was, Duncan saw a moment later, the most vicious bull of all.

"Go!" he yelled at Hadley. "Find McGregor!"

"Run, Duncan!" Conawago gasped.

But Duncan did not move. "No. I am too weary," he said, then a glance at his friend showed him Conawago understood the real reason. Most of those approaching from the kitchen door carried muskets. If they spotted Duncan fleeing they would fire into the Iroquois camp.

From the light of the torches his escort carried, Duncan could see that Lord Ramsey had thinned in the past months, his plump face now much harder, though his fleshy jowls had not entirely receded, giving him an unflattering, half-made appearance. But his burning eyes, lit by arrogance and hate, had not changed.

Not even his escort, four militia soldiers and two rough men with the look of stevedores, seemed prepared for Ramsey's wrath. The lord, shoving the man in front of him out of the way, stepped to Duncan and began beating him. "You worthless pig!" he cried in a cracking, high-pitched voice. "You Scottish scum! You damnable worm!" He slapped Duncan, then slapped him again, before pummeling him with his fists. Another curse came with each stroke. Duncan did not react, did not move. The great lord could put little power behind the blows, and any resistance would only invite his escorts to join in. Duncan staggered, taking the blows, returning Ramsey's malevolent stare until Conawago finally seized Ramsey's collar and pulled him away like a misbehaving child.

Ramsey turned on the old Nipmuc now, striking him with an open hand on the jaw, shoving him so hard that Conawago tripped and fell to the ground. Duncan watched as two, then four of the Iroquois braves leapt from their blankets, reaching for their war clubs. The militia soldiers uneasily closed in front of Ramsey, who gestured one of the street bullies toward Duncan. The man pulled a set of manacles from his belt.

"'Tis an ungodly clamor for the time of night," boomed a voice from behind them. "Ye'll have the poor inhabitants of the city thinking the Hurons have attacked." Sergeant McGregor was stepping out of the kitchen, six of his kilted men at his heels.

"We are finished here," Ramsey spat. "I am taking my property and leaving."

"Ye are leaving, aye," McGregor declared as he reached the circle of men. "I am charged with maintaining order and protecting the treaty delegation," he added.

"You have no authority over me!" Ramsey spat. "McCallum belongs to me! Do not interfere!"

"I have authority, y'er lordship, over anything that disturbs the delegations." Mockery was thick in the Scot's voice.

Ramsey turned on the burly sergeant. "You Highland scum! We should have finished you off in the last uprising!"

"Ye should have tried," McGregor shot back in a hot whisper.

"I don't know what fool decided to put you kilted apes in uniform!"

"That particular fool, y'er honor, would be the king."

Even in the dim light of the torches Duncan could see Ramsey's face flush. "This mongrel is mine!" he insisted. "I have warrants."

"I be not bound by warrants, y'er worship," McGregor replied in a level voice. "Only the orders of my general."

Ramsey's eyes flared. Grabbing the manacles, he viciously slapped them across Duncan's cheek, then opened one of the wrist restraints to place on Duncan. The sword that suddenly pressed down on the chains seemed to materialize from thin air. "If ye wish to test a Scottish blade against y'er Philadelphia bulls," McGregor growled, "I'm y'er man." The militia soldiers nervously tightened the grips on their muskets. The rest of McGregor's squad pressed close, making sure the muskets would be of little use.

Ramsey dropped the chains and retreated a step. "You are already my prisoner, McCallum," he reminded Duncan. "Take a step out of your savages' refuge and you are mine!" He grabbed one of the militiamen, shoved him toward the kitchen door, and followed him down the path.

Duncan watched Ramsey disappear into the house, then touched his cheek. Blood was dripping down his jaw, onto the chains below.

"You must flee, Duncan!" Conawago warned. "Now. He will have his men surrounding this place soon."

"To where?"

Conawago did not answer, just quickly walked to the little door in the brick wall, pushed back the bolt, and opened it. Marston stepped inside with a muffled lantern and nervously gestured for Duncan. "Our electrical friend says he has found us another sanctuary," Conawago announced.

Ramsey's men could be seen organizing themselves on the corner near the front gate as Marston, Duncan, and Conawago darted through the shadows. Duncan lost track of where they were, was only vaguely aware that they moved away in a wide curve from the lamps of Market Street for several minutes then back toward them. At last Marston led them to the back door of a house, fumbled with a key, then opened the door.

The first-floor windows of the house were cleverly rigged with dark canvas mounted on pins and pulleys, which Marston now lowered like sails to block out the glass before opening the screen on his lantern. "The owner is away," he announced. "He would not object to you borrowing the house. In fact he is certain to be delighted when I tell him the circumstances."

It was a simple, comfortable dwelling, its only trappings of luxury the scores of books in the front room. Not just a library, Duncan saw, as Marston lit more candles. Large Leyden jars stood in ranks along a table by one wall. Another table was cluttered with an odd assortment that included strange cast-iron shapes, stuffed birds, a globe, disassembled spectacles, two clocks, lenses, a dead dragonfly, and a wooden tray of lead type.

"You must not attract attention," Marston warned. "Beds are on the second floor, but no lights near the windows."

As they followed him up the stairway Duncan paused and looked at a strange leather hat hanging by the front door, shaped like a helmet but with a broad visor. "From the fire company," Marston said absently and gestured him on.

Conawago was next to pause, studying a strange device on the stairway wall. Two metal strips emerged from the ceiling and entered a wooden box, at the bottom of which was a small brass bell.

"We invented this detector several years ago. When there is a charge collecting in the atmosphere before a storm it will ring. His is likely the first in the world, though I have been trying to duplicate it in my attic."

"His?" Conawago asked, then his eyes lit with recognition, and he grinned at Duncan.

"As I said, he is in London as agent for the provincial government these three years past. What family is left has gone on a visit to Boston for several months. He asked me to watch things, lets me borrow such instruments as I may need."

Duncan's own eyes went round with awe. Conawago stared at the bell device with boyish wonder. Marston was hiding them in the home of Benjamin Franklin.

They were at a front-facing bedroom, confirming that the street outside was quiet, when Duncan recalled the books downstairs. "Is the library available to you as well, Marston?"

"Naturally. And to many of his friends. Dr. Franklin is responsible for the formation of a public lending library not ten minutes from here. He believes it is the duty of each citizen to continually improve himself."

"Mathematical books? Books on codes in particular?"

"Of course! The code on the trees!" Marston darted for the stairs, leaving Duncan and Conawago to find their way in the dark.

Franklin's peculiar organization of his books at first mystified Duncan, but Marston soon located a row of mathematical treatises on a top shelf, consisting largely of the works of Euclid, Descartes, and Leibnitz, along with a deposition on the variations in units of measurement in half a dozen European countries. But nothing on codes or cyphers.

"I am not sure he would classify the subject with mathematics," Marston said pensively. "But where . . . ?" he asked himself as he surveyed the shelves again. They searched through the books on religion, for Franklin believed early religious tracts contained hidden cyphers, then began a systematic search of every shelf. It was more than a quarter hour before Conawago uttered an exclamation of discovery.

"With the books on the printing press and typesetting," he explained, and he pulled out a slender volume entitled *Cyphers of the Ancients*. It was, to their chagrin, almost entirely about the Greek square, the numeric grid employed by Athenian battle commanders, and the Greek scytale used by the Spartans. Not a word about the pigpen cypher.

"Is there nothing else?" Duncan asked in disappointment.

Marston leaned over the shelf. "Nothing," he announced, then probed an empty space and extracted a slip of paper. "*The Cryptographer's Manual*," he read with new excitement. "On loan. I can just retrieve it from—" his words choked away. "It says," he announced, "that the book is at Lord Ramsey's!"

Duncan stared at the slip in disbelief. He felt the last of his hope drifting away.

"Can it truly be a coincidence?" Conawago asked after a forlorn silence.

"He is known for his great collection of books," Marston offered.

"The rot of the Ramsey house spreads to everything it touches," Duncan said grimly. Surely, he prayed, it had not come to this, surely after all he and the tribes had endured, the path of his own troubles with Ramsey had not converged with those of the murders. But in his heart Duncan realized that from the first moment he had heard Ramsey's name in Pennsylvania, something inside him had sensed the shadow of the treacherous lord, like some wraith stalking him.

"Evil finds its own," Conawago said heavily.

Duncan offered a reluctant nod of agreement. Ramsey viewed himself as above the law, in reality *was* above the law, and though he was one of the richest men in the colonies, his real currencies were deception and secret violence. He gazed at his old friend and considered what he had said. Conawago was pointing out there were others involved. Ramsey himself would never be touched by the law, but those who did his bidding could be stopped.

Duncan looked at the slip of paper with Ramsey's name on it. "Surely this is not the only such book in Philadelphia."

"I will make inquiries at the Library Company," Marston offered, "but it appears to be a rare volume published many years ago. Dr. Franklin often ordered single copies of works from a book-seller in London."

"Then someone must get into Lord Ramsey's library," Duncan concluded.

Marston looked startled. "Not any of us, surely. I am not of sufficient social rank to be admitted to that inner sanctum."

Duncan paced around the room, along the ranks of books and the table of Dr. Franklin's collections. His gaze lingered on an ornately carved box beside several ancient stone ax heads. "My pack," he said to Conawago. "You must retrieve it. If it falls into the wrong hands they will try to use that box of Townsend's with the turtle scratched on it to link Skanawati to his killing. Give it to Old Belt for safekeeping." He kept gazing at Franklin's little box as he spoke. "There is," he suggested in a contemplative voice, "a witness of sorts to what happened at the first murder."

"Ohio George is dead." Conawago was puzzled. "And now Red Hand."

"Burke sent Townsend into the wilderness, promised to publish his book, an offer more valuable than currency to a man like Townsend. So Townsend went to Shamokin, and out onto the Warriors Path because he trusted the Iroquois. Skanawati the elder was a warrior but no cold-blooded murderer. When he killed, he killed enemies of his tribe. He was deceived. If we understand that deception we may understand who was the deceiver."

"The only ones we know are dead," Marston pointed out again.

"The ones whose faces we know, yes. But there was at least one more."

"How do you know?"

"Because of the code carved on the trees. Townsend did not carve it as a sign of his own murder. Nor did any Indian. It was done by a European. One familiar with a code book brought to Philadelphia by Dr. Franklin. And there is a witness to what was done at that first tree, where Townsend died. He is locked in the prison not half a mile from here."

"The plunge in the river has left you daft," Conawago protested. "The Skanawati we know was not the Skanawati who killed Townsend."

"The plunge in the river reminded me of the Susquehanna. Stone Blossom said there is an essence passed from one Skanawati to the next. You have taught me that among the tribes the lives of spirits and the lives of men are intertwined." Duncan looked up at Marston. "I must see him."

His two companions stared at him as if Duncan had indeed lost his senses.

"And what?" Marston asked, "you will go throw pebbles at his cell window? The moment you are seen you will be arrested. You do not want to experience our jails despite the Quakers' best efforts."

Duncan looked at the scientist with new interest. "The Quakers?"

"The Quakers have a society for the improvement of prison conditions, the Benevolent Society, they call it. They have a notion that prisoners can be reformed, not just punished, that their bad habits can be healed like a disease. They have been of great help in relieving the squalor, even of some help to me."

Duncan weighed Marston's words a moment, then leaned forward. "Are you saying you have a connection to the prison?"

"They allow me to treat some prisoners, yes. They have even set up a treatment room in an empty cell."

"And how often do you do so?" Duncan could see the protest already rising on Conawago's face as Marston pondered his question. Duncan did not wait for an answer. "You are going to the prison tomorrow, and with a new assistant. I must see Skanawati."

Chapter Fifteen

THE STENCH HIT Duncan the moment he stepped through the heavy timber gate of the Walnut Street prison. The high brick walls of the foreyard gave little ventilation for the privies that lined one wall. For a moment he thought the men that sat along the other walls had been overpowered by the smell, then he saw that the debility on most of their faces was not physical. He had spent months in a king's prison, then a prison ship, and knew the great killer was no one disease but rather despair.

Marston paused to open a vial from which he poured vinegar onto his handkerchief before clamping it to his nose. Duncan, declining the offer of the vial, tightened his grip on the box he was carrying for the scientist and followed him into the building.

The Benevolent Society had cleaned out a corner cell on the top floor for Marston's sessions, and its high barred windows provided a modicum of air and light. The jailer, responsible for the entire institution, was a devout Quaker who, though he cast wary glances at the box Duncan carried, was an enthusiastic supporter of the Society. He greeted Marston courteously and gestured them toward a turnkey who silently escorted them upstairs. Though the prison was much more noisy than those Duncan had known—where outbursts were met with clubs and cudgels—as the prisoners saw Marston approach they grew silent.

"Sorcerer!" one muttered through the barred hatch of his heavy door. The moment another saw the scientist he began gasping in a fit of asthma.

Marston quickly unpacked the box Duncan had been carrying onto a table beside a smaller electrical machine the Society allowed him to keep in the cell. He showed his new assistant first how to line up the Leyden jars they had brought with others already there, the workings of the harness that suspended certain prisoners from the ceiling for treatment, then how to steadily turn the wheel that spun the glass ball on the machine. By the time Marston proclaimed he was ready the turnkey had the first patient at the door, an older man with a paralyzed arm. The man silently acquiesced as Marston gestured him to the wooden armchair by the machine, did not protest when the scientist tied the useless arm to the chair then carefully separated the fingers with small rolls of linen between each. Marston placed the hand close to the glass ball and nodded for Duncan to begin rotating the wheel that spun the ball. Moments later a stream of blue flame arced to the nearest finger.

The prisoner watched with an earnest fascination and did not react even as Marston, wearing a leather glove, moved another, then another fingertip to capture the electrical fluid.

"From the machine into your body, always from the machine," Marston murmured quietly to his patient as he worked.

"I think I felt something that time, doctor!" the prisoner exclaimed as he lifted his arm from the chair when Marston released him.

Marston nodded somewhat distractedly as he adjusted his device. "From the machine," he said again, as if it was a habitual refrain accompanying the treatment.

"From the machine?" Duncan asked as the prisoner left the cell. "But of course it is from the machine."

Marston looked up with a self-conscious glance. "There have been misunderstandings, about whether this work is for science or for the devil."

Duncan considered the words as he helped Marston adjust the jars. "Are you saying you have been accused of taking something out of your patients?"

Marston nodded hesitantly. "It is the inevitable burden of those who introduce new science. The immortal Galileo and Copernicus were denounced to the Inquisition." He winced under Duncan's inquiring stare. "There are those who say we extract a patient's soul to store in the glass ball." The scientist looked toward the cell door, as if hoping for his next prisoner to appear. "Fools," he murmured.

"Did this happen at Shamokin?" Duncan pressed.

Marston sighed and turned back to Duncan. "I was away, having Sunday dinner with the Moravians. Some Indians, Delawares and Shawnee, decided to use my equipment. There was an old Indian who had been feeling very weak in the chest, heart problems no doubt. They decided to treat him but had no notion of how to use the device. They let a massive charge build up then touched him in the chest. I am told there were sparks, a terrible smell of burning flesh, and he was rendered unconscious. When they examined him he had a molten lump of metal on his chest. When he regained consciousness he was weaker than ever, the sounds from his lips gibberish. He had clearly suffered some kind of collapse in his heart and brain. He died a few days later. They said my machine had extracted his spirit from his heart and melted it, leaving him an empty shell. When I investigated I found he had been wearing a copper medallion. They had no notion of the energy of the higher charges and so had melted the copper. It has happened numerous times, with lightning rods, with the swords of soldiers in storms, with nails on ships' masts. But they wouldn't listen, at their campfires they said I was a sorcerer, that I was planning to keep them from going on to the next world by reducing their souls to metal." Marston shrugged. "I was at the end of my work in any event."

The second prisoner arrived, a man with a pronounced limp. Duncan silently helped Marston prepare the man in the chair, and as he turned the wheel he listened to Marston's words again in his mind. The Indians, at least some of them, had decided a molten lump of metal on a dead or dying man was the work of witchcraft to extract and destroy his soul. Each of the dead men had had such a lump of metal, jammed in his throat. The killer knew it would have made the dead men taboo, too frightening to touch, would have kept other Indians away from the marker trees.

The next prisoner was the gasping youth. Introduced as a pickpocket, he shook with fear when Marston strapped him in, screamed a curse as the arc touched his hand, and screamed again as Marston touched a metal rod from one of the Leyden jars to his ear. "My patrons believe that there is part of the brain that controls criminal behavior," Marston explained over the young man's abject moans, "that if we can but burn it away the soul shall return to harmony." He gave, Duncan saw, but the lightest of touches to the ear, with the lowest of charges.

Marston stepped to the door as the pickpocket was led away, checked the corridor, and nodded to Duncan, who proceeded with a spent jar back to the waiting wagon. The jailer waved him out through the entry and waved him back in with only a glance up from reading a broadsheet.

Duncan moved quickly from cell to cell on the ground floor, stepping closer to the open hatches on the doors where no prisoner gazed out, ignoring the open cells whose occupants were outside. He paused at the end of the corridor, noticing a shadow in the corner that resolved into a stairwell as he drew closer. With a glance along the hallway he slipped down the stairs. The cellar extended only for half the length of the building, enough for half a dozen cells. Three of the heavy doors hung open, the fourth, judging by the dim lights of the two lanterns hanging in the corridor, held crates behind its locked door.

Duncan lifted one of the lanterns from its hook and held it closer to one of the remaining doors. A fetid smell wafted from the cell. A man growled, and another spat a curse as if Duncan was disturbing them. He moved to the next cell. The same rancid smell came from its hatch, but so, too, did a faint scent of cedar.

He gave a low call, the whistle of a warbler, that brought movement in the shadows. "*Jiyathondek,*" he whispered twice in the Iroquois tongue. *Hearken. Listen.* "It is Duncan. Conawago is close."

The chiseled face of the chief appeared in the dim light. Skanawati nodded in greeting. "*Niyawenhkowa kady nonwa,*" he said. *Great thanks that in safety you have come through the forest.* "Lamentable would be the consequences had you perished," he continued in an untroubled, solemn voice.

To Duncan's surprise, he recognized the words. They were from the traditional Edge of the Woods ceremony, in which Indian travelers greeted each other after traveling far to meet. He struggled to recall the words of response that Conawago and the rangers had taught him. "I have seen the footmarks of our forefathers," he recited after a moment. "All that remains is the smoke of their pipes."

For the first time since Duncan had known him, Skanawati smiled, then nodded his approval. "It is true, then," the Onondaga observed, "the forest is entering your blood."

This is absurd, something shouted inside Duncan. *There is so much to ask, so many mysteries to penetrate, and we are acting like we are picking berries in the wilderness.* But he found himself smiling back. "True enough," he acknowledged, then quickly added, "Marston is upstairs. He helped me."

Skanawati nodded again. "You must let them know back in our country that he is no enemy."

"There are other killers, Skanawati," Duncan blurted out. "I am gathering the truth."

"Truth?" the Indian asked. He grew silent, studying Duncan. "The truth is I want all surveyors to be gone from the world. They are always the beginning of the end for the land spirits."

"Men are not hanged for the sins nurtured in their hearts, only the sins committed by their hands." As he spoke Duncan looked behind him, thinking he heard the stairs creak. He lifted the lantern along the frame of the door, looking for a key. To his surprise, he found one, hanging on a post in the center of the corridor.

Skanawati hesitated when Duncan opened the cell door. He took only two small steps and lowered himself to sit on the floor against the wall. Duncan handed him a piece of sausage, brought from Marston's kitchen, half of which the chieftain consumed before stuffing the remainder inside his soiled waistcoat.

"Tell me something, Scotsman," Skanawati asked. "Is it daylight out?"

The question brought an unexpected ache to Duncan's heart. "It is early afternoon."

Skanawati nodded.

"I wish to understand about your uncle, the last chief. Why he would kill the surveyor Townsend. Was it because he knew of Townsend drawing a map? A great chief does not kill for no reason."

"The map had been destroyed by then," the Onondaga said. "It was an old feud. His wife and her family, all his children, were killed by Huron and French raiders many years ago."

"But Townsend was not French."

"My uncle often wore a scarlet soldier's coat. He had been given a medal from the English king when he was younger, for fighting for him in one of the wars."

Duncan struggled to make sense of the words. "You mean Townsend was with French that day?"

Skanawati nodded. "My uncle found them at the marker tree, saw how Townsend and the French Indians laughed and drank together. Above all, he hates traitors. It had been traitors, English trappers paid with French gold, who had led the raiders to his village all those years ago. He swore blood vengeance on all such men."

Duncan paced in front of the Onondaga, straining to connect Skanawati's revelation to the murders. "Who would know of your uncle's feud?"

"It was no secret."

"But why was he there that day, just when Townsend was with the French Indians?"

"Some Shawnee came to him, told him he had found a traitor who needed to be stopped before he inflicted harm on the Iroquois. When I heard this I did not believe it. Townsend was not an evil man."

"And Townsend, did he have a guide?"

"A Delaware called Ohio George."

No doubt, Duncan realized, Townsend never knew the difference between French and English Indians, had drunk with the French Indians because they had been friends of his guide. The first murder had been an elaborate trap, a test as it were.

"Outside," the chief asked, "have you seen a large black bird?"

"I—I don't know," Duncan admitted. He noticed a water bucket, filled the ladle hanging on its side, and handed it to the Indian, struggling not to let his frustration show. He reminded himself that seldom were conversations with an Indian conducted in a straight line.

"This cell," Skanawati said after a moment, "it is like a cave. It makes me think of my father."

Duncan leaned against the post, realizing this was the most he had ever heard the man speak.

"I never knew my father much," Skanawati continued, "no one in the village did. He never stayed with us except sometimes during the sugar tree or green corn festivals."

Duncan thought he understood. "My father had many responsibilities as well."

"No. It wasn't like that. He lived alone, in the woods, in the manner of what you Europeans call a hermit, except he did it to be close to the forest spirits. My people have a name for a man like that. A wild deer."

"It can be difficult to be raised without a father."

"An Iroquois boy is raised by his mother's family, by his uncle," Skanawati reminded Duncan. "But I find myself thinking more and more of my father. Once in a winter when I was young, he came and stole me away against my mother's wishes, took me to a high cave where he was living, just as a terrible snowstorm arrived. The morning after the storm he took me to the mouth of the cave,

where we could see for many miles. The world was white, everywhere, except for a single creature perched on an old dead tree
nearby, a raven. My father said he always sat there after snowstorms,
because it was a different world then, because in that world nothing
moved for as far as a man could see but the eye of that raven. He
said that bird was the most ancient of our gods. He said in all my
life the most important thing to remember was that the raven was
always watching me, seeing everything I did." Skanawati paused to
drain the ladle. "I see him sometimes, flying high above."

"In your village," Duncan said in a tone of wonder, "there was
a raven watching the ceremony of the dead."

Skanawati nodded, as if not surprised, then looked up. "Look
to the trail behind," he declared abruptly.

Duncan paused, thinking the Indian meant he had missed
something from their travels. Too late he heard the noise behind
and spun about. The club slammed into the back of his knees first,
so hard he collapsed onto the stone flags of the floor. Then he knew
nothing but a storm of boots kicking his belly, his legs, his neck,
his head.

The spirit fire. They were draining his life force, stealing the
spark that kept him alive. The odd tingling sensation in his hand
exploded into a hundred stabs of pain. His head shot up, and he
looked directly into the face of Lord Ramsey.

Duncan twisted against his bindings, gradually becoming aware
that he was back in the corner cell, suspended from the ceiling in
the harness Marston used for his treatments.

"In Pennsylvania," Ramsey lectured his captive, "a man who
escapes his indenture is a criminal. Worse, in the land of the
Quakers, you are a sinner, for you have broken your sacred word."

"My indenture." Through his spasms of pain Duncan could manage only a few syllables at a time. "Is in the name of your daughter." He saw Marston now, slumped unconscious in a corner.

"I have sworn out an affidavit that says otherwise." Ramsey nodded to one of the four men who attended him, and the man touched the shaft of a Leyden jar to a bleeding cut on the back of Duncan's hand. His head jerked back in pain. The man laughed, then touched the jar to his chin.

When he regained consciousness they had stripped off his clothes. They used all the jars, on every part of his body. The more he cried out in pain, the more Ramsey laughed. He saw the room in short bursts of vision between explosions of pain. A man spun the glass ball at a near blinding speed, generating more blue fire. Another man tried to get the rod of a jar into Duncan's mouth. Duncan waited until his torturer was close then jerked his shoulder violently forward, knocking the jar to the floor, shattering it as Ramsey applauded. Marston was naked from the waist up now, and a man applied one of the jars to his arms, which jerked compulsively.

Prisoners began shouting. Ramsey muttered something to one of his lackeys, who stuffed money into the hand of the turnkey. Marston tried to beat away his assailant. There was something on his arm. A metal wire was stretched from a glass jar to Duncan's belly, and he convulsed backward and forward. Marston's arm. He forced himself to focus on it. On the inside of his arm, above the elbow, was a scar in the shape of a lightning bolt.

"Burke!" he gasped, just as one of Ramsey's men applied one of the remaining Leyden jars to the bottom of his foot.

Ramsey slapped him into silence. "You will rot in this jail until the magistrates return you to me," he vowed to Duncan. "Then you will rot in a cell I am building in the cellar of my house. I think," he added, with a bemused glance at Marston's equipment, "we shall purchase some of these remarkable devices to keep you amused." Duncan faded in and out of consciousness. He twisted, flailed his legs. He was helpless in the harness, Ramsey's naked puppet. He made out voices in the outside corridor. Someone punched his belly. Marston, still on the floor, moaned. Duncan struggled against the pain, feeling the sharp stabs now even though his tormentors seemed to be gone. He fought an overwhelming fatigue.

The last thing he remembered was the fury on the face of Magistrate Brindle as he walked into the cell.

Chapter Sixteen

H E FELT SO assured by the tender stroking of his forehead, the soft singing near his ear, knowing his mother was at his side, that Duncan wanted to linger in the dark, quiet place. He tried to push away the painful moans from nearby, the drumming of infantry boots on cobbles, the strange tingling in his limbs, until a vision of limp bodies on a gallows invaded his dream. He pushed through his delirium, shaking his head violently, using the pain that followed to help him wake.

Finally he was back, gazing into the soulful eyes of a middle-aged woman wearing a white apron over an austere gray dress. As she dabbed at his face with a damp cloth she hummed a hymn.

"I always wondered what the first angel I met would look like," Duncan offered in a hoarse voice. His throat was dry as sticks.

The woman smiled. "You're not in heaven yet, Mr. McCallum. Only Philadelphia." She began checking the bandage that was wrapped tightly around three of his fingers. "All the angels I know are in the Benevolent Society for the Humane Treatment of Prisoners."

"Where do I join?" Duncan murmured.

His nurse smiled again, then lifted a small clay mug of water to his lips. Duncan winced at the effort of sitting up, then took the mug and drank as he studied his surroundings. He had not left the corner cell, but was on a cot now, and Marston's equipment, even the table that had supported it, was gone, the only sign of his experiments the ceiling hooks where the harness had hung. He looked back at his nurse, noticing a small Bible in the pocket of her apron.

"How long?" he asked. He pulled his legs to the floor, trying to stand, then sank back in a wave of nausea. Every extremity screamed in pain.

"You have been unconscious for nearly twenty-four hours," the Quaker woman explained.

"Conawa—" Duncan began then corrected himself. "Socrates Moon?"

"Your friend is safe. Last I saw him he was in the magistrate's library. It was he and the jailer who came to us for help."

"Was he arrested?"

"He is safe, as I said."

"I mean Ramsey. Surely he must be arrested."

The light left the woman's eyes. "There was no one here when the magistrate arrived. And Mr. Ramsey," she cautioned, "is a member of the council, and of the proprietor's private social club in London."

For the first time Duncan saw that the cell door was closed, with a guard outside. The despair that rose up at the sight caused more torment than all his injuries together. He was a prisoner. He would be a prisoner now for the rest of his life. When he looked back and saw the face of his nurse more fully, he realized he had seen her before.

"You gave me a glass of milk," he said. "How long have you been a member of the Brindle household?"

"I was born a Brindle and became a Bythe."

The realization came slowly through the fog in Duncan's brain. "Forgive me. I misunderstood. Your husband. I am so sorry."

"As we all are. It was his time to be gathered to God."

He saw the sadness in the woman's eyes, but felt helpless to deal with it. "The man who killed your husband was not Skanawati."

"They call it an accident now."

"He was murdered," Duncan said. "Like all the others at the boundary trees."

"There are teamsters who signed statements saying he fell on the rocks."

Duncan stared in disbelief. "Who would collect such statements?"

"A lawyer gave them to a magistrate. Not my brother, another."

"A lawyer working for whom?"

"That land venture. The Susquehanna Company."

Duncan closed his eyes again. "So in Philadelphia the truth has become a commodity that can be bought and sold."

Mrs. Bythe bit her lip but did not reply. She reached into the basket and produced a broadsheet. "Your friend from Virginia said you would want to see this."

The sheet was nearly covered with news of ship sailings and landed cargos. But at the bottom was a short article. *Shamokin Merchant Drowns.*

Duncan's mouth went dry as he read. *The body of Matthew Waller, merchant of Shamokin, was found by a river fishing vessel. Waller had been missing for two days and is now believed to have slipped from a wharf in the night.*

"The current can be very strong," Mrs. Bythe offered.

"He was killed," Duncan asserted. "He was killed because we were looking for him, because he was connected to the murders." Every door was being slammed shut. "Dr. Marston?" he asked after a moment.

"Recovering at his house by the river."

"I must see him."

"I can send a boy with a message, but I cannot tell if he will soon muster enough courage to return to the prison. And," she said, lowering her voice and looking toward the floor, "there are only formalities to be addressed before you are turned over to Lord Ramsey. Some papers to be signed. Once the signatures are sealed and verified by the clerks and the doctor releases you, you will be surrendered to your bondholder."

Duncan buried his head in his hands. Ramsey claimed to have built a special cell in his cellar for Duncan, was going to acquire electrical devices to use on Duncan. "He is not my bondholder. The document was signed over to his daughter. There were witnesses."

"He has signed an affidavit that says otherwise. He is a member of the council," she repeated, and she poured him another mug of water. She leaned closer as she handed him the mug and whispered, "It is his man on the door."

"The treaty," Duncan said when he had drained the mug. "Skanawati."

"The Virginians threaten to leave. The Indians are considering a huge price."

"For the freedom of their chief?" Duncan asked hopefully.

"No. For the sale of their land."

His heart sank still lower. "The formal negotiations for this have started?"

Mrs. Bythe rose, straightening her apron. "There are no meaningful formal negotiations until the informal ones are done." The
guard outside noticed the woman's preparation for departure and
opened the door.

"I wish you to borrow my Bible," she said pointedly, and
handed Duncan the small volume from her pocket. "Lord Ramsey
knows he must tolerate us Quakers. He allows us to hold prayer
sessions with his staff in his library from time to time."

He stared forlornly at the door as it sealed him in. Then
Duncan gazed at the little book, setting it down on the stool to dab
at the blood that began to ooze out the edge of a bandage on his
arm. He rose to walk to the cell door. Halfway across the cell his
knees buckled and he collapsed to the floor.

Later, after he had dragged himself back to the cot, after he had
passed out with only his arm and head resting on the cot, he lifted
the little book on the stool.

Inside the cover was a slip of paper with two sets of crossed
double lines with a letter and a dot inside the right angles, each
dot positioned differently inside its angle. On the reverse were two
triangles with letters and dots likewise arranged on each side of the
lines. He turned the page over and over. Every letter of the alphabet
was represented.

Duncan forced himself up, staggered to the window, and collapsed under it to hold the paper in the pool of light, understanding
the point of her parting words. The widow had been in Ramsey's
library. Conawago had spoken to her, and she had found the pigpen code. Duncan frantically patted at his waist, then crawled to
search the piles of tattered blankets at the end of the cot.

His pouch with his notes of the codes from the trees, along with
everything else he had had in his possession, was gone. But the signs
on the first tree were burned into his memory. With his finger he

drew in the dust on the floor the signs as he had seen them, beginning with the empty open-topped box, then an open-sided right angle tilted so its angle pointed to the center of the preceding box, ending with a complete, but empty square. His hand trembled as he consulted Conawago's chart. The first symbol was a B, the next a U. He quickly transcribed each letter, staring in confusion at the result. BURKE. The killer had simply recorded the name of his victim on the tree. It made no sense.

He closed his eyes against a tremor of pain and found the fingers of one hand twitching uncontrollably, his frustration now adding to his weakness. This is how his life would end, in Ramsey's cellar, more and more of his body twitching, convulsing, as he lost control of it. Each day more of his brain would be burned away. He had bet his freedom, his very life, on finding the truth, yet each piece of the puzzle was more useless than the one before.

He closed his eyes, adrift in despair, visited by a vision of the faces of those who had died on his prison ship. In the waking nightmare the dead came to life, each bloodless face turned to him in ridicule, pointing skeleton fingers at the paper in his hand.

Four paces to the far wall, four paces back. Duncan's hours were divided into journeys from one end of his cell to the other as he struggled to restore the power of his limbs. At first it was all he could do to stagger from one wall to the other, his knees and ankles protesting every move, his toes still tingling with a strange heat. He exercised thirty minutes by the clock of the State House visible through his window, then rested for ten, eating the stale bread and cheese left by the Benevolent Society, building such an appetite that he even emptied the bowl of thin gruel shoved through his hatch twice a day.

He tried to force from his mind his destiny as Ramsey's slave, recalling long discussions in the night with Conawago about war parties facing impossible odds against enemy tribes, how the warriors were taught to push away all fear, all thought of defeat, all thought of the morrow, to simply hold in their hearts the proud deeds of their forebears and the power of their gods. It was, he knew, little different from the training of the Highland clans, who had fought so many impossible foes through the centuries.

He often glanced at Mrs. Bythe's chart of letters and paused in his travail long enough to write more signs. He could not trust his memory of the other signs on the trees, so instead he encoded in the dust by the window the names of the dead. Cooper. Bythe. Burke. Townsend. Duncan leaned on the windowsill, facing out, watching the prisoners exercise in the small yard below, watching the spiraling smoke of a hundred chimneys. If he pressed close to the bars he could see masts above rooftops, remembering there were ships half a mile away that would take on an able-bodied crewman without question, ships that could take him to the Scottish settlements in the Carolinas, to New York, to Holland, where he had friends, to Ireland, where many Highlanders had fled after the purges. He lost himself again in imaginings of a different life, of how in the night he would slip out of the cell and over the wall, then sail away from all his cares. But when night came his despair bore down on him again, the black thing pressing like a heavy weight on his heart. He fought it by recollecting conversations he had had with Conawago.

His injured fingers kept curling up, and he considered, with the eye of the medical student, how the flow of electrical fluid affected even the smallest of muscles. Unwinding their linen bandage, he winced at the sight of the raw, oozing patches where his skin had been burned away, then pushed the fingers straight against the sill and watched them curl up again as if of their own volition.

He did not know how long he was being watched, but slowly the hairs on his neck began to rise. He limped back to his cot and sat, waiting. Moments later he heard the grating of the metal in the lock, and the door swung open. Marston limped into the chamber, leaning on a cane. The scientist stared at the turnkey, who frowned but stepped back into the doorway and closed the door.

Marston hurried to the door and closed the hatch. "You must not let them see you walking about."

"Sorry?"

"The best reason we have to keep you here is your medical condition. The jailer will not release you until you are healed. Ramsey is under the impression he has no need to hurry the paperwork for your transfer to his compound. I have food from Mrs. Bythe." Duncan saw now he carried a basket, which he placed by the stool. "And a message, from the physician who looked in on Skanawati. The chief wants you to know that he could not see the faces of those who attacked you. But he believes two were turnkeys, and a third man was giving them orders from the shadows."

"I must beg your forgiveness," Duncan said. "You were caught in Ramsey's trap for me."

Marston raised a dismissive hand. "We have survived. It was an illuminating experience to be on the other side of the jars. Illuminating," he repeated with a shallow laugh at his pun.

"Perhaps you could use less severe charges in the future."

Marston flushed. "I have already decided that the larger jars will no longer leave my premises."

"Your equipment is lost. I regret having dragged you into my problems."

"As I recollect it was I who sought you out that night," Marston said. "I have already written to Dr. Franklin. He will relish the exciting news from stale old Philadelphia. And the Benevolent Society has agreed to bear the cost of replacements."

Duncan could not help but grin at the scientist's good will. "I fear I have another request. Might you roll up your left sleeve?"

"Pardon?"

"Your sleeve. In the . . . in the confusion I thought I saw a mark. Like a bolt of lightning."

Marston grimaced, but began rolling up the cuff of the linen shirt he wore under his sleeveless waistcoat. "Our badge." He exposed his upper arm, extending the mark with what Duncan took to be pride.

It was a scar, a raised red scar in the shape of a jagged streak of lightning.

"This is identical to one I saw on the arm of Captain Burke when I examined his body."

"There are perhaps twenty of us in the Leyden Society. Natural philosophers interested in the advancement of the study of electrical fluids. Several of us," he added, "helped Dr. Franklin with his kites and lightning rods. We meet on the full moon and often send a kite up in a storm."

Duncan's mind raced. "How could Captain Burke of Virginia be a member?"

"He studied here. His father discouraged him, wanted him home, said his academics would be useless in running their estates. Once, when he was visiting, his father had him forcibly removed from one of our meetings. I think that's why he came back and joined us, an act of defiance."

"Came back when?"

"Last month Burke entertained us with that very story at our meeting. He was supposed to pick up maps in Baltimore and rendezvous with his troops at Fort Ligonier, supposed to take a boat from the James up the Chesapeake Bay to Baltimore. Instead he found a captain going up the Delaware Bay to Philadelphia, where better maps were available in any event."

"He came back to join your Leyden Society?"

Marston grinned awkwardly. "He came back to set the foundations for his new life, as he said to us. There was a party, where he drank and told us of his plans, perhaps more than he intended. His father also did not know he had a mistress here, did not know he had secretly accumulated enough money to buy a house in the city. He was a man of refined tastes, sent to boarding school in London as a boy, and after was never comfortable with the Virginia country life." He gazed down at his scar. "Joining the Society was his official welcome to Philadelphia. We have a little ceremony with a molded brass plate strapped to the arm through which we send a strong charge of electrical fluid. When we remove the plate the skin has been excited enough to produce the scar."

Duncan looked at his own bandages. "It would be painful."

"There is brandy involved."

"Where did he get such a large amount of money?"

"I don't know. It wasn't just the cost of a house. He was steadily buying shares in a merchant company, with the intention of supplying the frontier, was making regular payments to the owner."

"But you said he did not like the rough life."

"He was to stay in Philadelphia. He had some partner who was going to handle the frontier. There was final paperwork he had to sign here, based on the funds he already paid."

"But the money," Duncan pressed, "where would new payments come from if not from his family?" He considered Marston's words again. "Are you suggesting he was being paid by someone in Philadelphia?"

Marston shrugged. "A gentleman does not ask about such things."

Duncan turned and braced himself on the window again, gazing out over the busy city. "So Burke left from here to join his men," he mused out loud.

"Is that important?"

"Very." Duncan eyed Marston carefully, trying to judge just how far to trust him, then realized he had little choice. "Can you speak with the Benevolent Society again? Can you find Hadley?"

"Yes, on both counts."

Duncan began explaining what he needed.

The Benevolent Society arrived in force that afternoon, announcing a spring cleaning of the musty cells. Duncan watched as the jailer argued about the abrupt appearance of a dozen workers but saw his resistance fade before three Quakers matrons, including Mrs. Bythe, as they chided him. One went so far as to wave her Scripture at him.

He was in his cot when they came for him. Mrs. Bythe guided two large men who had fashioned a carrying stretcher out of a blanket and two long poles. Duncan feigned unconsciousness, kept his eyes closed as they carried him out and down the stairs, did not open them until he was set upon a pallet in a corner of the yard. Moments later two turnkeys appeared with a confused but compliant Skanawati. They argued only a moment before remitting custody of the Iroquois to Mrs. Bythe, who resolved their doubt with a coin pressed into each man's palm and a reassurance that they could watch their prisoner from the doorway. The Quakers, Duncan had decided, were as resourceful as they were devout.

The workers, most dressed in black or gray, many with broad-rimmed hats pulled low on their heads, began hauling soiled pallets and chamber pots out of the cells to the opposite corner. Two benches were arranged at right angles to the walls by Duncan and Skanawati, forming a small square by a cart of fresh straw that obscured them from the gate. The three women sat and began stuffing new pallets with straw as they sang a hymn. Skanawati, regarding the Quakers uncomfortably, had taken a step as if to retreat when one of the men in gray touched his arm and pushed his hat back.

"We give thanks you made it through the forest." It was Conawago.

The Iroquois slowly nodded, following Conawago's example as the old Nipmuc sat cross-legged on the ground beside Duncan.

Other workers gathered nearby with tubs of water and lye soap to wash the chamber pots, and more settled on the benches as if for a prayer meeting, further assuring their little assembly would have no unwanted onlookers. Duncan suddenly realized he knew all the new arrivals as they lifted their wide hats. Hadley, Marston, even Mokie, Becca, and her infant, Penn, were there. Duncan pushed back the thought that it was probably the last time he would see any of them and focused instead on the urgent need to draw the truth out. He leaned forward, handed Conawago the slip with Mrs. Bythe's chart of the code, then began to explain what he had learned.

They listened as he recounted how the killer had left codes that the fleeing slaves would carry, how the evidence had been contrived to cast suspicion on the Iroquois, how the codes were known to a small number of intellectuals in Philadelphia, how Captain Burke had joined his men on false pretenses, after secretly attending to his new life in Philadelphia.

"But why would the killer need to record the names of his own victims?" Hadley asked. He pulled a scrap of paper and a writing lead from his pocket, taking notes on his knee. He was keeping his own chronicle of the evidence.

"Because he was being paid for each one. Piecework. Because he was moving around unpredictably and could not report back in person each time he struck. Because Burke and his secret partner were obligated to make ongoing payments for their new business. And it was too dangerous to send a written message. So the escaping slaves carried the coded messages to Shamokin, where they would be received by the merchant Waller, who corresponded with a Philadelphia bank."

He ended by explaining how the raiders had taken Burke's body.

"But that was an act of war," Mrs. Bythe observed.

"That's what we were supposed to think," Duncan agreed. "Just as the first Skanawati, the one who died last winter, was supposed to think Townsend was dealing with French Indians. But they weren't French Indians. Some may have been Hurons, may have even traveled sometimes with Huron raiders, but they were outlaws working for the killer, who could not afford to have the body returned, since the scar would prove that Burke had recently been in Philadelphia."

"Even so . . . " Hadley began.

"Your cousin had signed a contract to buy a house here."

"Impossible!" Hadley rejoined. "He had been promised a large tract of the western lands. He had no funds to buy a house."

"He had a mistress here. He was never going to live on that tract. In fact his actions show that he had great confidence that the Virginians would never perfect their title to that tract. He did not know the depths of the evil he swam in. The money offered to him here allowed him to make a new life. He cared little if it meant helping to prevent the Virginia land titles being perfected for he did not intend to return to Virginia. He recruited Townsend, gave him a promise that his work would be published. He helped with the runaway slaves. But he knew too much. And he drank too much. Perhaps those behind the killings had intended to eliminate him all along. After all, for the rest of his life his knowledge would be a threat to them."

"But who would ever recognize such a scar?" Mrs. Bythe said. "There's only a small number of educated men in Philadelphia who would know the significance of this lightning bolt."

"Exactly," Duncan replied. The Quakers stared at him as his meaning sank in.

"But Mokie," Hadley put in after a moment, "surely they have nothing to fear from Mokie." The Virginian glanced at the girl, walking along the wall with her infant brother in her arms.

"Mokie knows something more," Duncan suggested, "information she probably doesn't think important. But something the killers fear. Keep her close."

Skanawati watched the clouds as Duncan spoke, seeming not to listen until Hadley leaned forward. "We have found a lawyer. He will write a formal opinion that Skanawati's confession is not valid."

"But it was given before so many witnesses," Duncan said with an uncertain glance at the Iroquois chief.

"The lawyer says that what is recited before a military tribunal at Fort Ligonier may not be used in a provincial court. The tribunal was convened by the commander of the fort. That Magistrate Brindle sat at his bench does not change the point of law."

"Surely," Duncan said, "the Virginia negotiators will never tolerate this. They must be placated for the treaty to succeed."

Conawago fixed Duncan with a pointed gaze. "Our Virginian friend and I have found a political solution."

Hadley leaned closer to Duncan. "Each of the three parties—Virginia, Pennsylvania, and the Iroquois—must obtain something of value from the treaty. The Virginians wanted the western tract, the Iroquois want their supplies, Pennsylvania wants security on the western frontier."

"Exactly. The Virginians will never give up on hanging Skanawati unless they get their land."

"There is, in fact, another condolence as important to them, something even more important to the citizens of Virginia. Wives and children."

"I'm sorry?"

"Conawago has spoken with the Iroquois chiefs. They calculate over two hundred Virginia prisoners are among the western tribes. Their return will be offered up. The treaty negotiators from Virginia would be tarred and feathered if they ever took land over the return of loved ones. The Iroquois will get their supplies, the Virginians will get the returned prisoners."

"And Pennsylvania?"

"Penn's colony will get the western fortresses it needs to secure the borders."

Duncan spoke loudly, slowly, to be sure Skanawati understood. "You are saying the treaty could be accomplished without any land being ceded by the tribes, without the Virginians taking the land they claim now, without a hanging?"

"All treaties involve compromise. Yes."

Skanawati slowly moved his gaze toward Duncan.

"You can go home to move your village," Duncan said to the Onondaga.

"The Virginians demand that the chief be held until the treaty is signed. For security."

"Then he needs to be removed from the hole he is kept in," Duncan insisted. "I will exchange cells with him."

Hadley and Conawago shared an uneasy glance. "The final negotiations are not to be held in Philadelphia," the Virginian declared. "The tribes are uneasy here, mindful of how many Indians who linger here die of European disease. Some Indians are already gone. And the city fathers are uncomfortable with so many Indians camped at the city edge. There are complaints. Last night there was a march of citizens to the State House demanding their removal. Lord Ramsey met with the governor."

"I don't understand."

"The negotiations are moving north, to the border of Iroquoia, to the town of the Moravians on the Lehigh River. The treaty is to be concluded at Bethlehem, the chief released there when it is signed."

Duncan finally grasped why his friends were not more cheerful in relating their news. With the treaty delegation moving north he would be in Ramsey's hands. He would be denied the final act of the great drama. "The Moravians are more welcoming to the tribes than any others," he said neutrally.

A new voice rose from the end of the bench, from a worker just arrived at the little assembly. "There will still be an inquest at the least into the deaths of Bythe and Townsend. And the Virginians insist we be ready for a trial if there is no resolution to the treaty. Mr. McCallum will be required as a vital witness." As he spoke the man lifted his hat so his face was no longer obscured. Magistrate Brindle's hands were white from the lime being used to scour the cells.

"I don't understand, your honor," Duncan said.

"The trail of ownership of the Susquehanna Company has been deliberately obscured in the official records. But Mr. Hadley's efforts have allowed us to locate several of the former owners, each with a peculiar tale of calamity that forced them to sell, each being called upon by Lord Ramsey's lawyers within days of the disaster." Brindle fixed Duncan with a pointed gaze. "I have this morning written an order for you to be conveyed to Bethlehem with us," the Quaker declared. "The order will be filed in the court when the convoy clears Philadelphia. Whether Ramsey likes it or not, a prisoner of my court is not released until I say so."

"Praise be to God," Mrs. Bythe declared in a loud whisper.

"And will Mr. Felton join us as well?" Duncan asked.

Brindle stiffened. "Of course. Why?"

"Each time we get close to one of the conspirators he dies. The last one was killed by your nephew in plain sight."

"He is a hero for doing so."

"Perhaps."

"You have suffered too many blows to your head, Mr. McCallum," Brindle observed as he rose to leave.

"Think of it, your honor," Duncan said to his back. "Consider the possibility that Felton works for Ramsey. You said he is making investments. How does he do so on the wages of a scout?"

Brindle halted, his head down for a moment, before proceeding out of the compound.

As the others began to leave and the turnkey escorted Skanawati away, Hadley dropped a newspaper on the ground beside Duncan. "All the world says he is a hero."

The front page of the *Gazette* held a crude print of a man firing a musket at an Indian with flames rising from his back. *A Fire of*

Fair Return, read the headline, over a story of how the brave Samuel Felton had saved a girl, and the city, from a murderous savage.

"I don't understand the headline," Duncan said, looking up at the Philadelphians.

"The poor boy got his revenge," Mrs. Bythe explained. "His turnabout."

"Revenge?"

"Don't you know? Poor Mr. Felton was a prisoner of the savages for many years."

Chapter Seventeen

I N HIS SCOTTISH prison, before being thrown onto his prison ship, Duncan had spent a week loosening the mortar of a single stone with a stolen nail, then calculated he had but to loosen another five hundred such stones and he would be free. Now as the prison wagon wound its way through the hills and valleys north of Philadelphia he could not help but consider again the many ways he might escape. His conveyance was merely a modified farm wagon, made for transporting livestock, the wooden slats on its sides susceptible to splintering with a well-directed kick, the roof planks weak with knotholes.

But each time he tested the wood he caught sight of Magistrate Brindle riding close, between the wagon and the Virginian soldiers, as if to protect Duncan and Skanawati. Brindle would be held accountable, Brindle would be disgraced if Duncan escaped. Once the treaty was signed there would be time, he told himself. There would be a return trip of two or three days before he was consigned to Ramsey's vengeful custody. Though it meant risking his life, though it meant he would be forever hounded by bounty hunters, he would make the attempt and flee to the deep wilderness, Felton at his heels or no.

In waking nightmares, he saw the ranks of conspirators. Ohio George, Red Hand, and Winston Burke hovered over him, with Ramsey standing behind, Felton fading in and out of his vision. Again and again he convinced himself that the Quaker was the missing link to Ramsey, only to recollect there was no real evidence, that Felton could have simply been playing the role of the bounty hunter, even the part of the civic hero in killing Red Hand. He had obscured his past links to the Indians. Yet no one who had been a captive of the tribes advertised the fact, for the stigma it would give them.

His companion in the prison wagon spoke little at first. After the first hour on the bumpy road Duncan had begun to recount to Skanawati the story of his visit to Shamokin and the chief's village, drawing a smile when describing Mokie's encounter with Rideaux's bear. He even hesitantly described the reburial ceremony, then his visit to the ancient shrine in the Susquehanna with Skanawati's mother.

The Onondaga had remained silent, though listening attentively, and later he asked questions about the reburial, making sure the old chief had been interred in the white fur Skanawati had trapped for him, and that his nephew Johantty had helped with the old chants. He looked at Duncan a long time. "There was a man who came and stared at me in my cell, a weak, pale man who wears lace around his wrists," he observed at last. "They say you are a slave to him."

"That is true." Duncan confirmed, then after a moment explained. "It was my punishment for helping my uncle when he sang the songs of our fathers."

Skanawati studied him in silence, then reached into a pocket on the inside of his beaded waistcoat and to Duncan's surprise produced a single, ragged strand of white wampum beads. Duncan did not move as the Iroquois draped the beads over his wrist. "Tell me more of this."

The story Duncan began took more than two hours to relay, as his companion constantly interrupted with questions. When Duncan spoke of how his clan's entire way of life had been outlawed for their resistance to the distant British king, Skanawati wanted to know what king his people had had before, and he nodded solemnly when Duncan said the Highland clans had never needed kings, had only needed to be left alone. When Duncan spoke of how his uncle, by then an aging, worn-out fugitive, had found Duncan at his medical college, the chief wanted to know the kinds of places where such men in their land hid, and whether the wise men of Duncan's school shared the wisdom of the Iroquois healers, who knew how the stars and moon affected the human body. When the chief asked how singing songs could condemn a man, Duncan finally explained how his uncle, the old rebel, hiding in Duncan's student lodging, had gotten drunk on his eightieth birthday and loudly sung out in the tongue of their people, which the king had also outlawed. "My uncle was hanged, I was imprisoned."

"Is it true then," Skanawati asked, "that your tribe is all gone?"

It was Duncan's turn to look away. He had had one of his recurring dreams the night before, of his grandfather calling him from down a long corridor. He looked down at the white beads, still sitting on his arm. "What I need of my tribe," he said, tapping his hand against his heart as he spoke, "is always with me."

He slid the beads off and draped them over Skanawati's wrist. "I have my own question, only one. Did you kill Captain Burke?"

"I am at war with all those who would take our lands."

"Did you kill Captain Burke?" Duncan repeated.

Skanawati looked out over the rolling hills. "There is nothing I would not do to save my people." Duncan saw that he had slipped the beads off his wrist and was cupping them in his hand.

They watched through the slats as the miles unfolded, passing farmers plowing with teams of oxen, entire families sowing seed in fields, small herds tended by boys who carried make-believe muskets carved of wood. As the farms begin to thin out, small armies of laborers could be seen felling trees.

"You English breed like mice," Skanawati observed in a flat voice. "It is as if you keep pouring out of the ground somewhere."

And that, Duncan thought to himself, was the crack in the world that Skanawati really was worried about. The shifts on the continent were all about population. The British would eventually win the war because their colonials totaled a million, while the French had at most sixty thousand. Pennsylvania alone contained two hundred thousand, while the entire Iroquois league numbered perhaps a tenth that number.

"When I was young," the Onondaga observed, "and first saw an entire valley cleared of trees by the Europeans, I was very scared. I was confused about the great magic it must have taken, since the tribes had never before done such a thing. It did not seem to me they had changed part of our world, but that they had laid down a whole new world and crushed ours underneath. My uncle took me to a debate in the Grand Council. Our wisest men, the oldest of the peace chiefs, were arguing about whether the spirits abandoned a land when all the trees were cut down. Some said the spirits died a small death each time any tree was felled, which is why we always say a prayer before taking a tree, why we speak to it when we shape it into a canoe or bowl or mask. Others said the spirits just moved so that the last trees in a land became very powerful, so much that sometimes in the night a tree might just get up and walk away."

"Trees grow back," Duncan suggested.

"But what we don't know," Skanawati countered, "is whether gods grow back."

So many light carriages and riders had passed their slow-moving caravan that Duncan paid little attention when the elegant coach and four with outriders passed them in the afternoon of the third day. It was only later that Duncan realized the coach and riders had not sped ahead, but were keeping pace with the treaty convoy, and with a sinking heart he realized there would be no chance of escape on his return to Philadelphia. Ramsey had come with his men to join the treaty entourage. The murders would have to be resolved before the treaty was signed, meaning Ramsey would place him in manacles the moment the document was signed.

Duncan had heard much of the Moravian enclave at Bethlehem, and on another day, in other circumstances, he knew he would have taken pleasure in roaming down its well-kept streets, past the massive stone-and-timber buildings housing most of the community's members. The town was renowned not just for its Christian living and training of missionaries for work among the tribes, but for its industry as well. The streets rang with the hammers of forges. Rows of clay pots from a kiln sat cooling in the open air. Planks fresh from a saw pit were being unloaded and stacked.

The elegant coach was standing in front of one of the largest buildings when their wagon finally halted. Duncan barely noticed the hands that reached out and guided the two prisoners into a compact stone building used as a summer kitchen, which had been cleared out to accommodate them. The bars over the solitary window and the heavy brackets for a timber to seal the door from the outside told Duncan it had been used for confinement before.

The two prisoners watched the busy traffic of the street from their little window. There were Indians here who taught the Germans the native tongues, Duncan recalled, and old Germans who set Christian hymns to those tongues. Teams of six and even eight oxen passed by, pulling wagons filled with black stones. The surrounding hills were rich in iron. Duncan touched Skanawati's arm and pointed to a group of Indians carrying quarters of meat to their camp by the river. Long Wolf was with them, carrying not meat but an elegant-looking fowling piece.

He was not surprised at the forlorn expressions worn by Hadley and Conawago when they followed the two Moravian women who brought their evening meal. They watched in silence as the women began arranging the food on the stone counter built over the cold ovens. Fresh cornbread, apples, pickled vegetables, dried venison, and buttermilk. Venison and cornbread. The Germans were attuned to the ways of the tribes.

Hadley waited until the women had left. "Ramsey is relentless, Duncan," the Virginian finally said. "Like a mad dog. One with the resources of Midas to back him."

"What has he done now?" Duncan asked, his heart sinking.

Hadley looked self-consciously at Skanawati, who listened without expression. "He's brought a Philadelphia lawyer with him, who heard of efforts to block the testimony about the trial at Ligonier. Now they have a dozen statements from witnesses at Ligonier stating they heard the confession, all sworn now before a different Philadelphia justice, not Brindle. Philadelphia witnesses, as it were, from a Philadelphia court. That judge issued a new writ for Skanawati. With a trial to be held, immediately. I don't understand the game he is playing," Hadley confessed. "He ignores the Virginians now."

"Because he believes the Virginian claims are defeated. They will have to be satisfied with the return of prisoners and nothing else," Duncan said, looking at Skanawati. His fellow prisoner had taken an apple to the window and was eating with no sign of listening.

"Now Ramsey needs the Iroquois to think it is Pennsylvania who controls the life of their chief."

"But why?"

"So Pennsylvania will receive the condolence offering, to the benefit of the Susquehanna Company. The tighter Ramsey makes the noose, the greater the offer when the tribes finally step in to save his life."

"The tribes have so little to offer a man like that."

"They have the only thing he desires," Conawago said. "Do you forget he has become the biggest shareholder in the Susquehanna Company?"

"The land," Hadley said in a hollow whisper. "It was always about the land, wasn't it?"

"Ramsey resents the fact that some of the noble families received proprietary colonies in the last century. He means to make his own." Ramsey, if nothing else, was predictable. He tried the year before to steal a colony for himself in western New York and was now seeking the same in the lands west of the Pennsylvania colony.

"He has made an understanding with the western tribes. He has told the Pennsylvania delegation that those Indians will rebel against their Iroquois masters if they must leave without treasure."

Duncan looked at Hadley in confusion. "No. I don't believe it."

Conawago shook his head. "Ramsey has a piece of paper with the marks of half a dozen western chiefs on it."

"My God," Duncan said, realization sweeping over him as he recalled the new fowling piece he had seen Long Wolf carrying. "He will flood the western chiefs with rum and guns to get their support. He means to drive a wedge between them and the Iroquois."

Duncan turned to Conawago. "You have to explain to Old Belt. You have to make him see the shadow descending upon the Iroquois, make him understand how Ramsey seeks to undermine him with the western tribes. Make him ask Long Wolf to look into his heart." He paused, looking to Hadley. "How do you know these things about Ramsey?"

"Mokie," the Virginian replied uneasily. "She hears things now."

"Hears things? I told you to keep her close."

"I tried. She was in Brindle's rooms in one of the great residence halls. But the Moravians in charge of the accommodations claimed she was needed to help with other guests, and she went away, willingly. We didn't know she was being dispatched to their most important visitor. Ramsey made a large contribution to the Moravians here, is not likely to be denied favors. Now she is in his household, for his tenure at Bethlehem. Ramsey was making light, saying what a valuable girl she is. He described how a mouse had appeared in his room and Mokie pulled a pebble from her pocket and threw it, killing the creature."

Something in his words nagged at Duncan.

"Ai yi," Conawago sighed and looked to Duncan. "With a bigger stone a man could fall."

The memory of their night at the ochre bed washed over him. "She was there!" he gasped. "In the camp of the renegades, the night before Burke was killed!"

An hour before sunset they heard the rumble of the bar being slid out of its brackets. The door cracked open to reveal the ruddy face of Sergeant McGregor. In his hand were two long sections of hand-wrought chain. "I have explained to the honorable magistrate that without fresh air ye may just wither like last year's roses," he said good-naturedly. One end of each chain was already affixed to a set of horse hobbles, which were quickly buckled onto the prisoners. Once the men were outside, the other ends were fastened to a heavy iron ring built into the side of the building. Sentries stood at a distance in front of and behind the building. Like dogs in a kennel, Duncan thought to himself, but he nodded gratefully, then even more vigorously when McGregor produced two clay pipes and a small pouch of tobacco and sent a soldier for a burning brand to light them.

Moments after Duncan and Skanawati had taken seats on upturned fire logs, smoking their borrowed pipes, two familiar figures emerged from the shadows. Duncan had forgotten that Reverend Macklin had left Shamokin for meetings with Moravian elders, but now Duncan stood for a warm handshake. Moses, at the German's side, bent and stirred Skanawati from his contemplation of the clouds. The Onondaga greeted the Christian Indian like an old friend, gripping his forearm tightly.

"I should have recognized that a meeting with elders meant Bethlehem," Duncan said to the German.

"I am grieved to find you in chains," Macklin replied. "I know you well enough to know it is undeserved."

"You do me kindness, sir," Duncan replied, then remembered one of the reasons Macklin had gone to the church elders. "Have you found your missing missionary, Reverend?"

"We have not," came the German's unhappy answer. "But Sister Leinbach has been appearing in my dreams. She calls me from a distance, as if in a long tunnel. As if," he added, "she has unfinished business." Macklin gazed up at the evening sky a moment then said unexpectedly, "It is why I asked those Scottish guards if I might speak with you."

"But I know nothing—"

Macklin held up his hand. "I have heard of the terrible end of that Shawnee in Philadelphia. He and Ohio George were the worse of a bad lot. Old Belt brought back his kit, from that barn where he was sleeping."

"I saw it," Duncan said. "A deck of cards. Some of those Shamokin nails. Ribbons."

"And a cross."

Duncan nodded as he remembered. "A simple gold cross on a strand of beads."

"He showed it to us because it seemed a missionary's cross. The sisters have confirmed it was hers, from her last mission with the Seneca. Sister Leinbach was wearing it when she left here nearly three years ago."

"I'm sorry." Duncan puffed on his pipe and looked over at the two Indians. Skanawati was looking up at the sky again as he listened to Moses speak in low, quick tones in their native tongue. "Red Hand gambled. On the frontier such a valuable could have changed hands twenty times in a month." Skanawati leaned back. Duncan followed his gaze toward a circling hawk. He was, Duncan realized, looking for his raven.

"But whom did he gamble with?"

Duncan lowered his pipe. "His band. Ohio George. Some Hurons they sometimes ran with in the wilds."

"And if I understand what Mr. Hadley has explained to me, someone from Philadelphia. A person who knew the comings and goings of Philadelphia surveyors. Suppose such a person," the Moravian said gravely, "also knew the comings and goings of our missionaries. I believe Samuel Felton was brought back to his family three years ago."

The kernel of truth in Macklin's words began to take hold. Duncan nursed his pipe a moment as he contemplated the genteel

Moravian town. "In Pennsylvania, if a European youth is freed from the Indians, might he come here, for the transition home?"

"It is not only possible, it is almost certain. The governor favors us with the task, knowing we have our feet in both worlds. Our schools have many children orphaned in raids, more than a few rescued from Indian raiders."

Duncan leaned toward Macklin with new interest. "Would your Sister Leinbach have worked with them?"

"Of course. It was, one might say, her speciality. The elders prescribe a regimen for all students that teaches them about the tribes. The Indians learn from us English and German, and returnees often need to be taught the same. It takes one who has lived among the tribes to truly understand the returnees. Sister Leinbach's husband was with the Seneca when smallpox hit them. He died tending to them, and she insisted on carrying on his work."

"Are there records showing which recovered captives were here, at the time she departed?"

"We are Germans," Macklin reminded him. "Of course there are records, in great quantities. I can probably find out which night three years ago the brethren were served shad, and which night dumplings."

As the two Moravians retreated, Conawago appeared, holding Mokie's hand. She wore the long dark dress of a house servant. Duncan instantly shot up, hands on the girl's shoulders, knowing the guards could take him inside at any moment. "Tell us true, girl, what did you find that night at the raiders' camp? We saw the guard you knocked down with a stone."

Mokie winced, like a schoolgirl caught in mischief. "Mama and I needed food. There's always food at those camps. If ever we saw one, Mama would hide and I would go borrow some."

"My God! You were stealing from the Huron raiders?"

"From anyone we saw on the trail."

Duncan shook his head in wonder. "What did you take that night?"

"That one I knocked down had an old pouch with a little dried meat and some cornmeal, is all." She reached into the folds of her dress. "And this. Mama said I could keep it." She raised the glass ball in her fingers so that it reflected the red light of the dusk.

Duncan stared in disbelief. "I think it would be safer with someone else, Mokie. Conawago will protect it for you. And you mustn't speak about it, or about seeing Indians that night. And go nowhere alone."

The girl frowned, clutched the ball close to her breast for a moment, then sighed and extended it to the old Nipmuc.

Duncan did not have the heart to tell her she had stolen one of the tokens Ramsey handed out to his murderers or that they too had worked out that she had secretly visited them the night before Burke's murder. As she walked away he revisited his memory of that night, and realized he had misunderstood everything about the moonlit camp at the ochre bed.

He woke abruptly in the middle of the night, his senses telling him that something was amiss. He lay without moving, gazing into the deep shadows of the makeshift jail, then leapt up from his pallet. Skanawati was gone. Impossibly, the Indian was gone. Surely Duncan would have heard if the door had been opened, surely there was no other way for the chief to leave the sturdy little building. He tested the door, tested the window. Both were locked tight. Then he heard a tiny sound, of particles falling from the chimney into the massive fireplace that took up the end of the building. The sole chair in the jail was in the fireplace, leaning against the rear wall.

He stripped off his shirt then slowly climbed the chair, balancing precariously as he used the slats on the back like a ladder, pushing himself upward until he was in the confines of the chimney itself. Ignoring the pain from his still-healing injuries, he wedged himself into the narrow space, pushing with his hands, bracing with his back. To his surprise he found he could inch upward, pushing alternately with his arms and back. He was up a foot, then two, ignoring the painful scrapes on his bare skin when he slid back against the stone. Finally, his back screaming in pain, his arms cramping, he touched the outside rim of the chimney. With one final, frantic effort he snaked upward another few inches, grabbed the top of the chimney, and pulled himself up and out onto the roof.

Skanawati sat on the peak, looking calmly into the night sky. Duncan scanned the stars. It was perhaps two or three in the morning, and the town and adjoining camp lay in silent repose. There were no streetlights, only lanterns hung at the doors of the large Moravian residence halls. The Onondaga offered no greeting. Duncan leaned against the chimney, scanning the shadows around the jail. Surely the chief must be holding back on his escape because he had spotted some passing sentry.

"When my mother found that crack in the world," Skanawati said abruptly, "she wept for hours. When she went back a week later, it was wider. She told me I must go on retreat for a month to speak with the spirits."

"Which is where you were when you saw Conawago and me at the cave, why you couldn't follow."

In the moonlight Duncan saw the affirming nod. "She said if the old gods did not understand that we still embraced them in our hearts, then the crack would keep growing wider and drain the river dry." Skanawati turned to Duncan, as if for an answer.

"It was gunpowder that made it," Duncan said, though the words seemed empty. He felt small and inadequate before a man he had come to realize was one of the most spiritual beings he had ever met.

"When I first saw it," Skanawati remembered, "it felt like a gash across my heart."

They watched the stars in silence. There were no patrolling sentries, Duncan began to realize. A meteor soared overhead, so close they could see a trail of smoke behind it. When the chieftain raised his hand to point at it Duncan saw that his arm was wrapped in a snake skin.

"My nephew Johantty will have a difficult time in the world," his companion suddenly said. "Conawago said the two of you know the old trail of the dawnchasers."

"We walked along it, cleared away what debris we could." Duncan recalled their three days on the trail, and his wonder over the treacherous drops down cliffs, the crossing of chasms on old logs, the swamps and rocky debris fields the ancient runners of the sacred trail had to endure.

"Johantty needs to complete that trail," Skanawati said, "the people need to see one of the young ones with the tattoo of the old spirits."

"We shall show both of you, Skanawati. If I am not mistaken it is near the site you chose for your new village. You will leave Bethlehem a free man, I swear it. You shall guide your nephew yourself."

"I would like that, of all things," the chief admitted, and he looked back at the stars. "Tell me about it, McCallum. In my mind, let me run that spirit trail."

Duncan found a small, sad grin tugging at his mouth. He leaned on the roof beside the Onondaga. His heart expanded with the honor done him, and the responsibility. "There is a great cottonwood at the edge of the clearing where it starts," he began, "so large that four men could not join their arms around it. An eagle sat in the tree the day we were there."

Skanawati offered a murmur of approval, and Duncan continued, seeing in his mind's eye the trail as he and Conawago had traveled on it, taking Skanawati up and down mountains, across rivers, along cliffs, past drawings of giant bears under sheltering ledges. When the chief asked if he had perhaps seen a bear by a particular mountain or a white otter at a river crossing, Duncan thought carefully and described as best he could the animals that had watched them that day. Skanawati listened for over an hour, once interrupting Duncan to point out another shooting star.

Each time Duncan paused, he looked for guards again, wondering when Skanawati would finally slide down the roof to freedom. The chief had freed himself from the little jail but was making no other effort to make good his escape. He had by his actions given Duncan his own freedom. When the hour came, it would now be the simplest of things for them to slide down the roof, onto the ground, and disappear into the night. Duncan made up his mind to stay with Skanawati when he finally slipped away, to do what he could to protect the chief.

But Skanawati just kept watching the stars. When at last he stood, stretching, there was a faint, gray hint of dawn in the east. Instead of sliding down the roof shakes he stepped back to the chimney and lowered himself inside. Duncan watched in disbelief. In his mind's eye he was already running, free, over the laurel ridges beyond the town. With painful effort he inched toward the chimney, casting one more longing glance toward the forest, then followed the Iroquois back into their jail.

The rattle of the timber bar the next morning brought Duncan to his feet instantly. He was halfway to the door when something in the window caught his eye. He halted with a shudder. A small squirrel hung dead. A piece of twine had been tied in a noose, suspending it. He touched it. It was still warm. It was one of the nocturnal flying squirrels, considered by some in the tribes to be a messenger from the spirit world.

He untied the twine, letting the creature fall to the ground outside, just as Macklin stepped through the door, closely followed by Mokie carrying a covered tray. As the girl uncovered bowls of cooked oats, fresh bread, and tea, she turned to Duncan with a determined glint. "He will be fine, Mr. McCallum, Mama and I will see to it."

Duncan lowered the spoon in his hand. "Who is going to be fine, Mokie?"

"Mr. Hadley. They came for us last night again, when I was returning to Mama's room. He wouldn't let them take us."

Macklin touched Duncan's arm. "The Virginians insist that Hadley sit with them as part of the treaty delegation. He is part of the Burke family, they remind him. He has taken notes from his travels with you, and they insisted on seeing them. Then the Virginians made Hadley go with them to the women's quarters, but when he realized what they were about, he resisted. They gave him a good thrashing, nothing too serious because he is family. There is a doctor here," Macklin added quickly. "No broken bones. Mokie nursed him most of the night."

Duncan now saw that the girl glowed. "What else, Mokie?"

"Sometime in the night, when he told me I should get some sleep, I told him it was right I tended him, after the way you and he helped deliver our precious Penn. That's when he said it."

"Said what?"

"He had me lean over him so he could whisper." The girl grew very serious, her eyes wide. "He told me I was his sister. He told me no matter what it cost him, Mama and me were done being slaves."

Duncan grinned. At least some justice was being found along the tortured path of the treaty convoy.

Macklin pointed Duncan to a corner as Mokie, to the chief's obvious amusement, presented Skanawati his breakfast with a curtsy. "I sat into the night reviewing the journal books in the Gemeinhaus, the main administrative building. Then later I found one of the teachers debating European politics at the Sun Inn down the street.

"There were four youths returned from tribal captivity that year. Sister Leinbach worked with all of them. Two eventually went on to Philadelphia, two were adopted by farm families. The names were Mueller, Rohrbach, Gottlieb, and Smith."

"No Felton?"

"I was as disappointed as you at first. No Felton at all for the past five years. But the teacher explained that those who were captured very young often forget their names. When that happens those who seem to remember some German get German names, those who seem English, English names. One of the boys, the one named Smith, was quite difficult. Rebellious, even violently so. The teacher recalls once Sister Leinbach gave him extra prayers to read as discipline, but," Macklin said in a tight voice, "the prayers were found the next morning impaled on an arrow, shot into the statue of the Holy Mother in our chapel. Still she was very patient with him, made him her special project that year. Improved his English tremendously, nurtured his soul, used the rod when she had to. Smith showed up at a Christmas service with stripes painted on his face.

"He had been brought back under duress from a Huron village by some trappers who thought a bounty would be paid for him. But no one knew who his family was, and they just left him here. It was only when Smith finally began to enjoy some of the pleasures of European life that he began to speak of memories as a small boy on a farm near Tulpehocken. They started to piece together the truth, although that took months. The elders came close to ejecting him many times. He would mock the Christian Indians, saying they had all been neutered by magic words out of a black book, he stole things from the kitchens. But Sister Leinbach persevered, as if the boy had become a spiritual test for her. Small mutilated animals would be found at her doorstep, once even in her bed. He seemed to nurture a particular hatred for her.

"Finally it was decided that all his immediate family had been massacred, so other relations had to be tracked down. When his Philadelphia relatives finally came he saw they were all somber Quakers and at first declined to see them. One of the brothers who was in the school says he thinks he dropped his objections to them when he saw they were wealthy, although others insist he finally came to be bathed in their Christian love."

A chill had descended over Duncan as Macklin had spoken. "Did he take his leave for Philadelphia before the departure of Sister Leinbach?"

"Two days after her departure."

Duncan stared at the piece of bread in his hand. He had lost his appetite. "And she was never seen again? Surely she had an escort."

"Sister Leinbach was a strong-willed woman, with a very particular vision of God's calling for her. Her only escorts were the mule she rode and a pack pony. She insisted on traveling alone to Shamokin for the first stage of her journey, to talk with God and build her spiritual strength for the challenges ahead. She meant to travel far into the Ohio country."

"Surely there was a search for her?"

"The road from here to Shamokin can be difficult because of the river crossings. There had been heavy rains. Sometimes in such weather our people will be taken in by a settler's family and shelter for a week or two. I waited a month before I decided to send a query asking when we could expect her. Many searchers were sent to look for her, but by then the trail was long cold, and the Huron raiders were getting active again."

Duncan watched Skanawati speaking with Mokie, smiling patiently as the girl traced with her finger the complex tattoos on his arm. When she was done he reached into his blanket and pulled out a little doll fashioned of straw from his pallet, expertly woven and pinched to give it shape. Duncan remembered seeing a similar one, made of corn husks, at the chief's village. The girl's eyes lit with excitement, and Skanawati glanced with embarrassment at Duncan as the girl hugged him.

"The treaty negotiators are at the end of their patience," Macklin declared. "There will be further conferring today. Magistrate Brindle has clerks in the Gemeinhaus preparing terms on parchment for signature. The trial may be tomorrow." Macklin looked uneasily at a group of men who were erecting a wooden structure near a corner of the main street. "Lord Ramsey has contributed a large sum for the expansion of the chapel here. That man in the lace collar who always sits with Ramsey isn't just his lawyer, Duncan, he is a judge. The one who has all the other witness statements. The one who is now to determine Skanawati's fate."

With those words the door was flung open. One of the kilted guards stood with an expectant gaze, waving the visitors out. Mokie solemnly shook hands with Skanawati, then Duncan. "Mr. Hadley says I must stay in my service for now, until it is over."

"Service?"

"With the great lord from Philadelphia. Lord Ramsey thinks he will buy us when this is over." The words were spoken not with foreboding but mischief as Mokie offered an exaggerated curtsy and skipped away.

McGregor soon appeared, the hobbles in his hand, gesturing Duncan and Skanawati outside once again for fresh air.

"Sergeant, have you heard of any other Indians camped in this valley?"

"The treaty followers have been drifting away. The villages need them for spring planting."

"I mean a small band, trying to be inconspicuous. Perhaps some from that barn in Philadelphia."

"I'll ask. That Moses seems to know everyone, German and Indian alike."

As McGregor moved purposefully toward the huge Single Brethren house where Moravian visitors stayed, Duncan stretched and caught a scent of spring in the air, of apple blossoms and fresh tilled earth. He wandered around the corner of the building, testing the length of his chain, and he was glancing back toward Skanawati when something slammed into his back. As he staggered forward his hobble was pulled out from under him, knocking him to the ground. It took only a moment for him to come to his senses, but by then Felton had seized his collar and had dragged him to the rear wall, slamming his back against it.

"You interfere with the affairs of your betters!" the young Quaker hissed. His eyes were wild. For the first time, Duncan saw a line of thin oval scars that ran around his neck like a necklace, an adornment used by some of the western tribes.

Duncan cast a desperate, searching glance for the sentry who was supposed be guarding the rear of the jail. The man lay in a heap against a stack of firewood.

"Not for a slave to decide anything!" Felton growled. He nodded at Duncan's hobble. "Now run."

The heavy leather of the hobble had been sliced apart.

"I'm supposed to trust you?" Duncan asked. "How many do you have waiting for me? I saw how you roasted your friend Red Hand alive."

"I shall wear those laurels for months," Felton boasted.

"Only among those who believe your ruse. I saw the calculation in your eyes that night. You could have shot me or Mokie. But Ramsey had claimed me, and you couldn't murder the girl with so many witnesses. Red Hand, on the other hand, was about to be captured and would have spilled his guts for a pot of rum. I wager you told your Indian friends the soldiers killed the Shawnee. But they will hear the truth soon enough. Watch your back."

"You have not a shred of evidence, Scotsman. And even if you did, a lowly slave of a great house will not be permitted to speak in the new court."

Duncan swallowed hard, realizing now that Ramsey had bought and paid for his new judge.

"Now run," Felton repeated.

"As you say, I am in bond."

"But here is an opportunity to stretch your legs, to have a taste of freedom for an hour or two before we track you. It's a handsome offer. A chance to soak up the light before being sealed into your rat hole for a few years."

It was a tempting offer indeed, and Duncan would relish a chance to meet Felton on his own terms in the forest. But Felton would not be alone, he would be with his pack of wolves. And the

offer was meant to assure Duncan would have no role in the final
act of the drama about to unfold in Bethlehem.

"I am in bond to Skanawati."

"Then you are in bond to a dead man!" Felton slammed the
end of the log in his hand into Duncan's belly. As he doubled over
in pain Felton seized him again, shoving him against the stone wall.
"It's a dilemma, McCallum. Ramsey offers a fine price to keep you
alive, but I begin to think you are worth more to me dead. I have
a place I could put your body, McCallum, a place no one will ever
dare look." As he swung the log again Duncan jerked forward,
ramming his shoulder into the scout, pushing him off balance a
moment. Aiming a kick at Felton's belly, he used the inertia of the
kick to drop and roll past the corner of the building. Instantly the
sentry at the front called out in alarm.

When Duncan looked back Felton was gone.

Chapter Eighteen

ORD RAMSEY WAS a man who lived with one foot squarely planted in another century. As Duncan was escorted, his hands tightly shackled, into the first-floor chambers of the Gemeinhaus now relinquished to Ramsey, he recalled his first visit to the patron's mansion in New York. The dominant portrait had been one of old King James. Here he saw that Ramsey had not just borrowed the room from the Germans, he had transformed it into a peculiarly English shrine. Two small oil paintings in gilt frames leaned against the wall on a sideboard, one of a castle, no doubt an ancestral seat, the other a likeness of William and Mary. On the sideboard stood ornate glass wine goblets and a pair of intricately brocaded gloves that once might have been worn by the dandy Inigo Jones in the court of a hundred years earlier. A fine lace cloth had been thrown over the plain German table, with an extravagant gold candlestick looming over maps and papers. It was these documents Ramsey and another elegant gentleman now perused.

Duncan did not resist when one of his escorts, all Ramsey men but for a single kilted soldier, jerked his manacles, propelling him to the edge of the table. He glanced over his shoulder at the Scottish guard, hoping for the sound of boots in the corridor. Another soldier had been dispatched to find McGregor when Ramsey's deputies had come for Duncan in the jail. He felt a new pressure on his arm. The man nearest him had put a leash on his arm, a metal plate that curved halfway around his bicep, tightened with a length of chain.

"Ah, McCallum," Ramsey said coolly. "At last we can chat in more relaxed circumstances. No more savage chaperones, eh?"

Duncan cast a pointed glance at the four rough-looking men hovering nearby. "That remains to be seen."

Ramsey lifted an eyebrow. "These men are deputized by our esteemed court."

Duncan eyed the stranger, an older man with the air of a courtier. "I look forward to experiencing such a court."

There was a quick movement at his side. The man holding the leash dropped a small object into the curved plate on his arm and began twisting the chain, tightening it. Duncan jerked back as a needle of pain shot up his shoulder. The man had dropped a little barbed ball into the harness to dig into his muscle. It was not a leash. It was a torture device.

"Save your ironies, McCallum. You have no audience for them here. In fact these men are charged with making certain your words have been subdued by the time we arrive back in Philadelphia. My disappointments in New York were all because I failed to see you properly broken to the harness. There is a special enclosed wagon arriving tonight, equipped with other useful devices," Ramsey announced with a cold smile. "It will be a memorable journey for you. I understand they have a team of deaf horses, so your screams will not startle them." Ramsey's thin laugh was obediently joined in by his minions. Duncan ventured another look backward. The

Highland soldier had been blocked at the door by two of Ramsey's deputies.

"We have put our idle time here to good use," Ramsey explained, emptying the glass of wine beside him. He pointed to a freshly drawn document, a new indenture. "We have of course given you credit for the time since you stepped off the boat. Six years and three months remaining."

"My indenture was assigned to your daughter. She has the document at the settlement in New York."

Ramsey gave a shrug. "So far away. The mountains between here and there are high. Everyone knows I brought a company of Scottish bondsmen from Britain last year. We just want to perfect the title, as it were, for the Pennsylvania province." The bespectacled man at his side nodded approvingly. Ramsey raised his empty wineglass and turned to a side door. "Where is that damned girl?"

The lawyer lifted the document and extended it to Ramsey, who ceremoniously lifted a quill from a silver inkpot and signed it as Mokie appeared with a freshly decanted bottle of wine. She glanced at Duncan then averted her eyes to the floor. She was breathing heavily.

Ramsey extended the quill to Duncan as Mokie filled his glass. The barb on his arm bit deeper. He looked dully at the pot of ink, gestured for it. As Ramsey pushed the pot to the side of the parchment, Duncan upended it onto the paper.

The little barbs digging into his flesh felt like a dozen knives. He groaned, closing his eyes against the new pain, hearing only Ramsey's furious curses at first, then a hammering like the drums of battle. Boots. Soldiers' boots. He heard a protest behind him, the sound of a quick blow, and a groan as one of the deputies doubled over. Suddenly McGregor was at his side, his face clenched in fury. He grabbed the chain on Duncan's arm and loosened it, throwing it to the floor, stomping on the curved plate. The barbed ball that rolled away was covered in blood. A moment later Magistrate Brindle stepped into the room.

"This man," he declared, "is remanded for assistance in concluding the treaty." Duncan glanced at Mokie. She had been running. Brindle's chambers were a quarter mile away.

"We conduct a purely private contract matter here," Ramsey observed in a level voice. "We do not require your assistance, Brindle." As he spoke the judge beside him dabbed at the parchment, trying to salvage it.

"The governor has directed that the treaty is the paramount purpose of our mission to Bethlehem." Brindle paused, looking at the blood dripping to the floor from Duncan's fingertips.

"Of course. And a grand celebration shall there be when you return with the signed treaty in your hands. I understand," Ramsey added in a pointed tone, "you are being considered for chief justice in the lower courts of Philadelphia. You are no doubt familiar with Justice Bradford, who sits on the Supreme Judicial Court for the entire colony."

Brindle would not be baited. "Should either of you wish to dispute me, you may send a petition to the governor in Philadelphia. In the meantime I shall conduct treaty business as I see fit."

The older judge finally found his voice. "The matter of the murders rests with me, Brother Brindle," he intoned in warning. His voice had the crisp, refined tones of London. He was, Duncan suspected, only recently arrived from England.

"A somber responsibility, your honor." Brindle returned the justice's stare. "I have no doubt you are consulting with God and your conscience to assure justice is served."

"These matters will not be settled in a storm of lightning and brimstone," the lace-collared judge put in, raising a snigger from

Ramsey. "We are ordained to do the justice of men, not that of the Old Testament." Not all the leaders of the colony, Duncan reminded himself, were Quakers. "My authority derives from the proprietor of the Penn colony," Bradford continued, "not the proprietor of heaven. And we shall see whose authority prevails tomorrow. With the dawn comes the time for king and empire."

Duncan saw the magistrate's fists tighten, the color rise on his face. McGregor gestured a soldier to Duncan's side before steering the Quaker away from the table.

"What did he mean?" Duncan asked the Highland sergeant as they left the building. "About tomorrow being a day for empire?"

"'Tis the last day," McGregor explained. "The governor and the general have decreed it, in a message from Philadelphia. Plans for the new western forts are finished. Construction must begin. Brindle has been charged with sending the treaty to Philadelphia with a fast rider by dusk tomorrow. They say they know the Indians will sign, provided a firm hand is taken."

Only when the jail door had been finally barred behind him and Duncan was once again the cellmate of Skanawati did he realize McGregor had stuffed a note into his belt as they had left the Gemeinhaus. It was from Reverend Macklin. *I have discovered that there is a book somewhere in the Gemeinhaus,* Duncan read, *that records the true names of the adoptees after their families stepped forward.*

The Gemeinhaus an hour before midnight had the air of an old German castle. Conawago had listened attentively at the side of the jail that evening, then dismissed Duncan's suggestion that they meet under the high moon behind the huge log building. But when Duncan had pressed, insisting that they first hide one of the long

Moravian coats and a black hat for him under a nearby oak then be
ready with Moses, he had acquiesced. Still he had seemed surprised
to find Duncan walking freely down the path in Moravian garb
and had pushed the coat back to reveal the soot from the chimney.
Even now as Moses led them by candlelight down the long hall of
the building Conawago kept looking back. From his expression,
however, Duncan could see that his real disbelief was that Duncan
would leave the jail and choose to delve into the secret vaults of the
Moravians rather than fleeing.

Reverend Macklin had been willing to explain the nature of the
journals they sought, and even offered to join them, but they would
not risk his being caught by the elders. There were two offices at the
eastern end of the second floor holding cabinets of books, the keys
for which were secreted on the top corner of each cabinet. Moses
led them through the heavy door at the entrance, into a large central hall that smelled of pine and beeswax. The two Indians moved
with instinctive stealth past the huge case clock at the rear of the
hall then into the eastern corridor, staying in the darkest shadow,
pausing at a sudden sound, continuing as they realized it was but a
twig scraping against a window in the spring breeze.

They made their way up the stairs and down the second-floor
corridor, into an office that overlooked the street. Conawago
watched the hall, Duncan the street as Moses opened a cabinet
and searched its shelves of ledgers and journals. After a few minutes Duncan joined him, starting with the top shelf. *Foodstuffs for
Single Brethren House 1755* read the title page of the first volume he
opened, *Linens and Sundries for the Sisters House 1758* on the next,
then *Supplies for Missions 1757*, and *Inhabitants of God's Acre*. The
Moravians were a fastidious people.

"God's Acre?" Duncan asked.

"The cemetery," Moses explained.

He quickly leafed through it. "Indians are buried there?"

"Those who wish it," Moses said absently as he surveyed
another book. "There is an old yard of Indian burial scaffolds two
miles up the river trail." He raised the journal in his hand. "*Rolls of
the Returned Souls,*" he read from the title page. "It's what the early
teachers called those returning from the tribes." He laid the book
on the table in the center of the room and pushed the candle closer.
The list grew longer each year, the names after the first two years
acquiring narrative descriptions under each. "1757," he recited
and ran his finger along the list. "Rohrbach," he read, "Mueller,
Gottlieb." His finger stopped at the last name. "Smith."

The first entry for the boy returned from the Hurons was brief,
in a feminine hand. Moses translated from the German as he read.
Estimated age 17, it read, *returned by trappers on the Ohio. Very little
English, no German. Apparently taken at an early age. After first bath,
found in kitchens covering skin with bacon grease. Refuses to sleep in a
bed. It required the efforts of four brothers to restrain him when we cut
off his long blond braids. I am convinced there is a deep soul trying to
come out if we can only reach it.* The entry was signed *S. Leinbach.*

There were more entries describing the classes, the program
for the Returned Souls. Smith was noted for remarkable progress,
but was also pulled from a hayloft while trying to fornicate with
one of the Moravian Indian girls and was repeatedly cited by Sister
Leinbach for missing prayer services, ripping pages from Bibles,
even releasing a snake in Sunday chapel.

"His adoption," Duncan said in an urgent tone. "We need the
adoption records."

Moses quickly leafed through the rest of the pages. "Not here.
A separate book apparently. They would not want the adopted
returnees to easily piece together their prior life. A clean break is
sought." He stood, returning the book, closed the cabinet, and led

them into the adjoining room, which judging by its furnishings was the office of an important personage.

"Leave everything as we find it," Moses warned, discomfort entering his voice for the first time. "This is the bishop's office."

Duncan and Conawago carefully opened the cabinet beside the large desk, finding financial records, birth and death records, ledgers of immigrants from Germany, even several Bibles of various sizes.

"The bishop interviews the families in great detail and records his findings," Moses whispered when their search proved fruitless. "The decision on adoption rests with him."

"And anyone who has been adopted would know this, would know the bishop kept such notes?" Duncan asked.

"Of course. And often the decision is made in the spring, before the summer work begins."

"Which means," Conawago said, "that he would be writing in the same journal now, making entries even today."

Moses nodded. "He often works late, making use of the evening light at the table by the window." The table was the one piece of furniture they had not touched. Duncan held the candle close, illuminating a long single drawer underneath. Conawago tried it and found it locked.

"Not locked," Duncan said, pointing to a small wedge of wood that had been jammed into the gap between the drawer and the frame around it. "Only made to appear so." He knelt, studying the lock carefully, pointing out the way the wood had been slightly splintered around it. Popping out the wedge, he pulled on the drawer. It was empty save for a few quills and a quill knife.

"I saw the bishop working at this table this very evening," Moses said. "He waved from the window. This tampering happened tonight, after he left."

"If you knew the building, and the routines of its inhabitants, what would be the safest way to steal the book?" Duncan asked.

It was Conawago who answered. "Enter while the daily business is underway and hide, then take the book and leave in the middle of the night. Perhaps take a nap, wait for the big clock in the central hall to strike midnight since many of the faithful keep working until they need sleep."

It was a long chance, but the only one they had. Duncan glanced at the smaller clock on the bishop's desk and lowered his voice to a whisper. "In a quarter hour."

"Then we must make ready now," Moses confirmed, and he turned to look back into the hallway. "Upstairs would be the place to hide. There is another floor, then an attic, neither used as much as the lower ones."

Duncan blew out the candle and quickly conferred with his companions. At either end of the second floor was a set of stairs to the third floor, then one central one to the attic, all three with doors into the stairwells. They quickly placed a tall chair stacked with books against the one at the west end, leaving Conawago to watch there. Then Duncan and Moses crept up to the third floor. The first two chambers were storerooms stacked with crates against the walls. They positioned themselves in the open doorways on either side of the hallway. As they settled in Duncan began hearing small sounds and occasional creaks of boards. Such a huge log building would have noises of its own, Duncan told himself, and no doubt hosted more than a few rodents.

The large clock downstairs chimed a hymn then struck the hour on a big bell that resonated throughout the building. Less than a minute later Duncan heard something new, a succession of squeaks from floor boards, and he ventured a look down the corridor. In the moonlight cast through the window at the far end of the hall was a new shadow, a figure creeping along the wall toward the far stairs. Moses was on his feet, ready to spring their trap once the man was forced to retreat to the stairs they guarded.

But the intruder did not retreat. Moments after he slipped into the stairwell, they heard the sound of pounding, then a splintering of wood.

"Conawago!" Duncan cried, and leapt down the stairs. By the time he reached the second floor the sounds of struggle were unmistakable. The old Nipmuc was holding his own, sitting against the door, pushing with all his might as someone on the other side hacked at the thin wood with a hand ax. "A table!" Duncan called, as he reached his friend's side. "I will bring a table to press against the door!"

But his words were enough. The sounds from the other side instantly stopped. Without an instant's hesitation Conawago flung the door open and was in chase, Duncan at his heels. At the top of the stairs they could see Moses silhouetted at the far end, his hand raised in signal. Their quarry was in one of the chambers off the hallway. Duncan darted into the first room, leaving Conawago to watch the hall. He found a broom and recklessly probed the shadows with its handle, aware that the intruder could be armed. But he had no time for caution. Every minute increased the likelihood he would be missed from the jail.

Finally, in the third room, a figure sprang out from behind a crate. Duncan jumped forward, seizing the man's leg. "The book!" he called to Conawago, who leapt toward them, knocking the journal from the man's hand then launching a stack of dusty ledgers from a small table as the two men fell.

"Bastard!" the stranger cursed in English, lashing out with his elbows, kicking off Duncan's grip, and slamming a fist into the old Indian's belly before grabbing his book and leaping up to flee along the hall. As he did so he uttered an urgent command in a tribal tongue.

"There are two!" Conawago warned, and an instant later Duncan heard a familiar hiss. He flattened against the wall as the arrow rushed by, not expecting the second arrow that quickly followed the first. He heard with dread the thud as the arrow hit, heard the gasp as Conawago dropped to the floor.

Duncan stood paralyzed a moment, stricken with fear for his friend, glancing at the shadowy shapes.

"Go!" Conawago groaned. Duncan willed himself to move forward, gathering speed as he ran down the hall. Suddenly a war whoop erupted and one of the shapes launched himself out the window. Then all was silent.

He was back at Conawago's side in an instant. His comrade leaned against the wall, an arrow protruding from his chest.

"Noooooo!" Duncan moaned as he knelt.

"It quite . . . takes the wind out of you," Conawago said, his breathing labored.

"They have a hospital here," Duncan said, cursing the low light as he lifted his hands to probe the wound, praying the arrow had struck in a rib and not a vital organ. "Where is the pain?" he asked.

"Like I said," Conawago said in a lighter, more level voice, "it takes the wind out of you." With a shove of unexpected strength, he pushed Duncan away then stretched out his hands, extending a heavy journal. As he did so the arrow too came away from his chest. A moment later Moses arrived with a candle, and Duncan could clearly see the projectile. It was embedded in the book, which had slammed into Conawago's chest with the impact.

"The fool took the wrong book," Conawago declared.

"Judging by these others," Moses said as he opened two of the journals scattered across the floor. "He made off with one of the annual reports of linen usage in the Sisters House."

A thin croak left Conawago's throat, then Moses chuckled, and suddenly they were all three laughing with abandon.

"The one who leapt out the window," Duncan finally asked. "Did he not know he was on the third floor?" It now seemed clear the second man had slipped down the stairs in the confusion.

"He must have assumed he would land on soft grass," Moses answered. "But instead it is cobblestone where he landed. And in the air his foot became entangled with his bow. He did not get up."

The Indian outside had broken his neck, Duncan confirmed as he bent over the body a minute later. He turned the head toward the light.

"One of those from the barn in Philadelphia," Conawago declared.

Down the street men had begun to shout. "Take the body to the Iroquois camp," Duncan said hurriedly. "Make sure Old Belt finds the other outlaws camped with this one. They are taking Ramsey money. Make him understand the truth, how they are all being manipulated by Ramsey and Felton. Take the book to Brindle, explain the truth about his nephew. I must get back to Skanawati."

"Surely you want to read the entry for Felton."

Duncan shook his head. "No time. And what happened tonight is all the confirmation I need."

Chapter Nineteen

ANACLES WERE PLACED on Duncan and Skanawati before they were escorted out of the jail the next morning. McGregor did not speak, and his men were equally grim as they flanked the doorway and motioned their prisoners forward. Skanawati took two steps and stopped so abruptly Duncan almost collided with him.

Duncan would never have guessed there were so many people in all of Bethlehem. They lined the pathway to the street on either side, they lined the street, past the new construction on the corner, lined the street all the way to the Gemeinhaus, scores of men, women, and children in the dark clothes of the Moravians. Mingled among them were nearly all of the teamsters of the convoy and several of Ramsey's rough private guards, along with at least fifty Indians. What had Ramsey's judge said? This was the day for king and empire.

To Duncan's surprise the guards did not lead them up the broad stone steps of the Gemeinhaus but walked around it to a large grassy flat bordered by elms and oaks. At the far corner were the rows of graves, some already many years old, of God's Acre.

In the corner opposite the graves, in front of a long stone stable, was an Indian encampment. In the near corner was a long plank table, on which lay maps and papers, Indian pipes and pouches of tobacco, law books and prayer books.

There was no air of victory, no edge of success among the treaty delegations at the table. Brindle, at the center of the table opposite Duncan, was flanked by two somber Quakers with three nervous clerks behind them. The magistrate stared into his hands as if praying. Hadley, bruised and bandaged, sat at the west end of the table beside the elder Burke representative and the other Virginians. Only Old Belt, sitting a few feet from the Pennsylvania delegation, seemed at ease. The Iroquois chief was alone at the table, with only his warrior escort and Moses behind him. Duncan did not miss the solemn, yet somehow reassuring nod Old Belt exchanged with Skanawati, nor the deep worry that creased Moses' countenance. On the table in front of Old Belt was a large hand-drawn map.

Behind the large table, chairs were arranged like a gallery. Two hundred feet away, closer to the cemetery, was another small grouping of seats facing a different direction. Duncan stared into the shadows they faced, seeing now that another, smaller table had been set up near the headstones. Justice Bradford sat there, wearing on his head one of the long curled periwigs favored in the courts, sifting through papers, casting expectant glances toward the treaty delegations. A throng of Moravians stood on the brick pathway at the edge of the broad square, watching from a distance, their group bisected by a richly dressed man on a bench whose presence seemed to repel bystanders. Lord Ramsey had a campaign table at his elbow, laden with personal refreshments as he conferred with another bewigged man in a blue waistcoat.

Magistrate Brindle stood as he noticed Duncan and Skanawati, gesturing them to sit in chairs opposite him before sitting himself.

They were not going, as Duncan expected, to Bradford's makeshift bench but to the treaty table.

"We commence this final day of negotiations for the glory of God and the mutual benefit of our peoples." Brindle's opening words had the sound of a well-rehearsed chorus. As he lifted a piece of paper Old Belt, now with Moses beside him, and the Virginians did the same, seeming to follow as the magistrate outlined the agreement thus far. Brindle reminded the parties as he did so that great parchments were already being inscribed in the Moravian school so the treaty could be properly signed after this final day of deliberation.

Brindle continued with a litany of the smaller matters that were the mortar that held agreements together. Pennsylvania had agreed that its settlers would not water their herds on the banks of the Conestoga River, which one of the Indian settlements relied upon for drinking water. Virginia trappers would not work the forests north of the Monongahela after the third month of the year. The tribes would grant safe passage to missionaries. Duncan watched the Virginians, saw how they cast suspicious glances at the Pennsylvanians, watched too as the man who had been conferring with Ramsey stepped behind Brindle and then conspicuously strained his neck to see the map Old Belt had apparently drawn. Duncan, too, studied it from his seat down the table. The map had lines drawn that divided much of the land west of the Susquehanna into three sections. Old Belt had accepted the inevitable and was ready to barter for Skanawati's life.

Mokie appeared, carrying a tray of wineglasses to Ramsey. The patron was preparing for a victory celebration.

"Gentlemen of Virginia," Brindle declared. "The Six Nations request you abandon your land claims in exchange for the return of the prisoners in the western lands, the details to be agreed by a special commission to sit at Fort Pitt. What say you?"

"Virginia," the senior Burke announced, "will reluctantly—"

"No!" the angry cry that interrupted came from behind. Ramsey was on his feet now, raising his fist at a new group that had appeared on the opposite side of the square. It was Long Wolf, along with the rest of the western Indians, leading horses with empty pack saddles. They were leaving, leaving without a treaty, without their expected bounty. Duncan looked back at Old Belt, who did not react, did nothing to betray his involvement in the desertion of the western tribes.

His guards gathered around Ramsey, who now shoved several of them toward the retreating Indians. But the men, knowing they were powerless, halted after a few steps. As Long Wolf reached the corner of the cemetery he tossed his expensive fowling gun onto the ground. Every Indian behind him likewise dropped something onto the pile. They were not only leaving without treaty payments but they were also returning the advance tokens given to them by Ramsey. Whispered curses rose from the Virginians as they realized the significance of the departure. It meant there would be no participation by the western tribes, and without them no return of prisoners.

Brindle watched the departing Indians with a grave face, though by his worried glances toward Old Belt, Duncan knew he was just as disturbed by the Iroquois chief's pointed disregard for the exodus. Conawago had done his work. Long Wolf and those who had taken gifts from Ramsey now were exposed, shamed in the eyes of the Grand Council. They were being cast out not by force but by the bonds of integrity that ran deep in the confederation. Skanawati watched the departing tribes without expression. One of the pillars of the treaty had just crumbled.

No one at the treaty table spoke, no one moved, until the last of the western Indians disappeared from sight. But Ramsey's imprecations could be heard from two hundred feet away, as he paced back and forth. Duncan, shifting the chains on his wrists, watched as the patron finally strutted to Justice Bradford, bending over him with urgent words. Moments later a youth sitting in the shade of a tree nearby was summoned to the table and given a coin by Ramsey before he sped away.

The colonial delegations broke into anxious whispers, the Virginians glancing up at Brindle, the Pennsylvanians at the bewigged judge. Duncan looked at his friends, trying to understand. Moses had turned his back and was still watching the direction taken by the defecting westerners. Conawago had taken a seat at Old Belt's side.

Duncan, still not certain why he and Skanawati had been summoned to the treaty table, watched in confusion as a number of the bystanders split away, moving toward the little shed that was being constructed on the main street, visible between a gap in the buildings. There seemed to be some sort of argument, with protests raised in German, as several of Ramsey's men began helping the carpenters.

Suddenly the senior Burke, who had been arguing with Hadley, stood up to seize the initiative. "The Virginian delegation," he announced, "is prepared to submit evidence that the murder of our brave Captain Burke was in direct retaliation by the Iroquois, who had been turned back by our citizens in the Shenandoah some years ago. There is the nailing of the hand. The nail itself. And a gear used to mutilate our noble officer, of a type hoarded by the Indians in Shamokin."

Hadley looked up with anguish at Duncan then buried his head in his hands. His companions were using his chronicle of the murders.

"This is no court of law!" a deep voice called out. Duncan turned to see Reverend Macklin standing before a knot of other Moravians near the table.

Brindle glanced at McGregor, who sent two of his men to Macklin's side. As he did so Duncan saw that another figure had joined the table. Justice Bradford had settled into a chair at the empty east end of the table, holding one of the polished squares of wood often used to pound courts into session. Macklin was wrong. The treaty negotiation was becoming a surrogate trial. The promise of returned prisoners had vanished with the western Indians. Now the delegates were competing to see who could pose the greatest threat to Skanawati's life, and the winner would get the condolence prize, the land that the Iroquois would have to offer to save him. The integrity of the Iroquois had forced the western tribes out, and they were now forced to surrender vast lands.

The Philadelphia delegate in the blue waistcoat stood, raising the bid. "We have a signed statement that Skanawati murdered the surveyor Townsend." He flourished a piece of paper in the air. Duncan suddenly recalled that Red Hand had taunted them by saying he signed such a paper. "We have the oath of the commander of Fort Ligonier that Skanawati was the murderer of Captain Burke!

"We have statements from teamsters in the convoy swearing they saw Skanawati send one of his warriors to kill Bythe!" the Philadelphia delegate continued. Brindle lowered his head, gripping his prayer book now. The speaker looked questioningly at Old Belt. As if to punctuate his words a sharp command rose from the construction on the street. A team of oxen, hooked to a hauling chain, was being urged forward. The delegates paused and turned as the animals strained in their yoke, lifting a timber frame. With a shudder Duncan recognized the structure. They were assembling a gallows, calculated to be in the sight of the Indian delegation.

"And how many statements were filed saying Bythe died by accident?" the angry words leapt from Duncan's throat unbidden. "No doubt your honor will wish to compare them to see how many of the same drunken teamsters signed both sets!"

"Those first statements are in Philadelphia with another judge," Bradford rebuffed him. "I am not able to recognize them here."

Brindle spoke, looking severe. "Not entirely true," he said as he extracted several folded sheets from an inside pocket.

The Philadelphia judge went rigid for a moment, glaring at the magistrate. He glanced at Ramsey before answering. "Those, then, represent a different inquest in a different Philadelphia court," he parlayed. "I have jurisdiction over all the Penn colony and set the rules in my proceedings as I see fit."

"The killing of Townsend was a misfortune of war," Duncan broke in again. "And the officer at Ligonier would accuse his own mother of murder if it offered a prospect of promotion! The nails and the clock gears were but ruses, so fingers would be pointed to Shamokin. The murders were done by several men," he concluded, "but all orchestrated out of Philadelphia."

Several angry gasps rose from the Virginian delegation. Brindle stood up. "If this treaty hinges on the killings, then let the truth of these killings be told!"

This then, was why Brindle had brought the prisoners to the treaty table. He had known that the western Indians were leaving, and he meant to end the game that had overtaken the negotiations. As the magistrate turned his head toward him, Duncan saw the anguish in his eyes, along with a new melancholy determination. He had finally glimpsed the current of deceit and murder beneath the surface of the negotiations. Brindle nodded for Duncan to continue. But as Duncan opened his mouth to speak, a deep, steady voice cut through the silence.

"It was Skanawati who killed the surveyor Townsend. It was Skanawati who killed Captain Burke." The Iroquois chief spoke of himself in the third person.

A sharp crack of wood turned every eye to the powdered judge at the end of the table. He was pounding the table with his polished block, exhorting his court to order.

"Surely there must be proof!" Brindle insisted.

The judge offered a petulant frown. "Are you this man's lawyer now, Brother Brindle?"

"If need be, yes!" Brindle shot back. "Injustice in this matter works injustice in the treaty."

"Any injustice here," Bradford corrected, "could always be remedied by a properly negotiated treaty."

"We do not play with lives, or the law, for personal greed!" Brindle barked.

The judge replied with a frigid stare.

"This man knows no details of the deaths," Brindle said. "How could a murderer not have the details of his work?"

"It was a midsummer day at a huge sugar tree," Skanawati suddenly declared. "That is where I killed Townsend. A blow to his head with a war ax was all it took. Nailing him to the tree was to remind his Virginian employers of their treachery in the Shenandoah."

"The killer carved symbols into the trees," Brindle interjected.

"A code that spoke the name of the dead to the Virginians, taught me by the Jesuits."

It was a lie. Duncan knew it was a lie. He glanced frantically at Conawago, who only looked into his folded hands.

"You were not there when Townsend died!" Brindle insisted. The chief reached inside his sleeveless waistcoat and pulled out a familiar wooden box, inscribed with a turtle. "I am chief of the turtle clan. The chief of the turtle clan was there." Skanawati slid the box down the table, to Judge Bradford, who picked it up with an uncertain glance at Ramsey, then turned it over to read Townsend's name. Duncan had handed the box over to Old Belt to be sure it would not be used by Ramsey.

Ramsey, satisfied, nodded to the judge.

The judge smiled. "Just as you have described," he said to Brindle, lifting a folded paper. With a sinking heart Duncan saw it was Brindle's notes, from the night in Philadelphia when he'd spoken to Duncan and Conawago about the murders.

Brindle was stricken, the color slowly draining from his face.

Duncan struggled to get words out. "He does not know . . ." he began in an anguished voice, then realized to his horror Skanawati did know, everything. More than once he had sat silently, feigning disinterest, as Duncan had explained the evidence to his companions. Duncan saw the steady, determined gaze between the two Iroquois chiefs as Skanawati revealed every detail Duncan had collected, and his heart lurched. At last he saw the truth that drove the two warriors, that had driven them from the start. The future was plain to see for two such men, in the settlements, in the rum that corroded their young, in the streets of Philadelphia. They knew the tribes were slowly being strangled, and they had determined to do what they could to save them for at least one more generation.

"Captain Burke," Skanawati continued in a level voice, "was at an old beech tree when I fell upon him, an hour after dawn. The blow to his head was not enough to kill but made him senseless enough for me to drive the nail into his hand." The Iroquois looked to the Virginians now as he spoke. "As any soldier of the Shenandoah deserved for the massacre of our warriors."

Most of the Virginians leapt to their feet, shouting and raising fists, giving every appearance of intending to snatch Skanawati away. McGregor's soldiers moved to the prisoner's side.

The judge slammed his wooden block repeatedly on the table. When the assembly had quieted, he surveyed the faces, glanced at Ramsey, and finally turned to Skanawati, motioning him to rise. "This court, having duly considered the confession and the evidence," he pronounced smugly, "does hereby sentence the defendant to be hanged by the neck until dead. Sentence to be carried out this day, at four hours after noon." He pounded once more, then turned to accept Ramsey's smile of triumph.

The silence among the spectators was stunned. But at the treaty table it was merely expectant. The deck had been played exactly as Ramsey had intended. All eyes turned to Old Belt. The revered chief had come hoping to return with a historic treaty and all the treasure it implied. Yet he had changed somehow since Duncan had first met him. Old Belt had always had a noble demeanor, but now there was something more, a deeper light in his eyes, a determined glint that was mirrored in Skanawati's own.

Fear rose inside Duncan, like a physical thing, pushing his heart into his throat, as he realized they had reached the end. The two Iroquois were not there for any of the reasons that kept the others at the treaty table. They acted on a different stage altogether. Duncan watched as Old Belt gazed into the sky a moment, as if he too knew about the ancient raven that kept watch on behalf of the spirits. The Iroquois chief stood and lifted the map in front of him, eliciting more smug smiles from Ramsey and his judge. At last Old Belt was ready to offer the great condolence gift to save Skanawati. He stared for a long moment at Skanawati then tore up the map, ripping it into small pieces and dropping them onto the table. As he walked away the hammering at the gallows echoed across the square. When Conawago rose to follow he had gathered the shreds of the map on the table and on the pile left three of the little glass balls.

Ramsey was speechless as he stared first at the balls then at Old Belt and the small procession of Iroquois who followed him. But he soon found his voice. "He'll die, you old fool! You don't think we will hang him?" the patron shouted toward the Indians. "Do not toy with us!" Ramsey cast a quick, uneasy glance toward Skanawati. The chief stared at him without expression.

"Just another scheming fur trader, you'll see," Ramsey said to Justice Bradford with a forced laugh as Old Belt disappeared. "We shall wait a couple hours, Brindle, then I shall show you how affairs of state are handled."

But no one else laughed, no one else believed Old Belt had any intention of reopening discussions. Brindle wrapped his hands around his prayer book, gripping it until his knuckles were white. All watched wordlessly as Ramsey hovered over Judge Bradford, directing him to a piece of parchment crowded with writing. Skanawati looked on with a curious expression as the Philadelphia judge signed his death warrant.

Chapter Twenty

I T WAS NOT soldiers who escorted Skanawati from the jail to the gallows but the remaining Iroquois. Duncan had been returned with the Onondaga after the death sentence had been decreed, but had been in the jail only a few minutes before McGregor permitted Old Belt to take Duncan's place in the little stone structure. Now Old Belt led Skanawati from the jail with his Mohawk guard at his sides. McGregor followed a few steps behind, carrying the shackles that he had removed from his prisoner.

Skanawati, seeming to know Duncan was to be removed, had solemnly addressed his cellmate. "You must not grieve, McCallum. Know this," he said, draping his strand of sacred beads over his own wrist. "On the night after I first met you and Conawago on the trail by Ligonier, I had a dream. In my dream I was being hanged as a murderer, and afterward my people returned to the old ways." Duncan could only stare at the beads forlornly. There had never been any hope, he knew now. The spirits had spoken to Skanawati, and dreams had to be obeyed.

The crowd by the gibbet had been gathering for hours, one group of Moravians reciting prayers in low voices, alternating with another group that sang somber hymns. Duncan had been in the custody of two of the Scottish soldiers much of the afternoon, but had been allowed to sit and talk with Hadley and Conawago, conferring in low, urgent tones as Ramsey paced along the street, futilely waiting for the chieftains to confer with him. They had seen the hangman, a thin scarecrow of a man, ascend the gallows, and they had watched, tormented, as the executioner had tested the rope and trap door with sacks of grain. Duncan had also seen the man's worried, troubled expression, seen how he fidgeted with his rope before descending to kneel in front of Reverend Macklin as the missionary offered a prayer for him.

The crowd's murmurs and prayers subsided as Skanawati approached, and the onlookers opened a wide corridor to give him passage. Duncan watched as Skanawati gestured for his escort to halt by the Scottish guards who kept the crowd back, twenty feet from the scaffold. He turned and went from man to man among the Iroquois, a hand on each warrior's shoulder in turn as, his face open and peaceful, he spoke a few words to each. Conawago was there, and Moses, and when the chief finished speaking with them he paused, searching the silent faces. Stepping to Duncan, he grasped his hand in both of his own, rattling the chains that bound the Scot.

"Remember this, McCallum," Skanawati said in a clear, untroubled voice, "the spirits intended that your clan and mine meet. I will seek out your old uncle on the other side and have him sing me some of those songs he died for."

Duncan, unable to speak past the swelling in his throat, nodded and offered a forced, anguished smile.

Last came Old Belt, who paused and pulled one of the eagle feathers from his braid and placed it in Skanawati's own hair. The

two chieftains stared at each other for a long, silent moment, then
Skanawati solemnly nodded and broke away. As he stepped out
in the pool of sunlight that bathed the gallows, head held high,
his body glistened with fresh oil that highlighted his many spirit
tattoos.

"Good riddance to murderers!" One of the Philadelphia men
called out, then threw an egg that broke against the chief's knee.
McGregor materialized before the man, hammered a fist into his
belly, and the heckler crumpled to the ground. Someone raised
a furious, high-pitched protest at the back of the crowd. Ramsey
was trying to approach the gibbet, but the Moravians and Indians
pressed together whenever he tried to enter, blocking his passage. One of the aristocrat's men loudly cursed and tried to shove
through. A kilted soldier swung a truncheon, dropping him senseless to the ground.

Several of the Moravian women began to sob as Skanawati
climbed the stairs. Mokie, crying uncontrollably, buried her head
in Hadley's chest. Conawago began a low chant.

It was all impossible, all unreal. For the past weeks Duncan
had been driven by the certainty that he would save the innocent
man in the end, that justice would intervene at the last moment.
But now the hour of death had arrived and Duncan was helpless.
The magistrate, tormented though he may be, was equally powerless. Now there were only Skanawati and the German hangman,
who nodded awkwardly at the Onondaga chief, before glancing at
Reverend Macklin below. With a stricken expression he regarded
the noose in his hand as Skanawati lifted his hands and held them,
open, over the German's heart a moment. Speaking a final prayer,
he placed the noose over his own head.

"My name is Skanawati, son of the Onondaga, chief of the
turtle clan," he called out in a clear, ringing voice that had no trace

of fear. He spoke not to the crowd but to the sky. "My people are the original people. They will not be forgotten." He paused, cocking his head, then an unexpected joy rose on his face.

High overhead, a raven was circling.

Skanawati looked back at the hangman, who seemed paralyzed. The German retreated a step. With a frantic hope Duncan saw he was not going to push the lever that dropped the hatch below the noose.

Skanawati offered the man a grateful nod. "My name is Skanawati," he called out once more to the spirits, then touched the fur amulet that hung from his neck and, with a long stretching kick, slammed the lever. The door opened and his body dropped.

The terrible silence as the body twitched, then went still, was like none Duncan had ever known. Half the bystanders openly wept, the remainder did not speak, could not speak. Every tongue, whether Indian, German, English, or Scottish, was numbed. The swinging rope creaked in the gibbet. From somewhere high overhead came the deep, throaty call of the raven.

The Iroquois warriors began a death chant. Under a nearby chestnut several Moravians began a quiet hymn.

Duncan forced himself to turn from the wrenching scene. He caught McGregor's eye, nodding for him to follow, then found Magistrate Brindle staring transfixed at the body, gripped his arm, and led him away.

Three hours later Duncan stood panting at the edge of a clearing by the river trail, rubbing the chafed skin where the manacles had scraped his wrists, anxiously watching the wide river trail, resisting the temptation to call out to verify the stage had been set as he had instructed. His freedom, his very life, had hung by a thread after the hanging, for Ramsey had been in a white-hot fury, in no mood to be denied anything. Duncan shuddered as he recalled the poison in Ramsey's eyes when he and Judge Bradford had come upon Duncan and Brindle talking, minutes after Skanawati's body had been cut down.

"You bungling fool!" Ramsey snarled at the Quaker. "You have lost the treaty for us!"

"I prefer to think of it as preserving our honor," Brindle replied in a quiet voice. "I daresay it will be years before the Iroquois speak to us again about land."

"The governor shall hear of this!" Ramsey barked. "The proprietor himself!" As he signaled for one of his men to retrieve Duncan, the patron's face flushed with rage. He would make Duncan pay for his losses, would start that very day.

"I am afraid," Brindle interjected, "that Mr. McCallum remains my prisoner."

"To hell you say!" Ramsey shot back. "He is *mine.* Your jurisdiction over him is finished." Ramsey gestured to his judge, as if it was Bradford's cue.

"There are still inquests into the other deaths," Brindle said, staring only at Ramsey. "He will be a key witness."

"Do not be so bold as to suggest you will keep him from me!" Ramsey put a hand on the shoulder of his judge, as if about to push him forward.

"I suggest you will not have him until I am finished with him. You will need an order from the governor, who shall hear from me of the strange dealings in the stock of the Susquehanna Company and the coincidence of calamities that forced the sales of its stock to you." The color began to drain from Judge Bradford's face. He retreated, stepping toward the coach that waited behind them. "We shall see you in Philadelphia."

Ramsey's face grew apoplectic. "You are ruined! No chief judge-ship, not this year, not ever! You'll be lucky to keep your post!" Ramsey spun about and climbed into his coach.

"He means it," Duncan said as they watched the dust cloud from the team.

"Men like that will not always have the power in this land," Brindle said quietly. It had the sound of a vow.

Duncan settled now onto a fallen log, pretending to be adjust-ing his moccasin but instead studying the long latticework shadow at his side and behind him. The old Indian cemetery, this one with aboveground scaffolds traditional to the local tribes, was exactly where Conawago had described. The tall wooden frames had been erected many years earlier at the bend in the river. Some had crumbled to the ground long ago, but at least two dozen still lay in the shadows, feathers and tattered pieces of fur hanging from many, the fur blankets used to cover the dead still intact on several newer ones. The ground was taboo to Indian and European alike.

Duncan was still sitting on the log when the lean blond man rode up and dismounted, calling out to the two Indian companions who had been running alongside him, following the conspicuous tracks Duncan had left from Bethlehem. The two Indians faded into the shadows, flanking Duncan, trapping him.

The timing had been a close thing. It had taken nearly an hour for McGregor to find a position out of sight of the townspeople but still in view of Felton's men who drank outside the inn. McGregor had played his part perfectly. Turning his back for a moment, the sergeant had provided the opening for Duncan to feign a blow with doubled fists onto his neck, dropping McGregor to the ground so Duncan could steal the keys to his manacles. Freed, Duncan had fled up the river trail, with just enough light left in the day for his tracks to be read.

He now watched as Felton paced around the pool of fading sunlight, letting him grow impatient, watched as Felton lifted a skull from where it had dropped from a scaffold, then picked up two sticks and pressed them together into a makeshift racquet. Lifting the skull like a lacrosse ball, he juggled it in the air then lofted it, smashing it against the log Duncan sat on.

"I should have known when I saw you performing lacrosse tricks in the tavern," Duncan said.

The Quaker scout's hand rested on the tomahawk on his belt. "You slipped your master again, McCallum. Please keep it up. I shall make a rich career of catching you and collecting the bounty."

"So it *was* you who hit me from the back in the Walnut Street prison."

"Of course. Twenty Spanish dollars for that one. I'll demand more this time. The market for your head increases every day."

"Your career is over," came another voice. Moses stepped from behind a tree.

"Come to offer me a prayer, old woman?" Felton sneered.

"Everyone was always looking in the wrong direction," Duncan observed, keeping his eye on Felton's tomahawk. "First suspecting the French, then the Iroquois as you intended."

"I hate the Iroquois. Always have."

"You were a Huron most of your life."

"I had taken five Iroquois scalps before I was fifteen."

"Then," Duncan continued with a shudder, "we kept puzzling over different bands of Indians who might be the murderers, wondering why Burke would have been involved. Of course if I had but known Ramsey had his hand in, I would have looked for bribery and subterfuge in Philadelphia from the outset."

"An outlaw and a dried-up old Jesus Indian," Felton said. "You're wasting your breath to complain."

"It was that connection between the violence and the band of Philadelphia investors that was so well-hidden. A killer in the wilderness who knew all the surveyors seemed so unlikely, a savage who knew the pigpen code impossible. Were you also involved in those accidents that beset the investors in the land company? There was a ship burned in the harbor, a warehouse leveled near the wharfs."

"A lantern through a cargo hatch, another thrown through a window. The work of a few minutes, for so very much money."

"And you and Burke needed money, for your new enterprise."

Felton looked back toward the broad river path, where his horse stood grazing in the moonlight with his rifle on its saddle.

"I doubt Lord Ramsey understands how fastidious the Moravians are about their records. Every orphan is recorded, every returned Indian slave, every former captive has entries, because they mean to keep helping those unfortunate souls whenever they can. Of course you had no need. You left them behind. You turned your back on their charity."

"They are women," Felton scoffed.

"They wrote things, in the interest of helping you. You were one of the most difficult of all the captives who returned from the tribes. They thought it was because of the trauma of shifting between worlds. Their hearts were too generous to see that it was because you had already become a predator years earlier, because you ran with Huron raiding parties for years and took scalps of settlers and Iroquois alike. You had a blood lust that would not be cured by soap and britches. A Huron raider in Quaker clothes. Your relatives in Philadelphia gave you every privilege, a scholar's education, rubbing shoulders with scholars, but there was a place inside none of that could ever reach. Even when you had decided to take on your Quaker mantle to exploit the pleasures of Philadelphia you couldn't resist killing Sister Leinbach."

"All the syllables in all their books," Felton said in a tone that sent a chill down Duncan's spine, "don't begin to equal the thrill of the war cry when you descend on an enemy camp."

"She was just a woman full of her God," Moses interjected. "There was never evil in her hand."

"She would beat me, invent punishments meant to shame me. A true warrior never forgets a captor who beats him. I had to gag her when I brought her here, to stop all those damned prayers."

The light was fading fast now. Duncan pressed on. "It seemed an impossible combination," he said, "the bloody violence and the scholar's code. It was a unique puzzle. And you are the unique solution."

Felton grinned and took a sideways step toward his horse. He was fast, Duncan knew. If he reached his rifle he could kill them both, one with a bullet, and one with his tomahawk.

"Did you kill them all yourself or just watch as your renegades did it?"

"You were there today. The killer was hanged, on the word of a senior judge, after a proper trial."

"Not a trial. A theatrical performance staged by Ramsey. You killed Burke. You were visiting your Huron friends just down the valley the night before. Mokie saw you. I saw you, the back of your head, though I didn't realize it until now. I had you in the sights of my rifle. You were expecting Van Grut at the tree. Finding Burke there alone was a bonus, a victim sure to heat up relations between the Iroquois and the Virginians. Your plan had already been launched, you had no need for Burke any longer. You could probably convince Ramsey to pay extra since Burke's death would mask crucial evidence and save Ramsey the considerable money promised Burke."

"He refused to pay. Because Van Grut was still alive."

"So you tried for Van Grut in Philadelphia."

"Interfered with again."

Felton glanced back at the trail and froze for a moment. His horse was gone. He retreated a step and gave a low whistle.

"It is blasphemy to disturb the graves the way you did," Moses put in. He was there not because of the murders on the Warriors Path but because of Sister Leinbach.

"I am beginning to change my mind about taking a bounty," Felton mocked them. "I can find enough room for both of you right here." He gave another soft whistle, then looked into the shadows with new unease.

"They're not coming," Duncan said. As he spoke four more men appeared, all Iroquois in the black coats of the Moravians.

Felton merely lifted an eyebrow. "Do you have any idea what Ramsey will want me to do to you when I bring you back?" he said to Duncan. "I might make more if I just sell the parts of your body to him, piece by piece. I believe I shall take you with us, find a quiet place in the woods to finish you slowly. Once when I was ten the Hurons brought back a Mohawk prisoner who was given to us, the children of the village. We tied him to a post and kept him alive for ten days, slicing a little more meat away each day. Don't cut any big blood vessels, was what the squaws taught us."

"I would gladly give up my freedom to avenge Skanawati."

"Avenge?" Felton snorted. "You and these women? I know these Christian Indians. If I told them I was going to chop them all to death right now they would stand in line waiting, reciting from their little books." Felton looked into the shadows again.

"Your band is gone, those two and all the others," Duncan explained. "They will be taken before the Grand Council as traitors to their nation."

Felton took a step toward the path, as if he were retreating, then crouched and spun about, cocking the little pistol that appeared in his hand as he brought it to bear on Duncan. He offered a victorious grin, but an instant before the pistol discharged his arm jerked up and the ball was lost in the foliage.

Felton gazed in disbelief at the arrow in his shoulder. Conawago stepped out of the shadows, holding his bow.

"I think," Duncan said, "you misunderstand something." He signaled to the men in the dark coats, and they dropped them to the ground. Their chests glistened in the moonlight, reflecting fresh war paint. "We only borrowed the coats so they could move about the town freely." The four men stepped out of the deep shadow. One of the Indians tossed something into the moonlight at Felton's feet. A painted turtle shell. Another raised a strand of beads, a sign of Old Belt's authority. Felton's eyes suddenly went round with fear.

"You no doubt know the chief's Mohawk escort. From the turtle clan, Skanawati's clan. And you just had more of a trial than Skanawati was given. I expect they will find a quiet place in the woods for you between here and Shamokin."

The color drained from Felton's face. He darted one way, then another as the Iroquois closed in, then one raised a small war club and gave him a blow on the side of his head that dropped him to his knees. When he rose they had fastened a leather strap around his neck, attached to a pole, the traditional way to transport war captives. One of his captors snapped off the arrow shaft, leaving the head in Felton's flesh to torment him. His last protest was choked away by a twist of the pole.

As Duncan watched the shadows where they had disappeared, another figure stepped forward. Magistrate Brindle had his collar turned up against the cool evening breeze.

"You'll never see him again," Duncan said.

The Quaker nodded solemnly. "I think," he said with a heavy voice. "I have never seen him. Sometimes," he added after a long moment, "we let our charity blind us to the evil in the world."

To Duncan's surprise Brindle stayed as a wagon pulled up bearing a coffin, driven by Reverend Macklin. The Quaker silently held one of the torches as Macklin, Duncan, Conawago, and Moses eased the remains of the dead Moravian missionary from the Indian grave scaffold and placed it in the coffin. He did not move even as Conawago and Moses returned and offered a low prayer to the disturbed dead.

The moon was high overhead when they finally had the wagon loaded. As Duncan began to climb up beside the driver, Brindle restrained him with a hand on his arm. "No, McCallum. This wagon goes south."

Duncan glanced in confusion from the Quaker to Conawago and Moses, who had appeared beside Brindle. "I will not dishonor you, sir. You are obliged to return me to Philadelphia."

"There are higher laws than those of Philadelphia," the magistrate said. Duncan now saw his own pack hanging from the shoulder of Conawago, his rifle in the Nipmuc's hand. "The new indenture Ramsey tried to force on you was never signed. And as a judge of this province I have received an affidavit in elegant handwriting from a highly revered man named Socrates Moon. He attests, has sworn before me, that he is an agent of a different bond-holder. I have been made to understand from him that someone on the New York frontier has a superior claim over you." Brindle extended his hand.

"You, sir," Duncan said as he accepted the farewell handshake, "are a noble man."

"No. There was but one noble man in this entire sordid affair," Brindle said, his voice cracking as he spoke, "and we hanged him today."

"The tribes will be furious," Duncan said. "It will be many years before they think of ceding land again. And that was what he intended from the start. No matter what we did he would have found a way to his noose." *Skanawati dreamed it*, he almost added.

"It makes it no less painful," the Quaker said, then climbed up onto the seat. "I have arranged a second wagon, and a second coffin. Would you see him to his home?"

They watched in silence as the magistrate disappeared down the river trail toward Bethlehem.

"What do we tell them in Shamokin?" Moses asked in a near whisper. "What do we tell his village when we arrive with the body of their greatest chief?"

"We tell them the truth," Duncan said. "Skanawati died so no more land would be taken from the tribes."

Epilogue

*T*HE WOODLAND ANIMALS seemed comforted by the low, steady throb of the drum, the squirrels and birds watching from the great cottonwood tree with curiosity, not fear, as the sound rose in volume. Duncan and Johantty had started an hour before dawn, beating together on the log drum, then Duncan had played his pipes as the young Onondaga brave continued the drumming. Lost in the music, the drum like the heartbeat of the tribe, the pipes conjuring visions of his youth, Duncan turned with surprise to find new onlookers. He had expected only Conawago and Moses to help him prepare Johantty for the dawnchaser trail, but most of the inhabitants of the new village hidden deep in the mountains had appeared in the gray light before dawn, sitting at the perimeter like monks in silent meditation. A cedar torch had been lit by the chimneylike formation of rocks, above a smoldering pile of the fragrant tobacco favored by the spirits.

Johantty stepped along the circle of villagers, receiving blessings from young and old, then moved to the central fire and stripped to his breechcloth and leggings. His body had been elaborately painted, not for war, but with the sacred signs of his tribe, a large turtle on his chest.

The young Iroquois offered a sober nod as Duncan approached.

"Today is the day we reconnect the gods," came a familiar voice at his side.

Duncan turned to face Stone Blossom. For the first time since they had arrived at their new village with her son's shrouded body, the grief had left her face. She had known they were coming, though had not expected Hadley or the Scottish soldiers, and had led them to a burial site that had been prepared below the ancient shrine discovered by Skanawati the year before. The Onondaga matron had kept a solitary vigil at the grave for two days and two nights. Returning, she had offered the first smile Duncan had ever seen on her wrinkled face when she had discovered Duncan, Conawago, Moses, Hadley, and half a dozen Scots working with the tribe to clear fields and build longhouses. Hadley had brought Becca, Mokie, and Penn with him, explaining that he was going to help Rideaux build a new school for the Indians, far removed from those who would hunt for runaways. McGregor and his men had stretched their orders as an escort for Skanawati to cover the return of his body and had a slip of paper from a friendly ranger captain passing through Shamokin that stated they were now pursuing a raiding party on his orders, a thin excuse but enough to cover them on their return to Ligonier.

With the new longhouses constructed and the crops now planted, a great weight seemed to have been lifted from Stone Blossom. She was radiant with pride for her nephew, but also clearly worried. The old tales of the daylong dawnchaser course said that runners often died.

"There now, madame, the spirits be watching over him."
Sergeant McGregor's brawny frame loomed over the woman. "Ye
be fortunate. I remember when I was a boy in the Highlands we
once had spirits who watched over us."

The words tugged open a chamber long locked in Duncan's
heart. Images flooded over his mind's eye, of his mother at the
hearth, his brothers roaming high in the heather among the
shaggy oxen, his grandfather playing pipes by the moonlit sea, his
sisters dancing at clan gatherings. He saw Skanawati, heard again
his words that their clans had been linked together, and in that
moment the dark weight that for weeks had been pressing on his
heart began to fall away.

Conawago was whispering directions in Johantty's ear, still
concerned that the youth would lose his way, when he looked up at
Duncan. His words trailed off. McGregor muttered a soft exclamation of surprise, and both men stared as Duncan slowly loosened
his buttons. Then suddenly the ragged old Scot's eyes lit with joy,
and he helped Duncan pull away his shirt.

Duncan worked quickly, tightening his moccasins and leggings,
letting Conawago tie his hair tightly at the back as the old Nipmuc
whispered prayers in his ear, not objecting when his friend took one
of the feathers from his own braids and tied it into Duncan's hair.
He became aware of a new sound above the pulsing drum, a sound
like the rustle of leaves, realizing finally it was the whispered prayers
of all the Iroquois in the circle. McGregor, wiping an eye, joined in
with his own Gaelic prayer. The old clans, Iroquois and Highland,
may be battered, but they were not lost.

He did not know how long he chanted with his companions,
blending the old magic of Gaelic with Iroquois words, but gradually
something quickened inside him, a new resonance, and he knew it
was now the pulse of the forest itself he felt. Suddenly Conawago

lifted a small red feather over his head, and every voice stopped. Johantty and Duncan exchanged exalted smiles then turned their gazes to the feather. Moments later the tip burst into color as the first rays of sun hit it, then side by side, running like deer, the two men slipped down the ancient trail into the shadows of the forest.

Author's Note

To those who have glimpsed the complex social structure and spirituality of the woodland Indians it should come as no surprise to learn that Skanawati was an actual Iroquois chief of the 18th century. As reflected in these pages, he alone faced the difficult challenge of being both a war chief and a peace chief, with the added responsibility of being an Onondaga and head of the turtle clan, which underscored his duty to protect the traditions and spiritual well being of his people. Although this tale of the Skanawati chief is fiction, it was in part inspired by an account from the historian Francis Parkman, who described an early war between the Iroquois and their traditional foes the Hurons during which the Skanawati chief entered the enemy's territory as a peace emissary representing the Grand Council of the Iroquois Confederation. When Seneca and Mohawk warriors, members of that confederation, invaded the Huron lands despite his presence, he felt his own honor and integrity so affronted, and the need to demonstrate the Iroquois commitment to peace so great, that he committed suicide in the Huron camp.

Honor and integrity were often stretched thin as Europeans began taking the traditional lands of the woodland peoples. During the first century of settlement, the colonial governments acknowledged the tribes as separate nations, and the European appetite for land was relatively small, largely confined to strips along the Atlantic coast. William Penn, the most significant of the early leaders in the region, exerted great efforts, including travel among the Indians along the Susquehanna, to assure that colonists and Indians would jointly inhabit a "peaceable kingdom."

By 1760 this dynamic had dramatically changed. Britain's imminent victory in the French and Indian War meant that the political leverage of the Iroquois—long a vital buffer between French and English—was disappearing. A massive increase in population was pushing farmers over the mountain ranges that had for decades served as the de facto boundaries for settlement. Indians were being cornered in taverns and persuaded over their cups to place their marks on contracts to cede land, contracts upheld in English courts despite the lack of tribal authorization. For years Virginian officials insisted the deed signed by the Iroquois to cede the Shenandoah country covered all the land to the Pacific. Provincial officials deliberately misplaced names on maps to deceive Indians when land was sold. While settlers often paid in blood for such official sleight of hand, the push for land was relentless. Competition among the colonies themselves was fierce. Connecticut laid claim to tribal lands in northern Pennsylvania, Virginia asserted preemptive rights over lands of western Pennsylvania, and one of the Pennsylvania governors himself surveyed and acquired lands along the Susquehanna for his personal estate despite prior treaty assurances that the lands belonged in perpetuity to the tribes.

The Iroquois leaders struggled to resist these encroachments, sending wampum message belts with depictions of axes smashing kegs to warn those along the Susquehanna to dump, not drink, English rum, circulating other belts that rallied the subordinate tribes to resist new land cessions. Leaders on both sides sought to alleviate tensions through treaty councils, which brought tenuous, intermittent peace, but the Iroquois chiefs well knew that every treaty conference was ultimately about the European lust for land, and that their centuries-old way of life was slowly, inexorably being consumed by that lust.

This was a time of historic change populated by many heroes, saints and villains, when worlds were being altered for European and Indian alike. The era offers not only a vital platform for understanding succeeding centuries in America, it also presents a rich tapestry of mixed cultures and stunning natural beauty. The people, places, and events woven into this story are all directly rooted in 18th century experience, from the use of symbols on trees, to the tribes' distrust of written words, the clandestine French support for runaway slaves, the Iroquois reburial of the dead, the massacre of Iroquois warriors by Shenandoah farmers, the kaleidoscopic town of Shamokin *(present day Sunbury, Pennsylvania)*, the unique intermediary role of the Moravians, even the fascination of some tribal members with clockwork gears. While the intervening centuries have eclipsed many details of Iroquois ritual and religion, it is not difficult to imagine how these very spiritual people would react to the petroglyphs found along the Susquehanna River, already ancient in the 18th century. The Susquehanna valley had one of the greatest concentrations of petroglyphs on the continent, and many survived well into the last century.

Seismic shifts too were underway in European science, as dramatically reflected in the rise of electricity as a field of scholarly study. Inspired by the work of Benjamin Franklin as much as by advances in England, France and Germany, electrical devices of the types described in these pages were indeed being used for experimentation and even medical treatment by the mid-18th century. Franklin reported that his life was forever changed by the gift of an "electrical" glass tube in 1746, and his years of research that followed resulted in a number of important discoveries—including the existence of positive and negative particles—that had a lasting effect on Philadelphia's burgeoning community of scientists.

While Scots certainly played a role in science—and Duncan McCallum's own training reflects the preeminent role of Scotland in the medical science of the day—it is the Scottish connection to native Americans that drives the central characters in this book. Doubtlessly a shared martial tradition and a common generosity of spirit contributed to this link, but ultimately that connection is one of those fascinating quirks of history that cannot be fully explained and perhaps can only be fully appreciated in retrospect. Scots adapted and integrated into cultures all over the globe—the wandering Scot was a fixture in many countries even in medieval times—but the link between the Scots and the woodland Indians of America is unique in history. While it began among the northeastern tribes when Highland troops and Iroquois served together in the French and Indian War, a Highlander born on the shores of Loch Ness, Lochlan MacGillivray, became the leader of the southern Creek nation, the chieftain of the Indians who decades later waged a bloody campaign against Andrew Jackson was a red-haired Scottish warrior named Weatherford, and John Ross, the revered chieftain of the Cherokee who led his people for thirty-eight years, was seven-eighths Scottish by blood.

Ross led his tribe on the infamous Trail of Tears, marking the final chapter in the destruction of the woodland Indians' way of life. That process was very much in its opening chapters in 1760, and real life heroes did indeed struggle to forestall it, though soon the chieftains would look back in disbelief at the violent transformation in relations with the Europeans. Some were no doubt present in 1763 to sift through the ruins when twenty peaceful

Christian Indians were massacred at Conestoga, Pennsylvania by a mob of settlers. In the ashes of the burnt buildings was found one of the original treaties signed by William Penn, its words still legible, including the promises that both people would live "with One Hand and One Heart," and that the settlers would for all time "shew themselves true Friends and Brothers to all and every one of ye Indians."

—Eliot Pattison

Timeline

1731   Library Company of Philadelphia is formed as the first public library in America, with Benjamin Franklin as a primary sponsor.

1741   Moravian missionaries from Germany establish a permanent settlement at the confluence of the Lehigh River and Monocacy Creek in Pennsylvania. The new community, called Bethlehem, becomes a center for Moravian missionary work among the woodland tribes.

1742   The Moravians negotiate a treaty of friendship with the Iroquois Confederation, providing for protection of missionaries working among the tribes, a pact the Iroquois steadfastly respect for decades.

1744   Virginia signs a treaty with the Iroquois Confederation to secure certain lands traditionally controlled by the tribes. The Indians later insist the pact transferred only the Shenandoah Valley and other areas east of the Appalachians, while the Virginians insist it gave them all the western lands to the Pacific Ocean. Land companies begin to be formed, competing for development of tracts in the Ohio country, including much of what is now western Pennsylvania. Surveyors begin working in those lands, often in secret.

1745 — Moravians establish a mission at Shamokin, the large Indian community at the forks of the Susquehanna.

1746 APRIL — At Culloden Moor, near Inverness, the Scottish Jacobite rebels, including many Highland clans, are defeated by British forces, breaking the rebel army and forcing the Jacobite leader, Bonnie Prince Charlie, to flee into exile. In the aftermath of Culloden, the British send punitive expeditions into the Highlands, destroying many traditional Highland clan communities. These campaigns, and the concurrent Act of Proscription, which outlawed the bearing of arms and even the wearing of Highland kilts, effectively ended the traditional Highland life for many clans.

Early in 1746 the first true electrical capacitor capable of storing an electrical charge is developed at Leyden University using a glass jar with metallic wrapping, water, and metal terminals. The Leyden jar becomes a platform for extensive experimentation with electrical fluid, or electricity, in Europe and America. Upon the gift of an "electrical tube" this same year, Benjamin Franklin sets aside his commercial pursuits and dedicates several years to scientific study, most of it focused on electricity, during which he discovered positive and negative charges and invented the lightning rod. During these years Franklin also ventured into electrotherapy, exploring the use of electrical charges to treat a wide range of medical maladies.

1752 JUNE — Franklin conducts his kite experiment, demonstrating that lightning is a form of electrical discharge.

1754 MAY — As British settlers moved into the Ohio Valley during the 1750s, the French deployed troops to protect what they considered their domain. The Virginia governor reacted by sending a small militia force into the region led by twenty-three-year-old George Washington. In May 1754 Washington raids a French camp at Great Meadows in what is now western Pennsylvania. The action marked the opening of armed hostilities between the French (and their allies Austria and Russia) and the British (and their ally Prussia), which spread to the Caribbean, Asia, and the African coast in what became known as the Seven Years War or, in North America, the French and Indian War.

1754 JULY   At Fort Necessity, erected by Washington near Great Meadows, an overwhelming force of French soldiers and Indian allies attack the Virginian troops. Washington is forced to surrender the fort and leave the Ohio country. The defeat galvanized the British government, which began deploying regular army troops along the western frontier.

1755 JULY   Near Turtle Creek, along the Monongahela, the British army under General Braddock is defeated by combined French and Indian forces. Of the front column of twelve hundred men, a thousand are casualties. This defeat, in which Braddock was killed, painfully demonstrated that rigid European military tactics would not succeed against the wilderness style of combat, resulting in new emphasis on irregular ranger forces and light infantry. The French and British began cementing relations with Indian allies— the French with Hurons, Ottawa, and Abenaki, the British with the Iroquois tribes, the Seneca, Tuscaroras, Cayugas, Mohawks, Oneidas, and Onondagas.

1755 SEPTEMBER William Johnson, who had forged close ties with the Iroquois, leads a mixed force of colonial soldiers and Mohawks in defeating French forces at the southern end of Lake George. Iroquois chief King Hendrick (Teyonhenkwen), who was part Mohawk and part Mahican, died at the age of eighty leading a Mohawk attack against the French.

1756 MAY   War is formally declared between England and France.

1756	AUGUST	French forces under General Montcalm attack and seize the British force at Fort Oswego, on Lake Ontario.

1757	AUGUST	General Montcalm attacks and captures Fort William Henry at the southern end of Lake George. After the surrender of the British forces, French Indians, ignoring Montcalm's orders, massacre retreating British troops. This battle and the ensuing massacre were immortalized in Cooper's *Last of the Mohicans*.

1758	MAY	British forces under General Forbes set out from Philadelphia to attack Fort Duquesne in what is now western Pennsylvania. Against the fervent objections of many Virginians, including George Washington, who wish the army to open a road from Virginia into the Ohio Country, Forbes constructs the first east-west road across the Pennsylvania mountains. Soon after, Forts Bedford and Ligonier were established along this road, which opened up the region to rapid settlement from eastern Pennsylvania. During this campaign the British embarked on a strategy of negotiating with tribes allied with the French to keep them from actively supporting the French.

1758	JULY	A vastly superior British force under General Abercromby attacks the French under Montcalm at Fort Ticonderoga. After a series of costly mistakes, including ordering Black Watch Highland troops to charge heavily manned entrenchments without artillery support, Abercromby withdraws with heavy British losses.

After a monthlong siege, British forces capture the French port of Louisbourg on Cape Breton Island, the strongest fortress in North America. In retaliation for the massacre at Fort William Henry, the British expel eight thousand colonists from Cape Breton.

1758	OCTOBER	British Fort Ligonier in Pennsylvania repels a French attack. British troops advance again on Fort Duquesne. The outnumbered French retreat from Fort Duquesne, burning it as they leave. The British rebuild the fort, renaming it Fort Pitt.
1759	JULY	British forces attack French Fort Niagara, seizing the fort and moving on to occupy Forts Venango and Presque Isle, eliminating the last French operating bases in the western theater. The French blow up Fort Ticonderoga and withdraw as General Amherst advances with a large British force. Amherst dispatches Rogers Rangers on a long-distance raid to destroy the Abenaki operating base at St. Francis.
1759	SEPTEMBER	After a bloody three-month campaign, British forces capture Quebec. In the final battle on Plains of Abraham, both the French and British commanding generals, Montcalm and Wolfe, are killed.
1760	APRIL	After enduring a winter-long siege in Quebec, British forces are attacked by the French and win a second battle on Plains of Abraham.
1760	SEPTEMBER	Montreal is captured by British forces, the last significant engagement in North America.
1761–1762		Fighting continues in India, the Caribbean, Europe, and the coast of Africa.
1763	FEBRUARY	The Treaty of Paris formally ends war, granting Great Britain control of North America east of the Mississippi River.